LOVE WILL FIND ITS WAY

JOSIE AND MIKE'S LOVE STORY

DECEMBER 9, 2019

Ivy Blacke

Ivyblack888@gmail.com

Dedication:

I have so many people to thank, but I will try and keep this short. First to my husband for believing I can do anything and standing beside me to make it happen, I love you to the beach and back baby.

To my "Mamma Bear" Cheryl- you rock. Thank you for helping me with editing and supporting me through this process. You and my "adopted sister" Cass have helped me so much! Love you guys

To my huge friend support group, you guys are my world. Thank you for putting up with me and helping me make this dream real by reading, rereading and crying with me through this crazy process. Suz you have been my best friend forever and I couldn't have done this without you and your support, Luv ya girl!

Also to my family, God where would I be without all of you. I love you all so much and I can't wait to share this ride with you all. To my brother and his wife, special thanks for reading my book, telling me I can do this and for helping me market and manage this crazy thing! Also bro, thanks for volunteering to cover model, but ummm, I got it! Mom and Dad thanks for not telling me I'm crazy and hugging me extra hard. To my Dad in heaven, I love you and I miss you. I know in my heart I've made you proud.

Special thanks to Leah Holt. You are so patient with me and as a fellow author I thank you for guiding me and helping me to make this dream a reality. You rock on so many levels. I can't thank you enough.

To all of you for buying my book, wow....thank you!!!! I can't wait to share more with you all.

Chapter 1

Josie sat in her hospital bed thinking, "How could this be happening? What did I ever do to deserve this?" Her whole life was crumbling around her and she had no idea where to go from here. The last 48 hours had been a whirlwind. One minute she was cooking dinner, the next she was a crumpled bloody mess on the floor. Officers handcuffed and hauled Jack away while the paramedics carted her to an ambulance. Josie's face was bloody, with cuts and scratches across it. She had bruises starting to form on her cheeks. She also had a swollen eye that was turning a deeper purple by the minute. She had glass shards in her arms, legs and back. Her arm appeared bruised, possibly broken. So much damage, but all the outward scrapes, scratches and bruises would heal. The emotional bruises would be harder to heal.

Josie was an attractive thirty-one-year old woman, about 5'5", hazel eyes, brown shoulder-length hair, normally she had an athletic build. Over the past few years she wasn't able to keep up her workouts so she wasn't as strong as she once had been. She was now softer, curvier than she had wanted to be. She was about 20 lbs overweight and for her height, she felt every last pound of that. She had enjoyed running to keep herself in shape. So how did her life turn out this way?

Eight years ago she met Jack at a party, but she never let go of her past. Her heart was broken by a man who held the key to her heart, one man that would forever hold her heart. In turn she never wanted to give her heart again.

Jack seemed harmless enough when she met him. He was sweet, charming and wanted to be with her. He was handsome in his own way, but not really her type-he had dark brown almost black hair, brown eyes and a medium build. He was muscular, but not overly so. He was strong and lean. Just looking at him anyone could tell he worked out. After dating for a year, Jack expressed thoughts of marriage, but she was unsure about the idea. She enjoyed his company and had some fun with him, but her heart just never opened to him. She gave him credit. He diligently pursued her with determination.

Although Josie was unsure if the year of dating was long enough for her and Jack to get to know each other, she agreed to his proposal, and through the justice of the peace she became Mrs. Jack Morris. Their first year of marriage was rough, trying to get used to one another's quirks and issues. But it was no different than anyone else in a marriage, wasn't it? She had nothing to compare it to, and her friends were slowly disappearing from her life because Jack consumed her whole world. Even her running and walking took a back seat. She would work and come home to spend time with him to work on their marriage. They had arguments, didn't always agree but somehow they were making it work. Year two of marriage things shifted a little. He became obsessed with where she was, who she was with and what she was doing. It seemed like all he wanted her to do was go to work at the diner and come home. She was taking some night courses for medical assisting. She wanted to help people. She didn't want to wait tables forever.

Jack worked odd jobs, he had his own business. He pretty much could do anything, he painted, he fixed things, he mowed lawns. Whatever people needed he did. He had a small weight room in the house and he would work out there when he was home. He always seemed to be home and Josie spent the days working, then would come home to him, make dinner and clean up the house. She was frustrated. When she started her night courses, he seemed to become agitated all the time with her and constantly wanting more from her. Jack would complain about the house being a mess, that she wasn't cooking good enough meals for him and that she never had time for sex.

The next two years of their marriage things dramatically changed. She couldn't seem to do anything right. She completely stopped running and walking; she felt like she was not healthy anymore. She felt her body getting softer, not as toned as it was before. She didn't like herself but continued trying to just keep her husband happy. If he was happy she would eventually be happy, right?

Jack became more agitated and impatient with her. He controlled everything. The friends she once had faded into the background because she didn't have any available time for them. She was disappointed in them for not sticking by her when she needed them, but she was also disappointed in herself for allowing the separation. She was very confused by her marriage because her husband was supposed to come first. Wasn't he? Jack became more forceful with her; he was pushing her all the time for sex. She was tired after her day and sometimes just not in the mood. Jack would tell her that it was her duty as his wife to fulfill him. He wanted sex and she had to oblige. She was trying to do things right but she seemed to lose more and more of herself as every day passed.

Josie had to answer for every minute of the day she wasn't at home. She went to work, came home, made dinner then headed to school to finish her classes. She graduated and had her degree as a medical assistant, but it didn't do her much good, as she didn't have time to search for a new job. He didn't want her to find anything else. He wanted her where she was.

The last three years of their marriage became a nightmare. He started to get physical with her. She got held up at work one night, got home late because the other waitress had a family emergency and didn't get to work on time. She stayed to cover, when she got home he was in a rage. He didn't believe her, he demanded to know where she was. She was tired and just not in the mood for his drama. She tried to walk away from him, he grabbed a hold of her spun, her around and punched her in the face across her left cheek.

Josie felt like her eye was going to pop out of its socket. She thought her cheek was smashed into a million pieces. The left side of her face felt like it just exploded. She thought time froze in the instant he hit her and she didn't know what to think. She was in shock that he had hit her. She didn't quite know what to do. Tears sprang to her eyes, she turned and ran to their bedroom. He didn't follow right away. But an hour later he came in, threw a bag of frozen vegetables at her and said in a voice she learned to fear, "Don't ever lie to me again." He left her alone but an hour later he was back demanding sex from her. She refused; he was angry, "Like fuck, Josie. You are my wife and we are going to have sex. Take your clothes off, now!" He had started stripping his clothes; she didn't move. He came to her, slapped her in the face then ripped her clothes off of her. He had sex with her while she cried.

After that the beatings got worse. She had broken ribs from him punching her and she just suffered through. Her friends would ask her about the bruises on her arms and face but she wasn't sure what to say. She would lie to them, tell them that she fell or tripped down the stairs carrying laundry. She tried to explain every bruise. He was trying to hide the bruises better by hitting her in the stomach, ribs and legs where they would be covered by her clothes. It eventually got to the point where people didn't even ask about the bruises anymore.

The night her life finally changed was the worst. A neighbor actually heard Josie's screams and called the police. Had the neighbor not done that, Josie was sure she would not have survived. She was making dinner. "What's for dinner?" Josie didn't turn to look at him. She just spoke, "Spaghetti."

Before she knew what was happening he pulled her by the hair away from the stove and punched her in the head. As she tried to protect herself he was screaming at her. "You are a lazy piece of shit. You whore! You are nothing but a piece of trash who couldn't satisfy a man if your life depended on it. I have to take sex from you because you never perform your wifely duties. Do you know what that's like? You are my fucking wife. I deserve to have you when I want you and you should be more than fucking willing to meet my needs. You fucking whore! You need to learn some respect."

Jack continued punching her in the head; when she moved her hands, he would punch her face. He hit her eye, her cheek and caught her under the chin a time or two. He then started punching her in the left side, right side and square in the center of her abdomen.

When she fell screaming to the floor, he kicked her in the leg, and she thought her leg flew off her body. Then he kicked her in the ribs. He stomped on her arm and it felt like it was completely disconnected from her body. She felt the blood rolling down her face, which unfortunately was a normal feeling for her. He stopped kicking her and started ransacking the kitchen, throwing pans, plates, glasses and silverware at her.

Josie laid in a heap on the floor rolling in and out of consciousness. By the time the police got there she was surrounded by glass, broken plates and pots and pans. He came back at her when he heard the sirens. He was kicking her again then dropped to his knees. He pulled her up, the last memory she had was him yelling. “You are my God damn wife and I will do whatever I want to you. Do you hear me! You need to learn respect. I will teach you how to respect me." Then he punched her so hard on the left side of her face that she thought her head came off her shoulders. She heard a scuffle and Jack's voice. "You stupid cock suckers, this is my home, my wife, I can do what the hell I want. Get the fuck out of my house." "Help me! I don't want to die like this!" She didn't know if she spoke the words out loud or if she dreamed it. Then the world went black.

Josie heard sirens as she tried to come out of the haze she was in. Someone was touching her but not the way Jack had. She thought she was finally dying and done living the hell she'd been in for the last seven years. She felt like she was floating, like she was finally safe. She thought it was weird how she could have so much pain but feel like she was safe. All she thought about the last seven years through all the beatings was her past. She had once known love like nothing else. The memories of the only love she had ever known; Michael. What would her life had been if he did not walk away? As she faded in and out of consciousness Josie dreamed of Michael. His face was there in front of her. His blue eyes piercing her soul, while his blonde hair wrapped around her fingers. He was what pulled her through the horrible times, the pain, the raping she suffered at the hands of her husband, the miscarriages and the general suffering all because of Jack. The love she had with Michael she knew she would never have again. She would never love that way or give her heart away like she did with Michael. Jack he was a mistake. One she paid dearly for through the years. The broken bones and bruises would heal. Josie's broken heart from Michael never would.

Chapter 2

Josie laid in the hospital bed, a brace on her arm and a boot on her leg. Luckily nothing was broken, only bruised and sore. The police came in to take her statement. Fortunately for her Jack punched the officers. Now he was being charged for resisting arrest, assault of an officer and with the new domestic violence laws he was being held for trial. They requested her signature for evidence, medical records and offered her an attorney. She was finally ready to end this chapter in her life. She lived through the worst beating and she wanted her life back. She wasn't going to be a victim any longer. She was going to see this through, get out of this town and start over in a town where people didn't stare at her with pity in their eyes. All her old friends, the people at the diner and her neighbors all stared at her with pity on their faces. She couldn't stand it. She wanted to make something of herself and find happiness. She would never have that here.

Josie wanted a divorce and enough time to lose herself. The lawyer was good, but Jack refused to sign divorce papers. The bastard got three years in jail. Most likely to only serve two. Josie was devastated, but she knew she at least had two years to change her life and get as lost as she could. She went home, packed up her clothes and took a few personal items she hid from Jack, the only things she had left of the love she once shared with another man. She got in her car. The first and only stop she made was at the bank. She couldn't close her account out as it was a joint account with Jack, but she took as much money as she could out of the account and away she went. She left Springside, Maine, in her rearview mirror and all the pain she felt while living there.

Josie drove until she couldn't drive anymore. She slept in her car at truck stops when she could to save money, and other times she got a room in a rat trap motel. She stopped in towns when she saw help wanted signs. She worked for a month or so, replenish some money then took off to the next town. She passed through town after town, searching for something but unsure what that something was. She cried herself to sleep some nights for the empty life she was living, and she pushed through some days hoping and wishing that there was something else out there for her. She longed to find friends again, this time friends who would stand by her when she needed them and ones she could trust with her secrets without having pity in their eyes.

Josie drove from town to town for a year. Every town she stopped in didn't feel right. She stayed for a while then moved on.

She never got close to anyone, she never felt like she wanted to. In her whole life Josie never felt a closeness to anyone except her Grandma and Michael. Her parents didn't ever really seem like they wanted a child. They moved to Florida right after Josie moved out on her own. She never called them and they never called her. It was sad. She had a love with her Grandma, though. It was a special bond that Josie was eternally grateful for. That bond helped her become who she was. It helped her to love Michael.

Josie felt like she drove halfway across the world, but she finally stopped in a cute little town. The town had brick sidewalks. There were antique shops, a general store and some unique clothing stores. There was a diner but also some other restaurants ranging from steakhouses to seafood grills. There was a park with benches with a fountain in the middle. The place really spoke to her, it screamed home. There was a gym in the town. There was sadly an orphanage that she passed on the way in through town. It broke her heart thinking of the children living there without someone to love them. She thought this town would be a nice break for her. This place would give her a chance to replenish some funds but could it be more? She found a job at the diner. She made some good tips, she learned some of the local folks' names. She came across a really inexpensive apartment. She was healed physically, just some scars here and there. She was starting to think that this was where she was meant to be. She was happy here. She knew when the time came for Jack's release she had to be ready to move at a moment's notice. She knew he would never stop looking for her. But for now she had a little under a year to enjoy life for a while here in Wellsprings, North Carolina.

Josie loved the town. She could walk everywhere. She even started getting back in shape again. She started running again. She was working her way back into her old routine, the routine before Jack. She was taking time to figure out who she was and she liked who she was finding. The only thing she needed and wanted was friends. She was a little lonely but filled her time with running and walking through town. There were old buildings that looked like log cabins; some had been refurbished. Some had additions to them, but kept the character and integrity of the buildings.

Her apartment was in one of the old buildings on the main street of town. It had a small stoop in front with two steps. The exterior was stone with wood beams running through it. It looked like it was a small cabin that was reinforced with the beams and stone.

There were a lot of older buildings in town and they were all so charming to her. She loved the character of them. It must be the rustic feel that they had.

Josie and Michael loved the cabin in the woods, mountains and all of what nature had to offer. Okay she didn't like the bugs, snakes and possibility of bears, so this town was just perfect. A little rustic charm without all that other stuff. Her apartment was very cute. Just inside the front door was a flat area with hooks for coats and hats, then to the right two small steps to her living room. The apartment came with furniture. She had a beige love seat and a glass coffee table. There were some glass shelves on the wall for decorating. A chair sat opposite of the loveseat, it was also beige. She had a beautiful window that she looked right out from her living room onto the main street of town.

Josie's apartment had one bedroom, perfect for her. She had a small kitchen with a very small wooden table and two chairs. She had her appliances: dishwasher, stove, oven and microwave. The kitchen was small with no fancy décor or high end appliances. Josie always loved cooking and this kitchen would be more than what she needed to start cooking again. She had a hallway leading from the kitchen to the bedroom and bathroom. There were hardwood floors in most the house, except the entry way, kitchen and bathroom which were tiled. The bedroom had a dresser, night stand, closet and a bed. The apartment was simple, plain and nothing fancy, pretty much just like Josie.

Josie saw a medical office one day while she was out for her run. She had been in town a couple of months and she thought she should probably get a check-up, to make sure all was healed or at least get herself established with a local doctor. When she walked in the lady behind the desk was talking and laughing with another woman. When they saw Josie they greeted her warmly and by name. "How did you know my name?" The woman behind the desk just laughed as she responded, "You are the only person in town that we don't know so we figured you were the elusive Josie we've heard about. We've heard so much about you, it's like we already know you. Hazards of a small town." Josie liked this woman immediately, she had a way about her that just seemed genuine, her smile was open, warm and traveled all the way to her eyes. It put Josie so much at ease. Even though it seemed more of a formality, Josie stuck out her hand, "Well anyway I am Josie Morris, and you are?" The woman took her hand and smiled. "I'm Sarah Blake. This is one of the doctors here, Miranda Porter. We are both pleased to meet you." The other woman came forward to shake

Josie's hand as well. "So what brings you into our office today?" Josie smiled at Miranda, "I'm looking to get an appointment for a check-up. Since I am staying here in town, I thought it was best to get established with a local doctor."

Miranda came out from behind the desk and waved her down the hall. "Well, now would be good. How 'bout we go in the exam room and get some information from you, then we'll check you out." Josie was shocked, she stuttered "But I don't have my wallet or anything with me. I was just out for a run. I thought I would just set up an appointment." Miranda just laughed. "I believe that the apprehension I see on your face is more than likely going to keep you from ever coming back in the building. I know people, and you definitely don't like doctors, exams or even being here right now." Miranda continued to guide Josie into the treatment room. "Now is as good a time. We had a lull in the schedule so all works out. You're here, might as well take care of you now instead of you never coming back. This is a small town, Josie we take walk-ins all the time." Miranda smiled and Josie tried to relax. Miranda was correct getting Josie back into the office for her appointment probably would take a small miracle.

Miranda handed her some paperwork to fill out and a gown to change into. She excused herself, as she stepped out of the room briefly. She came back in just as Josie was finishing with the forms already changed into the gown for a quick physical. Miranda had locked up the office as Sarah was leaving for the day. Sarah only worked a few hours a day since she had her baby. "I just had to lock up the office so no one came in while we were here. All the other doctors are rounding or off today. Sarah's been sticking it out for now until I find some new help. She's taken pity on me and my disorganization, plus she's my best friend practically since birth. She's hoping I find a replacement soon, as she's anxious to just be home with her little girl." Miranda saw what looked like apprehension on Josie's face. "Is everything okay, Josie?"

Josie was accustomed to people staring at her, but this woman didn't seem to be staring at her or looking at her with pity. Josie knew that some of her scars were visible in the gown. She was feeling really uncomfortable, but she plunged ahead anyway. "Yes I'm fine. You know Dr. Uhmm... I'm sorry all I caught was Miranda." Miranda held her hand up and smiled, "Miranda is fine." So Josie plunged on, "Well, Miranda, I'm a medical assistant. I don't have any office experience, but I'd love to interview for the position if you are in need of some help." Miranda's eyes lit up as she smiled, "How about we get through the reason you're here, then we can talk about it." Josie figured that was fair, but after her sordid tale and medical history, she was sure the interview would be postponed forever.

Josie went through her medical history explaining what was necessary trying to keep out what wasn't. Miranda was looking at Josie with concern for what she had been through. She could tell that there was more that she wasn't ready to share. Josie was keeping her at bay. Josie liked the woman, but could she trust her? Could she finally open up and let everything out that she had been holding in for so long?

All Josie had ever wanted in life was to have a family. She dreamed of that family so many times. Almost as if on cue Miranda asked her, "Have you ever had children?" Josie shook her head. She wanted to trust this woman. She wanted to finally be free of all the things that she suffered at the hands of her husband. She started slowly, "I miscarried twice. I was only a few months along both times. My husband is currently in jail. He was physically abusive to me." Miranda paused from writing in her chart to look at Josie. "I believe the miscarriages happened from the things he did to me."

Miranda was looking at her encouragingly and Josie continued. "He repeatedly forced me into having sexual relations. He would tie me or shackle me to the bed because I would otherwise not have allowed it. I tried to fight but it only made things worse for me. I am unsure with all that my body has been through if I will ever be able to have children. After the two miscarriages I never got pregnant again. I assumed children will never happen for me." Josie hung her head and a few tears escaped.

Miranda didn't say a word. She stood up silently grabbed some tissues and placed a hand on her shoulder. "No one should ever have to suffer as you have. I'm sorry." Those words from her were all Josie needed to dissolve into tears. Miranda placed her arms around her to let the woman cry. She needs to be allowed to let it go, yet she guards herself completely.

Josie straightened herself and pulled her emotions in. "I'm so sorry Miranda. I've made a fool of myself. I don't know why, I mean I never usually...." Miranda held up her hands, "Please don't apologize. You are human, and you probably have never allowed yourself to mourn those two babies you lost, let alone mourn your loss of freedom. It's okay to have emotions after all you've been through. We all have our scars and burdens. Some are easy to tolerate, others, well they fester, grow and take longer to come out." Josie looked at the doctor and smiled a weak little smile. She thought Miranda was a nice person and Josie was thinking how happy she was that she found herself in this town. Miranda made her feel at ease, comfortable, and she felt safe. It wasn't often in her life that she felt safe, but here in Wellsprings she did.

Miranda performed a complete physical for Josie. She listened to Josie's heart and lungs, looked in her ears, throat and eyes. She had her lay back. She did a breast exam, checked the abdominal area for any pain, tenderness or any evident issues. "Ok Josie you do not seem to have any tenderness, but I would like to do an internal exam, then we are all done." With all she'd been through, having anyone touch her was bad enough, let alone having a pap smear. She only knew Miranda for a few minutes. She was not afraid of her. In fact, she liked the woman. She just didn't know if she could follow through with the internal examination. Miranda guided her into position and advised her, "I will tell you everything I am doing before it happens; if anything hurts, you tell me and we stop. You need to try and relax, okay?" Josie verbalized agreement and closed her eyes, while tears roll down her face. She was tense and needed to find a way to relax her body.

Josie's mind had a way of allowing her to escape from what was happening to her. It was the only way she could cope with the things that happened to her. Whenever Jack was beating her, having sex with her, or sexually torturing her, Josie's mind would wander. As always her thoughts drifted to Michael. His smile, the laugh and the way he would place his hand on her back to guide her into a room. He would gaze down at her with a look in his eyes, and a crooked smile that always made him even sexier to her. He looked at her like she was important, special, like she was loved.

Josie was feeling discomfort from the examination. Miranda was trying to be quick and careful. "We're almost done Josie; hang in there with me." A few times Josie was ready to tell her to stop. It was terrible for her to be so vulnerable. She felt a lot of pressure from the speculum inserted in her, and she felt every scrape of the brushes collecting tissue for the slides. "All done Josie, just slide yourself back a little." She did as she was told and Miranda came beside her. "I'm sorry if I hurt you. I know that was not easy for you. But you did great. Why don't you get dressed then come on out to my office so we can talk." Josie nodded her head. She waited for Miranda to leave the room before getting off the table and getting dressed.

Josie found Miranda sitting behind a small but practical desk and she motioned Josie in. Miranda was writing in what Josie assumed was her chart. She sat back and waited. Miranda put her pen down and looked across the desk. "So physically Josie, things are fine. Health-wise you are in good shape. Your body has been through a lot. You've suffered a lot, but I can tell you from a medical standpoint things are right where they should be." Miranda looking at Josie said, "As far as that job goes: I'm looking for front office help basically making appointments, answering phones, keeping me organized; and I will train you for some other things as they come up. If you are interested, I'd love to start having Sarah train you right away." Josie looked at her like she just told her she won the lottery. "The pay is $15 an hour to start, with raises based on job performance. Some days may be 5 hours, others may be 10 hours. You never know. I do rounds at the hospital, having an extra pair of hands is helpful. If you are interested, I'd love to have you as part of my team."

Josie was in shock. She looked at Miranda, all she could think to say is, "Are you kidding me?" Miranda laughed, smiling at her,

"No I'm not kidding you. Look, I need the help. I feel a connection with you. You seem like a genuine, hard-working woman who hasn't really had many breaks in life. You deserve one, so what do you say?" Josie couldn't think. Things like this didn't happen to her. She stood up and put her hand out, "You won't be sorry. I promise you. I would love to work for you. I'm willing to learn whatever you will teach me. I'm waitressing at the diner, but I'm sure I can work something out with them. I'll be here tomorrow. What time do we start?" Miranda laughed and told her eight am would be great. Miranda showed her around the office. Josie left there on cloud nine. She knew this town was right for her. She ran home with the first true smile she'd had in years beaming across her face.

Chapter 3

Josie got home, took a shower then headed to the diner to talk to her boss. She worked out things at the diner. Turns out they weren't in need of full-time help any longer so her hours were going to be cut. They offered her some shifts on an as-needed basis. Once she got her work schedule from Miranda or an approximate schedule she could let them know at the diner to work out some extra hours there if she wanted them. Then she headed to one of the local stores to buy some scrubs to go to work at her new job. She was so grateful to Miranda for giving her this chance.

Josie was not paying attention on her way out of the store, she ran right into Sarah and her husband. "I am so sorry Sarah. I was in a fog. I wasn't paying attention." Sarah laughed, she waved it off. "Not a problem at all Josie. I'm so glad we ran into you. Miranda told me you'll be starting at the office tomorrow. I'm so excited for you, well and me. I can't wait to be home all the time with my baby girl, Bella." Josie smiled down at the beautiful little girl in the stroller. She was so cute as she smiled up at Josie. Josie reached out her hand to Sarah's husband, after tearing her attention away from Bella. "I'm Josie. It's nice to meet you." He reached out his hand smiling, "Nice to meet you Josie. I'm Chief Ted Blake of the Wellsprings police department. This town has been buzzing about you." Josie's smile dropped when Ted said he was the police chief. She knew she'd have to meet up with the local police eventually but she really hated that Sarah's husband was the police chief.

Sarah noticed the exchange and thought it strange the way Josie reacted to Ted. "So Josie, we're going to go to the Heartbreak Bar on the outskirts of town tonight. Would you like to come out with us? Miranda and Rod are coming as well." Josie hesitated at first, then thought why not. "Sure that would be fun. I haven't been out in forever." They made arrangements to meet at the office and they could all go together. They decided to meet at seven, that would give Sarah and Ted time to grab a bite to eat after dropping Bella off at the babysitter.

Josie headed back home. She was off to a good start she had a new job, with a boss who knows all the crazy details of her marriage. The other friend she met, her husband is the police chief in town and he's going to know as well. Oh boy she picked the wrong people to try and be friends with. Hopefully all would go well and she wouldn't lose the only friends she had in town. She tried to think positively but what were the chances that this would all work out. In her lifetime only one thing was ever right and he ran away from her. She drove the love or her life away and now she didn't think she'd ever love again. She tried not to go there with her thoughts but it was too late. She couldn't stop dwelling on Michael or Mike as everyone but her called him. He was always the one who protected her.

Josie met Michael as a teenager he was a bouncer at an under 21 place called Club Escape, where all the kids hung out. She was almost seventeen when she met him and was pretty much a free spirit. Her parents didn't bother with her much. Once she was in high school, they pretty much did their own thing. They had their own lives, Josie cooked for herself, she got her own lunches together, but they would leave her money to get groceries when they were out of town. So she pretty much took care of herself. When they were home they never knew if she was home or not. She was at Escape Club when her boyfriend, Joe walked in with another girl.

Josie confronted Joe and the girl. She really didn't care all that much that he was cheating on her as she heard the rumors, but it mattered that he thought so little of her and her feelings to treat her that way. She ended the confrontation by saying, "Someday I'll know what real love is, but you, well I don't hold my breath that you'll ever find true love. If you do get lucky enough to find your true love, I hope she's smart enough to drop you on your ass and laugh while she walks away." She turned on that note. When she went out the front door she didn't realize that the bouncer was following her.

"Hey beautiful wait a second." Josie stopped and turned around. Surely he wasn't talking to her. When she spun around she saw a rather large gorgeous blonde haired man coming toward her. She didn't know what to do, so she just froze. "Hey. I heard you in there. That was pretty classy. You could have gone all crazy and wild on them but you handled that like a classy woman." Josie still starring at him, wasn't sure what to say at first. "Thank you. I knew he was cheating on me. It didn't really matter that much. He was just a stepping stone to my pond awaiting."

The gorgeous giant smiled at Josie. She felt her knees go weak. "I should go. I don't want to keep you from your job." She turned to walk away but he kept following after her. "Where are you going? You don't have to leave. You could stay. Maybe keep me company. The closest I've ever come to a fight here was you in there tonight." He chuckled, she turned and smiled back at him.

Josie walked toward the gorgeous giant. He reached out his hand to her. She took his hand and thought a lightning bolt came out of the sky and struck her where she stood. It was the most powerful feeling she'd ever experienced. She came beside him and he dropped her hand. He placed his hand on her lower back guiding her back to the porch of the club. “Wait here.” He went inside and brought out a bar stool for her to sit on. He leaned against the building as they talked for what seemed like hours.

Josie was so entranced by Michael she never saw anyone come in our out. They both seemed to only have eyes for each other. She asked him his name and she’ll never forget his answer. He reached his hand out to her, “I’m Mike. At least that’s what everyone around here calls me. My mother, called me Michael. I never really felt like I deserved that name. It felt strong and important.”

Josie took Michael’s hand in hers and stepped off the stool. She moved up close to him. She felt a need to be closer to him to make him see how important he was. He stood straight up when she moved off the stool to head toward him. She tugged his arm as he bent down to her. She kissed his cheek softly. He turned his head to her. She could feel his breath. She whispered, “It’s nice to meet you Michael. I’m Josie.” She doesn’t know how long they stood there that way, but the spell didn’t break until someone came out and yelled, “Yo Mike, what up dude?” She saw a flicker of irritation maybe, anger at the interruption. She dropped her head and moved away from him slightly. Michael mumbled to her “I’ll be right back.” He stomped toward the group that interrupted them and she climbed back up on the bar stool. She watched him walk away and thought wow! How did she get so lucky to meet this man? He was gorgeous and, had beautiful blue eyes that lead to his soul. He paid attention to her and wanted to spend time with her. No one, not even her parents wanted to spend time with her. Why this man?

Josie brought herself back to the present slowly. She could almost feel Michael's touch, his breath and his hand on her back. So many times these past few years she swore she could feel his hand on her guiding her. She knew it was all in her mind but God how she wished some days that he really was there guiding her. She got herself dressed and ready for a night out with her new friends. She just hoped for the best.

Josie left her apartment walking to her new place of employment where she found everyone waiting for her. Miranda introduced her boyfriend, Rod and they all climbed into the Suburban belonging to Sarah and Ted. Everyone chatted on the way to the Heartbreak bar. The girls talked about the office and how excited they were to have Josie part of the crew. The guys were busy talking police business in hushed voices. Miranda said she was really glad Josie was going out tonight.

She thought it was a good start. Josie smiled and nodded. She sat and listened to the conversation between Sarah and Miranda. Josie was smiling and interacting but her mind was still thinking about Michael.

It only took 15 minutes to get to the bar it was on the outskirts of Wellsprings and in the next town technically. The town was Kellersville, North Carolina. They all climbed out of the car to head in. The ladies went through the open door that Ted held for them and Josie followed them to a table next to the dance floor. The guys went to the bar to get drinks for the ladies.

Josie looked around and it was really a cute place. It was very rustic. There was a stage for a band and a nice size dance floor. The bar was spacious and surrounded with twinkling lights and a beautiful granite top. The floors were wooden. The table tops looked like they were made out of large trees stained to preserve them. The tables were her favorite. They were beautiful and she couldn't stop herself from rubbing her hand over the table they were seated at.

The guys were at the bar where they saw the owner. "Hey Mike, how's it going?" He came over with a big smile and shook hands with Ted then Rod. "Hey guys. Where are the ladies tonight or are you flying solo?" Ted laughed, "Are you kidding, they live to go out on the town. They're over there with the new girl in Wellsprings, Josie."

Mike's eyes shot up and over in the direction they were pointing and he saw Josie. She was rubbing her hand over the table and smiling. She was saying something to her friends. He saw her lips moving but he couldn't hear her. He watched her talking and longed to hear her voice. She was just as beautiful as the last day he saw her. Her long brown hair flowing over her shoulders, he couldn't see her eyes but he remembered them, they were hazel with flecks of brown in them. Her skin was lightly tanned and her body was more mature and beautiful than he remembered. Her eyes were bright and beautiful and he remembered them every time he thought of her. While he watched her lips moving he remembered how they felt against his. He looked at her and yes she had changed, she matured. But she was just as beautiful as the day she walked into The Escape Club. She wasn't as thin as she was back then but her body held beautiful curves. He felt his body react to seeing her. He never could get enough of her. He had wanted her just as much now as he did back then.

How was Josie here? He knew she was in Wellsprings, he heard people talking about the new girl. It's a small town and word travels over to the next town. He went to the diner where she was working just to be sure it was his

Josie they were all talking about. He stood outside watching her, through the big windows. He nearly crumbled and ran to her begging forgiveness. He watched her and remembered the times they had together, he could never forget her. He loved her, then and now.

Mike knew it was possible Josie would come into the Heartbreak bar, but he wasn't ready yet. He needed some time. Then he thought time for what? Weren't the last eleven years, enough time for him to think? "What's wrong Mike? You look like you've seen a ghost." Mike chuckled, he ran his hand through his hair as he leaned in to the guys, "You could say that. Hey, do me a favor, don't mention me to Josie, ok?" The guys looked at each other, then back at Mike. Ted spoke, "Sure, but is there a problem?"

Mike shook his head. "No not a problem, just a past. I need some time till I come face to face with Josie. She's an incredible woman, and well, you guys know my past. I don't think I'm ready to own up to that with her." Ted looked at Mike, he shook his head. "Someday you have to let go of the past. You did your time dude. You've turned your life around. Cut yourself a break, but you got it, for now we won't mention your name." Mike said thank you to the guys then he turned to head back into the shadows to watch.

The guys headed back to the table and discussed how odd the conversation was they had with Mike. "Ted did you see how he was looking at Josie?" Rod was voicing the concern that Ted had been thinking as well. "Yes I saw it. I don't know what is going on but I sure think we need to figure it out. I've never seen Mike react that way to anyone. It's very strange. It's like he has known her his whole life." Rod agreed. They stopped the discussion as they reached the table.

They delivered the drinks to the women and Ted put a Rum and Diet Cola down in front of Josie, wine for his wife and Miranda. Rod had his beer and they all sat down getting to know each other. Josie sipped at her drink as she hadn't had a drink in almost ten years. She didn't drink much normally, after her eight years with Jack, she learned to despise the smell and what it brought out in him. She must have gotten a dark look on her face as Ted leaned toward her, "Everything ok?"

Josie gave Ted a weak attempt at a smile, "No but it will be." He let her comment go for now but he was feeling his inner detective coming out. First Mike acting so strange and now Josie, something was definitely going on. Things were just not adding up with this woman. Between the way Josie reacted when she found out he was the police chief, the conversation he and Rod had with Mike, now the look and comment Josie had made, he wished he knew what was going on.

Josie was enjoying herself. She watched Sarah and Miranda dancing they were waving her to come out too. She wasn't a big dancer so she just shook her head. She had a feeling she was being watched. The hair on her neck was standing up and she was feeling electricity in the air. It was the strangest feeling. She found herself looking around the room wondering why she felt so uneasy. She turned toward the bar, she saw someone in the shadows of the bar but she could only see a silhouette. Ted saw her looking that way and tried distracting her. "So Josie, what brings you to our town?"

Josie turned her attention back to the men sitting at the table. "Well as a matter of fact I wanted to come talk with you. I've just been putting it off. I wanted to try having a normal life for a change." The guys both seemed to completely turn their attention to her. Rod spoke up this time. “What’s going on? Are you in trouble?” Josie waved her hand at him, “Not really. It’s nothing like that. I’m actually running away.”

Josie saw the guys exchange a glance and she continued on before she lost her nerve. “I’m running from my husband. He was physically abusive for the last three years of our marriage. The last beating he gave me had me in the hospital for a while and we ended up in court. He was sentenced to three years but could get out within the next six months for good behavior, serving a total of only two years. I tried to get him to sign divorce papers but the judge wouldn’t force him to sign. I’ve spent the past year and a half fighting him in court, recovering then trying to lose myself somewhere so he can’t find me. I’m still married to him, so I’m sure when he does get out, he’ll be looking for me. I’ll be on the run again. I wanted you to know Ted, being that you are head of law enforcement here in Wellsprings. I don't want to bring trouble to your town so I will try and move on before he finds me, which I hate because I really like it here. I really don't want to be any trouble." Ted and Rod looked at each other.

Ted rubbed his face and said in such a tone she was kind of afraid, "What is his name?" Rod was looking over his shoulder toward the bar and wondering what Mike knew about this or if he somehow was involved in it. Time frame wise it was impossible for the husband to be Mike but how was he connected to this woman. Josie looked at them and answered the question, "Jack Morris." Ted looked at Josie, he went to take her hand in his and she flinched but didn't pull away. Ted didn't miss the jerk of her hand but he tried to keep his hand on hers. "You don't worry about being trouble. You are no trouble at all. Besides you are becoming part of our family.

We will worry about Mr. Morris, so help me if he ends up in this town and sneezes too loudly we will personally escort him out. I have no tolerance for men like that. There is no excuse for what he did to you." Rod nodded in agreement. "You are the victim and do not need to run anymore. You are home. Besides Josie, you can't run forever, eventually the past catches up to you."

Josie looked at Rod, "No I guess I can't run forever, but it's hard to sit knowing he's coming for me. At least if I am running my mind is occupied on where I'm going and what I'm going to do next. Some of my past I wouldn't mind if it showed up, but the last eight years are better off staying in the past." Her eyes filled up with tears. Ted was still holding her hand, he gave it a squeeze and pat before removing his hand from hers.

Josie couldn't believe her luck meeting these people. They were unlike anyone she had ever met before. They were the friends she had been looking for her whole life. Ones who stood beside her and didn't leave her standing alone and afraid, she really didn't want any harm to come to them so it surely would be hard to leave them.

Josie pushed her chair back, she excused herself to go to the ladies' room. She was trying not to cry but a few tears were betraying her and rolling down her cheek. She wanted to move away from the group before they saw it. Her mind was turning the whole way to the ladies' room. Once there she wiped her eyes, fixed her makeup and just thought about the friends she had made. She was missing only one piece of the puzzle to her life. It was the big center piece, Michael. If only she still had him she would finally have the life she'd always wanted and needed. If what Rod said was true, that the past eventually catches up with you maybe someday she would find Michael again.

Mike had been watching the exchange, he couldn't stand to see the tears in Josie's eyes. He pounced as soon as she was out of the room. "What the hell guys?" Ted and Rod stood to Mike's words. "What is going on, why was she crying? She was crying wasn't she?" Rod was filled with a rage at what he just heard and Ted was trying to figure Mike's place in this equation. "Mike, how do you know this woman? I need to know." Ted was pushing his friend for answers and Mike wasn't the kind of guy who liked to be pushed. Mike ran his hand through his hair, he looked so distraught that Ted was starting to think he was involved with her.

"Look Ted, I can't get into it right now. Not with Josie possibly coming out here at any moment. How bout I come to the station tomorrow and I can fill you in." Ted slapped him on the shoulder and nodded agreement. Mike turned so he could head to the shadows again right as Josie came out of the ladies' room. "Hey guys. Who was that?" Rod stammered, "Who, that guy? Oh uh, he's the owner. Matt I think his name is." Josie smiled, took a sip of her drink. "I think I'm going to give it a try on the dance floor. For some reason I feel, free." Ted and Rod smiled at her as she turned heading toward the dance floor. "Smooth Rod, really smooth." Rod looked at his friend and chuckled, "She caught me off guard. What was I supposed to say?" Ted shook his head, "I need to go make a call. I'm going to get some information before Mike comes in tomorrow. I'm going to find out what happened to our girl there and find out what I can about Jack." Rod nodded as Ted stepped out of the bar to get the information he needed.

Ted dropped Josie off at her door. He was on his way to take his other passengers home as well. Miranda, who never misses a thing, said "So who's going to tell us what's going on?" Rod and Ted laughed. They knew if they didn't spill the information she wanted she wouldn't rest until she knew. Rod started to tell her about the abusive husband, "I know all that. I want to know about what happened at the bar, with Mike." Rod looked at Miranda. The woman never ceased to amaze him. Of course she already knew about the abusive husband. Miranda had a way of getting people to open up. Look at what she had done to him.

Ted spoke up about Mike. "I'm not sure what is going on with Mike yet but don't spill any information to Josie about Mike. Not even his name." The girls both looked at each other, then at Ted and Rod. "Mike's rules not ours. He's coming to see me tomorrow so hopefully

I'll know what's going on then. So until I know what's happening, zip it ladies." Miranda and Sarah were both stunned. They've been going to Heartbreak bar for the last few months. They had seen the owner there but he really kept to himself at first. He purchased the bar about a year ago. Max was present first during the construction and then Mike showed up about six months ago. Mike seemed like a stand-up guy. He had really cleaned up the bar and made some beautiful changes to it. Mike changed the bar's name, and the doors opened officially about the time Josie came to town. Coincidence? Or Planned? Miranda's mind had started rolling. Miranda couldn't wait to know more.

Chapter 4

Josie was so excited. She was up at five am, went for a run, came home, made herself some coffee and scrambled eggs. She showered and dressed in her new scrubs. Josie was on her way with her new life. She was thrilled. Josie couldn't wait to get to work, her first day at a new job, and her first day with her career. Josie actually had a career now and she was free to explore where her schooling was going to take her. Josie walked, almost skipping all the way to the office. Her smile was genuine and she beamed at how her life was finally becoming what she had always wanted.

Mike got out of bed. He stood staring out the window. How was he going to fix this? How was he going to make things right again? Was there a way? Mike shook his head to try and clear his thoughts. He headed to the shower to get ready for his meeting with the police chief. Mike had a lot of explaining to do and he wasn't quite sure where to start. It was going to be a long day. While Mike showered, he remembered Josie and all the time he spent with her back in Springside Maine. He had never been as happy as he was back then. Mike loved the time he spent with her. Walking away from her nearly destroyed him. He hadn't been with another woman since Josie, and Mike didn't plan on ever being with anyone again. Josie owned his heart and soul.

"Good morning Sarah." Josie bounced into the office and Sarah looked up at her with a huge smile. Sarah was curious about this woman but she really liked her. She felt an instant connection with her and so did Miranda. It's like Josie was already part of their family. Sarah just hoped that Josie would stay. There was something so wholesome about her. Josie had a sad look in her eyes that made people wonder what she had gone through in her life. When Josie smiled it didn't quite reach her eyes. Almost like she was broken, like she didn't know how to be happy anymore. Sarah hoped that she would find her happiness again. Everyone deserved happiness and love in their lives. "Hey Josie, are you excited?" Josie nodded her head and geared up for her day of training.

Josie didn't see Miranda until closer to ten am. By this time, she learned so much from Sarah, she was just soaking it all in. Miranda came in she smiled at the two of them behind the desk. "Good morning ladies. How's the first day of training going?" Josie couldn't contain her excitement. "Oh it's incredible. I've been learning scheduling. I've been filing and getting familiar with the office. I've even answered the phone." Miranda laughed at the enthusiasm pouring out of the woman. "Well when the pope shows up show him in." She winked heading to her office laughing. Sarah and Josie laughed as well. "I guess I was a little too excited." Sarah smiled and made a small gesture with her two fingers, they laughed some more but continued on with the training.

When Josie got home from work she was exhausted. She was happy with all she learned today, it was a lot of information, but she was feeling really good about everything. Josie climbed into a nice warm bath leaning back with a deep sigh. She had put the radio on and listened as Adele sang the song that tore at her soul. That song just brought back so many memories.

Music made Josie emotional, especially when the lyrics of songs reached her soul. This song brought her to her knees. It played in her head when she thought of Michael and it tore at her soul, for she wanted one more night with him, a night to get the answers she needed, a night to hold him in her arms and beg him to stay. A night that would have changed the last years of her life.

Josie closed her eyes thinking about the days she spent as a teenager. Josie went to school every day, worked part time in a pizza/sandwich shop but she found a way to see Michael almost every day. They would meet at Escape after school or after she got done with work, once she graduated from high school. Josie didn't have a car so she would walk there. It wasn't far from her house and work. This was when she first started running. She first did it so that she had more time to spend with Michael. But Josie began to love it and she would find reasons to run, she even had Michael running with her on days he didn't have to be at the club. The only time she hated running was in the rain and snow, although she would walk through fire to be with Michael.

Josie didn't realize all the kids that hung out at the club even when they weren't open. People were coming and going all the time at first when she and Michael started hanging out, but then it seemed to become less and less. Josie commented to Michael once about it and he puzzled her with his response. "Sometimes you do things you're not proud of." Michael got up and moved pacing the floor in front of her. "You're just so set in your ways you don't know any different." Michael stopped in front of Josie, taking her hands, "Then you meet someone and you feel like you want to be better. You need to be better for her. But you're scared and don't know how to be the person she deserves."

Josie stood up, she reached to take Michael's face in her hands. "Michael, I'm not your mother. I am proud of you just as you are. In case you haven't noticed, I'm in love with you." Michael looked into her eyes, "God knows I don't deserve you, but I really want to believe that I do." Michael kissed her. They had kissed before but, this kiss was a soul stealing light every fiber of your body on fire. Michael's hands tangled in her hair as he pulled her head back while his tongue danced with hers. They stopped kissing and Michael leaned his forehead against hers. "Josie girl, I love you too. I don't know what I did to deserve you but I treasure every minute I have with you." Josie smiled at Michael as she leaned in to kiss him again.

Josie and Michael had been together almost a year. They would meet at the club. They would kiss, talk and hang out there. One night, just prior to her turning eighteen she said to him, "Michael, I want to be with you."

Michael stopped kissing her neck. “You are with me.” Josie looked at Michael, “No. I want to be with you, all of you. I want you to make love to me. I want to be part of you.” Michael looked at her stunned by her words.

Michael walked away from her, he turned his back. Michael was silent until finally he turned to Josie, “Why? Why do you want to be with me?” Josie didn’t know what to say to him at first. She just looked at him with tears in her eyes, “Because until I met you I felt like I didn’t exist, like I was no one on this earth. You are the reason I feel like I am someone. You make me feel special, loved, wanted and needed. Why do you find it so hard to believe that I would want to be with you? You are special Michael. You make me feel whole when I’m with you. You are my missing half. I want to be with you forever. Don’t you want that too?”

Michael was silent just watching Josie at first, then he walked back to her. He took her cheeks in his hands and kissed her. "You deserve so much more than I have to give you but I would give anything to be with you forever. I want to be with you so much it hurts, but I don't want to hurt you. I want you to be sure and ready." Michael stood there holding Josie's head, looking into her eyes. "You give me too much credit Josie. You are special. You are bright, funny, caring and your heart is so beautiful. How I got you is beyond me but I do treasure every minute I have with you." Josie leaned up to kiss him and held him to her. She pressed her body against Michael and just breathed him in. "One thing you need to know Josie, you are stronger than anyone I know. You are a beautiful soul. You can conquer the world, believe in yourself always. Promise me." Josie nodded her head at him.

Josie knew Michael was it for her. No one would ever compare to him. Michael was her soul, he made her complete. Michael was the man Josie needed in her life. No he was the man she deserved in her life. Josie may have only been seventeen going on eighteen but she knew Michael was it for her. She knew that with her whole heart. Michael pulled away, "Just give me some time, it won't be long. I don't think I can wait much longer. I've wanted to be with you since the first night I met you. I'll make it happen. I just want things to be special for us. I want you to have something nice. Not here at the club and not in my car. You deserve more than that."

Josie dipped her head as she said quietly, "This isn't my first time. I wish it was. I made a total error in judgement before we met and truly regret it now. I'm ashamed but it was only once." Michael tipped Josie's head up to him. She refused to look at him now that he knew the truth. “Look at me Josie.” Michael waited for her to comply. “It will be the first time for both of us.” Josie looked at him smiling. Michael kissed her gently on the lips, then he sent her home. Michael relayed he had work to do and Josie was a distraction.

Josie brought herself to stop the foolish reminiscing and got out of the tub. It was a million years ago. Michael was probably hundreds of miles away and besides why should she care anymore. Michael obviously didn’t care as much as she did. Hell Michael probably didn’t even remember her or their time together. It was a hard lesson to learn but Josie had to find a way to just let it all go. Michael walked away and never looked back, no explanation, worst of all no good-bye. Josie was left alone, confused and heartbroken. She would never understand why. She walked to a restaurant in town called Soups and Such. It was a favorite of the locals. They made homemade soups, breads, sandwiches and desserts. Josie had heard from around town that it was run by a family, a mother, father and daughter. The daughter, Taryn was the one who created everything, homemade. The word around town was that Taryn was very withdrawn due to something everyone referred to as the incident. Whatever that meant, Josie didn't care, she hated gossip. She ordered her food, then went to sit on the benches in the park at the center of town. She watched the fountain, relaxed a little and watched the people around town. Sometimes being alone was overrated for all her mind did was wander over her past and wonder where she had gone wrong.

Mike showed up at Ted's office. He walked in the front door of the police station.

Chills ran up and down his spine. He never wanted to see another police station in his life. He remembered the day he turned himself in at the police station. He walked into the police station, right up to the desk of the detective he was to turn himself into. "Remember the deal is me and you leave Josie alone. I want to clarify that this is going to be honored." The detective nodded to him in agreement. Mike sat and gave them all the information he promised them he would.

Mike's mind was deep in thought when Ted saw him and came over. He shook his hand and ushered him into his office. Rod was at his desk as they passed by, Mike nodded at him but he continued following Ted to his office. Ted closed the door, "Have a seat Mike. We have a lot to get caught up on."

Mike sat down, clasped his hands in front of him as he leaned forward with his elbows on his knees, head bowed down. “I never wanted to see the inside of one of these again.” He laughed a nervous laugh then sat back to look Ted in the eye. “I have plenty to be ashamed of but Josie was the best part of me. She is the reason I wanted to clean up. But when I decided to clean up it was too late. I had fallen so hard for her, I couldn’t, no I didn’t deserve her. She deserved so much more than I had to offer. What was I going to give her? I had nothing but a life I was ashamed of.” Ted looked at him and waited. “I’ve spent every night thinking about her. I laid awake plenty of nights cursing the day I followed her out of The Escape Club. She was so beautiful, so pure, so.... I should have just let her go.”

Ted couldn’t help himself, “Why do you feel you don’t deserve her? To me it sounds like she changed your life for the better. Every man deserves to find a woman that helps make him a better man. Sounds like that is just what you needed. Didn't she know what you were doing?"

Mike stood up, he started pacing in the small confines of Ted's office. He ran his hand through his hair. "That's just it Ted, she had no clue. I was at the club pushing drugs on those kids. I was the bad guy. I made money selling to them and that's all I had, drug money. You met her, you've seen her. She deserves better. From the first night I met her I hid it from her. I felt dirty, like I was the devil. She was so sweet, caring and wholesome. I didn't want to soil her with that. They all knew at the club when "Mike's girl" was there, stay away. No one was allowed to talk to her and tell her what they were doing there. If they did, they were done. I tried to protect her."

Ted listened to Mike, he just shook his head. "Dude, you need to lighten up. I hate drug dealers but you aren't that person. You haven't been for a long time. You never forced those kids to do anything either, you weren't out there bringing them to the club. They came to you and if not you it would have been someone else. The guys you worked for they were the ones who were the devil. I've seen your reports. You came here when you first rolled into town and registered with my office. I read all your files. You helped put those guys away and closed that place up but refused a lighter sentence for it. Why?" "I didn't deserve it. All I did was tell the truth." Mike explained.

Mike stood staring out into the police station with his back to Ted. "They wanted Josie too. They thought she was part of it. I told them the only way I'd help was if she was out of it. She had nothing to do with any of it. She was just unfortunate enough to be with me. I don't understand why she's here. How did she find this town? Why this town?" Mike went back to sit in the chair. "I heard she was married, why isn't her husband with her?" Ted stood up and motioned Rod to come in. Once he was in the office Ted told Mike the truth.

After the conversations Ted had with Josie and Mike he called in a few favors. He wanted to know what the husband had done to Josie and what to expect when and if he arrived in his town. He was appalled at the things he read. Rod and Ted combed through the files and the court records as well as Josie's medical records, prior to Mike showing up. It was amazing how this woman survived all the things he did to her. The police report of the last beating was heartbreaking. The police officer that was on the scene had commented that in all his years he had never seen anyone take such a vicious beating. The blood was everywhere. Somehow the woman pulled herself out of unconsciousness to look at him and beg him, “Help me! Please don’t let me die. I don’t want to die like this. Save me.” Then she went back into unconsciousness.

Rod and Ted both read the file. They just couldn’t believe the things that happened. Her medical chart and court report revealed some gruesome things sexually that she had gone through. They had found shackles in the bedroom, and devices that the gynecologist would use upon giving exams. The reports of the sexual abuse she endured was sickening. She relayed in her court transcripts how he would tie her or shackle her to the bed, cut her body with a knife and on occasion hold a gun to her. Once he even took the gun sticking the barrel of it inside her. Josie’s report on that incident was heartbreaking. She stated to the court that she prayed the gun would go off so she could just stop enduring the torture he devised against her every day. She just wanted to die, versus put up with anymore.

Rod read this and threw the file at Ted, "I can't read any more of this shit. I want to kill the son of a bitch. He is one sick bastard Ted. How could someone like this get away with doing this? He did all this to her and he didn't get put away for life. Where is it fair?" Ted didn't disagree but he reminded Rod that they needed to think of Josie and protect her. They couldn't focus on what she had been through at the hands of a mad man.

Mike was off his chair, it tipped over and he was trapped between the two men. Rod took him by the front of the shirt, "Chill dude. Relax. You going wild and getting yourself into trouble is not going to do her any good. Sit back down." Mike paced a little and started to breathe more naturally. He righted his chair and sat back down. He spoke with anger dripping out of him, hands balled into fists, his face red from the anger. "He doesn't deserve her. He should be beaten the way he beat her. How much time did he get?" Ted shook his head, "You really don't want to know." Mike looked at him, "Tell me!" Ted told him that his sentence was almost up for good behavior. He was given three years but he was going to only end up serving two years. He also told him that she pushed the courts for a divorce but it was not granted, he refused to sign the papers. "He's going to get out and come for her. I can most likely guarantee it."

Mike could feel his heart hammering in his head. The pulsing was showing in his neck as well. "I'm not going to let that happen, I don't care what it takes. He will never touch my girl again. How could this happen? All the years I served and he walks away with a slap on the wrist. He nearly killed her. How can he walk away barely serving any time, he deserves to rot in jail for what he did to her, I'll kill him if he touches her!"

Rod held up his hands, "Wait a minute. First of all, you aren't going to do anything. The Department will protect her, nothing will happen to her under our watch and secondly you need to stay away from him if and when he comes around. You are not going to get yourself back in trouble for trash like him. Besides, don't you think Josie has suffered enough? Finding you again then losing you again would destroy her." Ted nodded agreement.

Mike shouted, "What am I supposed to do, sit here and let him hurt her again? That won't happen. I'd go back to jail before that." Ted slammed his fist on his desk and rose up leaning forward to Mike, "You damn well are going to back off! This is none of your concern.

We will handle this." Mike furious stood up and leaned into Ted's face, "The hell it's not my concern I love her and I will never stop! I will not let her suffer anymore!" Ted sat back down and smiled at Mike, "So you love her. Are you going to clue her in? Or are you going to keep hiding from her?"

Mike sank back down in his chair. Rod patted his shoulder and quietly left the room, he was called in to help control Mike through the anger of learning the truth. His job was done it was up to Ted to convince Mike to face his past and claim what he never allowed himself to fully have. "How can I tell her? What right do I have? I fucked up. Did she tell you how I left her?" Ted shook his head no.

Mike sat there and watched it play in his head. "She came to the cabin looking for me. I had just blown up at Chad and told him I was done. I warned her to never come to the cabin without me because Chad was evil, I never knew what he would do. Chad was furious with me he had been for months because I stopped producing. After the night Josie and I made love, I wanted away from that life. Truth was I didn't know what else to do. I knew the cops were watching me and waiting. But when Josie showed up she was angry, she pounded on the door. I told Chad to tell her I was gone. I hid from her I couldn't face her. I watched her to be sure Chad didn't touch her. "Chad, where is he? I need to see him." Chad laughed, "He's gone. He's done with you little girl." Josie was furious, she didn't believe him she pushed past him and headed to my room, crying and screaming my name. Chad was laughing, "I told you he's gone." She was angrier than I had ever seen her. She had her back toward where I was so only Chad could see me. She was shaking and crying so hard, "Where is he? I have to be with him, he wouldn't leave me especially not without saying good bye." Chad laughed, "You're just a stupid kid. Mike's moved on. Don't you get it? You were fun for him, now it's over." Josie slapped him across the face and I smiled. That was my girl, she was definitely feisty. Chad grabbed ahold of her, he shook her then growled at her. I poked my head out of the closet I was hiding in and he then just pushed her out the door. As soon as that door was closed I went after Chad and I knocked his ass out."

Mike sat silent for a minute. Ted saw the pain in his eyes and the clenching of his jaw. "She didn't deserve that but I was too chicken shit to face her. I knew if I saw her or tried to talk to her I wouldn't turn myself in and change things for the better, for us, for her. When I was with her I couldn't think straight. I just wanted more and more of her. She was so mad because I had been avoiding her for almost two weeks." Mike stood again. He looked out in the police station. "I was heading to the police station from the cabin but I had to go by the club. I parked up the road and walked in through the trees. She was there sitting on the steps to the club her head in her lap and she was sobbing." Mike turned back to look at Ted, "I could have gone to her then but I didn't. I just watched her. Several people walked past her, they never stopped. I must have watched her for an hour crying. She finally stood and started walking through the parking lot. She got close to where I was standing. It was the spot where I first approached her and fell in love with her. I heard her say "I love you Michael, wherever you are please come home to me." How do you just walk away from that?" He went back to the chair. He fell, defeated into it.

Ted understood his pain, he felt it. Hell he lived it. "Mike all I can tell you is you need to tell her you're here and explain to her what happened. She'll be angry I'm sure but she'll forgive you if she still loves you, then you can be together and start over." Mike shook his head, "No. I don't deserve her forgiveness and no one tells her I'm here." Ted nodded, "Whatever you want. But you're making a mistake. After all that woman has been through, she deserves a man who loves her, who will treat her the way she deserves and who's not afraid to face his past. She's stronger than you think. I also believe that her nature is forgiving Mike. You need to give her and you a chance. None of us are going to lie to her forever. You have some time, but the girls I can't control. You know Sarah and Miranda are very fond of her already. It's only a matter of time till she finds out, she deserves to find out from you."

Mike got up turning to leave he stopped. He couldn't face Ted all he could do was say, "I appreciate your help. Maybe I am making a mistake but I've made so many with her that I don't even know where to begin to pick up the pieces. If I hadn't left her she would never have endured the things she did, how could she ever forgive me for that now? I caused her more heartache and physical pain with my actions. I truly will never deserve her now." With that Mike opened the door and stormed out so fast that he didn't even acknowledge Rod along the way.

Rod headed to Ted's office, "That went well. I'm sure glad you didn't tell Mike about the sexual abuse. There would have been no stopping him." Ted shook his head, "I know. He truly loves her and that information would have put him back in jail. He would have never contained his fury. Hell, we're not in love with her and want to rip the guy limb from limb. If Mike can get through his stubbornness they would have a shot."

Rod started laughing at his friend, "Spoken like the King of Stubborn Land." Ted filled him in on what he had missed and the two men sat silent for a few minutes. Rod was the first to speak. "What do you think will happen if he finds out about the things you didn't tell him. I mean all of the things she endured? There will be no controlling him, will there?" Ted nodded his head in agreement, "No he will lose control. We just have to hope he never finds that out or if he does, it's from her and she can control him. I have a feeling that Josie holds all the keys to that one, only she has the power to control the beast that lies inside that man." They were silent for a moment and then there was a knock at the door.

Chapter 5

Mike was furious with all he'd just learned. How did he not know that Josie's husband was beating her? He had people reporting back to him about her, keeping tabs on her. At least that's what they were supposed to have been doing, the last few reports had been kind of repetitive and now come to think of it his spies all seemed nervous when reporting to him. He gave up his life of drugs, but it was still handy to keep around some of the people he used to know. He headed to his apartment above the bar and made some calls. That boy would be lucky if he could walk when Mike was done with him. He had contacts on the inside. Jack Morris was going to find out what it was like to have the shit beat out of him.

"It's Mike. I need a favor. I want to know all there is to know about Josie's husband. I know the truth." The person on the other end was stammering, for fear of what would happen to him for not revealing the truth. “I don’t care if you knew or didn’t know. Now is the time to make up for it. Find out where he is and I want him beaten. I want him to feel her pain. I want to send a strong message. Tell him to divorce her and let her be or fear the wrath of me. I will find him and I will take care of him if it’s not done. I also want any information you can find on her. Don’t leave out anything. I want it all this time. If you leave anything out, I’ll come after you when I’m done with Jack Morris.” Mike was pacing and listening to the man on the other end. “I don’t care, if I end up back in jail so be it. I will not have her saddled with him for the rest of her life. I want her free to move on, and not always worrying about when he finds her. Got it! Just do it. Let me know when it’s done.” Mike hung up the phone. He hated that world but for her he would do what it took to get her free of her husband forever. It was the least he could do for her. He headed to the bar to get ready for the evening crowd.

Josie sat just watching the town. It was so peaceful. Not much traffic on the road and not many people milling about. She was restless sitting there. She thought she would just go home, but it was early. It was only six thirty. She thought of the bar they were at the night before and how nice it was there. Josie went home, got her car and headed there. Something about that place just seemed warm and welcoming.

Josie walked into the bar and ordered a Diet Cola. She really didn't drink much and besides she was just there to enjoy the surroundings. There was a juke box against the wall and the place was fairly empty. She went over to the jukebox and looked at the selection, great range of music a lot to choose from.

Someone came up behind her. She turned, it was the bartender. “Here’s your Diet Cola.” Josie moved away from the jukebox and took the drink. “Thank you. I’ll just grab my purse.” He waved at her, “No, that’s ok. It’s on the house. I heard you’re new in town.” He stuck his hand out and introduced himself. His name was Max. Josie shook hands with him, but trembled when her hand touched his. “It’s nice to meet you Max. I’m Josie. I heard the owners name is Matt. Is he here tonight?”

Max was confused at first but then realized she must have been told a different name to keep her from questioning. “Matt’s not here yet. He’ll be in shortly. Is there a problem?” Josie shook her head, “No just the opposite. This place is incredible. I hear he just purchased it and redid all this.” Max gestured her over to her seat and sat down with her for a few minutes. He told her that he was a partner but Matt designed everything. He was particular about how the place looked. Max explained to her that he had started the construction on the place to Matt's specifications and waited for Matt to get to town to take over. The bar had only been open a few months. Josie gushed, "Well it's wonderful in here. I wish it were busier for you guys." Max waved off her concern. "No worries. We're just getting started. We have a karaoke night coming up and we have bands coming in so, it'll pick up." Josie smiled at him. Max stood up, "Well, I better be getting back to work. It was nice meeting you and talking with you. I hope to see you around." She smiled at him, "Nice to meet you as well. I'll be here for that karaoke night. I think it sounds like a lot of fun." Max headed back to the bar and in the shadows saw Mike. Scowl set. Was that anger in his eyes or jealousy?

Mike stood in the shadows watching his friend talk to the only woman he ever loved. Mike was jealous. He watched Josie, she stood with her back to him looking at the jukebox. She had jeans on and a shirt that came just to the tip of her waist where her jeans rested. Mike watched as Josie moved, her shirt would lift ever so slightly. He begged it to raise just a little higher. It was torture seeing her so close and not being able to touch her, especially after all he'd just learned. Mike wanted to go over and wrap his arms around her waist, reach under that shirt and touch her skin. He wanted to take away all the pain Josie had suffered. Josie had turned and was talking with Max. Mike watched her mouth move as she talked with him. Mike missed those lips. Josie smiled at Max and Mike wished the smile was for him. She looked around the bar, he wished he knew what she was thinking. Ever since the other night Mike couldn't stop thinking about her.

He couldn't stop the ache he felt in his body, he couldn't stop wishing things had been different all those years ago.

"What was that about?" Mike nearly growled the words to his friend. "Relax Mike. I just introduced myself. She thinks your name is Matt. Josie loves the bar by the way, said she'd like to talk to Matt and tell him what she thinks about the place. She's also in for karaoke night. I think she's going to be coming here a lot. You better figure out how to get a handle on this, whatever it is you got going on here." Mike just stared in her direction while his friend talked to him. Max was right, they all were right but he just wasn't ready yet. Soon, he would have to figure it out. Max was a good friend. He was one of his correction officers in jail. Max knew all about Josie. She was all that he talked about in jail. Josie consumed his mind. Max helped him to feel better about himself, talked him through a lot of things during his time in jail. Max was a good friend and didn't deserve Mike's anger now. Mike was just so torn up over Josie's suffering. Seeing her so close and not being able to do anything about it made it even harder.

Max knew a guy back in his home town of South Carolina. The guy was an old high school friend, he knew of places for sale, businesses that were in trouble or owners who were running their places into the ground. Max's friend had said that there was a bar that a man wanted to sell. The man wasn't advertising as he didn't want the place ripped down. He wanted it saved and back to the potential he knew it had, he just didn't have the energy or funds to turn it around any longer. Max wanted to get out of the correction system, retire and move closer to home. Max had money but he didn't want to invest alone in something this big. Mike and Max talked about it. Mike wanted a fresh start when he got out and the bar seemed like just what he needed. A new town where no one knew him and a chance to start over. Mike had transferred money to Max and Max "retired" a year prior to Mike's release. Mike really missed his friend that last year there, but Max had the plans and was getting things ready to go. Max purchased the bar. He had started the construction alone but Max and Mike finished it together.

When Mike was released he wanted to see Josie before he left town, but no one knew where she was. All of his contacts seemed to have lost her. Little did he know that she was going to be heading right to him. Talk about fate. Mike was so caught up in watching her so entranced by her being so close he nearly missed that she was heading his way. Mike sunk back to the safety of the room behind the bar.

Max went to her, “Need a refill Josie?” She perched up on the bar stool, “That would be great. One more and then I gotta head home.” Mike stood behind the wall that separated him from her and he could hear her talking. Max had gotten her to laugh. Mike thought it was a beautiful sound. Just hearing her voice again stirred him in ways he hadn’t been in years. “So what are you doing in town? I know you’re new so you didn’t grow up here.” Josie got a faraway look on her face. “I’m trying to find who I am again. I lost myself for a few years. Now I’m just hoping to have a new start, a new me and the life I deserve.” Josie had tears in her eyes as she spoke.

Max smiled at her, “Well then I hope all your dreams come true little lady.” Josie smiled back. “I had a dream once. It was my own fairytale, now I just want honest and true. Simple enough right?" Max shrugged and walked away to tend to another customer. "It sounds so simple but yet it's still not what I had with Michael." Josie spoke to herself or so she thought but Mike heard every word. "What have I done Josie?" That was all he could say, and he could only say it to himself.

Josie drove home from the bar smiling to herself. It's so strange how comfortable she felt there. It felt like home. Josie felt safe there and she felt like this whole move was right. Josie was starting to feel like a normal person again. The weeks passed and then a month. Josie was loving her new life in this town. Josie knew with every passing day Jack's release was getting closer but she was finally feeling like she had a place again. Josie had a home here in Wellsprings, she had friends. Real friends who cared about her and wanted her there despite the risk of Jack coming for her.

Josie's training at the office was done and she was flying through things like a pro. Josie even started going to the hospital with Miranda. She was so tired after working that she hadn't really had time to go to the bar or work at the diner. Miranda kept her busy, but she loved it. She was learning so much and felt a real connection with the people. She had purpose again.

Miranda stopped by her desk on the way out. "Are you good to lock up?" Josie nodded. "Alright then I'm out of here. I'm going home to spend some time with Rod. We've been so busy here that it's been so late when I get home, I feel like we haven't had time for each other. Have a good weekend Josie." Josie looked at her friend, "Don't forget next weekend is karaoke at the Heartbreak."

Miranda made a face, "I don't know how you talked me into that but I won't forget." Miranda laughed and waved on her way out of the office.

Josie finished her work. Turned off all the lights and locked up for the day. Josie headed home. She was thinking maybe a good run, a shower and bed. She needed to make it an early night, she was bushed. She was getting ready to change into her running clothes when the phone rang. "Hello." There was a familiar voice on the other end. A voice she had hoped to never hear again. "You, stupid bitch! You cleaned out the bank account and skipped town on me. You had my ass beat up in jail, had me threatened to give you a divorce. I'll give you a divorce over my dead body. I'm coming Josie. You can run but you can't hide. I'll find you and teach you how to respect your husband. You're going to pay for walking out on me. Mark my words, you are going to pay." He cackled into the phone then the line went dead. Jack. He found her, he was coming. What was she going to do? Josie needed, what did she need? Josie hung the phone up, changed into her jeans and t-shirt. Josie needed the safety of the Heartbreak Bar. That place always made her feel better.

Chapter 6

Mike got a call the day after Josie was in the bar. His message had been sent. Mike hoped that sick son of a bitch learned his lesson. He wanted to mess with his Josie well he was going to have to go through him first and that abuser would never touch Josie again, not if he could help it. Mike was missing her as she hadn't been in for quite some time. Mike checked with Ted and found that she had been working hard at the medical office and Josie was doing fine. No word on the husband other than he got the shit kicked out of him. "You wouldn't know anything about that would you?" Mike laughed through the phone, "Not a thing but I'd like to shake the hand of the man or men responsible." Ted smiled on the other end. He knew Mike pulled some strings and got that ass a dose of his own medicine. Ted informed Mike that they would all be there for the big karaoke night. Josie was dragging them all out. Mike was thinking about her and next thing he knew Josie was walking in his front door. She didn't look right. She looked scared, frazzled. Not at all like the Josie he had seen here previously. Something was wrong. Mike pulled into the shadows as she came up to the bar.

Josie pushed her way in the door of the bar. She didn't notice anything not the people in the bar or the owner watching her as she approached. "Hi ya Josie! Haven't seen you for a while. Would you like a Diet Cola?" Josie looked at Max her eyes looked scared and distant. "Rum shots and a Diet Cola. Keep the shots coming." She slapped $40 on the bar and waited for her drinks to arrive. Josie was skittish, she kept looking around. She was pounding the shots like water. She'd had three and was working on number four when Max went to Mike. "Something is wrong dude. You need to talk to her." Mike grimaced. "I can't! Not like this. Something happened. I'm calling Ted." Mike headed to his office and called Ted's cell phone. As soon as he picked up all Mike said was, "Is he out?" Ted was silent. "Ted she's here at the bar kicking back Rum shots and barely drinking her Diet Cola. She's not a drinker. Jack found her. I would put money on it." Ted said he couldn't come to the bar he had the baby, Bella, but he would call Rod. He would be there and handle things. "I'll make some calls Mike and see what I can find out. I'll keep you informed." They hung up and Mike headed back to the bar to see how Josie was doing. "Hold on Josie girl. No one will hurt you again. I promise you that." Mike talked to himself wishing he could talk to her.

Josie was starting to forget why she didn't like to drink. She was enjoying herself then she remembered. "You know Max, some people can't hold their liquor. They get mean, they hit and they hurt you. I don't know why they get that way. I'm feeling, happy. Better than I did when I first got here. You got a good crowd tonight. Does your boss ever work? He's never here. What does he think he's too good to work? Bring him out here I'll set him straight. You're awfully busy he should be helping you." He waved Josie's rambling off, "Ah Josie, I'm fine. He's a hard worker. He just has some issues right now. He's a good man. He's here when I need him. We're partners, he just handles the business end of things. You just relax and maybe slow down on those shots?" Josie smiled at him, "Pour me some more Max." So much for slowing down he thought. Max obliged only because he knew she'd never drive home from the bar. Mike would take her himself before he'd let her leave. Whatever was ailing the little lady sure had her running scarred.

Rod walked into the bar to find Josie sitting on the bar stool, propped up against the wall. She was talking to herself as there was no one sitting next to her. Max was tending other customers. He knew she was pretty plowed. "Hey Josie how are you?" She looked at him, "He's coming for me. I can't live through that again. I don't know how I survived the first time around with him. I just can't do it again Rod. If I can't run and hide from him, I would rather not live at all." Rod nodded to her, he saw Mike over her shoulder in the doorway. He heard. "How do you know Jack's coming Josie? What happened?" Josie told Rod about the phone call. He could see the fear in her eyes. Rod also saw the anger flaring in Mike's. Mike was so mad he felt responsible now for Jack's phone call. Mike fucked up again by having him beat up. Now Jack was going to take it out on Josie. Mike couldn't let that happen

Josie excused herself to stagger to the bathroom. Mike came out from the back. He shook Rod's hand, "Thanks for coming. Do you know if he was released?" Rod shook his head. "Ted just called me. He told me he's still in but he's being released next week. He's setting her up to start worrying. He's trying to terrorize her. It's how guys like him operate. It's a cat and mouse game. He's trying to see if he can get her to run. He wants control. He wants to play with her." Mike hung his head. "What are we going to do? She's a mess. She's been pounding the shots, she's had at least eight or nine. She doesn't drink. She's going to run and I'm going to lose her again." Rod shook his head. "No. Josie's not going anywhere. She loves it here. She'll stay, but you are going to have to pull it together. I think a bigger problem is that she doesn't want to live through the torture again. She could do something worse than running. You are going to have to let her know you are here. The longer you wait the harder the truth is going to be. She needs you now more than ever. She needs something to live for, something to not fear."

Josie was heading back to the bar and Mike went back to the shadows. "How about a drink Rod? I'll buy." Rod shook his head no and tried to convince her to let him drive her home. She wasn't budging. "You go home Rod. I know Miranda was looking forward to spending time with you tonight." Josie winked at Rod. He thought about the woman who waited at home in their bed. Max filled up another drink for her. This was the start of her eighth or ninth shot she thought, she kind of lost count. She was on her second Diet Cola.

Rod was secretly impressed for someone who doesn't drink she was holding her own. She was definitely doing pretty good. It was funny these little ladies could put it away. His Miranda had a few too many one night, but held her own. Rod was impressed with her too. Damn women! Such complicated but beautiful creatures. No wonder men couldn't live without them. Rod couldn't remember a moment without Miranda. He didn't know how he survived so long without her. He knew how Mike felt. Rod would never let anything or anyone hurt Miranda. He'd do anything to protect her. Now Mike had to step up and do the same for Josie.

Josie was rambling about losing the battle. She was saying how sometimes things just don't work out like you planned. Rod was listening to her, trying to piece together the conversation. "You know I loved him. I gave him my whole heart. I wanted to spend my whole life with him." Rod said, "I know, but he changed. I know it's been rough Josie but you'll be ok. Jack's not going to hurt you anymore." Josie looked at him like he was speaking a foreign language. Josie shook her head, "Not Jack. God I could barely stand the sight of him. I never loved him. I meant Michael. He's the love of my life. I'll never love like that again. He was the one. The first time I told him I wanted to make love to him, instead of just ripping my clothes off he planned it all out."

Josie got a far-away look on her face, continuing. "Michael took me to his cabin. He prepared dinner. He wasn't very good at cooking but I figured I'd do the cooking anyway going forward. But he was good in the romance department. He had it all figured. He got me flowers. No one ever gave me flowers. Did you know that?" Rod feeling a little uncomfortable with where this conversation was going, only shook his head no. Mike was still standing where Rod could see him. Rod saw the pain on Mike's face listening to her. "He got rid of his roommate for the night so we had the whole place to ourselves. He kissed me and when he did my body just melted. All he had to do was touch me and I felt the sparks flying. His touch just made me want more. He told me he loved me, that he never wanted to let me go. He held me so tight I thought he meant it. I would have walked to the end of the world for him. But instead he walked away from me. He never came back. Who does that?"

Josie's eyes were shiny and glassy. Rod wasn't sure if she was going to cry or if it was the alcohol. "We made love for the first time that night. It was all I'd dreamed it would be. He was gentle and loving. He took his time with me. He was in no hurry. I wanted the night to go on forever. I wish I could have frozen time. I would give anything to be back there again, in his bed, his arms just to have his love again."

Rod looked up at Mike. Mike was reliving every word she spoke. Rod saw the haunted look in his eyes. "We were making out on the sofa. Things were getting awfully heated. One minute he was on top of me kissing me, stroking my body. The next minute he was carrying me to his bed. He laid me on the bed moving next to me." She was rubbing her hand up and down her other arm continuing her thoughts. "He stroked my whole body. He touched my face, his hand traveled down my neck, my shoulder, my arm to my hips." Josie's arm was idly running back and forth on her neck just above her breasts. "He told me how he dreamed of this night his whole life. He said he'd never met anyone like me, he could never love anyone more. He was lighting me on fire with his eyes and words. I wanted to touch him. I had only ever been with one person before him. My hands were shaking. I touched his face with my hand. I took my hand down his face slowly, it was my way of trying to say I love you without words. It was me trying to pull his thoughts from his mind. I touched his lips with my finger and trailed my fingers down his chest. When I reached his pants I froze. I looked up at his eyes and I saw it. He did love me. I could see the heat there. He was waiting for me to make the move. He didn't want to scare me or push me. He wanted me to be in control."

At that moment and much to Rod's delight Max interrupted. "Another drink?" Josie looked confused for a moment then looked at Rod horrified at all she'd just told him. "Oh my God! What was I thinking? I'm so embarrassed." Rod put his hand on her arm. “It’s ok Josie. It’s fine. You’ve done nothing wrong. It’s a beautiful memory.” She looked at Max. “Hit me again Max. I still can think. I just don’t want to think anymore.” Rod nodded to Max. He went to get another shot. He placed it in front of her turning to walk to the other side of the bar. Rod looked for Mike in the doorway but he had moved away.

Josie sat there looking like she was unsure of what to say. Rod just smiled at her, he offered her a way out. “You don’t have to say anything Josie. I’m here to listen if you want to talk or I’m here to watch you drink and take you home when you’ve had enough. I’m your friend. You don’t need to be embarrassed.” She looked at him, “Thank you for being here for me. I really love you Rod. I mean, like a brother. God I don’t feel romantically about you.” She laughed and Rod smiled. “I feel the same way Josie. You’re like a sister to me, I love you that way. I will protect you, you know that right?” She turned her attention back to losing whatever she could in the alcohol, ignoring his statement. She still wasn’t sure what she was going to do, but she picked up another shot starting her tenth shot and Rod could see her teetering on the bar stool. Even the wall wasn’t stabilizing her any longer. She looked toward Rod because by this time she couldn’t even focus anymore. “The room is spinning. When did we get on this ride?” She kind of laughed, before he could react Mike was there. He scooped her up off the barstool, as she passed out, he headed to the front door. Rod followed. “I’m going to drive her car home. Can you give me a ride back here after we settle her in at home?” Rod nodded his agreement. They headed to her apartment.

Mike put Josie in the car belting her in. Mike drove with her next to him. All he could do was curse himself for being so stupid, for hiding from her when she needed him. He needed to figure this out and soon. Mike couldn't stand back watching her this way too much longer. It was tearing him apart inside. He pulled up in front of Josie's apartment and looked over at her. God how beautiful she still was. Josie was even more beautiful now. Mike reached over, he touched her cheek. He saw Rod's headlights pull in behind him. He got out of the car heading over to the passenger side.

Mike carried Josie into her apartment. He made his way to her bedroom. Mike laid her on the bed, found a bucket placing it next to her. Mike also poured a glass of water, putting that and a bottle of headache pain reliever on her night stand. Josie was going to need it. Mike sat on the edge of her bed. He rubbed his hand on her cheek, down the side of her neck. Mike could see the scars now that he was closer to her. He had every inch of her body memorized. He would have never forgotten any of it. Mike listened to Josie tonight he heard her telling Rod about their first night together. Mike remembered it like it happened yesterday.

"We can stop if you want to Josie. No one says we have to do this if you're not ready." Josie shook her head. "I'm ready. I've been ready. I just don't want to do it wrong." Mike smiled at her, he reached over touching her face with the back of his hand, "It all feels right to me." Josie continued touching him. She pulled his shirt up touching his bare skin. Everywhere her hand went left a trail of fire running after it. Mike trembled, when she went to pull away, he held her hand where it was, "No Josie, don't stop." She kept rubbing his chest until he couldn't stand the restriction of where she could reach. He sat up and pulled his shirt over his head then laid flat on the bed. Josie hesitated a moment before she climbed on top of him. She straddled his hips. She started to touch him again. Josie rubbed her hands up and down his arms coming back to his chest. She took her hands down to where their bodies met. Mike couldn't help himself he was pushing himself up to her. He moved his hips, he could see the flare in her eyes. Mike sat up holding her back as he slowly lifted her top over her head. He didn't have much more control left. "Josie I'm going to lose this battle. I don't know how much longer I can hold back." She nodded, she was trembling herself. Mike eased her off him lying her back down next to him.

Michael got out of the bed, took off the remainder of his clothes. Josie just watched him. He climbed back into the bed, taking the rest of her clothes off. Once they were both naked he took in every inch of her body. Mike touched everywhere he had been waiting to touch. He needed her, more than the air in his lungs. He couldn't wait much longer. Josie reached for him, taking him in her hand. He groaned. She was killing him. She stroked him, familiarizing herself with him. She was ready.

Mike slipped on a condom as he was kneeling between Josie's legs. He touched her, slipping a finger inside of her. Josie lifted herself off the bed to him. "Oh my God!" He kept stroking her. Mike delved into the depths he waited so long to explore. He was throbbing. "Oh God Josie! You are ready for me. I can't wait anymore." Josie whispered to him, "I've been waiting my whole life for you.

Now Michael, I'm ready now." That's all he needed. Mike was up and over her. He kissed Josie and as he kissed her he eased inside of her. Mike pulled back to plunge in further. Her hips answered him as she raised higher to him. Josie's knees raised. She pushed to take more of him. Mike pulled back, then buried himself into her. He tore his mouth from her swearing, "Shit Josie! It's like you just fit me. I'm going to lose every ounce of me to you." She couldn't respond as she was moving under him having an issue with her own control, causing Mike to lose control even faster.

Mike started moving, stroking her inside, each time plunging into her, falling more and more under her spell. Mike pulled back. He was trying to gain some control. Josie went wild, "No Michael, more I need more. Please I can't I'm going to die if I don't have you." Mike took his hand to her face,

"Shh Josie, I'm right here. I'm not going anywhere. I'm here." Mike kissed her. As he kissed her again he drove himself into her with a force he didn't mean. Josie continued to go wild beneath him. She was moving against him taking more than he had to give and she was stroking him, pulling him. Their movements together were erratic. He felt her tensing, "Let it go Josie, just let it go." Mike moved with her. He drove in and out of her. He took one last drive fully into her as he felt her explode around him. She was saying his name, "Michael, Oh God Michael. I love you." Mike felt her release. He felt her giving all of herself to him. He was done. Mike exploded right along with her. He rolled to his side pulling her with him. Mike wasn't ready to lose their contact. He kissed her nose, "I love you Josie Girl." She tucked her head under his chin, idly stroking his chest. "My Michael. Oh God, I can't wait to do that again. I love you." Josie drifted off to sleep. Mike laid there holding her promising her he'd be a better man for her.

Mike got up off her bed. He started to walk out of the room but he just couldn't leave. He turned back heading to Josie's bed. He bent over to her whispering in her ear then kissed her on her lips. Josie stirred and mumbled, "Michael." He looked down at her face. She was out cold, fast asleep. He wondered what she was thinking. He turned heading back out of her apartment being sure her door was locked before climbing into the car with Rod.

Chapter 7

Halfway to the bar Mike looked at Rod, "Thank you for doing this." Mike was slightly embarrassed about him hearing his personal business. Rod nodded his head. "Josie was really upset tonight. I can't believe that jack ass is getting out of jail. He should rot there for all he did to her." Rod was gripping the steering wheel trying to curb his tongue but he just couldn't. "You know he should rot but he's not going to. He's coming for her. Where are you going to be? Hiding in the shadows watching, damn it Mike, I just sat there tonight listening to that woman pour her heart out about the love of her life. Doesn't that mean anything to you? She obviously is still in love with you even though you broke her heart. Don't you think you two deserve to try and work things out? A chance to be happy, together? Don't you think she deserves the truth from the man she's clearly still in love with?" Mike shifted uncomfortably in the seat next to Rod.

Mike knew Rod was right but he had no idea where to start. "I heard her. It broke my heart to just stand there. You gotta know that. I just don't know where to start with her. I don't know how to tell her." Rod pulled up at the bar. He put the car in park. He looked at Mike, "Man up, start at the beginning. Tell her the truth. Trust her love for you to bring her back to you. If she truly loves you, forgiveness will come." Mike sat there silent for a minute. "What if I don't deserve her forgiveness? She trusted me, she believed in me. All I did was lie to her from day one. I'm no better off now than I was then. I have no home. I live above the bar. I have nothing to call my own. I caused her so much pain, if not for me leaving her she would have never married that monster. How could she forgive me for all the pain and torture she endured?"

Rod was getting frustrated with him, "You know poor me doesn't really suit you. You should really grow a pair. We are sitting in front of your bar. Once you get this place off the ground you will buy some land, build a house, maybe buy one here in Kellersville or in Wellsprings, but you have a start. You cleaned up your act, served your time, redid this place and started a new career. That's improvement. Stop second guessing everything, talk to her. After all Josie has been through, don't you think she deserves some truth from the one man she obviously can't forget about? The one she loves more than you probably deserve right now. If she can still love you after leaving her, then I imagine the only one blaming himself for her horrendous marriage is you." Mike was angry at his words. But then again the truth hurts. Mike mumbled thank you to Rod, got out of the car heading back into the bar. Rod drove home wondering if Mike would ever stop putting himself down. No one blamed him for his past, but he couldn't let it go. If he didn't let it go, his past was going to ruin the best thing that ever happened to him and his entire future.

Josie was dreaming. She had to be. She saw his face, she felt his arms around her. She heard his voice, "It's ok Josie girl. I'm here. I'll protect you and take care of you. I love you. I never stopped." Josie heard it. She felt him. She had to wake up. Josie opened her eyes. That's when the pain started. "Oh God, what happened to me?" Josie sat up. She felt her world tilt. Her head was throbbing and she wasn't sure her roiling stomach was going to settle anytime soon. She saw the water and pain reliever on the night stand. She spun her feet to the floor sticking her foot in a bucket. "What the hell?" She sat there a few minutes to get her bearings. She needed to take that whole bottle of pain reliever but settled for three for now. Josie didn't trust herself to stand up so she just sat there a few minutes trying to get her brain to work.

Josie remembered the phone call and going to the bar. She talked to Max. She started drinking. Rod was there, no he came later, he talked to her. "Oh my God! What did I tell him!" She remembered the conversation she had with Rod about Michael. Why did she do that? Why could she not let the man go? Wait, she heard him. He was talking to her, he kissed her. He touched her, she felt him. He couldn't have. Could he? "What the hell happened last night?" She said to herself. She got up heading to the bathroom. Josie splashed cold water on her face. She heard the knock on the door. She grabbed a towel, dried her face, "Michael." She went to the front door opening it.

"Good morning sunshine! How are you feeling today?" Miranda, was all perky, looking absolutely gorgeous, with Rod hanging behind her. He looked at her and waved. Josie stepped back letting them in. She was truly humiliated. Josie looked at Rod, "I don't even know what to say to you right now. I am so embarrassed. I have no idea why I told you all those things." Miranda looked at the two of them. She saw Rod blush, and had to ask, "What happened? What did you tell him? I'm dying here you two. He wouldn't tell me anything other than you were hammered, carried out of the bar and driven home." Josie sank down on her love seat hanging her head.

Rod, bless his heart whispered, "I'm going to make coffee. You guys catch up." Miranda moved next to her. "He told me about the phone call. I'm sorry honey." Josie looked at her friend bewildered. "I was starting to feel safe, comfortable and like I finally had a family. Now I have to give it all up. Where am I going to go?" Miranda was outraged that she thought she had to leave. "Josie you most certainly are not going anywhere. This is your home. He is not welcome in this town. That will be made clear to him. Don't you ever talk about leaving us, we are family." Rod came out of the kitchen and sat down.

Josie sat there silent for a few minutes. How could she stay bringing that trouble to Wellsprings? She didn't want the people of Wellsprings looking at her like they did back in Maine. "Miranda you don't get it. He's going to find me. Anyone who gets in his way is going to get hurt. I don't want to see any of you get hurt because of me. Besides I left Maine because I couldn't stand to see the pity on everyone's face when they saw me. I don't want people's pity. I just want my life back."

Miranda stood up, "You are not leaving this town! If you want your life back, then take it the hell back! Make your stand and stand here with us." Rod chimed in, "You can take some self-defense courses at the police station. There is a gym in town, go with Miranda and Sarah. Get strong physically. In the process you will make your mind stronger." Josie sat looking at her friends. She never had anyone care enough to take a stand for her or with her. She didn't know what to say. Tears started rolling down her face. Rod grimaced, "Not the tears. I hate when women cry. I'm going to get the coffee." Miranda looked at Josie. The two couldn't hold back the laughter.

Rod's face was priceless as he spoke. He was a really sweet man. He had a real soft spot. He wanted to come off all rough and tough, but he really was just a big teddy bear. Josie started to explain, “You know Miranda I would love to go the gym and take those self-defense classes. Maybe that would help me feel safer stronger more in control.” Miranda sat back down on the sofa with Josie. She started telling her about the classes and all the things the gym had to offer. Josie was starting to feel like she just might be able to stay in this town, making it home.

Miranda was eager, “So Josie, I’m dying here. What did you tell Rod that had him blushing?” Josie started telling her some of what she remembered about last night, when Rod walked in with coffee mugs. “Oh no, not again. I can’t listen to these things again.” The two women dissolved into a fit of laughter. Once they were able to control themselves Josie said, “I’m sorry Rod. I usually am not the type to divulge such personal matters. I don’t know what it is about the Heartbreak Bar but I feel such a connection there. I feel all these memories coming back to me. It's just so strange. It's like last night, I saw Michael's face, I felt his arms, I heard him talking to me. I woke up this morning half expecting to see him. It's just weird. I can't explain it."

Josie brought herself back to the present looking at Miranda and Rod. They both had a very strange look on their face. "What? Why are you guys looking at me like that? You brought me home right? Rod what happened last night? Who brought me home?" Rod looked at Miranda. She was the one to speak. "Rod didn't drive you. Matt did. He drove your car here, carried you into your place with Rod's help. Rod just took Matt back to the bar." Rod looked at Miranda like she just spilled trade secrets. "Well then I guess I owe both you guys. Whose idea was it to leave me the bucket next to the bed, water and headache reliever?" She chuckled smiling at Rod. He cleared his throat, "That was all Matt."

Before they left Josie and Miranda set up a time for later to meet at the gym. Rod told her the date and time of the next self-defense class. Josie asked him to sign her up. She would be there. Josie apologized to him. She told him she would try to never let her embarrassing moments happen again. Rod smiled uncomfortably at her. "It's not a big deal. Just promise me you're not going to drink like that anymore." Josie laughed, made a cross on her heart. She smiled and waved to them as they drove off. So what's with the elusive Matt again? She was going to pay him back somehow. She just wished she could meet him. Josie was starting to wonder who the mystery man was. She had an idea on how to pay him back. She looked at the clock. "Plenty of time," she smiled to herself. She went to get a shower.

Josie got dressed and presentable. She still felt awfully crappy but she did it to herself. She was not going to wallow in self-pity. She was going to push through this. She got in her car headed to the grocery store. She was going to make some meals and take a care package to Max, Matt and Rod. She loved cooking but she rarely did it anymore because it was no fun cooking for one. Now she had a reason to cook. She had just enough time to do some shopping, get the stuff home and meet up with Miranda. This was perfect, she was so excited.

Chapter 8

Miranda was panting, leaning on her treadmill. "I hate you! What are you super human, bionic or something?" Josie was running on the treadmill next to her. She smiled at Miranda's words. "Nope, I just love to run. I used to run every day before Jack. As a teenager I walked everywhere. I had no car. If I wanted to go somewhere I had to use foot power. Then I started to run." She started to slow her pace and got herself to a walk to cool down. "I've been running in town again. I try and get out every morning before work, sometimes again afterward." She stopped her treadmill and grabbed her towel. Miranda was watching her. "How is it that you just ran all that time on the treadmill? I walked and I look like hell but you look like you're ready to keep on going. I thought I was in shape. I guess I have a lot to learn. Teach me well, Obi Wan."

She bowed to Josie and the two dissolved into laughter. Once they stopped laughing they headed to the weights.

The trainer was hovering over them at the weights and machines. He was explaining to Josie how to use the equipment properly and was adjusting her weight. He watched her to be sure she was operating on the machine correctly. He made some adjustments for her to the machine then told her if she needed anymore help to just ask for Steve. As he walked away the two women admired him as they watched him go. They looked at each other laughing. Miranda said, “He so totally could be my son. He was flirting with you Josie.” Josie waived her comment off.

Josie was taking this gym thing seriously. She thought if she could get stronger and faster then she would have a chance at protecting herself with Jack. She and Miranda spent an hour and a half at the gym. When they were done, they sat on the floor stretching out, drinking some water. "You know Josie Jack doesn't have control of you anymore. You have a life here, friends and a career of your own. You're not the same person you were when you were with him. He'll see that, he won't stay. He'll see he can't control you anymore. Now that you've become independent so there is nothing here for him anymore."

Josie looked at her friend. She folded her legs in front of her. "The weird thing is that I don't know why I didn't fight harder or run sooner from him. It's like I thought he was all I was worth. I felt like I didn't deserve any better. I loved once, he ran out on me, so Jack was all I could hope for." She shrugged and stared off into the distance. Her friend looked at her. Miranda asked the hardest question

Josie ever had to answer, "What would you do if Mike came back to you? I mean what would you do really? Do you see yourself taking him back or pushing him away? You don't have to answer me but I'm asking because it seems like you never really let go of him. You've used him as an excuse, 'no one would ever love me' or 'I don't deserve any better'. I mean do you really believe that shit? If that's how you feel, then you will never find anyone. No one wants to be with someone who doesn't believe in herself." She paused, she saw her point was sinking in. "You're a strong woman Josie, you're smart. You're better than that. Take the driver seat in your life, see where it takes you." Miranda stood up and left Josie to her thoughts.

What would Josie do if Mike ever returned to her? So much has happened to her since he left. She decided in her mind that if he would come back she would need to know why he left before she could ever decide to take him back. She also had to stop blaming him for the choices she made. Miranda was right. He's her excuse to not move on. He's been her scapegoat of sorts. She is the one who never allowed herself the things in life she deserved. She was the one who had the pity party for herself. She made herself believe that because he left her behind with no explanation that she was not worthy of anything or anyone. She's the one who did this to herself. How did she let that happen?

Josie wanted to blame Mike for leaving her, for her being with Jack, but the truth was she chose Jack and Mike had nothing to do with it. She never allowed herself to see the good in herself. She let Mike walking out on her consume her and define her. She was the one to blame for feeling like she was not worthy of anything better than Jack Morris. That was going to stop now. She was done letting someone else define her life. It was time she took responsibility for her actions, and time she saw the woman she was. She needed to stop being the woman who Michael walked out on. She got up and went to gather her things.

Josie caught up with Miranda at the desk. They ended up walking out together. "Thanks Miranda. I needed that. I guess now I just need to figure out what I want in life. I need to take control of my own life. No more excuses, no more feeling like I'm not worthy of the good things in my life." Miranda smiled, "I didn't want to be harsh but you need to look at yourself in the mirror Josie. See the woman the world sees, embrace her. Don't let her fade into the background. Keep getting stronger and figure out what Josie wants for a change." They reached Miranda's car said good bye, but before they parted decided to hit the gym same time tomorrow.

Josie was restless when she got home from the gym. So she started cooking. She was making lasagna. She had it layered in the oven. She made a garlic butter and cheese mixture to put on the French bread she bought. She also had some steaks marinating. They were going to marinade over night. She would make them tomorrow night with sweet potatoes in the oven. The guys were going to love this. She would take the lasagna to the bar tonight for them and tomorrow she would just cook the steaks, she'd keep them warm for the trip to the bar. But before she took the lasagna she had to make desert. She was going to bake her grandmother's chocolate chip cake.

Josie remembered her grandmother making the cake when she spent summers at her grandmother's home. Josie would always do things with her grandmother to help her. Josie's grandmother wanted Josie to be self-sufficient so teaching her how to cook, sew and clean were a necessity. Josie's grandmother was a hard woman but she was always very loving with Josie. Josie was grateful for the summers she spent with her grandmother. When Josie had to go back home after summer break she missed her grandmother a great deal. Josie never understood why her grandmother was so hard and seemed so uncaring about certain things, but Josie never felt unloved or like a burden with her grandmother

. Josie's grandmother was a private woman. She only shared what she wanted to. Even on her death bed she never disclosed much about her life. Josie sat by her bedside every day until she passed away. She remembered their last conversation. "Josie, my dear don't mourn me when I'm gone, just go on and live your life.

Make something out of yourself, follow your dreams. Always, be proud of who you are. Don't ever live life with regrets. Answer to yourself. Hold yourself accountable for your life. No one else has the power to decide your life and dreams for you. Remember that. I love you, Josie. Don't ever forget that or doubt the love I have for you." She held her grandmother's hand and cried as she drifted off to sleep. Those were the last words she spoke. A few days later her grandmother was gone from her life. Josie wiped the tears that escaped her at the memory. She thought about the conversation earlier with Miranda. Funny how two people in her life who didn't know each other essentially gave her the best advice of her life.

Josie took the lasagna out of the oven. The cake was baking when the doorbell rang. She went to answer it. She was face to face with Ted. She welcomed him in, he followed her to her living room. “Boy it sure smells good in here.” Josie smiled, “I’ve been cooking. I’m dropping some lasagna off at Miranda and Rod’s place for taking care of me last night. I’m taking the rest for Max and Matt at the bar. They were all good to me last night. What better way to repay them but with a home cooked meal?”

Ted smiled at her. Josie was a very generous and thoughtful lady. He could see why Mike was so in love with her. “Well I’m not going to keep you but I wanted to let you know I’ve been checking on, your husb..... um, Jack. When he makes a move and gets released we’re going to know it. Rod and I will be here for you. We will keep him from you. We don’t want you to leave us.”

Josie hung her head then looked at him. “I’m lucky to have found Wellsprings and you guys. I just hate that I'm putting you all in danger with him. Am I being selfish because I don't want to leave?" He looked at her. "Josie I don't think you have a selfish bone in your body. Look at what you are doing for Rod and Miranda. Not to mention Matt and Max. You are part of this town, Wellsprings is a better place with you in it." Josie wanted to believe him but she feared what was coming. Her timer beeped, Ted stood to leave. "No Ted, wait. Have a seat. That was my grandmother's chocolate chip cake. Let me take it out of the oven, I'll send some home for you and Sarah." He smiled, "It smells so good I don't know if it will make it home to Sarah." Josie smiled, "Your secret would be safe with me." They both laughed. Ted thought for a moment, "You know Josie, there is a girl in town, Taryn. Her family owns Soups and Such. She's quite a cook and baker. She's had some hard times. Maybe the two of you should meet some time.

She's a sweet person. Sarah and Miranda were friends with her for years. Taryn just kind of withdrew. They tried and tried but Taryn just kept pulling further away. I know they miss their friend. I think all of you ladies together would be an unstoppable force." Ted smiled and Josie said, "What happened to Taryn?" Ted shook his head, "That's Taryn's story, talk to her." Josie nodded.

Ted sat for a minute looking around her apartment. Josie had no personal touches to it. Josie left it plain, just the furnishings that came with the apartment, empty shelves on the wall. She hadn't changed or added anything. There was not even a vase of flowers. Josie was a woman on the run. She didn't plan on making a stand. Would she change her mind?

Josie came out with a plate and handed it to him. "Thanks Ted for all your doing. I appreciate it." Ted took the plate. "No problem. I'll be sure you get your plate back. But Josie, would you do me a favor?" She nodded, "Sure Ted anything, name it." Ted smiled and told her "Just let us do our job and you start settling in here. Make this your home. Make this your place. Let us see you, Josie Morris in this apartment. Not just blank walls." Josie followed his gaze around her blank canvas of an apartment and she saw what he saw. No roots, no plans to stay. Is that what she wanted? Ted turned and let her to her thoughts. She never really had a place of her own. Her house with Jack was not a home, it was a house with nothing of her in it. She never allowed herself to make it a home. Now she had a place of her own. It was a place for her to make home.

Josie packed up all the food she made and drove to the Heartbreak bar after stopping at Miranda and Rod's to drop off her goodies.

She couldn't stop thinking about what Ted said. He was right. She was saying this was home but she was afraid to make it home. Well, that was going to have to change. On her way home she was going to treat herself to a few things. She didn't have a lot of extra money to spend but a few touches would make it home. Then each week she could add to it. She needed to find herself. What better way than starting with her home?

Josie pulled up at the Heartbreak. It was fairly empty in the parking lot. It was after all before dinner time. Hopefully later it would pick up. Josie loved this bar, it was so welcoming, the rustic charm the inside had, it felt so inviting. Josie loaded up her lasagna, cake and bread. Max saw her coming and she saw a man head toward the back of the bar. She figured it must have been Matt. He always seemed to be avoiding her. Max greeted her, "Well, Josie how are you feeling today?"

Josie laughed at him, "I wasn't feeling so great this morning but I didn't let it slow me down. I appreciate you and Matt taking care of me last night. I was really a mess. I'm so sorry. I'm not a big drinker." Max started laughing, "You could've fooled me. You were slamming them down." Max looked at all the food she had and asked. "What is all this?" Josie placed all the goodies on the bar. "I've made you guys some home cooked food. Lasagna, garlic cheese bread and chocolate chip cake for dessert. You'll have to heat up the lasagna but it's all ready to go." Max looked at her stunned. "Wow, how nice is this? You didn't have to do all this, but can you come and get drunk every night if this is how we get repaid?" Josie laughed. She put her hand to her head, "Oh no, this girl isn't doing that again anytime soon." Max laughed, he carried the food into the back.

As Max passed by Mike he said, "If you aren't going to tell her you're here I'm going to run off with her." Mike grimaced and growled a response to his friend. Max headed back out to Josie. They talked for a few minutes. She was going to leave to let him eat something before the Saturday night crowd rolled in. "Hey Max. One thing before I go. I noticed my $40 I laid on the bar was still in my purse this morning. Who paid for my drinks?" Max being cornered, not wanting to lie to her, he told her the truth, "Matt." She smiled. "Tell him thank you for me. Someday I'd like to thank him myself. That is if he'd ever give me the chance."

Josie turned and walked away. Mike appeared next to his friend to watch her leave. "That is one special lady. I don't know how you've stayed away from her so long." Mike shook his head, "It hasn't been easy." Max slapped his shoulder and headed into the back to try the bounty of food she brought for them to eat. Mike just stood there watching the empty space and doorway that she just walked through. "Definitely hasn't been easy." He spoke to the empty space.

Josie was good on her promise to herself. She took her car home first. She walked through town and stopped in some of the little shops. She saw a woman walking her dog. Josie recognized her from the restaurant, Soups and Such. She saw the way the woman walked, looking around, not letting her guard down. Josie wondered about the hell this woman had been through. Josie recognized the sadness in her eyes, the loneliness when she turned and they met gazes. The woman turned back and kept moving. Josie was going to go after her, remembering her conversation with Ted but today Josie needed to do some things for herself first. She was no good to anyone else, and no good to give advice if she was always going to run the other way herself.

Josie went on and found a few things to decorate her home. She couldn't wait to get them home. She looked around the town. "Home, I really am home." She smiled heading to her apartment ready to make her stand. She was starting the self-defense class in the morning, then hitting the gym again in the afternoon. She was getting her life back. No one was going to stand in her way. If only, no she wasn't going down that road again. But someday maybe she would find Michael again. What she would do if she got the chance to see him again, still remained to be seen.

Josie got into her apartment. She put her stuff down stretching her arms. She almost regretted taking the car home and walking with all her purchases. Some of them were a bit awkward to carry. She bought some pictures, with cabins and trees in them. Josie had one she particularly liked. It was a cabin, with a stream flowing behind it. There was a deer standing in front of the cabin looking out over the stream. It was so beautiful it just drew her in. She could almost feel herself being a part of that picture, almost like she was in that cabin.

Josie bought some cute little figurines to put on her shelves as well. They were woodsy animals to match the pictures. She bought a couple of little deer, raccoons and bears. They were so cute she just couldn't pass them up. The woodsy theme made her remember simpler times, times with Michael. She had even bought a few little crystal vases. She was going to go get some flowers for them, to give the apartment a little more of a homey appearance. She stood back and looked around. "Now it feels like mine, rustic and charming." She thought one of Matt's tables would look perfect in here, she wondered if he'd miss one, then she smiled at the thought. She was so pleased but she still had too much energy. She was so excited about her decorations, and her new resolve. She was going to go for a run.

Josie hit the street starting her run. She was pushing hard. She was feeling more and more like her old self. She was running and thinking. Before she knew it she was at the Heartbreak bar. She was really hitting her stride again. She paused for a minute, checking her pulse rate, catching her breath. That's when she saw him, Matt.

He was a figure in the distance, in the shadows as always. She didn't realize how big he was. He looked so tall and muscular. He had a swagger about him as she watched him climb the stairs beside the bar. She couldn't help but watch him. There was something about him that drew her to him. He was so mysterious. He never came out around her. It was like he was hiding from her. There was something familiar about Matt but she just couldn't put her finger on it. She was so lost in thought that she didn't notice he had stopped, turning her direction. She smiled, waved to him and he raised his hand in a wave to her. He turned heading into what she assumed was his apartment above the bar. She was too far away from him to see his face or to speak to him. Someday, hopefully she'd get to meet him. There was something about him. She wondered if it was just the mystery since he never came around her, or was it something else with him. She turned starting her trek home. She was going to sleep well tonight.

Mike watched Josie run away. Mike couldn't believe when he turned around she was there. He had been thinking about her, then there she was, again. Mike held Josie last night and it was killing him. He wanted to hold her again. He was so close to her, he felt her skin against him he touched her lips with his. Mike wanted her back. He wanted his life back, all the time he lost with her and all the things he missed with her. He just wanted it all back. But was it too late? Rod was right. He had to man up and take control. Josie deserved to hear the truth, he owed her that much. He destroyed her and he truly hated himself for it. How could he expect her to welcome him back into her life after all the pain he'd caused her? He owed her though. He had to stop thinking of himself and think of her. The truth is what she needed to hear. Only he could give her that.

Chapter 9

Josie was restless in her sleep. She was dreaming of Mike. Mike was with her. They were both laughing. He had his arms around her. He was teasing her about something when someone came through the door. "Mike I want to talk to you. Get out here." Mike stiffened, he told her to stay in his room. Mike left the room closing the door. The voice she had heard was Chad's. Chad seemed really angry. Josie heard hushed voices. The men seemed angry. She couldn't hear what they were saying but she knew it wasn't good. It seemed to go on forever, and she wasn't sure what to do. She went to the door, she turned the knob to open it. She heard Chad say, "You need to cut her lose. She is ruining you. You don't do your job. I'm losing money. You're going to have to make a choice. Her or the job." Josie saw the anger move across Mike's face. She saw it in his eyes. She had never seen that side of him. Mike had grabbed a hold of Chad's shirt. He was in his face. "Don't you threaten me. Don't you ever talk about her. If it's a choice I have to make, you would lose every time. Don't push me on this Chad." Josie saw Michael shove Chad away. He started heading her way. Josie closed the door. She went back to sit on the bed. Josie woke up. She hadn't thought about that night in a long time. Chad left after he and Michael argued. Michael seemed distant for the rest of the night.

Mike told Josie to never come to the cabin without him. Josie had wondered why. Now she knew he was protecting her, Chad didn't like her. But she didn't understand what was going on. Why was Chad so mad at Mike, and why was he losing money because of her? Josie asked Mike when he came into the room what was going on. He told her "Don't worry about it, it was just business. Don't ever ask me about business, it's nothing you need be concerned with." Mike told her Chad was overreacting to a situation.

Josie was sure Mike wasn't telling the truth but he seemed so angry she didn't want to push him. She stood up, moved off the bed heading to him. She started taking her shirt off. She was unbuttoning her pants when she saw the desire flicker in his eyes.

Mike closed the gap between them. He picked her up, Josie wrapped her legs around him. Mike started kissing her, devouring her as if he had never had her before. He turned her. Josie's back hit the wall. Mike braced her against the wall as he kissed down her throat and her chest. Josie held his head to her as she tried to put what she heard out of her mind.

Mike pulled her legs down from around him. He quickly, stripped off the rest of her clothes and his own. He hiked her back up around him. "I love you Josie girl and I need you. Forgive me for this." He seemed so sad, so desperate for her. She whispered his name, "Michael." He pulled back and drove her into the wall. He entered her with a fierce desire, like he would die if he didn't have her right then. "Forgive me Josie." Josie had thought he was asking for forgiveness for the force with which he took her, little did she understand he was asking her forgiveness for what was about to happen.

Josie wasn't scared, she was excited. She never feared anything Mike did to her. She trusted him, she loved him. Two weeks later she lost him. He was gone. That night after their lovemaking he held her to him. Josie joked with him. "I'm not going anywhere Michael. I'm yours forever." Mike squeezed her tighter, knowing that this was the last night he would allow himself with her. He needed to protect her from him, his life and the people around him. After that night he made sure they weren't alone again. That was the last night that they made love.

Josie got out of bed. She was going to shower but figured it was pointless. She was heading to self-defense class, then the gym. She would shower after that. After all she showered before she climbed into bed last night. She drove to the police station. She was guided to the gym area. When she arrived there she smiled so hard she thought it would be permanent. There stood her friends. Sarah, and Miranda. Josie ran to them hugging them. "What are you guys doing here?" They laughed. Sarah said, "Supporting our friend." Rod looked at them, "Alright ladies let's get started." Josie looked around, there were a few other faces from town she recognized. She noticed way in the back of the group the face she had seen the other day in town, Taryn.

After class Josie was going to talk to Taryn but she practically ran out of the building, so Josie went to talk to Rod. "I know I keep saying it but I'm so sorry about the other night. I hope I haven't made you uncomfortable." Rod smiled, he told Josie there was no problem. "If you need to talk Josie, my ears are always open." She was sure it embarrassed him the other night, as he slightly blushed whenever she brought it up. But she knew he wasn't going to hold it against her, he really was a good listener, with good advice. He was the brother she never had.

The girls were ready to hit the gym. The three took off together down the street. They headed to the weights first. They each chose their starting point. The trainer from the other day, Steve, started their way. "Uh oh, Josie here comes lover boy." Miranda burst into fits of laughter after speaking those words, while Josie blushed and shushed her. Sarah had no idea what was going on as she couldn't meet them the day before. "What? Who? Hey, no fair keeping secrets guys!" They were all laughing when the boy approached Josie again. He went through the instructions, adjusted her weights, he went to touch Josie to correct her movement. Something in her snapped.

Josie jumped off the bench, there was fear in her eyes and voice, "Don't touch me." Miranda was up moving beside her. She talked to her in a calm even tone. "Josie, it's ok. Relax. Breathe. We're here, just relax." The boy not sure what was happening, backed away and moved on. Josie looked at her friends, fear apparent in her eyes.

"I could feel him touching me. Like I was back in that house. He was trying to get me to bed with him. He would never take no for an answer. I hated him, but I feared him. He would push me down, no matter how I fought he was always ready for it. He tied me down. He would tie me to the post of the bed. When I would kick at him it made him angrier. Once I was all tied down he would cut my clothes off laughing. He'd use the knife as he held it against me. He cut me that I bled just to keep me from fighting him. The pain of that was minor compared to the pain of having him touch me. He found new ways to torture me every time. He'd pull his gun out and point it at me to keep me from fighting him. He had all kinds of things he used on me, inserting them into me. He had a bag with things. I don't know where he got them, he had a speculum in there. He used that on me, stretching me open. He would take his fingers inside of me, he even had vibrators and things he used on me. I hated him, I feared him. I never knew what would come out of that bag. Once he took his gun after he put shackles on me, he put it inside of me, I wished he would have just pulled the trigger. Then I wouldn't have had to endure it."

Sarah gasped at her friend's words. She was shocked at what Josie suffered through. Josie continued as though she never even heard Sarah. "I wouldn't be afraid of people's touch if he'd just shot me or slit my throat with the knife." The tears had started trickling down her face, not that she was actively crying but more the pain escaping her. She just had a lost and stony look to her.

Miranda knew Josie had suffered but not the extent of the torture just explained. No wonder she was terrified of the touch of anyone. She deserved better than that bastard gave her. No one deserves that kind of treatment. Miranda was livid and angry about how the justice system worked. It failed Josie and it failed her old friend Taryn. To think that animals like Josie's husband could induce so much fear and pain then could be free, roaming about the public to hurt again.

Sarah and Miranda both had tears in their eyes for the pain she had suffered. Miranda moved in front of her. "Josie, you are safe now. He's not going to hurt you anymore." Sarah chimed in, "That's right. Ted and Rod are not going to let it happen. They will be sure to protect you. That's what they do." Josie looked at her friends. Josie tried to curve her lips into a smile. She excused herself, she needed a minute to compose herself.

Josie stood in the bathroom with water dripping off her face. She looked at herself in the mirror. Would the demons ever leave her? How was she ever going to be whole again? She knew Jack would be coming for her. She would rather die than to suffer under his hands again. She would kill him before she would let him touch her sexually again. How would she ever be able to be with anyone again? After all he had done to her, would she ever feel whole again? Would she ever be able to make love to a man again?

Miranda and Sarah were at the treadmills waiting for Josie to take the one between them. Josie hopped on. “Ok ladies how fast do we want to run today?” Sarah looked at her. “Run?” Miranda laughed at her response, “Fasten your seatbelt Sarah, save yourself, don't try and keep up. I learned my lesson yesterday." Josie just looked at her friends and smiled. Josie hit her on button and away she went. She was running so hard that she was starting to hit exhaustion fast. She was lost in her head, she was remembering all the things Jack had done to her and she just wanted to forget. Josie wanted to be whole again, to not fear someone's touch. Josie ran harder. She just wanted the pain to stop. Josie was so tired from the emotions and the thoughts she couldn't escape. Sweat was running off of her. The sweat was mixing with the tears that kept escaping her. She couldn't stop the tears so she pushed herself harder. Josie's legs were burning and her breathing was becoming more labored, but still she pushed further.

Josie kept running like she was possessed, then finally felt she couldn't push her limits any further. Josie had that big run last night so when she finally shut down her run the girls both looked at her. "What? I'm a little worn out today. I ran to the bar last night and home." Miranda looked at her shaking her head laughing. Sarah said, "Holy crap! Your tired? Really? You ran to the bar last night and home? Are you super human or something?" The three women started laughing. Josie looked at them, "I'm so glad you guys are my friends." They hugged, but Josie had things to do. She made her way out of the gym. She had dinner to cook and deliver to the Heartbreak again tonight. She was hoping tonight would be the night she would get to meet Matt.

Miranda looked at Sarah as they watched Josie leave the gym. "That girl is one tough cookie. Can you imagine surviving the things she went through? I think that was only the surface of things that she went through." Sarah shook her head shuddering. "I can't even imagine the horror of what she had to endure. How did she ever survive?" Miranda put her arm around her friend, "True love pulled her through. That is the only answer. It had to be the love she has for Mike that pulled her through. You know how strong love like that is." Sarah smiled at her friend, she shook her head in agreement. Sarah spoke, "Maybe Josie is the missing link we need to bring Taryn back to us. Do you think?" Miranda smiled, "It sure as hell couldn't hurt. I sure do miss Taryn. We had a lot of fun growing up." Sarah and Miranda silently remembered their friend and how it hurt when she turned them away.

Josie walked into the Heartbreak bar. She had hot steaks, sweet potatoes with butter, cinnamon and a cup of brown sugar for them if they'd rather the sweetness of that. "Hi ya

Max." He looked up smiling. "Hey Josie, what do you have there?" She told him what she had for dinner tonight for him and Matt. Max was salivating as she spoke. "You are spoiling me. That lasagna was delicious last night. I think we ate the whole loaf of bread too." Josie laughed at Max, he turned to take the food in the back. Josie sat down on the bar stool waiting for him to return. Josie was lost in her head again, thinking about earlier at the gym, the things she revealed, to her friends, she didn't know how to forget.

When Max returned he was chewing. "Oh God I think I've died and gone to heaven! I think I need to marry you." Josie laughed, she ordered a Diet cola. She sat there for a few minutes then asked Max what she had been wondering for a little while now. "Have I offended Matt? I mean every time I come here he isn't in the bar or he disappears into the back. Matt never comes out to talk to me. It's odd. Isn't it?" Max just shrugged his shoulders. "Matt does a lot of paperwork, with just starting up he's been lining up gigs, trying to figure out ways to make the place better. I'm sure it's just a case of bad timing." She sat there pondering for a little bit. Meanwhile Max went into the back to get more to eat.

Josie sat at the bar drinking her Diet Cola, thinking. She was making some great changes in her life. Josie started the self-defense classes, she was going to the gym now. She had a great job and a cute little apartment that she was making her own. She even started cooking again. Things were going so well. She was just waiting for the next thing to happen. Josie knew Jack was looming somewhere, he would find her. Josie was just worried what would happen when he did find her. She was deep in thought never noticing the figure in the doorway watching her.

Mike stood there watching Josie. Mike wondered what she was thinking. She looked worried, sad. She was deep in concentration. Mike wanted to go out there and talk to her but he just wasn't ready yet. What if Josie turned him away? What if he told her the truth and she ended up never wanting to see him again? Mike couldn't take that. Plus, with all that was happening for Josie, with her husband getting out of jail, Mike was sure she had enough to worry about. Mike surprising her was the last thing she needed right now, wasn't it? He wanted her back in his life. She was so beautiful and the more he saw her the more he wanted to touch her. The food she had been bringing was so good. She really knew her way around the kitchen. He was hoping someday he'd be there watching her cook. He was just looking at her and he was getting aroused. Mike needed Josie, and only Josie. He had to find a way to tell her the truth. He was getting ready to move from the doorway when he saw Max approaching her.

Max walked over to her with another Diet cola. She smiled up at him. "Thank you Max. Did Matt tell you that I saw him last night?" Max shook his head no. "I went for a run. I was so restless last night that I started running and didn't stop until I was here. Matt was going up the stairs I'm assuming to his apartment. He turned, I waved to him and he waved back. That was the only time I ever saw him, Well, I guess I didn't really see him. He was in the shadows. I could only see his silhouette in the dark, but there was something familiar about him. It's strange, but I just can't put my finger on it. I really hope I get to meet him, one day."

Max looked toward the doorway, he saw that Mike was no longer standing there. Max thought to himself, I hope you heard that buddy. He patted her hand. Josie pulled her hand away quickly as if Max had burned her. He, knowing some of her history didn't make a big deal over it and just continued what he was saying. "Matt's a very private person. Like I said he's got a lot going on right now so don't take it to heart. I'm kind of curious though about this run you took. Do you do that often? I mean I realize by car it's not far from Wellsprings, but on foot?"

Josie looked at Max laughing. Josie didn't understand why everyone around there was so surprised that she liked running. "I used to walk everywhere I went and I used to run all the time. I enjoy it. It has a way of relaxing me. Besides, I feel like I am really starting to get back in shape. I've been running since I got into town. Last night was the farthest I've run in quite a while. It felt really good." Max just grinned at her. "Hey whatever works for you, I am not a big runner. I like lifting weights and keeping in shape, but I have no desire for running. But I will say you look incredible so maybe I should start training with you." She started laughing and reached out her hand. Josie wanted to reach out to him but she was unsure, so she pulled her hand back. She looked at him, "You are a really sweet guy. Thanks." He looked at her. Max didn't miss the reach with her hand nor did he miss her hesitation to touch him then pull away.

Max went into the back and Mike was standing there waiting. "Seriously dude, you are killing me. What is going on with you two?" There was anger in Mike's eyes. Max just looked at him before saying, "You know you are seriously pissing me off. That woman is still in love with you. You are too busy hiding from your past to see it. You are going to lose her. Not to me but someone is going to see how wonderful she is soon because let's face it that woman's body is smokin'! So don't question me if there is anything going on, get off your ass and do something about it. Make a move and see what happens." Max spun on his heels, heading back to the bar just in time to see Josie going toward the door. Max hollered out to her another thank you, she waved back to him. Mike came through the doorway in enough time to see her going through the door again. Mike knew his friend was right but how was he supposed to tell her.

Chapter 10

Josie opened the door to the office. She was ready to start another busy week. She straightened up and checked the office messages then headed into the back to brew some coffee. Miranda came in behind her which was a surprise as she normally headed to the hospital Monday mornings. After the weekend and the things Josie revealed, Miranda thought a day at the hospital would keep her mind busy, help her keep the demons at bay. So much pain, Miranda had thought all weekend, how could someone endure so much pain yet be so wonderful inside. Josie's soul was just amazing. "Hey Josie, can you make two coffees to go?" Josie turned around, "Absolutely." This was great. She was getting to go to the hospital with Miranda.

On occasion Josie would go to help with charting. It was faster for Miranda to have

Josie help her but it was also nice because Josie got to learn a lot. They talked on the way to the hospital, and Miranda was filling her in on what the morning would entail. Once they arrived at the hospital Miranda went into a couple of rooms and Josie followed charting as Miranda did her assessments. Miranda was very thorough with her patients but she also talked to them on a personal level, she had a great bedside manner.

Miranda came out of a patient's room and Josie knew they were going to take a detour. The patient Miranda had just seen, said her granddaughter was upstairs on the pediatric floor. Miranda had a real soft spot for kids, she promised the woman she'd stop to say hello to her granddaughter. So when they went to the elevator Josie wasn't surprised. "Hey Josie take five, I'm just going to pop in here and say hello." She was standing in the hallway debating whether or not to go in and visit too. After all she loved kids, but then she heard a little voice singing. Josie followed the voice, she knocked on the door. When she looked in the room, she saw the cutest little girl. She had bright red hair up in pigtails, she was holding a doll on her lap singing contently to it. Josie walked up next to her bed, “Hello, my name is Josie. What is yours?” The little girl looked up at her with the most beautiful green eyes and a smile that lit up the room. “My name is Rachel.”

Josie sat down on the chair next to the bed and said, “Don’t stop singing. It was so pretty.” Rachel looked up at her, “I don’t really know any songs, I was just making that up.” Josie laughed at the little girls’ honesty. “Well that’s ok honey. How ‘bout we just talk. Or I can sing you a song about fireflies?” Rachel nodded, “I get to go home soon. The doctor says I'm all better. I was sick, I had to come here for some medicine. Now I'm all better. Sing!" Josie laughed, "Well I bet your mommy and daddy are so happy they get to take you home." Rachel just looked down at her doll, she seemed sad all of a sudden. Josie didn't know what she had said wrong.

Rachel looked at Josie, "I don't have a mommy or daddy. I live in a home with a lot of kids that nobody wants. But that's ok cuz one day someone will be looking for a little girl. They will come and get me." Josie was so shocked. She hadn't realized or known, but how could she have. She reached out her hand, brushed it over Rachel's cheek and smiled at her. "That is going to be one lucky mommy to have you as her little girl." True to her word Josie started singing,

The Faith Hill song always made Josie feel good, made her dream, and right now she wanted this little girl to be able to dream and imagine her world differently than how it really was. She was the most precious little being Josie had ever met and her heart was breaking as she just poured her soul into singing to Rachel.

Rachel's eyes lit up. "Again!" Josie sat talking to Rachel for a little while and one last time sang Fireflies to her. She heard Miranda come in behind her. "Well, Rachel looks like my boss is here. I have to go, but I will stop in and see you. Maybe I can find you another doll and bring it when I visit." Rachel's eyes lit up and she smiled, "That would be so much fun, we could sing, make up songs, you can sing Fireflies and we can just play dolls, because then I would have two. One for me and one for you. You know where I live right?" Josie nodded, before she could leave, Josie bent down and kissed the little girl's forehead. "You be a good girl Rachel and I will see you soon." Josie turned at the door stopped and waved again.

"Wow, Josie. You can sing. That was so sweet and beautiful." Josie turned to her friend with tears in her eyes. "How can someone not want that beautiful child in there? I would love to have a child of my own and there are people who just throw their children away? How does this happen, tell me Miranda, how?" Josie's face was red with anger and the emotions running across her face were there for all to see. Josie definitely wore her heart on her sleeve where children were concerned.

Miranda pulled Josie into a private area instead of the hallway to have a discussion. "Josie, think about it. Some of these kids are the product of rape, some had parents who were drug addicts and some were in a family with people who simply didn't want a child but couldn't stand the thought of abortion. Do you really want any of those children to be raised by the parents who brought them into the world? As harsh as it sounds they're better off waiting for a family who wants children, who will provide them love, provide safety and stability, instead of heartbreak, beatings or worse." Josie knew her friend was right but it really broke her heart. She had been putting some money aside. She was going to keep putting as much away as she could afford, then buy some things for those kids.

"Seriously Josie, where did you learn to sing like that?" Josie waved Miranda off. She said, "I appreciate the change of subject but I don't sing. I just was feeling something and it spilled out. It wasn't that good." Josie paused for a moment thinking about days with her grandmother. "I sang in church choir in the summers when I visited my grandmother. I never learned how to sing, I just did what felt natural. When I feel something if just pours out." Miranda laughed at her friend, "Ok we'll see about that this weekend at karaoke." Miranda started moving to the stairs and said, "Did you ever sing for your old boyfriend like that?" Josie smiled, "Not really. Sometimes I would sing out the hymn we were working on in church, but only a verse or two. I've always been pretty shy about my singing, never felt like I needed to share it. Except for with the one who gave me the talent. It made my grandmother happy, that's all that mattered to me." Miranda nodded her head. They finished their rounds, headed out of the hospital and back to the office.

At the office Miranda and Josie saw the usual things, sore throat, sprained ankles nothing too serious. Today was a quiet day and Josie found herself thinking a lot about that little girl. How could she not have found a home? She was the sweetest little thing. She was so adorable. It really tore Josie up inside. She was going for a long run tonight. She needed that more than the gym.

Miranda came out of a patient room and found Josie staring at the blank computer screen, she knew her mind was still on that little girl. Josie had the heart of an angel. She was going to have to talk to Mike. This was ridiculous, they both loved each other, whatever happened in the past needed to be discussed. They needed to move on together. Josie needed healing. All the things that she endured and suffered through, she deserved to be happy. Seeing Josie today with that little girl Miranda knew it brought up old wounds of her beatings, her two miscarriages and the life she was not supposed to have. With that lunatic ready to be released Josie really needed something true and wonderful. Mike was that for her. Josie deserved happiness, she deserved the life she'd always wanted and was ripped out from under her. The next chance Miranda got she was going to talk to Mike. Miranda was tired of seeing her friend hurting. She was tired of having to lie to Josie about Mike.

Josie was so glad Miranda let her leave work early. She was ready to hit the road with her sneakers. She really needed to think and running gave her that. Josie grabbed her iPod, changed her clothes and hit the road. She was hitting a great stride. Her mind was racing. Jack would be out soon. She was afraid of what that was going to mean for her. Josie thought about this town and the people in it. They were all so wonderful. The town was beautiful. She loved all the things about it. Josie thought about her new job that she loved. Going to the hospital with Miranda gave her a learning experience and in the office she had been learning more and more. She smiled as she thought about her apartment because she now had something of her own. Josie also thought of that little girl in the hospital. She was so beautiful. Rachel was so sweet, God, Josie had just fallen in love with her little voice. She just couldn't help but be drawn into the beautiful green eyes, the fiery red hair, her cute little smile.

Of course Josie's thoughts went to Mike. Always Mike. So many things had happened between them. Josie remembered all the times people would see her and say, 'that's Mike's girl', or times when she would be with Mike, someone would start to approach them but changed course. Kids would say, 'hi' then scampered off. Josie always found it odd but she figured they didn't want to disturb them or

Mike didn't want to be bothered by anyone when he and Josie were together.

After the first time Josie and Mike made love they had been together as often as possible. Usually at the cabin so they could be alone, but one night Josie was with him at The Escape Club and she was angry about a discussion they were having. Josie didn't remember all of what it was about, but she was angry about how cavalier he was about her view point. He seemed to not even care what she thought. They got awfully heated with each other.

Josie yelled at him, "You are the most irritating, frustrating, pain in the ass." Mike looked at her getting all mad while she yelled at him, "I'm serious Michael. You are the most stubborn, frustrating person on the face of this earth. You are such a fucking dumb ass. You have such a closed minded view point. You don't even care what I think. How rude! How completely aggravating, I thought you were better than that. What the hell? Are you even listening to me?" Then she saw the glint in his eyes. "Oh no you don't! Don't you even act like that. I'm mad at you! Looking at me that way isn't going to change anything. You are so inconsiderate sometimes Michael. I'm tired of you acting so, uh God, you make me so mad I can't even finish yelling at you. Aren't you going to say something for yourself?"

Mike chuckled, he rubbed his face, took his hand through his hair. "Oh yeah I'm going to say something. Run sweetheart, cuz when I catch you I am having my way with you and where I catch you is where it's going to happen." Josie looked at him like he was mad, but the desire was brewing inside her as well. Just the tone of his voice, the way he looked at her. It was almost like he could stare the clothes off of her, bringing her to an orgasm, all with just one look. How did he do that? "Michael," Josie hated that she sounded breathless. "Be serious." "Oh I am." Mike gasped. "You got to the count of five for a head start,1, 2, 3."

Josie stood staring at him. Mike was serious, Josie saw it in his eyes. She turned and ran. Josie headed for the woods behind The Escape Club. As soon as her feet hit the gravel of the club, Mike yelled "5". He was hot on her heels. Mike was the only person who ever challenged her on a run. They would run together some nights when the club was quiet. Mike would run with her when he took her home instead of driving when the weather was nice. Mike didn't like the idea of her being out late at night on her own.

Josie hit the tree line. She weaved around them. Josie was laughing now, the anger totally gone. She could almost feel his breath behind her. It didn't take long and Mike's arms were coming around her from behind. "You are a cheater. You never finished counting." Mike turned her in his arms, he covered her mouth with his ending the protesting and the fight. Mike held her tight to him, he made quick work of her clothes. Josie was just as greedy working at his clothes. Mike laid her down on the ground, under the moon lit sky.

Mike took Josie's breath away every time she was with him. She gave him her heart and soul. The moon was bright and Josie could see Mike's face. She knew she saw the love she felt for him reflected back in his blue eyes. Mike was stroking her breasts, he trailed his hand down between her thighs. "I am only whole when I am here like this with you. I don't know how I'd survive a minute without you Josie girl." Josie gasped at Mike's touch. She wanted more. She grabbed him to pull him to her. She took his mouth while Mike took the rest of her. She was over the edge in seconds. Josie felt every pulse in her body explode. She felt like she was standing on the edge of a cliff just letting herself fall backwards. Josie was tingling all over, she was enjoying the feel of him as he thrust into her. Mike was off her in seconds cursing, "Damn it." Josie sat up. "What's wrong, are you ok?"

Mike was perched on his knees next to her. She could tell he was trying to gain control. "I'm fine. You're killing me Josie. No condom." She realized then he stopped before his release to keep her from getting pregnant. Mike was always so cautious. He wasn't prepared for this tonight. Quite frankly, neither was Josie. She came up on her knees in front of him. She started stroking him with her hands. Mike reached out to stop her. “Please Michael. It’s not fair to you.” Mike moved his hands taking her face in them. He pulled her in to kiss her, with that she could feel his release under her gentle stroking. Mike stopped kissing her, he leaned his forehead against hers. “Don’t ever get angry with me again Josie. I don’t like it when you are mad, but I do like the fire you get in your eyes. That and your chest heaving as you were yelling at me. Damn, everything you do turns me on. I’m just lost without you. How will I ever survive without you?”

Josie ran harder, she pushed harder. Before she knew it she was at the Heartbreak bar again. She stopped running as she paced in the parking lot. She pulled her ear buds out. She got madder with every step. Damn him! Mike was planning on leaving her. Was their love only one sided? Was she a joke? Was

Mike playing her for a sucker? No, she was being ridiculous. Mike loved her. Josie was sure of it. Didn't he? He had to, she saw it in his eyes. His eyes were like as they say, a window to his soul. She saw everything in them. Mike couldn't hide that. It wasn't a lie, or was it?

She was so lost in her own thoughts she never heard Max come up behind her. "Josie?" She spun on her heels, pulling her fists up ready to throw whatever necessary to protect herself. "Whoa, Josie! Relax, it's me Max." Josie relaxed as she stared at him for a minute. "Holy shit Max. I was ready to hit you!" Max laughed a little nervous, "What are you doing out here? Are you ok?" Josie relaxed, slowing her breathing down. She was mad at herself, she really needed to be more careful than to let someone sneak up on her like that. She was just so lost in her thoughts, she needed to be more careful. Damn Michael and his memories.

Josie looked at Max, "I was out for a run to clear my mind. Obviously it's not working or you would've never had the jump on me like that." Josie laughed then smiled at Max. He smiled back at her asking what was troubling her. Josie told him about the worries she had with her husband, how she loved the town, about the little girl she had met today. Josie then told him about the lover who abandoned her so many years ago. She was still wrestling with the abandonment she felt from that. "I wonder sometimes Max, was I so naïve and dumb? Or did I really mean something to him? Right now I feel stupid, cheap. I feel like a fool. I mean if he really loved me, where did he go? Why would he have gone without a reason? A good-bye or even a kiss my ass would have been nice. Instead, I wonder all the time what I did wrong. Was I good enough for him? Why didn't he want to stay?"

Max was feeling really awful about the pain his jackass partner was causing this poor woman. Josie was the moon and stars to Mike, he was just too stupid to set things straight. Max paused for a moment pondering how to answer. "Josie all I can tell you is sometimes for whatever reason life gets in the way. You know, things were going great for you two. You weren't wrong about him. He probably loved you, if he's smart he still does love you, but sometimes things happen that can't be explained without causing a lot of pain to both people involved. Maybe he thought he was sparing you the pain of I don't know, the truth? Maybe he had a secret life or something that you didn't know about."

Josie laughed, "Michael? A secret life? I don't know, seems too far-fetched. He was so easy going, he didn't have much. Michael lived with his boss, he drove a junker car, and besides if Michael loved me he should have been able to tell me anything knowing that I would've loved him, no matter what." Max smiled at her shrugging. "Well then my only defense for this man is he must have been really stupid or out of his mind to walk away from you." Mike was one stupid bastard. This woman would have sold her soul for him. Actually it sounds like she already did. Josie laughed at Max for his kind words, but in her heart she knew, she was never going to be over Mike.

They talked for a few more minutes about the bar, the upcoming weekend of events and Josie was excited for the weekend out with her friends. The karaoke night was going to be fun for them all. She reached out, completely out of character for her, throwing her arms around Max hugging him. Josie caught him off guard, since generally she avoided personal contact with people, pulling away even when he placed a hand on hers. Josie was pushing herself out of her comfort zone, she needed to, it was time for her to get back into the world, time for her to feel something good again. She also needed the comfort of someone's arms around her. Max swayed a little when she launched herself at him, lightly putting his arms around her, so he wouldn't scare her or make her uncomfortable.

As Josie pulled away from him she kissed his cheek as a sister would kiss her brother, "You are a really great guy. Thank you for talking with me. I appreciate the thoughts." Max patted her shoulder, "Just think about it Josie. Be careful on your way home." Josie turned, nodded put her ear buds back in her ears, starting off on a slow jog to get warmed up again. Max watched as Josie headed off. He didn't need to turn around to know that Mike was watching. Max sighed heading back to the bar and his angry partner.

Chapter 11

Before Max could get a word out Mike punched him in the face. Max the one who thinks before acting was angry. He grabbed Mike shoving him up against the side of the building. “You, stupid fuck! I know you’re mad but if you would calm down, think about what you just saw, nothing happened. Even if it did, what do you care? You’re the jackass hiding in the shadows just watching and waiting. Fuck that Mike! Get over yourself. Tell that woman how you feel before someone else sees how wonderful she is, taking her away from here and away from you.” Mike was fighting mad, “Nothing happened! And you call me a jackass. You had your hands all over her. You kissed her.” “Oh no I didn’t, Mike! Josie kissed me and Josie hugged me. The kiss was a kiss on the cheek like a sister kissing her brother. The hug was a thank you because I was trying to help her sort her feelings over some jackass that broke her heart years ago. You wouldn't happen to know who that jackass is would you? Josie was beating herself up over it, thinking he never really loved her and played her. So did you Mike? Did you play her? Or did you and do you still love her? That woman deserves to know the truth. Josie deserves to be happy, not questioning the love that she felt for you! God you are so stupid Mike! She's been hurt enough by you and her ass of a husband. Isn't it time for her and you to be happy again?" Max gave him one last shove to get his point across turning to head into the bar. Max stopped turning to Mike first. "I've grown quite fond of the little lady. In fact, I'm liking her a whole lot more than you these days. She is one tough and brave little lady. Maybe she does deserve better than you. That hug she gave me took nerves of steel on her part. Not long ago in the bar I touched her arm and she pulled away. She is making progress, what about you? Can you say the same?" Max turned back heading into the bar.

Mike sauntered over to the steps of his apartment to sit down. Max never spoke to him that way. He was right though, he had his head up his ass. He needed to fix this and fast. Did Josie really think that he didn't love her? How could she? Everything he did, he did for her. He tried to spend as much time with her as he could, he spent days and days with her, talking, laughing, making love. Mike loved her so much it hurt. Hell he left her to protect her. He left her to……He hung his head. He left her to protect his ego. To save face because he wasn't the man she thought he was. Mike wasn't half the man she needed or deserved. He left her because he was a coward. He needed to tell her the truth. Mike owed her that. He owed them a chance. He robbed them of that chance before, he had no right then and he had no right now to do so. Josie deserved better than that, better than him. But she also deserved to know the truth, the truth that he loved her, his whole life. The truth that he fucked up. All he could do was hope she could forgive him.

Mike headed back into the bar, to his friend, Max. If Max never spoke to him again it would be too soon. “Max.” He spun and Mike could see his eye swelling already. “I know I’ve run my limits of I’m sorry, but I am. I just can’t think when it comes to her. Josie’s all I think about all I want. Now that she’s here I’m more and more irrational, and...” “Irritable, unreasonable, foolish, stupid, in need of serious anger management. Dude you punched me!” Max finished for him. Max was mad, he had every right to be. Mike told Max that he was going to tell her the truth. Mike realized that he was being a coward. Josie deserved better than that. "Finally, when are you going to tell her? If you leave now you can catch her, just run and run fast." Mike laughed at that, while Max grinned at him. Mike got a far-away look in his eyes. "Soon. I just need the right moment. I will tell her everything."

Josie finished her run in record time. She felt great. She ran so hard on the way back she didn't have time to think. She left it all pounded into the pavement on her way back to the apartment. She walked in her front door, heading for a shower. She was going to soak in the tub but, decided against it. She wanted a shower and bed. She wasn't even hungry, she was exhausted. Josie just needed some sleep. In the morning she was going to hit the gym before work. After work was self-defense class. Josie took a nice warm shower. She climbed under the covers, the cool sheets touching her skin as she didn't even stop for her PJ's. She just climbed naked under the sheets. Josie smiled as a memory came back to her. She drifted off to sleep dreaming.

Josie and Mike had just finished making love. They were in the cabin, ready for sleep. Josie went to grab Mike's T-shirt to put it on when he grabbed her arm. "Where are you going? And if it's not for food get back in here." Josie laughed. "I'm going to get a T-shirt to put on." Mike growled, rolling to grab ahold of her with both hands. He pulled her naked body up against him. "You don't need a T-shirt. Feel the sheets against your bare skin, feel me against you. A T-shirt just makes me angry cuz I have to work around it to touch you. Besides give me twenty minutes, you'll be naked on top of me, taking this bull to the championships." Josie laughed at him she swatted his arm playfully. "Oh Michael, you are something else." He was true to his word that night. He was sometimes so eager to touch her and make love to her. It was like he couldn't get enough. Josie couldn't get enough of him either but Mike, what he wanted and when he wanted it he took it.

Josie woke up with thoughts of Mike again. She laid there for a few minutes just thinking. She thought about what Max said last night. She thought about her own thoughts, her feeling like she was played the fool. Josie decided that she probably would never know the truth. Maybe what Max said was true. Who knows, but she didn't want the memories of the love they shared tainted by thoughts that Mike didn't love her. Mike had to have loved her. No one had ever touched her the way he did and no one ever would again. Of this she was sure. Josie didn't think she could ever have someone touch her that way again, not without thinking of Jack and the things he did to her.

With the thought of Jack, she decided it was time to get moving. She got dressed heading to the gym. She did a full round of weight training and also did some crunches on the balance ball. She was working her abs when she saw the girl from the restaurant. She was on the treadmill. She was walking quite a fast pace. Josie wondered what it was that made her so sad. Josie wanted to go talk to her, but she really needed this workout and had to finish up so she could get to work.

Josie just kept going through her routine. She did rotating crunches working all her muscles. She was burning in a good way, every muscle was screaming at her and she pushed on. She was going to finish up with a run on the treadmill, but she caught someone out of the corner of her eye. It was Max. Max was lifting weights in the corner of the gym where the free weights were. Josie smiled at him but he wasn't looking her way. Max looked very deep in thought. He was watching something over by the treadmills. Josie followed his gaze, she smirked. The soup girl, so that was Max's kryptonite.

Josie headed to the treadmill just as Taryn was getting off, Josie smiled and Taryn dropped her head, not making eye contact. Josie shrugged it off and thought another time, when she had more time but for now, she had a date with the treadmill. Josie only did 5 miles as after her run last night, her weight training today and self-defense class tonight Josie thought she was pushing the envelope a little. She felt really good but who knows how she'd feel later. Josie finished up her run heading home for a quick shower and some food before work.

The week continued fairly uneventful. Josie continued her gym workouts and self-defense classes. She was walking home from work on Friday when she saw the cutest dress in the window of a dress shop. She rarely dressed up or splurged on her wardrobe but she thought, "what the hell." She went in. She tried on three other dresses, plus the one in the window.

She ended up not getting the one in the window, it was just not her, but she settled on a simple black dress with spaghetti straps, it came mid-thigh on her, which really accented how hard she'd been training. Josie's legs really looked great, all the running was paying off. She thought the dress looked simple, elegant, it made her look absolutely beautiful. It hugged her curves, she felt a little self-conscious but she needed to break out of her comfort zone a little more.

She smiled at the reflection looking back at her. She thought other than the scars, she looked good. Josie would just wear a shawl around her to cover some of the scars on her arms. She couldn't hide the scars forever so she might as well get used to them. She was thinking about her closet at home, she knew she had some cute little silver sandals but no jewelry to highlight her ensemble. Josie bought the dress and headed home. She was going to the gym to meet Miranda so she'd ask to borrow something for Saturday night.

After the gym Miranda insisted on seeing the outfit so she drove to Josie's apartment. Miranda insisted she wasn't walking as she'd had enough exercise for one day. Josie just laughed getting into the car. At Josie's apartment Miranda told Josie to put on what she was going to wear. When Josie came into the living room Miranda's jaw almost hit the ground. There was nothing special about the dress but with her figure, all the hard work she'd been putting in at the gym it hung and accentuated every curve it needed to accentuate.

"Wow! Josie, you look fabulous! Really! Amazing!" Josie blushed fidgeting a little. "I don't know do you really think I look okay?" Miranda gasped, "Okay? Josie you look hot in that dress. I have the perfect necklace and earrings you can wear." Josie remembered that she had a necklace tucked away in the box of treasures she hid from Jack. She smiled at Miranda, "I think I have the perfect necklace. I almost forgot about it." Josie hadn't thought of that necklace in ages. But when she came out with it and clasped it, Miranda squealed with delight. "It's perfect. What is that, a butterfly?" Josie reached down touching it she nodded and Miranda knew there was a story but didn't ask. "Well, I have silver diamond studs that I can loan you to wear. They will be perfect. They will sparkle like that necklace."

Josie felt a little foolish being all dressed up. "Are you sure it's not going to be too much?" Miranda shook her head no. Miranda knew that once Mike saw her in that dress he was going to have no choice but to tell her the truth.

Miranda left Josie and headed to the Heartbreak bar. It was time she had a talk with Mike. Miranda needed to set some things straight. When she got there she saw it was pretty busy. Miranda went up taking a seat at the bar. She ordered a glass of wine and waited. Miranda saw Mike come from the back. She waved him over. He walked over to her looking around cautiously. "She's not here, but she will be tomorrow night. If you don't drop this shit of not telling her who you are then you're a fool. Josie is going to be looking hot. New dress and a little something you may recognize." Mike replied, "Cut the shit Miranda. What are you doing here? We're kind of busy." Mike knew she was giving him a hard time.

Miranda, she was a feisty one. She always said what was on her mind, whether people wanted to hear it or not. "Look I want to talk to you." He gave her a look. "Alright come in the back. I can't stand out here and actually listen to you with all this action." Miranda got off the bar stool following him in the back. Miranda looked around, she was impressed by how organized everything was. Mike really was keeping his place orderly. By the crowd out there tonight, he was finally giving life to this old place. Miranda really liked this guy but she wasn't going to let that sway her conversation with him tonight. "What can I do for you Miranda?" Mike motioned to a chair for her to sit on. He stood waiting for her to tell him what was so important.

Miranda began speaking, “I know you are hiding from Josie. That’s fine if you want to do that, but we have grown quite fond of her. She’s family to all of us, especially Rod and me. Your deception has now become ours and I don’t like it. We are also keeping a secret from her because of you. She told me once that she left the town in Maine she was in because everyone looked at her with pity on their face. She didn’t want that. She wanted a fresh start where people didn’t know what she had been through. She has that here, only now we’ve all betrayed her.”

Mike started pacing. Miranda was right. Mike was single handedly destroying Josie’s new life. It’s like lie after lie and no way out, except the truth. Mike just kept pacing.

Miranda was getting tired of wondering what was going through his head. "Seriously, Mike! What the hell! Are you going to tell her what's going on or not? Josie deserves that much. She deserves to have," Mike spun around and looked at her, "She deserves to have better than me! I get that Miranda. I know I don't deserve her. Who knows maybe when she hears the truth she'll go running out on me like my sorry ass deserves. Maybe she'll give me a taste of what I did to her. I deserve it, I know I do."

Miranda was speechless something that rarely happened. She watched him. She heard the anger and self-contempt he was feeling. He truly believed that he was a horrible awful person. Miranda held her hands up to him. He stopped to look at her. "Mike honestly, cut yourself a break. You made mistakes. Everyone does, we're human. The thing is, you paid for your mistake. You are making a good, honest life for yourself." Mike looked at Miranda. She actually felt sorry for him, Mike had a sadness there. "You know Mike, all I wanted to say was Josie deserves to have the truth from the only man she's ever loved. Josie deserves the life she always wanted, with you. You really need to pull your head out of your ass long enough to see the woman she has become. She's a loving, forgiving person who just wants to understand what happened to the love of her life. You're a dumb ass if you think she'll never forgive you. She may need some time to think, to see you for who you are now, but I have no doubt in my mind that she'll want to be with you again. Think about it." Miranda turned to leave, but stopped, "By the way, you better pull your shit together, because she's about to do a number on your sorry ass when you see her. I'm just sayin', you'd better be prepared."

Mike stood there just staring. Miranda was right Josie deserved the truth. Was he really that man to her? He didn't know, that was the thought that kept him up at night. Does she love him enough, or will he lose her forever? Regardless he had nothing to lose, only to gain. If Josie turned her back on him forever he would be no worse off than he is now, but if Josie could forgive him, he could have it all again. He could hold her in his arms, he could spend the rest of his life making love to her and making her happy, reminding her of how much he loved her every day. Mike wanted to hope but he knew he had no right. Pull my shit together, Miranda said. Mike chuckled a moment, what was his Josie girl planning?

Mike's phone rang. He answered it with a tone harsher than he'd meant to. On the other line was one of his informants. Jack was free. Mike hung up the phone. He cursed under his breath. Mike finally got the truth from the guys who were supposed to be watching her. They were terrified of what Mike would have done had he known what was happening so they left the details out. Mike told them he wanted all the reports. He had files delivered to him within a few days. They were filled with all the information that was held from him, the horrors of what Jack did to her. Mike nearly destroyed his apartment, if it hadn't been for Max, he may have. Max sat with him, looked over the files and couldn't believe what he read. Max wanted to go with Mike to kill the sick son of a bitch responsible for all those heinous acts against that sweet woman. Mike wanted to find him and kill him for what he did to his Josie girl. The man didn't deserve the air that he breathed let alone five minutes of Josie's time.

Max came in the back, “I’m getting slammed dude. I could use a hand.” Mike came out of his thoughts heading back to work. He really needed to hire some more help. He had applicants, he just had been so consumed by Josie that he hadn’t been really interested in looking at them. That was the first thing he was doing tomorrow. Mike needed to get this place straightened out. He needed to get help in here for tomorrow night.

Chapter 12

Josie woke up deciding to head to the orphanage. She wanted to see if Rachel had returned. If not Josie was going to the hospital to see her. She grabbed a shower and headed to the orphanage with a doll in hand as promised. She got there and it wasn't as bad as she imagined but still it broke her heart. Josie signed in at the entrance and told the worker that she worked with Dr. Porter. She mentioned meeting Rachel at the hospital. The desk clerk told Josie that Rachel had made it back home. She would probably love to see Josie. They took her to the play room where Rachel was. Josie walked through the door and Rachel looked up seeing her immediately. "Josie! You came to play dolls with me!" She ran over to Josie, hugging her legs before Josie could get down to her level for a real hug. She took Rachel's hand as she took her to the play area. “Fireflies! Sing!” Rachel was so excited she was clapping her hands, rocking back and forth. Josie smiled laughing. “Ok I will sing Fireflies, but only if you will let me braid that beautiful hair.” Rachel stuck out her hand to shake, “Deal!” She was beaming from ear to ear. Josie started singing. Before she knew it there was a crowd of children sitting around her rocking back and forth, smiling up at her.

Rachel was true to her promise, she let Josie braid her hair. While she was brushing it and preparing for the braid, Rachel talked non-stop making Josie laugh at the excitement she had about everything. She was so wonderful and sweet. All at once Rachel was quiet. Josie was afraid something had happened. Josie was braiding her hair, so she leaned down to her ear to ask, “Are you ok Rachel?” She whispered softly, “Yes.” Josie finished braiding her hair, turning to look at her. “What’s the matter sweetie? Don't you like the braid?" Rachel looked up at her with such sad green eyes, it just tore her to pieces.

"Josie?" Rachel said in a very small quiet voice. She smiled at the little girl. "Yes?" Rachel stood in front of her and looking like she was ready to run away. "Can I ask you something?" Rachel came up on her knees and nodded her head yes. "Why can't you be my mommy?" She finished the words, threw herself at Josie, burying her head in her shoulder. Josie's heart was melting, it ached for this little girl. She hugged her so tight. She hated to let go. "Rachel, I wish I could be your mommy but..." Josie stopped, why couldn't she be her Mommy? She was a loving person who had a roof over her head a job. Why couldn't she adopt Rachel? She hugged Rachel, "I have to get going honey, but I promise you I will be back soon. Okay?" Rachel nodded to her. She leaned over to give Josie a kiss on the cheek. The simple act of love brought tears to her eyes. “You be a good girl. I will see you soon.” She hugged her again, grabbed her things and headed for the administrator’s office.

Josie was so excited when she left the orphanage. She couldn’t go home. She headed to Ted and Sarah’s. Sarah opened the door welcoming her in. She looked around, the place was quiet. “Where is everyone?” Sarah had explained that Ted took Bella to the babysitter, who was a retired lady who used to be a cop with Ted. She was going to keep Bella overnight so they didn’t have to rush home tonight. He would be back shortly she had told her. “So what’s going on with you? I haven’t seen you this happy since Miranda hired you at the office.”

Josie couldn't contain her excitement any longer. "I applied to be an adoptive parent. I went to visit Rachel from the hospital, I'm sure Miranda told you." Sarah nodded and Josie continued. "Well, while I was there she hugged me. She said she wished I could be her mommy. I was ready to tell her why I couldn't when I realized there was no reason I couldn't so I went to the office, filled out an application. Now all I have to do is wait. I know adoptions can be complicated but I am hoping for a smooth process on this one." Sarah smiled at her. She was very excited for her friend. "Really, that is wonderful. We can do play dates, go shopping together. Oh I'm so excited. How long do you have to wait?" Josie said the application process was a little lengthy but she could continue going to see Rachel. Once she was approved through applications, then the final phase was home inspection and if she passed that then Rachel was hers. All in all, it could take months to become official but Josie had said she didn't care. She could wait as long as it took as long as she ended up the mother to that sweet little girl. Sarah squealed, "Josie I am so excited for you. This is wonderful news."

The front door slammed and a curse rang out, "Son of a bitch! Are you sure?" Ted looked up. He saw his wife and Josie starring up at him. "I gotta go. Yeah I'll take care of it." He hung up the phone. He looked at the smiles on both women. He really wished he didn't have to make them go away.

"Ted really, you don't come in the house swearing like that. What is going on?" Sarah walked over to him. He looked right past her at Josie. Josie's heart sank, she knew. "Jack's coming isn't he?" Ted walked over to her leaving his wife to trail behind him. "No Josie. He was released though." Josie hung her head,

"When?" Ted told her that he was a free man as of an hour ago.

Josie stood. She started pacing the living room. She stopped to look at Sarah with tears in her eyes, "I almost forgot about him. There isn't anyone in the world that would give me a child with him in the picture." Sarah walked over to her and hugged her while she cried. Ted was confused. He looked at the two women and was ready to ask when his phone rang.

"Chief Blake," It was Rod on the other end. He had gotten the same phone call from Mike that Ted had. "I don't know how he found out." Ted walked out of the room to talk more privately with Rod, "I don't know but I am going to ask him that's for sure. Mike got the information before we did. I know he still has connections but he shouldn't. Damn it Rod I don't care either but we gotta make sure that he stays on the straight arrow, he can't slip up. Mike's future depends on it. Yeah Josie knows. She's in my living room with Sarah. Alright we'll see you tonight." He hung up the phone and cursed again. He dialed Mike's number, he needed answers. Mike answered on the first ring, "I'm on my way to the bar, I want answers Mike."

Ted headed back into his living room. He told Josie not to worry, Jack was not going to hurt her again. Josie looked at Ted with tears flowing down her cheeks, "He already has." Sarah hugged her as she cried. Ted told Josie he had to leave again. Sarah told Josie she'd be right back as she followed to the front door.

"Sarah what's going on?" Sara filled Ted in quickly. She told him about the adoption that Josie was working on, the little girl she had fallen in love with. "Can't you do something for her?" Ted shook his head, "I have to go Sarah. I have other issues right now to deal with. I will think about it. You know we have to deal with the fact that this lunatic most likely is coming for her first. I am heading to talk to Mike. He is the one who told me that Jack is out. I didn't even get official word yet but Mike knows. I don't like it. I don't want him sucked back into that world." Sarah kissed Ted. "Be careful sweetheart." She turned to go back inside to Josie.

Sarah and Josie talked. Josie did calm down but she was still upset. It seemed that Jack was always going to win. She hated him. She didn't want to put Rachel in danger so she was going to have to forget about adoption for now. She should cancel the application but she just didn't have the heart. Josie assured Sarah that she was fine. She just needed to go for a run to clear her head before getting ready for tonight. Sarah walked her to the door hugging her, “Don’t give up hope Josie. Sometimes hope is all we have. When you least expect it, dreams come true.” Josie looked at her. She smiled a weak smile. She thanked Sarah, leaving her home to go to her apartment.

Ted arrived at the bar. Mike was waiting for him. He held his hands up before Ted could say a word. “I’m sorry. I know I should not have used my contacts. They owed me.” Ted looked at him. “Is this how you want to start your future with Josie? You don’t want to tell her about your past, you’re afraid of losing her but yet you’ll risk it all for what, the idiot who isn’t worth anything? You are more important to her than Jack. You need to remember that. No matter what, don’t fall back on what you knew back then. Let me do my job and protect her.” Mike shook his head at Ted. “I can’t help it. I feel helpless. Those guys who called me were supposed to check in on her for me while I was in jail. They did but they were afraid of me. They left out the part of him beating her."

Ted sat talking Mike out of using his old contacts. He owed Josie that. He couldn't fall back into those old habits. "I don't want to Ted. I'm not trying to. I want a life that she can be proud of, a life full of the things she deserves. But how can I do that with him looming about, with not knowing what is happening with him? I swear Ted I would risk a life with her to be sure she was safe. I need to protect her since I wasn't there before to protect her. I feel responsible for all the hell she went through. My sources got me all the reports." Mike shook his head. Ted could see the pain in his eyes. "Do you know all that she went through? I mean all of it Ted? I read it and I damn near destroyed my apartment. I wanted to go find him. I want to hurt him the way he hurt her. I just feel like had I known I could have done something."

Ted shook his head, "You are not responsible. Only the man who did this can be responsible for it. You couldn't have done anything. You were serving your time. Those guys did you a favor not telling you. Had you known you would have gotten yourself in more trouble. You could have ended up serving more time depending on what you did. You need to keep yourself out of this and out of trouble in order to give Josie the things she needs now. Josie wants a life and if what my wife tells me is true, which I'm sure it is, she wants that life she never got to have with you. Don't do anything that would take you away from her again."

Josie started her run in the usual fashion. She had her earphones blaring. She was trying to drown out the thoughts. She increased her speed and increased her speed, before she knew it she was full on pounding the streets with her feet. Josie was openly crying as she ran and she didn't care. Josie needed to just keep running. She was so angry. How could Jack still keep screwing up her life? It's not fair, she had suffered enough. Now she was just a sitting duck waiting for him to come for her. She wondered what life would be like if Mike wouldn't have left. No, that wasn't fair. Yes, Mike left her but she chose to marry Jack, why she would never know. Had she not married him would she have found this place, these people? Would she have ever felt the love in her heart for that little girl? Josie would never thank Mike for leaving her but it was a process. It was how her life was meant to go. What was the plan now? Was she supposed to continuously suffer? Why? What did she do that was so awful that she was doomed in her life? She was crying so hard by now that she could barely see. She stopped running and hit her knees. She covered her face, just kneeling on the ground crying.

Mike looked out the window of his apartment, he saw Josie in a heap on the ground. He was ready to run out the door when he saw Ted leaving the bar heading toward her. “Josie? Are you hurt?” Ted was on the ground next to her. He put his arms around her holding her to him. Ted looked over her head. He saw Mike standing in the window. Ted waited for Josie to calm down. When she finally did he helped her up and into his car. Josie stared out the window watching the town go by. Ted told her to not give up. Things were going to get better. Just because Jack was released didn’t mean that he was going to come after her. Ted really wished he believed that but he needed her to believe. He intended to keep Jack from getting to her. If Ted didn’t succeed in keeping her husband from getting to her, he knew Rod was dedicated to that as well. Josie and Rod had a special bond, he worried about her, he cared about her. Ted found it odd, but he questioned Rod about it. Rod assured him, it was not a romantic interest. There was just something about Josie that drew him in. He felt the need to take care of her, he felt like he was responsible for her, like she was his sister, nothing more. Ted was glad that Josie had someone she felt close to as well. He knew with sexual abuse cases, that in most cases, the victims didn't let anyone get too close. He was so glad for Josie that she wasn't letting this man break her.

Josie buried her sobs, "I'm so sorry for being so much trouble Ted. I guess I just don't know how to handle any of this. It's like I'm on the roller coaster from hell. My life is good, then I lose Michael, crashing down I go, I marry Jack life is ok, he beats the hell out of me, life sucks, I run away find a home, job, friends and a daughter. Jack is back, everything is being pulled away from me. Seriously, whose life is like this? I feel like a fool. I really do wish I'd never met Jack Morris, even if my path wouldn't have found this road. I just wish I could have a normal life." Ted smiled at her, "Give it time Josie. It will happen, trust me. Good always finds a way to good people. Just believe."

Ted pulled up at her door. Josie got out of the car. As she was heading toward her front door Ted hollered out the window. "Someday ask Sarah to tell you our love story. It may surprise you. Try not to worry Josie. We'll be by to pick you up at seven." With that he drove off giving Josie something else to think about besides her troubles. She stood there staring at Ted's car drive off wondering what he'd meant by that.

Josie heard her phone ringing, she figured it was Miranda so she ran to catch it. "I'm coming bitch. Don't think you can hide from me." Josie was done cowering to him. "Jack! You son of a bitch! Don't you threaten me! I'm ready for you, do you hear me? I'm ready for you. You can't hurt me anymore. I won't allow it. I'm in control of my life now, not you. You may have controlled me once but not anymore. I won't let you destroy me or hurt me anymore. It ends now." Jack laughed in the phone at her, "I'll tell you when it ends you whore!" then the line went dead.

Josie meant it, she was done being his victim. It was time for her to take control of her life again. Josie took a shower. She started to get ready for the night planned with her friends. She was ready to have a good time and leave Jack for another time. Josie dressed humming to herself. She curled her long brown hair, she let the curls just hang soft and light. She put her makeup on using brown eyeshadow, a black eyeliner with mascara and just a touch of blush. Just before her friends arrived she picked up her necklace, remembering simpler times, beautiful sweet memories.

"Michael, you didn't have to buy me anything. What is it?" He laughed at her. "Open it and see." Josie looked at him then the package. She tore into it like a five-year old on Christmas morning. She opened the lid of the box. "Oh Michael it's beautiful. Look how it shines and sparkles. Put it on me." Josie handed it to him, he brought it over her head. She lifted her hair as he hooked the clasp. He started kissing her neck. Mike turned her around to look at her wearing the necklace.

Josie touched the necklace with her fingertips. "No one has ever given me jewelry before. I'll wear it forever." Mike bent his head to kiss her. They had held on to each other under the stars and moon. Even in the moonlight it glittered and shined. "Nothing can compare to your beauty Josie. You are the most beautiful thing in my life. This butterfly is to remind you of me, of the beauty you have inside your heart and your soul. I love you Josie girl, I'll love you forever."

The knock on the door interrupted Josie's thoughts. She grabbed her purse and keys. She opened her door. Rod was standing there. "Wow! You look amazing." Josie dipped her head and blushed. Rod reached out his arm to her. She grabbed ahold of it laughing. Sarah and Ted said how wonderful she looked. Miranda winked at her and said, "I told you hot." Everyone laughed, all Josie could think was she wished Mike could see her. She reached up and touched her necklace. Miranda smiled as she watched Josie touch the necklace, she thought to herself, hang in here Josie, he won't be able to resist you tonight.

The group all chatted on the way to the bar. Josie told them about the little girl and her application for the adoption. "The only thing I forgot about was the fact that I'm still married to a psychotic maniac." Rod looked at her, "There is no guarantee he's coming here. If you want, we can work on getting you a divorce." Josie didn't want to tell them about the phone call but she figured she hasn't kept any secrets from them so, "Jack called me tonight." Ted hit the brakes and pulled over. "Josie, why didn't you call me or Rod? What did he say?" She told them the conversation and Ted looked at Rod. A silent conversation happened between the two. Rod spoke first,

"You know Josie how bout we meet up tomorrow afternoon, go over some self-defense moves. I want to make sure that you are prepared just in case." Josie smiled at Rod. She confirmed a time to meet with him. When they reached the Heartbreak bar, Ted stopped Rod on their way inside.

Ted was concerned, "Rod you need to head to Mike. Let him know about Josie's phone call. Make sure he doesn't know anything else about it. Tomorrow we'll meet up and talk more. We need to keep that girl safe." Rod nodded, "Agreed, I'm not letting another criminal run free to hurt someone again. We need to be ready Ted." Rod rushed ahead of the ladies to get the door. They all giggled and Miranda leaned up to give him a kiss. "There's more where that came from later." With a wink she headed into the bar. "Promises, promises." Miranda smiled at Rod, "Oh that's a definite promise babe, count on it." Rod grinned and watched her move inside. He caught up to her and pulled her to his side, wrapping his arm around her waist. He pressed his fingers into her hip and her eyes met his. "Counting the minutes." Rod bent his head down to brush her lips. Miranda's eyes closed, she savored the touch of their lips, finding herself counting the minutes as well. Rod patted her ass then moved to the bar as planned, while Ted went with the ladies to their table.

Josie walked to their usual table. She sat looking toward the dance floor. She pulled her shawl around her a little self-conscious with her scars. Nowhere to hide them with the dress. She noticed a few people glancing her direction and she felt a little off kilter. She didn't really like the attention. She smiled and waved at Max on her way to the table. She noticed the stunned look on his face. Josie giggled at the way Max looked at her. When he winked at her she dipped her head again to hide the blush.

Rod was at the bar. Max looked over at him. "Holy crap! Wait until Mike sees her. If he doesn't make a move, I will." Rod grinned at him, "Where is he?" Max went in the back room. Max was back in seconds. Mike came out cautiously, looking toward their table. Mike saw Josie. His heart slammed against his chest. He felt a rush of heat all over his body. Mike could feel his instant reaction to seeing her. He thought he would die if he didn't touch her.

Mike's thoughts were interrupted by Rod. "Mike we need to talk." Mike turned his back to the beautiful vision to give Rod his undivided attention for now. Rod told him about Josie's phone call. I'll kill him if he gets close to her." Rod told him to settle down, but to keep his ears open on any unfamiliar people coming to town also to keep them informed of any other phone calls he may receive on the matter. Mike agreed he would, but he promised he was not going to follow that road, Josie deserved better.

Rod said, “Josie is quite a woman.” Mike looked over his shoulder at her. “Josie met a little girl at the hospital, she’s an orphan. She went to visit her at the orphanage. She filed adoption papers. She’s afraid that Jack will hurt her chances of getting her. She really loves that little girl.” Mike looked at him then hung his head. “I’m not going to be much better for her.” Rod looked at him, shaking his head.

Rod disagreed, “You are not a bad person Mike. People who have records have been known to adopt children, depending on their crime. You have made donations to the orphanage and you've more than paid your debt to society. I didn't tell you to make you second guess your decision to tell her the truth. I told you so you would know what's at stake with Jack, and to prepare you for fatherhood. At least I hope you're wanting to be a father since you two belong together." Mike nodded, "I just hope she wants me as part of that life after I tell her the truth." Rod shook his head, "If you don't believe in yourself how do you expect her to?" Rod turned to go back with his friends, when he did he noticed her sitting in the corner by herself, Taryn. The one woman he didn't save. Rod was going to make damn sure Josie wasn't added to that list. Max brought them a round of drinks and noticed the Taryn hiding in the corner as well.

"Josie you look fabulous." Max was putting her drink on the table, "Now go easy with this tonight." They all laughed. Josie promised a two drink maximum. They were sitting and talking when the karaoke DJ came over to their table with a catalog of the songs available to sing. He was playing dance music in between the karaoke. He was going to keep playing dance music in order to keep things from getting dull. The girls were excitedly looking over the book. “Sarah just wait until you hear Josie sing. She is going to blow you away. “Josie looked at Miranda, “What makes you think I’m going up there singing? I’m not good with people staring at me. It was different that day I sang in the hospital. It was just Rachel and me. I felt something, the words just flowed. I have to feel it.” Miranda smiled. “So pretend you are singing to just one person and not a whole room full.” Josie looked at her friend rolling her eyes, like that was even possible. The bar was packed, people everywhere, but if she could she’d sing for him. In her heart she wished her heart could conjure up the man from her past, the only man she'd ever loved, the only man who could make her body melt with one touch, the man that she would sell her soul for just one more night. If singing could bring him to her, she'd stand naked in front of that room and sing, but that couldn't happen, he was gone.

Ted and Rod were just watching the three women, while exchanging glances between each other, and watching Mike at the bar. This was the first time he'd been out in sight that Josie could see him. She was really not paying any attention to the bar, Josie started having a distant look to her, like part of her was somewhere else, but eventually she would look over at the bar. Would she recognize him or not?

Chapter 13

They were having such a good time, laughing and singing along with the music. Miranda put in a slip with the DJ to sing 'Girls Just Wanna Have Fun' and they were up next. The guys couldn't wait to hear them. They were joking with them about getting out their ear plugs. They were all laughing while they headed up to the stage. All three had a microphone and Miranda was their leader. Sarah was extremely nervous and Josie she just tried to look out into the crowd. The lights on the stage really made it impossible to see anything. Everything was just shadows. Halfway through the song Sarah and Josie started to relax and have fun with it. As they finished and turned to go off the stage Josie handed the DJ her request. While the other girls laughing all three left the stage.

The DJ went back to playing some music. The girls were dancing up a storm. Ted and Rod talked while they continued to dance. "I told Mike what's going on. He promised to let us know if he heard anything but he wants us to do the same. I'm worried about him. Mike is wanting to kill this guy for what he did to Josie. We are going to not only have our hands full protecting Josie but we are going to have to get control of Mike too." Ted looked over toward the bar and said, "I don't think so. I honestly believe that once Mike tells Josie the truth he isn't going to risk losing her by going back to jail."

Mike was watching the guys, he saw Ted looking over at him. What was he supposed to think about the conversation he had with Rod? A father? Him? He always thought someday he'd have kids. But adopt? He wasn't sure about that. He donated money to the orphanage and still continued to do so. The original money he donated was what was left from his old life. He didn't want that money. He bought his pick-up truck, this bar and that was all he needed. The rest went to the orphanage. He wanted to earn his money now, honestly and without destroying lives. Rod was also right, he had to believe in himself, accept that he made mistakes in life and paid for them. He was ready to tell Josie the truth. God help him, he didn't want to spend any more time away from her. Especially now with that sick son of a bitch coming after her, he didn't want her to be alone. Who was he kidding? He didn't want to be alone anymore, not with her so close, so beautiful, so sexy. Damn he loved her with every ounce of his soul. He had to tell her the truth.

Mike watched her with her friends dancing and having fun. He watched her on stage singing. He was smiling from ear to ear. Max was telling Mike how he didn't know he had teeth that he never saw them before. He was smiling so hard. Mike shoved him good naturedly then focused on her. Mike had been watching her all night. She would occasionally get a far-away look on her face and look almost like she was going to cry. She kept reaching up to her neck touching her necklace. Mike couldn't see the necklace from there but it seemed to mean a lot to her.

They were getting drinks out at the bar as quick as possible. Mike heard the DJ restart karaoke. This really seemed like a good night. They were busier than they'd been in a while. He was glad he hired a few people who started tonight. Everything seemed to be going well. Mike went in the back for a few minutes, when he came back out he looked around. He'd finally made something honest and it was working out. Soon he'd be able to look around for some land. Mike hoped he'd be able to build a home with Josie. First he had to get through telling her the truth.

Josie was sitting on pins and needles. She didn't tell her friends what she was doing. She was just going for broke. She sat there laughing with her friends and she sat back a few times feeling like someone was watching her. She reached up to her necklace. She just imagined that he was there, that he was watching her and protecting her.

Josie was nervous about singing in public. She'd never done that, other than at church, but she wanted to sing to Michael. She felt the need to let her emotions out. She was ready to start letting go of all the baggage she'd been carrying around. She wanted to free herself from all the pain. She wanted to remember all the good times but she needed to heal. To do that she had to stop thinking about him every minute of every day. This would be her release. Her way to free her heart to start moving forward again. Her goodbye to Michael, her fresh start, her new beginning.

Mike was pouring drinks, helping Max behind the bar when he heard the DJ announce …'and up next a little song from Josie. She's going to sing All I ask made popular by Adele.' He overflowed the glass, "Shit." Max was right behind him. "I got this."

Josie's friends were shocked. Josie stood to go up on stage. Josie could hear her friends cheering her on. Josie hit the center of the stage. Mike's gaze was on her. Josie turned to the crowd. It was like she was looking right at him. Josie swallowed nervously. She thought about her friend's words, 'pretend you're singing to one person.' The music started. Josie started very timidly at first.

Then she imagined he was there, in front of her.

As Josie headed into the chorus she reached up to her necklace and when she did Mike saw the shimmer and he knew, the butterfly. She was wearing it. She still had it. He had almost forgotten about that. He bought it for her, so she would never forget him, so he could set her free, let her spread her beautiful wings and soar. God she was beautiful.

Josie's voice started to hit full stride now. Mike felt her words hitting him, she was singing to him and only him. He felt every word, every verse, it destroyed him. Josie squeezed that necklace in her hand. Mike could feel her squeezing his heart. Josie was singing to him. This was meant for him. Mike was mesmerized by her. He didn't even hear or care about anything else around him.

Max was staring at Josie then at Mike. He didn't know who to watch. She looked amazing up on the stage. She sounded as beautiful as she looked. Rod and Ted were in shock at her voice. It was beautiful. Then Ted had a thought. He thumped Rod, "Mike." They both turned to see how he was handling this. Rod said to Ted, "He's definitely going to cave. He isn't going to let her walk out of here tonight without telling her." Ted nodded in agreement. They turned back to their other halves who were by this time crying and smiling all at the same time. The men both put their arms around their ladies pulling them close.

Max turned his attention to the woman hiding in the corner. She was wiping tears out of her eyes. There was something about that woman, he needed to know who she was. There was such a sadness in her eyes, Max was drawn to her and he didn't even know who she was.

Josie sang the chorus and she just poured her heart into it. She was ready to let it out. She wanted to sing to Michael. If she couldn't well, she could pretend she was. This song always made her think of him. She sang out the chorus, just one last verse.

The crowd erupted into applause, whistles and shouts of encore. Josie stood for a moment. A few tears rolled down her face, she whispered to him, wherever he was, "Goodbye Michael." Josie turned and she left the stage. The DJ was speaking into the microphone "Let's hear it for Josie." The DJ cut to dance music. Josie headed back to her friends. Ted and Rod were on their feet and Sarah and Miranda were jumping up and down to hug her. Ted and Rod reached out to her, "That was incredible." Josie was quite embarrassed over the attention. Josie needed a moment to compose herself, “I’m going to the ladies’ room to freshen up.” Sarah headed behind her, “I’m coming too.”

Sarah was holding on to Josie’s arm asking questions like a firing squad. “Where did you learn to sing like that? Oh my God, was that for your lost love? Have you ever thought about singing professionally?” Josie started laughing, “Take a breath Sarah.” Sarah started laughing too. As they walked into the bathroom Josie went to the mirror to freshen up her face. “That was my goodbye to Michael. He was the greatest love of my life, but it’s time for me to move on. Holding onto him is never going to bring him back to me. It’s not healthy for me to keep holding on. It’s killing me.” Sarah looked at Josie, she shook her head. “You can never give up on true love Josie. Love will always find its way back to you. All you have to do is believe, allow your heart to feel what it feels, never give up hope, hope is all we have sometimes. I agree that you need to let it happen on its' own, but Josie, don't ever give up on your true love."

Josie didn't know how to reply to what Sarah had said to her. She thought she was finally ready to let go of that part of her, but after listening to her friend she felt like she would never really be ready to let go of that part of her life where Mike was. She felt like Sarah was right don't give up on your true love, but considering it's been over ten years she felt like her true love had given up on her. This thought put a sadness in her heart. She truly felt lonely.

Miranda turned her attention to the bar in enough time to see Mike look over at them. Then headed out to the DJ. He came past them on his way back to the bar. "I'm going to need some time with her tonight. I'd like to take her home." Ted nodded to his friend. Ted could see Mike was visibly shaken to his soul. Josie rocked him to his core tonight. Miranda couldn't help herself, "I told you she was going to be hot." Mike turned smiling at her, "She is scorching, more beautiful than anyone I've ever seen in my life." Mike moved back to his place behind the bar. Poured himself a shot of whiskey letting it burn all the way down.

Max was watching him. "Did you know Josie could sing like that?" Mike shook his head no. "I knew she could sing, she used to sing to me when we were alone, but that, I was not prepared for. Josie used to spend summers with her grandmother, she would sing in her church choir but I thought it was just to please her grandmother. She never sang around anyone, I always thought she had an amazing voice, but that up there tonight, God she was killing me. Did you hear her? Did you see her? God she's gorgeous." Max looked at him, "Are you ok Mike?" Mike just stood there poured another shot of whiskey and shook his head, "No, but I'm trying." Mike slugged the shot back as his eyes caught her coming back from the restroom. Max was worried, he'd never seen Mike so tore up. Mike's hands were shaking he looked lost, dazed and scared. Max just slapped his shoulders, "I got this tonight, no worries." Mike smiled a weak smile to his friend as he moved more in the shadows.

Sarah and Josie headed back to the table. When they sat down Josie saw Rod staring at her. She didn't know why, then he grinned and winked at her. Josie smiled at her friend and she relaxed a little. They all chatted for a few minutes when a slow song came on. The couples looked at each other. Josie saw them. "You know it's ok to get up and dance with each other. I'm fine guys, I promise. I'm not going anywhere." They smiled at her, as they stood and headed out to the dance floor. Miranda was spouting off to Rod, "Oh my God that was even more incredible than the day in the hospital. I hope he listened to her. She was breaking my heart up there. Can you believe...." With that Rod leaned in and kissed her. She pulled back looking at him, "Why did you do that?" Rod smiled at her, "Because sometimes Miranda you just talk too damn much." Rod leaned in and kissed her again. Miranda moved back to look in his eyes, "Just wait till I get you home, Rod. I'll show you no mercy." Rod smiled again, "Promises, promises." He bent to take her lips once more, he knew he was in trouble, because when Miranda promised no mercy she delivered. God he loved that woman.

Ted pulled Sarah close to him. He looked toward Josie, "Do they remind you of anyone we know?" Sarah followed her husband's gaze. She laughed, "Yes they do. The stubborn man thinking he was protecting her, when all the while all she needed was the man she loved." He bent his head so that his forehead was touching hers. "You are right as always. Beauty and brains, I'm the luckiest man alive. I just hope they can overcome like we did." He bent his head to kiss his wife. He was a lucky man to have forgiveness and love from the only woman he ever loved. He could have lost it all, but his Sarah was a good woman, she loved him. That was all he needed. Once he knew she still loved him, he didn't give up until she was his again. Ted lost a lot when he walked out on Sarah to protect her, but he was grateful he got his second chance with her, but he'll never get the second chance with his son, that was something that will haunt him till his dying day.

Max looked over. He saw Josie sitting there, then his attention was drawn to the woman in the corner again. Max saw her stand up, she looked at the dance floor, she had tears in her eyes as she turned. Their eyes met briefly, until she dropped her gaze then headed out of the bar. The woman was moving like her life depended on it.

Josie sat there rocking to the music, two men approached her asking her to dance but she turned them down with a polite thank you but not tonight. Josie sat there, she never saw him coming behind her. The music changed and Journey came on with a familiar song, 'When You Love A Woman.' Josie sat straight up in her chair. Tears were in her eyes. It was their song, hers and Michael's

"Josie girl." She looked up. No one called her that, no one but, "Michael?" Josie stood up and came face to face with him. Mike reached out his hand, "I will explain everything, but first they are playing our song. Dance with me. I need to feel you in my arms, it's been too long." Josie's hand was trembling as she reached for his. Mike took her hand guiding her to the dance floor, his arm came around her, his hand took its place on the small of her back like he had done so many years ago. He guided her to an empty space on the dance floor and turned her to him as he pulled her in close.

Josie leaned her head against his chest. She felt her heart hammering so hard. She didn't know if she was going to make it through this dance. Mike's arms were strong around her and his head was resting on hers. Josie could smell him. The familiar scent of him filled her head, woods, pine all man. She was getting lightheaded, dizzy.

Mike felt her heart hammering just as he could feel his own matching her erratic beat. He held on to her as he could feel her trembling. He was afraid she wasn't going to be able to finish the dance. He kissed the top of her head. She brought her face up to look into his eyes. "Easy Josie girl, just let it flow. Just dance with me."

Josie looked at him with tears in her eyes, "Please tell me I'm not dreaming?" She reached her hand up and slowly drug her fingers over his face like she had done so many years ago. "Is it really you?" Mike stopped moving, he leaned down to kiss her mouth. "Does this feel like a dream?" Mike kissed her so softly then he moved back to look at her face. Tears filled in her eyes. One rolled down her cheek. Mike reached up to brush it away.

Mike cupped her cheek with his hand as he stared into her eyes. Those beautiful hazel eyes. They were burning him to his core.

Miranda, Rod, Sarah and Ted were mesmerized by what was unfolding in front of them. It was straight out of a movie. They watched Josie, and how Mike handled her. He knew her and it was like no time had passed between them. They knew each other's movements. They knew each other's bodies. They stopped moving and they kissed. The group of four looked at each other. They held their breaths and watched.

Josie was confused by him being here, "Michael, I don't understand? Where? Why? How? I mean...." He reached his finger up to her lips, "Shh, Josie. I will explain. Just please dance with me first." Josie held her questions for now and just went back to letting him hold her, trying to not think beyond the dance. The music stopped and they stood there for a moment as the dance floor started to empty. Josie looked up at him, “You’re not going to disappear again are you?” Michael went to brush her cheek with the back of his hand and she flinched. It caught him by surprise. “Josie, I’m not going to hurt you. You have to trust me.” It tore his heart out that she flinched with his touch. What did that son of a bitch do to his girl?

Josie stood there looking at Mike. She started to realize that people were leaving the dance floor and she moved away from him. She smiled at him and didn’t know what to say. She dreamed of this moment and all she could say was, “I want you to come meet my friends.” Josie reached out to take his hand. He didn’t move. She looked at him, “Michael?” He shook his head, “Josie we have to talk. I have a lot to tell you.” Josie was puzzled. “Okay

Michael, but I need to get my things and they are with my friends so come with me and meet them. I really think you are going to like…" Mike cut off her words, "Josie I know them. They know me. Shit, this isn't how I wanted to do this. Will you please come with me so we can talk?"

Josie let go of Mike's hand. She looked at him, then at her friends. They lied to her. Josie was the fool again. "How long have you known them?" Mike looked at her, "Josie please?" "NO! How long?" Mike hung his head. "I met them when I moved to town, a few months maybe. This bar, it's mine." Josie let the words sink in. They've known him and they lied to her. They told her his name was Matt. Everyone was laughing at her. Josie turned to walk away from him. "Josie…." She spun around, "No! Don't touch me. You've been here all this time. You let me think you were someone else. You hid from me. Why? How and why did you get my friends to lie to me? Was this a game? Was I a joke to you, to them?" Mike shook his head, "No Josie. It wasn't like that, I wanted to tell you I was here. That first night you walked into my bar I couldn't breathe. I wanted to tell you, but it's not that simple. I have things that I have to explain to you. Please just come with me." Josie turned and looked at her friends watching them. Josie turned back to him, "I need some air." She turned back all but running out of the bar.

Miranda met her at the top of the steps by the dance floor, "Josie." She held her hands up, "You all lied to me, how could you?" Then Josie headed full steam to the front door, not even waiting for an answer. Josie hit the door so hard she thought it would come off the hinges. Josie took a gasp of air into her lungs as she moved toward the side of the building. Josie was leaning up against the building, her head was spinning and she wished she could figure out what had just happened in there.

Mike started heading in the direction Josie went. Rod had moved to Miranda's side, she was hurt by Josie's words and worried she was losing her friend. Miranda grabbed Mike's arm. "Fix this Mike. We are her family and love her. Don't hurt her." Mike looked at her, "I don't want to hurt her. I've loved her, my whole life. I just don't know how to fix what I've done." Mike went to move away to head after Josie but Miranda persisted. "Mike, it's time for the truth. Don't hide things from her and don't lie anymore. All truth, this is your one chance, so make sure you do it right." Mike looked into her eyes, he could see the concern there. Mike nodded at her as he headed after Josie. Josie heard the door slam and heard heavy footsteps coming her way. Josie knew it was him, her Michael.

Chapter 14

Mike headed out the door, he didn't see Josie. Mike's heart was hammering, ready to jump out of his chest. Mike was ready to call out her name when he saw the shadow. Mike headed toward the side of the bar where his apartment was and there she was. She was leaning up against the bar with her head back and eyes closed. "Why Michael? Why have you lied to me? Why have you turned the only friends I've known against me? And why do you turn up tonight of all nights," Josie opened her eyes, looking at him as she continued, "the night I finally think it's time to move on. The night that I finally realized I'm not giving up on my true love, he gave up on me."

Mike moved closer to Josie. His heart was breaking hearing the pain in her voice, hearing her say that he gave up on her. "You got it wrong Josie. I never gave up on you. I never stopped loving you and I never will. Your friends care about you. Don't blame them for my mistakes. They only did what I asked but my time was running out with them too. They didn't want to deceive you but I made them promise not to tell you. It was my place to tell you."

Josie stood up straight she looked at him with such pain in her eyes, Mike hated knowing that he put that pain there. "You're right Michael. It was your place to tell me. I've been waiting for an explanation for over ten years. So tell me Michael, tell me why you broke my heart, ran away from me found me again, hid from me, had my friends lie to me and mostly Michael tell me why I should give a shit or why I shouldn't kick your ass right now for all the hell you put me through! Tell me! How could you hurt me this way? Why did you do this to me? Didn't I mean anything to you?

Didn't you love me the way I loved you? Damn you Michael!" Josie's voice was reaching a level of angry like Mike had never known.

Josie's words stung. She was mad as hell at him. The last time she was mad like this at him they made love in the woods behind the club. Josie turned him on when she was angry. There was something in her voice, her face became red and her lips firm thin lines that begged him to kiss them. Then there was her chest which heaved at the force with which she yelled at him, he couldn't help it, he was completely turned on now. He had missed her body, he had missed her. There wasn't much about her that he hadn't missed. The way she said his name, Michael. Never Mike or anything else, just simply Michael. Mike loved the way Josie looked at him, the eyes searching him, reaching into the depths of his soul.

Josie's lips, how they curved, they were soft warm and begged to be touched by his lips.

Josie saw the glint in his eyes and the desire brimming, she felt hers rising too from the way Mike was watching her. Damn him! How did he do that? Josie started counting in her head. She had to get the flames out. She was mad at him, Mike lied to her. Mike looked so damn good, God why did he look so good? Josie cleared her throat but he still heard the huskiness of it. "I know what you're thinking, but it's not happening. I'm angry Michael. You hurt me and you disappeared from my life so many years ago as quickly as you just appeared. How could you even think that I would want to have sex with you. God you are so unbelievable! What the hell happened to you? I deserve to know the truth."

Mike looked at her, he took a deep breath. "You are right Josie, but damn I've missed you and your lips, your eyes, the way you say my name, the way you look when your angry, God there isn't much about you that doesn't turn me on. I'm sorry but that's the truth. You do deserve the truth. There hasn't been a day I didn't think about you and about those days and nights with you. It's a long story. If you want to kick my ass, I can't say as I blame you. I won't resist." Mike reached out to touch her arm. Josie side stepped away from him. Mike stepped toward her again. "Don't!" Josie looked at him with fear in her eyes. Mike cursed, "Son of a bitch! What did he do to you?"

Josie's head snapped up. "You knew? You left me there to suffer? You, son of a bitch!" Josie lunged at him and caught him with a right that would have made Sugar Ray proud. Mike caught one in the face and he caught the second before it made contact.

"Josie, damn it stop!" Mike yelled, "I didn't know. I only found out a couple of weeks ago. If you just give me a chance. I need to start at the beginning." Josie was furious, "A chance! Chance for what, to steal my heart, run off with it with no goodbye, fuck you or anything and then come strolling back expecting me to take care of your business for you. I mean that might have worked when we were kids, but damn it Michael I'm not a kid anymore. I've got a husband who beat the hell out of me, raped me, made me feel like trash and he's coming for me again. So if you don't mind I really don't have time for your, bullshit! You, big dumb ass!" Mike had a hold of her and she struggled under his grasp, Josie wanted to hit him again. Mike couldn't blame her.

Mike had a hold of her arms, she was furious. Josie stomped her foot on his. Mike loosened his grasp on her arms and she pulled one arm free to punch him in his stomach. Josie caught him off guard, but he recovered quickly. Mike grabbed her arms and turned her so that her back was too him, he pulled her tight up against him. Mike took a deep breath, "Josie please, just give me a chance to tell you what happened. I know I don't deserve any of your time after all I've done to you but," he paused. Josie sneered at his comment, he was sure she rolled her eyes at him. God how he even missed that about her.

"The beginning Josie." Mike explained, "I need to start there. The night I met you at the club. I heard you with that guy and girl, you caught my attention. You were so beautiful, you handled yourself like a lady. You had class. I told myself not to follow you out but my feet just didn't listen, neither did my heart. You were way out of my league, even then I knew it. There was something about you, I just couldn't let you walk away. Then in the parking lot when you spun around and looked at me I was done. It may have been fourteen years ago, but I remember it all like it was yesterday. I've lived that moment in my head for the last ten years."

Josie gave him a snort, "Yeah, I meant so much to you, that's why you walked out on me without an explanation." Mike let go of her, turned his back to her and ran his hand through his hair. "No Josie! I ran out on you because I'm a coward. I was not the man you thought I was. I was nothing but low life scum." Mike turned back around. Josie had turned as well to face him. He saw confusion in her eyes.

Ted rounded the corner at that moment and said, "I don't want to interrupt but we are leaving. I trust that you will be sure she makes it home alright?" Mike turned to him and nodded. Ted looked at Josie, "You're good with that?" Josie looked at him like she wasn't sure what to do. Ted moved over to her. Hugged her then quietly spoke just for just her. "He's a good man Josie. Listen to him. Give him a chance. You'll be safe with him. I promise you." Ted pulled away, she nodded. Ted handed her the things from inside the bar then turned to Mike. Quietly to Mike he said, "Talk to her. Do not hurt her again." Mike nodded at him. Ted left them, Michael looked up into Josie's eyes and she shivered.

Mike moved toward Josie but she stepped away. Mike cursed himself, "I promise Josie I'm not going to do anything to you. I just want to talk. Then I'll drive you home. Or if you'd rather I'll drive you to your place and we can talk there." She looked at him. "I want to go home." He stepped over to his truck he started it up. He came back to her. Put his hand in the small of her back guiding her to the passenger side where he opened the door for her and helped her in. "I will be right back. I need to let Max know I'm leaving." Mike disappeared through a side door of the building.

Mike stormed into the back room heading right to the bar. Max was wiping up the counter. "Hey Max, are you good?" Max looked up surprised to see him. Max nodded, "Are you?" Mike shrugged, "She wants to go home. I'm not sure what that means. She's afraid of me because of that bastard. She punched me twice already, I don't know how this is going to go." Max looked down at the counter then back up at his friend, "Be strong, and remember you're not that guy anymore. You turned your life around. She's not stupid Mike. She'll see it. Just give her time, and a few more punches." Max smiled at his friend. Mike nodded and grinned back. He grabbed a bottle of her favorite rum and headed out the door.

Mike climbed in the truck. Josie saw the bottle and laughed. "Is that for me or you?" Mike looked at Josie and smiled back, "Maybe a little of both." Josie couldn't believe Mike was sitting next to her. God she missed him. But what was going on, where had he been and how did he know about Jack? "Okay, do you need directions to my apartment?" Mike shook his head, "No Josie. I've been in town. I know where you live. I've been there."

Josie turned her attention back to stare out the passenger window. "Son of a bitch! The night I got drunk. You carried me to my car. You drove me to my apartment. You put me to bed. You kissed me. I thought I dreamed it. They told me it was Matt. You're

Matt." Mike eased the truck into reverse while he listened to her putting pieces together. Mike made the fifteen-minute drive to her apartment but if felt like it took a lifetime to get there. Mike didn't know how to respond to what Josie had just said. He didn't think she was looking for him to comment, Josie was trying to sort her own thoughts, as well as the lies he and her friends had told.

Mike and Josie pulled up at her apartment. She reached for the handle to open the door. Mike reached out his hand, placing it on her leg. "Josie please wait. Let me get that." Josie dropped her hand, within seconds Mike was out the driver's door on her side opening the door to help her down out of the truck. Mike walked Josie to the door with his hand securely placed on her back. He took her keys opening the door. He handed her the keys then he turned to walk back to his truck. "Where are you going?" Mike stopped, turning to look at her. "You said you wanted to go home." Josie rolled her eyes at him. "Yes. I was cold and tired of standing outside, dumb ass. I wasn't going to go into your apartment when I'm not familiar with it. I've waited over ten years for answers, how much longer do I have to wait? Grab the rum and get your ass in here. I have a feeling we're going to need a drink, well at least I am." Mike turned back to the truck smiling to himself, "I'm in!" Mike wanted to dance a little jig right there on her sidewalk but he just grabbed the bottle then hurried to her door before she changed her mind.

Josie waited for him, when Mike came through the door he reached to close it and their hands touched. They looked at each other and the sparks were flying. Josie pulled away moving into the room. Mike closed the door then turned the lock. He looked around the room and thought it looked too plain for Josie. She had a few pictures on the wall that were nature pictures, pictures of deer in the woods with a cabin, she had some shelves on the wall with figurines on them. Mike could tell she was afraid to make a start, to make this home. Josie dropped her keys and purse on the table.

Josie told Mike, "Make yourself comfortable. I'm going to get some glasses and change." Mike said, "You're changing?" Josie turned to look at him. "It's just that, you look beautiful Josie." Josie smiled turning into her kitchen, grabbed two glasses and two cans of Diet Cola. Josie filled the glasses with ice then headed back to the living room. She put the drinks down and sat on the other end of the love seat from him.

Mike leaned forward poured some rum into their glasses, opened the Diet Cola and added that. He watched as Josie took her shoes off, rubbed her feet, then tucked her legs up underneath her. Mike handed her a drink, he saw her shiver. Mike got up took the blanket off the chair and covered her legs with it. "You really surprised me tonight Josie. That song, it was beautiful. You sang it so perfectly. You looked absolutely stunning up on that stage. It felt like you were singing right to me." Josie smiled, "I was singing to you. Every time I hear that song all I think about is you. You're all I've thought about since the day you left me." Josie paused for a moment, reached up to touch the necklace. She simply said, "I'm ready to listen."

Mike watched her touch the necklace with her hand, his eyes dipped below her hand, he took a deep swig of his drink to distract himself from the thought of touching her body, "Back in those days Josie I did a lot I'm not proud of and the day I met you I realized just how disgusted I was with my life. I needed to be better. You deserved so much more than I was." Josie looked at him confused. "You knew I worked at Escape as a bouncer. But what you didn't know was that I worked for Chad. Escape was a front for his drug business. I was one of his dealers." Josie was stunned. "That's not possible. I mean you never, I never saw you..." Josie stood up and moved across the room. She turned her back to him. "I never saw you do drugs, how could this be true?"

Mike's heart broke when she walked away from him. "You're right I never touched the stuff. Once I experimented, I didn't like it though, but I still sold it. Josie you have to know I hated myself. The only thing good about me back then was you. I hated what I did and everyone knew when you were there, they were to steer clear. I didn't want that around you. I kept that part of my world as separate from you as I could. I was so consumed by you I needed to spend as much time with you as possible so that cut down the amount I was selling. I wanted out, but Chad wouldn't let me. He said I owed him and I did owe him, but I was done living that life. I wanted better for you, for us."

Josie laughed a half laugh, "Well I guess that explains why Chad hated me." Mike shot up to his feet and walked closer to her. "Chad hated that he was losing money, that I wasn't producing, plus the heat was on. The cops were on to him and were watching us. Josie turned to look at him, "Watching us?" He dropped his head, "They were watching Chad and me. But because you were always with me they assumed that you were part of it. Yes, they were watching you too." On that last sentence he was looking her in the eye. He saw horror, fear and shock in them. “Oh my God, Michael, they thought I was doing drugs? What the hell did you drag me into?” Josie stopped for a moment.

Josie looked away from Mike. “So everywhere we went and everything we did they watched. That’s creepy that we were being watched all the time. How could they do that? I mean ...... Oh my God, Michael!” A horrified look came over her face. Josie turned looked at Mike, and said, “They watched us, I mean they watched us in the woods the night we made love.”

Mike was feeling so dirty. How could he have put her through all of that? “Josie, I don’t know what they saw. It doesn’t matter now. I can’t change things that happened back then. I’m truly sorry for all of it but I turned myself into the police. I told them you were not involved and that you never were. I tried to make things right. I told them your only crime was, loving a guy like me."

Josie looked at Mike. She saw for the first time ever, a defeated look on his face. He was strong. Mike got what he wanted, when he wanted it, he never showed weakness. Who was this in front of her? Never had she seen him look this way. Mike hung his head. He didn't look at her now. He was different. He wasn't her Michael, he was broken. Or was it her that was breaking him?

Mike continued talking to her. "The last night we made love. I knew I had to break away from you but I had no idea how. I was getting my personal things in order. I was trying to tell some of the kids that bought from me to clean up. They didn't need the shit. I wanted them to get out of that life. Chad caught wind of it, he was mad as hell, the night you came looking for me I was at the cabin. I told Chad to lie to you. I waited until you left to be sure Chad didn't hurt you. After you left I knocked his ass out. I hated him. I hated the way he talked to you. He tried to cheapen our love, he tried to hurt you."

Mike started pacing the living room now. Josie went to get her drink and sat back down on the loveseat. Mike continued talking, "I left there, I went to finish up some things at Escape. I found you there. I parked down the street. I walked through the woods and that's when I saw you were there. It broke my heart that I had hurt you but I had no choice. I went to the police station that night. I made a deal telling them everything they wanted to know. I gave them everything Josie. I shut Chad down. But I had to pay too." He turned to look at her. "I served ten years in jail." Josie gasped and covered her mouth with her hand. "That is where I have been."

Mike saw in Josie's eyes how he no longer was the man she thought he was. He saw the horrified look on her face and he knew he'd lost her. "While I was in jail, I made friends with the guard. He wanted to retire and move away from town. He told me about a bar that was really run down in a small town. He wanted to buy it, fix it up, start over, but he didn't have the money so I told him I had the money. He and I became partners. Max retired before my sentence was up, he took my designs for the bar and started to make it come together until I could get out to be there to help. I'm not proud of where the money came from to build it but I'm proud that we're making a go of it. I never stopped thinking about you."

Michael stopped. He turned to look at Josie, "I had people checking in on you. They told me you had married and that was where the communications ended. They were afraid to tell me about him hitting you. I didn't find that out until after you came into the bar." She looked up at him, he saw the surprise in her eyes. He couldn't believe that she thought he would have just forgotten about her. He never would forget her, he couldn't she was burned into his soul.

"How did you find out about Jack and the beatings?" Josie asked. Mike looked at her then continued his story. "When I came to town I figured since I was opening a bar in the town next to this one I should see the local police, tell them who I was that I had served my time. I wanted to be free. I was done with that life. I didn't want the past to come back and bite me in the ass. I stopped at the police station and met with Ted. I told him about my past history at Escape, my serving time and about the Heartbreak bar. I offered him to come in to look around anytime, no warning, no warrants. I had nothing to hide. I did my time, I wanted a fresh start, an honest living. So when you hit town and you guys came in the bar, I asked them not to tell you about me. Ted was suspicious, he asked me to come down to the station. I agreed. I went to the station the next day. At the station Ted questioned me about how I knew you. I think at first he thought I may have been the one hurting you. I guess when I told him our story he knew how I felt about you he called Rod in and they told me about Jack."

"I swear to you Josie. I am done with that life but when they told me I couldn't help myself. I called some old contacts. I really wanted to kill Jack. I made sure they sent me the information that everyone was too afraid to give me back when this was happening. I swear Josie if I'd have known I would have found a way to stop it." Josie just looked at him. She wasn't quite sure what to think about all she had just heard. It was a lot to take in. He moved back over to the love seat and sat back down. He freshened up his drink and hers.

Josie sat there quietly, not quite sure what to say to Mike at first. "Everything back then seemed so simple. I never knew any of what you were doing. I moved out of town after Jack. People looked at me with pity because of Jack but I imagine they all thought I was pretty stupid since I didn't know you were, well doing what you were doing." She took a deep breath and just sat there staring at him. "It seems like my whole life I've lived in my own little fantasy. With you I thought we had everything, but I never knew what you were doing. I never asked either. I guess that was stupid of me. But I loved you, that was all I needed to know. Then I met Jack. I thought I could make it work. I thought he was," Josie paused and looked at Mike, "enough."

Tears formed in her eyes, he wanted to reach out to her but he knew he would scare her off. He sat and waited. "I never loved Jack. I had no room in my heart for him. My heart only belonged to one person. I have heard what you said Michael. I still can't believe how blind I was to what was going on around me, but I loved you. The things you hid from me I wouldn't have condoned but I wouldn't have been able to stop loving you. I don't understand why you wouldn't have been honest with me."

Mike reached out to take Josie's hand in his, but she pulled back. "I love you Josie girl. I never stopped. I met you and my world changed. I wished I wasn't the person I was. I needed to do something to make myself better.

I wanted you to be able to be proud of me, not ashamed. I hated that I hurt you but I didn't know how else to get out. I had to serve my time. I had to close that place down to be rid of that life. But never once did I ever stop loving you. I just didn't deserve you." Tears rolled down her face. She was listening to him and she loved him, but how could she forgive all he did to her? Josie stood up. Mike stood as well.

Josie looked up at Mike's face. She reached out with her hand to run her fingers down his face. "God help me Michael, but you are the only man I ever loved." His heart was about to beat out of his chest, then she spoke again. "But I need time. I need to process this. I need to figure out where to go from here. You lied to me Michael. You walked out on me, you broke my heart. I can't just forget that."

Josie was looking into Mike's eyes and speaking from her heart, "You didn't trust me to tell me the truth. How do I know that you will trust me now? What changed? I'm still the same girl that you didn't trust back then. I'm the same girl, I believe the same things I did then. I just don't know why you had to push me away. What happens now? I mean what happens if something else big happens in your life that you think I shouldn't be around. Do you walk away from me again? Do you stay and stick it out? I mean I just don't know. I feel like I can't trust you to believe in me. I feel like you don't know me at all and," She paused dropping her head to look at the floor, then looked him in the eye, "I feel like I don't know you anymore."

Mike dropped his head looking at the floor, defeat drooping his shoulders. Josie spoke again, "I didn't say it was over, I just said I need some time. I just need to sort out the things in my head. Maybe we need some time to get to know each other again." Mike looked back up at her, "Can I see you while you are thinking about things? I would love to start over getting to know the woman, who is standing in front of me." Josie moved away from him. She shook her head no. Mike felt his heart sink. "I'm asking for a few days, maybe a week or two. But I need time, time without you in it confusing me. I will come to you one way or the other and let you know what I decide. Besides, you know what I've been through. I'm a broken woman Michael. I'm not sure I'll ever be able to be the woman I once was with you."

Mike moved to Josie, "I'll wait as long as it takes. You are all I want in life Josie girl. You are all I've ever wanted. I know who you are Josie, and if we're being honest with each other you know who I am too. I never lied to you about my heart, or who I was. I just kept the ugly side to myself. Now that you are here and we are together, I want to share everything with you. I would not hide anything from you, now or ever again. I heard what you said. I believed in you, I just didn't believe in myself. I didn't believe that after all the things I did that I deserved to have someone like you in my life. I won't make the same mistakes, Josie. I promise you, when you are mine again, I won't let you go. As far as you not being the woman you were, I don't believe that. With time we will have all that we had before. He may have done unspeakable things to you, but deep in your heart, you know me, you will believe in our love again and together we can face your fears." He leaned down before she could protest, he took her in his arms and kissed her. He pulled her tight against him.

Mike's lips were soft at first against Josie's lips, then more urgent and demanding.

He delved his tongue between her lips and he felt her tongue touch his. Her arms moved around him and her hands were burning an imprint into his back. He continued the kiss as he pressed himself, hard and throbbing against her, he could feel his control slipping. He softened the kiss and pulled away. Both of them breathless and panting, “Oh hell yeah, I will wait, and it will all be okay again. I love you Josie, don’t forget that and don’t forget to think about that kiss.” With that, Mike turned to leave, but he stopped, turned back around then he took his hand and tangled it in Josie’s hair. He pulled her head back, as he leaned in for one more kiss. He couldn’t get enough, he needed just one more kiss from her sweet lips. “Damn Josie, I still can’t get enough of you.” Mike turned this time for the door. He left with her standing there trying to calm her beating heart

Chapter 15

Josie lay awake in bed tossing and turning. She couldn't sleep. She got up, she walked around her apartment. She made some hot tea and honey. She sat to think. She couldn't believe she never knew what Mike was doing. She never really questioned him about what he did. She didn't really care back then. Why did she care now? Why should it matter? He turned his life around, right? But he lied to her. No he never lied, he kept it from her. He never lied because she never asked. Right? She sat her tea cup down and paced the living room. This was crazy. But he did hide from her and he ran out on her without an explanation. He should have told her. Then what? Would she have gone to the jail to visit him? Would she have stood by him? This was impossible. How was she going to figure this out?

Josie needed sleep but when she laid down on the love seat, all she could think about was that last kiss. How could she still react to Mike that way? Why couldn't she control herself around him? It's like her body had a mind of its own when it came to him. It was maddening! But that kiss, how he took her, the passion behind those lips, the power of him just taking control of her like that. It wasn't rough but it was, erotic, and she wasn't afraid. Damn him, he could always charm the pants right off of her. But she wasn't a kid anymore, and she needed to remember that. She needed to think with her brain not the hormones that started running through her body since he first said her name. Besides, could she ever be with him sexually after everything Jack did to her. Josie's body shivered at the thought, what if she could never tolerate Mike touching her again. After all Jack did to her, the scars, the pain the torture..

Josie got off the love seat and ran to the bathroom, she threw up at the thought of what Jack did to her, and the knowledge that Mike knew the things Jack did to her. How could Mike want her after what that sick bastard did to her. Jack always told her he was hers, nobody would want the slut she'd become. He told her that she enjoyed it because she was wet and ready for him. Did she want him? Why had her body reacted to Jack? Was it just the way the body was, or was it true, did she like it? No, Josie hated Jack and what he did to her. But would Michael believe her, or would he think she was a bad person? That thought was what kept her stomach churning till there was nothing left but her dry heaves, while she hung her head over the toilet.

Mike drove home thinking about that kiss. Josie still loved him, she had to. That kiss was hotter than he ever remembered. Her lips were so warm, her body so willing to melt to him. She fit him in exactly all the right places. It had been a long time for him. He was lucky he was able to come back from that second kiss. He should have never gone back for more. He was starting to feel the desire ready to explode after his lips first touched hers, then he had to go back and take her mouth again. Damn if he didn't want to scoop her up and take her to bed but he knew she was not ready for that.

Mike needed Josie to remember the love they had. He needed her to trust him again. He needed to make her fall in love with him again. But how? She wanted to be alone. She told him to stay away. He needed a way to simply state his feelings to her. But how? He pulled up at the bar, got out of his truck. He slammed the door shut heading in the back door. He stopped. "I got it!" Max was coming in the back room, "Got what?" Mike just waived him off. Max asked his friend, “How did things go?” Mike rubbed his neck looked at his friend, “Better than I thought, but I have a long way to go.” Max nodded. They talked a little business then Mike told Max to head out he’d finish up. It’s not like he was going to get a lot of sleep anyway.

Josie had fallen asleep at some point and woke up on the love seat. She had a terrible kink in her back. Her stomach was rumbling. She got up made some coffee and tried to get her head around everything. She needed a run. She put her workout gear on and ran to the gym. She did a workout with her weights and then hit the treadmill. She was running with her headphones on. She was pushing her limits. She was staring into space not really paying attention to anyone around her. She was trying not to think. Sweat was pouring off of her and she could feel her legs burning. Her lungs were burning too, they needed air but she pushed further. Finally, she slowed her pace to a jog then slowly to a walk, then stopped. She was wiping her forehead when the young trainer approached her.

"That was some run you had going there. Wow!" She just looked at him. "Thanks." She huffed out still trying to catch her breath. "You have really gotten into great shape. You're doing extremely well. Anything you need help with in the gym?" She looked at him she thought, he's a nice kid but she needed to stop this. "No, thank you. I'm fine really. Hey look, I appreciate all you're doing for me but I really just like to come, work out and go home. I'm not looking for anything else, if I need any help though, I will be sure to ask." He looked at her, started to say something then thought better of it. He nodded walking away. She was glad she finally just told him. She had enough to deal with. She didn't need any more complications.

Josie walked home showered and dressed. She wanted to see Rachel. She drove to the orphanage. She was told where to find Rachel, who was having a tea party. She was sitting at a little table with her back to Josie. She had her two dolls sitting with her. "Is this a private tea party or can I join in?" Rachel spun around jumped out of her chair and launched herself at Josie. She was so excited to see her. "Josie! You're here! I'm having a tea party. Well not really cuz they won't give me any tea. But I'm having a party anyway. Come sit! Let's play!" Josie was laughing at the facial expressions, eye rolls and pouting mouth that Rachel showed her. It was meant to convey the complete exasperation she felt about not having real tea, but Josie found it endearing, funny and well, simply put, Rachel.

Rachel was full of questions. Where had Josie been? What had she been doing? When can she go home with Josie? It was hard to keep up with the questions, but the hardest to answer was when Rachel could go home with her. She never told Rachel that she filled out an adoption application as she was afraid to get her hopes up. So she tried to side step the question.

Josie began, "Well last night I went out with some friends. I got all dressed up ...." Rachel was clapping her hands, "What did you wear? Was it a dress? What color? I bet you were the most beautiful lady there?" Josie was laughing. She told her all about the dress, the necklace and Rachel insisted she wear it the next time. She would just die if she didn't see it. Josie laughed moving on with her story. "We danced and sang. I stood up for the first time to sing in front of people. I ran into an uh, old friend and I went home."

Rachel gasped covering her mouth, "Was it a boy?" Josie was trying not to laugh. Josie nodded. "Tell me, tell me! I want to know more. Is he handsome, does he like you? Do you think he'll like me?" Josie didn't want to tell her a lot but it was hard to limit information as she asked so many questions. Rachel was so excited. Josie told her about Michael, that yes he's very handsome, that they once liked each other very much, in fact she thought they'd get married someday, but they didn't. Josie reached out her hand to smooth Rachel's hair, "Of course he would love you! What's not to love about you? You are my favorite person in the world." Rachel got off her chair to climb on Josie's lap. She laid her head on her shoulder, "Then I will have a mommy and daddy. I hope he really does love me too." Josie squeezed Rachel in her arms she let a tear slide down her cheek. She loved this little girl.

The administrator, Megan Tate watched Josie with Rachel. They had such a bond and connection. Rachel lit up whenever Josie came to visit. Rachel was a beautiful child full of love but whenever adoptive parents came to see her it was like she just closed herself off. It seemed like Rachel was protecting herself from them, especially men. Rachel was terrified of men. She didn't seem to warm up to them easily. But with Josie there were no barriers, just Rachel being herself. She could see the love Josie had for her and she knew that Rachel loved her as well. As an administrator what was she going to do? What could she do?

Josie didn't think she'd ever be able to adopt Rachel. With Jack and now with Mike's history, she was sure if she chose Mike she was going to lose Rachel. She stayed an hour longer and got Rachel to play with the dolls. They sang silly songs but Josie had to go. Her lack of sleep was catching up to her, she needed to head home.

Josie pulled up at her house and Rod was sitting on her front step. "Oh shit!" She got out of her car rushing over to him. "I'm so sorry, we were supposed to work out. Oh damn! I kind of didn't sleep last night, I went for a workout this morning. I'm just coming back from seeing Rachel. I just needed to see her." Rod smiled. "No worries. I was just sitting here enjoying the day." She sat down next to him on the steps. "Do you want to talk about it?" He asked. She nodded yes. She spilled the whole story. Rod knew most of the details but he wanted Josie to talk it out.

Josie sat quietly for a few minutes then she told Rod her fears. "I'm scared Rod." He turned to look at her, "Of what?" She stood up to pace the sidewalk. "Well I'm scared because of Jack. I'm afraid he will find me. I'm afraid of what I feel for Michael. It nearly destroyed me the last time he left me. How do I survive that again? Mostly I'm afraid because of Jack and Michael I will never have what I really want in my life, Rachel." She moved to sit back down next to him. He was silent for a few minutes. Rod got up and walked over to a motorcycle, picking up a helmet. "Wanna go for a ride?" She stood up and nodded. "I've never been on a motorcycle before. Let's do it!"

Rod guided her onto the bike and told Josie to hold on. She put her hands on his hips at first but as soon as he pulled away from the curb she wrapped her arms around his waist and held on with a death grip. "I have to breathe Josie," he laughed and she loosened her grip. "Relax and just go with it." She did, soon she was riding behind him like a pro. They went past the Heartbreak Bar and around some windy roads. They hit a dirt road that seemed like it never ended. In front of them she saw five beautiful cabins come out of the trees. He stopped the bike. She was so mesmerized she got off the bike still wearing the helmet looking around.

"What is this place?" Josie asked. Rod came over to her to get her helmet, she laughed. "Sorry, it's so beautiful here that I didn't even know I still had the helmet on." He went to put their helmets on the bike. "This is where I grew up. My grandparents lived here. They raised me here. I love it, it's my favorite place in the world. It's hard to get out here with Miranda's schedule, but we do get out on occasion." She went up the steps on the porch of one. "I love it! This is incredible. I would want to be here all the time if these were mine.

What's behind the trees back there?" Josie pointed ahead of them where there was a lake. Rod fished there as a kid. She ran off the porch steps and headed that way. He followed her. "Oh wow! This is beautiful. How incredible this is?" She stood on the bed of the lake just looking up and down. He found the large rock on the shore and perched on it. He called the rock his thinking rock. He spent many days and nights perched on that rock wondering where his life was going to go. Josie stood there wrapping her arms around herself. "What am I going to do Rod?"

Rod sat there watching Josie for a moment. "You know Josie, Jack is a problem that we are going to help you deal with. You don't have to worry about him. As far as him causing you to not get Rachel that's hogwash. You will get a divorce from him and that part of your life will be over. No one will fault you for his actions. You were the victim." She looked at him and shrugged, "I don't think I'll ever be rid of him. He's a horrible person. The weird thing is that when I first met him he was very sweet and nice. I don't know whatever happened other than the drinking. But then again, I guess I was naïve. I was with Michael for almost three years and never knew what he did." She laughed at herself. "I must be a really horrible judge of character."

Rod stood up to walk over to her. "Josie, you are a very sensitive and caring person. You cannot take the blame for Jack's actions. When a person has a problem with alcohol he can be very sneaky and hide a lot of things. You can't blame yourself for that." She shook her head. "No I am responsible for my decisions. I married him. I didn't love him and I knew I didn't. I should have walked away but, I didn't. I didn't want to be alone. I wanted

Michael, but…" She trailed off. He shook his head. "Josie you did the best you could, you can't beat yourself up. You need to let it go. You need to forget about what happened in the past and figure out what you want for your future. That's where your focus should be. You can't change the past. Should've, could've and would've doesn't' get you anywhere. It's funny, you sound like Mike. All he does is beat himself up over his past." Josie looked at him. "What do you mean? What is Michael beating himself up over?" Rod looked at her. "He blames himself for your pain and suffering. He wishes he would have told you everything. He wishes he'd never gone down the path he did. He has a lot of regrets. A lot of should've, could've and would've. He did his time Josie and he turned away from that life. He made a place for himself here. He's a good man. Maybe you both need to let the past go and move forward. Start fresh, forget the past. Just move on."

Josie stood there looking at Rod for a moment. Then she turned her back to him. "That sounds good in theory Rod, but it's not that simple. "How do I choose between the man I love and the daughter I found?" She turned to him with tears in her eyes. Rod looked at her. "No one says you have to. If you love Mike, if you want to be with him then be with him, things with Rachel will work out." He shrugged. Josie looked at him. "I'm serious Rod. Do you think they'll ever give me custody of her with a boyfriend who has a criminal record?" He rubbed his neck. "If they were smart they would. Do you know what Mike did?" Josie looked at him. "Yes he was a drug dealer." Rod shook his head. "Sit down Josie, it sounds like you need to know more about the man Mike is."

Josie walked over to sit on the rock Rod had been sitting on. He moved closer to her. “Mike did deal drugs but Josie you have to know what else he did. When he found out that the police were watching him he approached them. He told them he would turn himself in and all the people he worked for. All he wanted was for the police to leave you alone. They told him they wanted you too, he said, ‘no deal’. He told them that you had nothing to do with what was going on. You were dating him. He told them he hid it all from you. He swore to them he would give them all they needed to shut things down but he needed a little time to wrap up some loose ends. Mike went back to the Escape Club, he talked some of those kids into straightening up. He did all he could to turn them away from that life. He was true to his word though. He walked away from you, turned himself in and gave the authorities all the names they needed, all the information needed to shut down the whole operation. The police offered Mike a deal. He refused it. He told them he would serve the time he deserved. No deals."

Josie sat there looking at Rod like he was crazy. "I don't understand. Why would Michael do that?" Rod shook his head, "Because he's a truly honest man. My assumption is that he didn't feel he deserved a break. He wanted to be the man that you deserved. The only way to do that was to serve the time he was sentenced, no deals, no breaks. He was honest and true, holding himself accountable for his life, for his decisions. That's a man with integrity, heart, and courage."

Josie started crying. Rod just stood there. He let her feel what she needed to feel. He walked back to the cabin so she could think. She sat there and cried for what seemed like hours, but she knew it wasn't. What did she do now? Mike didn't tell her any of that. Why would he not tell her that part of things? She really needed to think about things. She knew she loved Mike. That wasn't the issue. The issue was he had lied to her and now she had to think of not just herself but Rachel. She really loved that little girl. She didn't want to lose her. She was really torn. Now what did she do? She got up to head back to Rod. She asked him if he could drop her at the Heartbreak bar. If Mike didn't tell her all of that, what else was he not telling her?

Josie walked into the Heartbreak bar. She went to her usual spot at the bar. Max came from the back room. "Hi Josie. What can I do for you?" She looked at him. "I need some answers." Max shifted uncomfortably but nodded agreement. She asked him first if Mike was hiding in the back, Max said no he was running some errands. Josie took a deep breath then started asking him about Mike's life in jail. Max told Josie that Mike never got into trouble. He kept to himself, he talked about her all the time. Max told her that he felt like he knew her before he met her because of how much Mike talked about her. Josie sat there for a minute. "Why didn't he contact me? Why didn't he tell me? I just don't understand."

Max looked at her. He walked away to get Josie a Diet Cola. He placed it in front of her. "He was ashamed Josie. He spent his whole life just trying to make a go of things. He worked menial jobs for little cash. He couldn't make ends meet. His mom walked out on him when he was young. He started working when he was twelve doing whatever he could. He mowed lawns, shoveled snow. He did all he could to survive. He slept wherever he could and he still went to school because he didn't want to drop out. He wanted to graduate. He stayed out of trouble because he didn't want to get taken away. When he turned 16 he worked some pizza and sandwich shops, then after he graduated he had the misfortune to meet Chad. Mike was tired of working his ass off not being able to have anything. Chad pounced on him. He gave Mike a roof over his head and food. He let Mike live there for months before having him start to sell. At first Mike didn't see the harm in it as he wasn't pushing anyone into it. Buyers were coming to him. He started to get into a rhythm, he had some regular customers then Chad opened the Escape Club. He hated the things Chad was doing. He tried to distance himself but he knew he owed Chad and didn't know how to get out. Then Mike met you. He had a reason to become more."

Josie was shocked. "Michael never told me about his mom. I thought he had a good life. When I first met him he told me his mom called him Michael, that he never thought he deserved that as it sounded important and strong. He never told me that he grew up alone." Max looked at her, "I imagine there are many things Mike never told you. He kept the ugly side of his life private. He never let it cloud what he had with you. It sounds to me like you and Mike have a lot to talk about." Josie nodded, "Indeed we do. But I need some time first. I feel like the man I love doesn't really exist."

Max shook his head, "You got it wrong Josie. The man you love is still there, it's you that made Mike who he is. The good was in him, but you showed him a love with no strings, a love that he never had before. That man is still there. The layers' underneath are the ones that almost broke him." Josie didn't know what to say. She looked at Max. She saw truth and honesty in his eyes. "I just don't understand why Michael hid so much from me. I feel like he didn't trust me." Max shook his head, "He trusted you Josie, he was just ashamed. He held you up on a pedestal. He had it in his head the things you deserved and needed. He felt like he fell short on that." Josie stared at Max, she was so confused. "I don't understand why he felt I deserved to be on a pedestal. I made mistakes in my life." She sat silently for a few minutes, then she looked up at Max. "Thank you Max. I appreciate the talk." Max nodded at her. She got off the bar stool to head home. She needed time to think. The long walk home would give her time to gather her thoughts.

Chapter 16

Mike pulled up in front of the orphanage. He went to the administration office. He sat down with Megan Tate. He told her that he knew Josie. He was hoping to meet the little girl that she visits. Megan was a nice lady, younger than he expected her to be. She had to be his age. He was thirty-seven now. But then again maybe Megan was closer to Josie's age. Mike and Josie were five years apart, Josie was younger. Megan took Mike to meet Rachel.

Mike walked into the room where several kids were playing, Megan led him to a cute little girl with beautiful red hair, who turned to tentatively look up at him. Rachel wasn't sure about the man in front of her, as she never saw him before, but she wasn't afraid of him like she normally was of strange men. She reached out her hand and said, "Hi! I'm

Rachel. What is your name?" Megan watched Rachel with Mike and was surprised how well she was responding to him. This was all new, Rachel never reached out to any man before, she never showed an interest.

Mike bent down to sit on the floor so he could be more on her level. "I'm Mike. I'm a friend of Josie's." The little girl was standing, she started jumping up and down, covered her mouth then she launched herself right at Mike. He caught her and started laughing. Megan moved away and continued to watch from a distance. She had never seen Rachel take to any male. This is part of why she hadn't been adopted. She was afraid of men. But this man she responded to, as she did with Josie. Rachel didn't close herself off to either of them.

Laughing Mike pulled Rachel off his neck to sit her in his lap. She sat down clapping her hands with excitement. "Can we play dolls?" Mike looked at her smiling. "Okay, but I don't know how, I'm a boy you know." Rachel giggled, "I'll show you." She ran off to get her dolls. She handed him a doll and started talking away. He felt really uncomfortable at first then he just followed her lead, soon they were both laughing.

Rachel looked at Mike. "You are silly!" He laughed at that. "I am?" She was looking at him suddenly with a serious look on her face. She stood up to move closer to him. She climbed on his lap again then touched his face. "I knew I would like you." Mike not sure what she was talking about asked, "What do you mean?" Rachel looked at him. "Josie told me about you. You're going to be my new daddy." Mike's heart started hammering out of his chest. Josie said that? Holy crap! Did she make a decision about him already? "Rachel, what did Josie say about me?" Rachel told him what Josie said to her about meeting her old friend. Rachel told Mike that Josie told her he would love her. Mike was a little deflated but Josie was right. He loved this little girl after only a short time. He felt like he was complete with Rachel and with Josie, he would be whole again. He cut his visit short with her and promised he would be back soon. Rachel clapped her hands and hugged him so hard around his neck that he didn't think he could breathe.

Mike left the orphanage. He headed to the police station. He needed to talk to Ted. When he got there the staff told him that Chief Blake was off. After checking with the Chief, the receptionist gave Mike Ted's home address. He went to Ted's house, knocked on the door and Sarah answered. "Hi Sarah, I'm sorry to bother you guys at home but can I talk to Ted for a minute?" Sarah welcomed him in. He followed her to the kitchen where Ted was holding a small child. Mike was guessing she was about two. Ted stood up moved toward Mike offered him a hand. “Hey Mike, what’s going on?” Ted shook Mike’s hand smiling at the little cherub looking up at him. “Who is this?” Mike asked. Ted beamed. “This is my little angel Bella Marie.” She reached out to Mike and said, “Hi!” She smiled, she seemed quite proud of herself. Mike held his hands out to her, she came to him easily. “Well, hello there beautiful! You are such a sweet thing.” Sarah snorted behind him, “For thirty seconds she’s adorable. Just wait till she screams her head off or throws a temper tantrum. She’s a real peach then. She tends to have her daddy’s temper.” Mike laughed and Ted just frowned at her. Sarah took Bella Marie so Mike and Ted could head out on the patio to talk.

Ted said, "So what can I do for you Mike?" Mike looked a little uncomfortable. "Ted I haven't known you that long and already I've asked you to lie for me so, I can understand if you say no, but... Well, you know Josie just adores the little girl at the orphanage. I met her today and I think she is awesome." Mike's face lit up talking about Rachel. Ted didn't miss how happy he looked. Mike continued, "I don't want to be the reason Josie doesn't get Rachel, but I want to be with her. So I was hoping you would be able to go with me to the orphanage and speak on my behalf. I don't know what to expect, but I'm sure if the staff there knows about my record, I'll be out on my ass in no time."

Ted looked away from Mike for a moment, then spoke as he turned to look at him again. "I would gladly do that. I think you would be good with kids. I will do all I can for you. I told you previously, I pulled your records, I believe in you. You let me know when and I'll be there. Honestly though I don't think you'll need my help. I think you are worried about nothing." Mike stood and shook his hand. "Thanks, Ted for everything. Now all I have to do is get Josie to forgive me and maybe we have a shot." Ted followed him to the door. "Don't give up. I didn't and look what I have to show for it." Mike turned to look at him. "I don't understand?" Ted said, "Another time my friend. But know I understand. Just don't give up." Mike left as he thanked Ted again. He headed back to the bar. He was thinking no way in hell was he giving up. In fact, his first shot at winning Josie back should be arriving at her door any minute.

Josie got home after her long walk from the Heartbreak. She headed into her apartment and went for a water bottle. The run from her place to the Heartbreak never bothered her, but the walk sure seemed to have taken forever. She took her shoes off and was just sitting down when the doorbell rang. She opened the door to a man holding a vase of white roses. “Josie Morris?” “Yes that’s me.” She took the flowers and headed into the house. She unwrapped them and pulled the card out. It read, ‘First we must become friends.....again, Michael.’ She held the card to her chest. “Oh Michael.” Tears stung her eyes. She just sat there thinking.

Josie truly loved Mike. Was he really to blame for his actions? What kind of role model did he have? I mean her parents weren’t Ward and June Cleaver but Mike’s mom? How could she just abandon her child like that? Then she thought about Rachel. How could her mother abandon her? What did Miranda say, would you rather the kids be raised by someone who doesn't want or love them? Poor Michael. Was that what happened to him? His mother just walked out with no reason or explanation? Did she not want him? Even though she didn't raise him he still grew up with such a wonderful heart. How did that happen? "His soul is pure, and loving. My Michael." Josie spoke out loud and then just laid her head down to cry for the only man she ever loved.

Mike got back to the bar, things were slow. He headed up to his apartment to put together his next surprise for Josie. He had to win her back. He also wanted to work on a letter for the orphanage. He needed to get some things down on paper so that he didn't botch things when he went to plead his case. He was going to get Ted to go with him early next week so that he could get things rolling. He wanted Josie to have everything. He needed to get her all she'd ever wanted. He owed her that. He was writing his thoughts when he just stopped to think about Josie.

"Someday Michael, you'll marry me and we'll have a dozen kids. We'll live in the mountains, hike every day and make love every night. I'll cook for us. You won't ever want to let me go." Josie and Mike had just finished making love, Josie was all curled up against his side. Her arms and legs were wrapped around him. Mike laid there smiling at what she said knowing that he was leaving soon. God how he was going to miss her. He hoped to hell he had the strength to leave her. "Josie, you'll kill me before we can have those dozen kids. Feel my heart. It's racing out of my chest now." Josie looked up at him and put her hand on her heart. "Mine is racing too. It's because you love me so much. Mine beats like that whenever I think of you." He looked into her eyes. She was killing him. "Josie girl, remember always that I love you. I would give anything to be with you forever." She smiled at him. "It's settled then. You're mine forever!" She raised herself up and kissed him on his lips ever so gently. He grabbed her arms and pulled her on top of him. He wrapped his arms around her and deepened the kiss. Their tongues delved into each other and the desire rose quickly between them. Mike couldn't help himself, whenever he was around her he couldn't stop. He needed her and he had to have her. One last time.....and another and another. He was never going to be able to walk away from her. How could he?

Mike flipped her onto her back, he groaned, "Josie," That was all the encouragement she needed. She grabbed ahold of him, all hard and ready. She guided him to her. Her sweet, soft, silky center was ready and waiting for him. He was going to remember this forever. She was burned into his soul. Her touch on him was enough to make him lose his control. He let her guide him and once there he drove deep inside her. She answered with every fiber of her being and thrust toward him. Beat for beat, stroke for stroke, they were one. Then Josie surprised him flipping the tables. Before he knew it she was on top of him. "Slow down Michael. I don't want this to end." She slowed down the pace and he was growling at her, "Damn you woman! What have you done to me?" She rocked back and forth on him. She took her hand down his chest to where their bodies met. "I've made you my soul mate forever. Love me Michael. Just love me." She bent down to kiss him and he was a broken man.

Mike shook his thoughts, returned from his memory and a tear escaped him. "Damn!" He got up deciding he was going to go down to the bar. The memories tore his heart out. There was a knock at the door. Mike opened the door to Max standing there. "Josie called." Mike's heart skipped a beat. "She said she didn't have your number so she called the bar. She wants you to come over." Mike could have kissed him. "What did she say? When? I gotta shower. Oh man, she wants me to come over!" Max held up his hands. "Slow down Romeo. She made me promise to stress, as friends and to talk." Mike's face dropped a little. "It's a start. Right?" Max looked into his friend's hopeful eyes placing a hand on his shoulder. "You gotta start somewhere. Just listen to her." Mike nodded then Max was gone. Mike took a deep breath. He went to take another cold shower. He was starting to hate them. He was going to let Josie talk and he was going to calm himself. No touching. If he touched her he was afraid, he wouldn't stop. He couldn't help but smile. "I'm going to see my Josie girl. Hot damn!" He got dressed and went down to the bar to hang out with Max until it was time to go see her.

Josie hung up the phone and regretted it. "What are you thinking? You can't even think about Mike without wanting him. This is a mistake." She sat there talking to herself. She invited him to her apartment. What was she going to do once he was there? This was ridiculous. She was going to have him over to talk, to get to the bottom of things. She had questions about things that they needed to talk about, the things she learned from Max and Rod. That's all, no more. She needed to remember that when he got there. "Damn! Why does he have to be so handsome?"

Josie thought back to when she and Mike were together before. She would just stare at him and smile. Mike would say, "What?" Josie would look at him, "Nothing."

Mike would catch her staring at him all the time. Once she was staring and he said, "If you don't stop staring at me I'm going to be forced to do something you may not like." She frowned at him. "What do you mean?" He walked closer to her and wrapped his arms around her. "When you stare at me like that I get all hot. I see your eyes on me, I want your hands and lips all over me. You are going to be in trouble if you keep it up."

Josie giggled at Mike and swatted his shoulder. He bent his head to kiss her. When he pulled back she moved her hands up to his face. "I can't help it. I want to be able to close my eyes when I'm not with you and have your face right there. I want every line, every twitch of your lips, every curl of your hair and your eyes embedded there. I don't want to miss a second of seeing you. I want you with me always, and since you can't always be there I have to remember every inch of you." She slid her hand down his face. "Why do you do that Josie? You always slide your hand from my forehead down to my chin. Why?" She smiled at him. "I'm trying to implant my love in your brain, trying to feel your face and memorize every inch of it. I want to leave a trail of my love across your heart and I do that through the windows of your soul, your eyes. My hand is my heart and when I do that I am giving you my heart." He bent his head to take her lips, which parted instantly for him and he hiked her up.

Josie wrapped her legs around Mike's waist. When she didn't think she could take anymore he pulled away. "I will never forget an inch of you. You're embedded on my soul. I'm in yours too. Don't forget that Josie. I'm always there." Josie slid her legs back down to the ground and told him she wanted to make love to him. "Here? Now? We're at the club, anyone could walk in. You're crazy!"

Josie unbuttoned Mike's pants and pulled the zipper down. She stepped away from him and unbuttoned her blouse. His eyes watched every button release, he was looking torn. She threw her shirt on the floor, then unbuttoned her pants and started to slide them down her hips. She watched him, fire was blazing in his eyes. She took a deep breath, unhooked her bra and when he saw her breasts released from the fabric holding them in place he knew he would lose the battle. She cupped her breasts with her hands lifting them, gently caressing them, he saw her nipples harden and he was done.

Mike went toward Josie as he growled at her. She looked up at him. "Do you want to touch me Michael? Do you want to feel me under your hands? Do you want me to surround you and milk every ounce of you into me? Come to me, make love to me, spill yourself inside of me, fill me with all of you." She was back up with her legs wrapped around his waist and he carried her to one of the tables. He sat her on the edge of the table. He slid his pants down around his ankles as he pushed her gently to lay back on the table. He was ready to explode. Her words, her body, and her touching herself just made him wild. He ripped the fabric of her underwear and slid into her. She remembered the heat that surged through her at the ripping sound her underwear made. But she didn't have to wait long because not a second lapsed before he entered her. He was driving her higher and higher. He was rubbing his hands from her breasts down to her stomach. "My God what you do to me woman!"

Mike reached under Josie and took her ass in his hands, to raise her ever so slightly.

He pulled her toward him driving deeper, harder inside of her. She raised her back up and exploded around him. He pulled her higher, driving into her again and again. Each thrust was harder, fiercer than the last until he growled and spilled himself inside of her. She laid there panting, trying to recover. She raised herself up to him, pulling him in for a kiss. He tried to go soft on the kiss, but she wasn't having it. She wanted it hard. She pressed her lips against his, forcing her tongue inside his mouth and making sure he knew how much he excited her. Mike broke the kiss, "God Josie, I could have hurt you. You bring out something in me that I didn't know existed. Are you okay?" She leaned back and saw such concern in his eyes. She pulled him in to kiss him again and whispered, "I love you Michael, you could never hurt me. I'm so glad we can feel each other now. I love to feel your warmth inside of me." Michael had taken her to the doctor and sat in the waiting room, because after the episode in the woods when he didn't have a condom, they decided they needed more protection. Josie told him she wanted to take responsibility for the birth control. She wanted to be able to feel him inside of her without barriers. Once Josie started taking the pill, their lovemaking moved on to fiercer heights. She loved every minute of it. Mike never scared her. He loved her. He never hurt her. Until he was gone.

Josie came back to the present and decided she needed to keep space between her and Mike. It was her only hope. She would just have to keep those thoughts out of her head, keep from touching him as well. She wasn't ready to forgive him or sleep with him. She needed to find out more. There was a whole lifetime of things he never told her. Whenever she asked him personal things in the past he changed the subject. She never pressed him for answers. Well that all ended tonight. There would be no more hiding from the truth. She wouldn't be put off. She deserved the truth, all of it and he owed her that. She waited what felt like a lifetime for the answers, she wouldn't back down this time. Their love was so powerful, she needed to know that he felt the same. She needed him to trust her completely and then she would know that it was real.

Chapter 17

Mike sat in his truck outside Josie's apartment. He was shaking. What did she want to talk about? How was this going to go? He was nervous. He rubbed his palms up and down his legs. He was pacing earlier in the bar and Max was tired of watching him. He told him to get out. He was driving Max crazy as well as himself. He was not sure what Josie wanted him to tell her. He told her about the dealing and jail. There wasn't a whole lot else to tell. He had to remember to keep his distance. He didn't want to get too close because if he did he didn't know if he could handle it. He didn't want to scare her away. The physical attraction was definitely still there. He was sure she was feeling it too. "Remember the note on the flowers Mike. First we need to become friends.....again." He took a deep breath, climbed out of the truck and walked up to her front door.

Josie was fussing about. She put some pretzels on the table, made two drinks. She thought they would be needed. She lit some candles and was second guessing that when the knock at the door came. "Too late now." She hoped he didn't misread the candles. She went to the front door and opened it.

"Hello Michael." He looked at Josie and didn't know how he was going to get through this without touching her. "You are the most beautiful thing I've ever seen." She dipped her head and stepped aside to motion him in. "Thank you for the flowers and the card. It was so beautiful." He turned to her. "I meant it Josie. I know I'm back too square one and I get that. We need to be friends again. You need to trust me." She nodded and moved past him to go into the living room as she spoke. "That's why I invited you over. I need to get some answers. We need to talk. We need to see what we do next."

Mike didn't know what to think about Josie's words. See what we do next? Was she kidding, he knew what he wanted to do next. He wanted to hold onto her and never let her go again, he wanted to touch that body of hers and make love to her as if his life depended on it, because it did. Without her his life meant nothing. He already spent way too long without her. He didn't intend to spend any more time away from her. She was all he needed for his life to be complete. God he was stupid! He waited way too long to find her. He needed to tell her whatever she needed to hear. He needed her and he never stopped wanting her.

Mike looked around the room, he saw the candles, drinks and pretzels. Josie was trying too. There definitely were sparks flying in that room, he wasn't imagining them. You could feel every ounce of tension, sexual tension between them. She sat down. He went to sit next to her.

Josie cleared her throat, with a trembling hand, that she silently cursed she picked up her drink to take a swallow. She put her glass back down. "I asked you here tonight so we could talk. I think there are a lot of things that we need to talk about. Things that we never discussed when we were together before." Mike nodded to her. She took that as her lead to continue. It was too bad all the things she wanted to talk to him about were running out of her brain while the smell of him and sight of him were replacing any conscious thought she had left. She cleared her throat again plunging forward.

"Why didn't you ever tell me about your mother?" Mike looked away from her. He really wished Josie hadn't asked that. Damn Max for telling her. He's the only one who knew the story of his mother, therefore the only one who could have told Josie.

It was Mike's turn now to take a drink with a shaky hand. He took a rather healthy swallow and moved uncomfortably in the seat next to her. He leaned forward as he placed his elbows on his knees. "I don't really like talking about it. I guess I thought it didn't really matter. My mother was there taking care of me, packing lunches, making dinners then one day she left never coming back. I don't know why or where she went but, well there isn't much to say about it. It happened, I moved on. I took care of myself. Why tell people, I don't want anyone's pity." He just stared straight ahead. He didn't want to look in Josie's eyes.

Josie sat quietly watching him. “It hurt you Michael. Your mom hurt you by walking out. I imagine you still wonder why?” He turned to look at her. “Josie it was so long ago. I did wonder why. I was angry but I had to find a way to survive. That took priority. It didn’t matter anymore why or where she was. All that mattered was a roof over my head and food.” Josie shook her head, “So that’s it? Big tough guy didn’t really care. Isn’t upset that she walked out on him, doesn’t have any resentment, wasn’t hurt. Okay, well it’s been a fun evening, I think you should go.” Josie stood up. Mike just stared at her back.

Mike stood up. “Damn it Josie, what do you want me to say? That I was hurt, I cried every night, I laid in bed begging God to bring my mom back to me. That I was so scared to go too far from our apartment because I didn’t want to miss it when she came back. That every day I curse her for the life I led and the things I did to survive because she didn't have the guts to stick it out and take care of me like a mother should. Some days I still have a hatred for her and I still love her all at the same time. Is that what you want to hear?" Josie spun around on him with tears rolling down her cheeks. "Yes Michael, that's what I want to hear. But not to hurt you, I just want the truth. Not the truth that you think I should hear but the God's honest truth, the good, the bad and the ugly. I need to understand why you felt you couldn't trust me to stand by your side."

Mike stared at Josie. He reached up to touch her cheek. Josie pulled back flinching like she was fearful he was going to hit her. He pulled his hand back and cursed, "What the hell did that jackass do to you?" Josie asked him to sit back down. She moved back to her place on the loveseat too.

“We’ll get to all that Michael, my house my rules.” Josie responded. “I’m not done yet with you and your past. You’ve hid a lot of things from me. You want me to be your friend again? I need to be able to trust you.” He nodded. “I don’t want to hide things from you Josie. That was never my intent. I will tell you whatever you want to know.”

Josie went on, “I want to know all of it Michael. How did you survive, where did you go, did you have anyone to help you? Why did you never tell me the truth? I want to know all of it. These things are the things that happened to make you the man you were when I met you. I want to know how you became the beautiful soul you were and are when you were abandoned by the woman who was put on the earth to protect and love you. I want to know how you remained so beautiful inside, how you didn’t turn hateful and hardened.”

Mike raised his hand and wiped a tear that escaped Josie's eye. "I will tell you whatever you need to know. But Josie you were the one positive in my life, the one thing I had that made me want to be a better man. You were the good inside my soul. The one thing I lived for, the one thing I needed." He dropped his hand back to his lap. He told her how he would go to local restaurants to get food from dumpsters. He had made friends with some of the kitchen staff at a few places. They would bring him stuff out in containers so he didn't have to sift through the garbage. He would sleep in the alley of their apartment but he had to be careful to not be seen since he didn't want someone to take him away. He didn't want to risk missing his mom.

Mike told Josie that when he let himself acknowledge that she wasn't coming back he tried to find a way to make some money. He took jobs here and there. Made some money but not enough to afford a place to stay and food. He had spent a lot of time while in school at the library. He would stay until they closed doing homework and reading books. He always enjoyed the time he spent there. He learned a lot and the librarian was really nice to him. She would help him with his homework when he needed it.

Once Mike got a job permanently after school, he missed the time he spent there. He told Josie that he graduated high school for himself. He wanted to be somebody. "Instead I met Chad, he took me in. I never realized what I was giving up to have a roof over my head. I thought I would just sell for a little while until I could get enough to have my own place and find a better job. I never meant to do it as long as I did. By the time I met you I was just in so deep with Chad that I didn't know how to get out."

Mike stopped and took a drink. "The night I met you Josie, my life changed. You made me feel smart. Like I was somebody, I mattered. That's when I knew I had to get out." He hung his head down. He spoke so softly that she wasn't sure she heard him correctly, "I didn't want to disappoint you." His head went up to look in her eyes, "I didn't want you to leave me too." He stood up and moved across the room with his back to her.

Josie didn't know what to say. She had tears that kept escaping her eyes. She didn't know how to make them stop. She stood up and moved behind Mike. She reached out her hand to place it on his shoulder. The connection sent fire throughout her body. Mike turned at her touch to face her. He didn't dare reach out for her, for fear that he wouldn't be able to stop at one touch. “So you pushed me away before I could hurt you, because your mother didn’t stay there was no way I would either. Right?”

Mike nodded. “I was in so deep Josie. I didn’t know how to tell you. So I figured you’d be better off without me. I would turn myself in, do my time and move on.” Josie looked at him. “Because you thought I belonged on a pedestal instead of beside you.” Mike shook his head yes. “You were beautiful and so smart. You deserved everything.” “No, I deserved the man I loved Michael. But you decided I belonged high on a pedestal you created. You put me there to fall off with no one below to catch me.” Mike just looked at her. “But there is more to your story because you did more than your time. You could have struck a deal for the evidence you turned in but you didn’t. Why?” She understood now how he could feel like she wouldn't have understood. His mother walked out on him so why wouldn't she. She got that, it was untrue but she understood. But she didn't understand why he put her on this pedestal and why he would serve more time than necessary.

Mike walked around Josie. He moved to the table to get his drink. He took another long drink emptying his glass. "I think I'm going to need more to drink." She laughed and took his glass. Her fingers brushed his and she almost dropped the glass. She went into the kitchen to fill his drink and he followed her. "I turned in the whole drug ring. I gave them the names of everyone. They were able to shut the place down. The police wanted to offer me a deal. I would have served half the time, but what did I have to rush home to? I had no place to live, no family and no you. I had money stashed away but it didn't mean anything. I had lied to you. I didn't want to see you looking at me with disgust in your eyes. I knew what I did was wrong. I knew you deserved better, so I told them no deal. They told me I was crazy but I told them, I did what I did and I deserved what I got."

Josie listened to Mike. She turned to hand him his glass. "You weren't very fair to me. How do you know what I would have done? I loved you Michael, I would have done anything to be with you. I would have stood by you. I would have helped you through all of it. It's not fair that you made my decisions for me. You chose my life for me. You should have trusted me. You should have loved me enough to know what my heart would have done." She moved to walk past him. He put his drink on the counter and grabbed her by the shoulders before she could pass him. "I loved you too much Josie to watch you spend your years coming to see me behind bars. I trusted you. I wanted you, I just wanted more for you. What kind of life would that have been for you?" She snorted and pulled away from him, "A hell of a lot better of a life than getting the shit kicked out of me every day. Plus at least I would have known I was loved. You say you loved me too much, well from where I was sitting it sure didn't feel that way."

Mike took a deep breath, "Josie what would you have done? Your family would have disapproved of me and my crime. Where would you have gone? I needed to protect you, I needed to love you enough to let you go. It killed me to walk away, but I did what I thought I had to do. You deserved a chance at a life." Josie moved away from him going back into the living room. Mike turned grabbing his glass, he guzzled that one down and made himself another. He took that one with him back to the living room and sat down on the loveseat. He waited for Josie to be ready to tell him what he knew was going to destroy him.

Josie stood in her living room with her back to Mike. She couldn't face him. She heard what he said, he was right where would she have gone? She wouldn't have been able to stay at home her parents wouldn't have approved but he should have told her. She heard him make another drink, she knew this was hard for him. The man didn't like to talk about himself. She heard him come into the room and sit down. He was going to need that extra drink for the things she had to share with him.

Josie said, "You should have trusted me Michael. I didn't belong on a pedestal. I belonged beside you, not above you. I wasn't perfect Michael. I made mistakes, but I loved you more than life itself. I was looking at apartments for us. I didn't know how we would make it, but I knew all we needed was a roof over our heads and each other." Mike shook his head, "I didn't know Josie. I wanted that life with you. I wanted it more than you'll ever know."

Josie took a deep breath as a tear slid down her cheek. "I waited for you to come and get me. I thought for sure you'd never leave me behind. I wanted to be ready when you came. I had a bag packed. I wore your necklace every day. I told myself if you really loved me you'd come for me. The days, turned to weeks, weeks to months and then I knew you weren't coming back. I was there the day they tore down the club. I cried for all the memories that we shared there. I cried for the love that I lost. I was angry but then I just tried not to care. I vowed I'd never give my heart away again." Mike was sitting and cursing himself for her pain. He didn't think how she would feel. He hoped she would just move on, that she would let go of him and move on. When he heard she got married, he was angry but he knew he had no right to be. He had left her with no choice, but to move on.

"I met Jack one night at a party." Josie explained. "He flirted with me and I just basically blew him off. After the party he came to the diner I was working at. Night after night he came, until I finally acknowledged him. He was a nice guy, so I thought. He took me out to the movies, dinner and to a few baseball games. Things were going okay. I liked him but I didn't love him. We dated for a year. I didn't sleep with him. I think it frustrated him, but I didn't want anyone else to touch me. That part of me still belonged to you." Mike was dying inside from her words. The devotion she had toward him, how could he have turned her away? "But after a year with him I gave up. I didn't want to be alone. He wanted to be with me. I didn't think I was worth anything. I thought, I didn't matter that much. So what did it matter if I loved him or not."

Mike shot to his feet. "Josie how could you think that? You were everything that was good about me, you were, are amazing. You are beautiful, so damn sexy and worth everything I have. How could you think you weren't worth anything?" She turned slowly to him with tears streaming down her face. Josie shot back. "Because I didn't mean enough to you to stick around. Because I loved you with everything I had and you ran away from me. Because all my life I wanted to be touched and loved the way you loved me, but you went away and never came back. I never knew what love was like until you, but after you left me I never felt that way again."

Josie sank down to the floor and Mike was by her side pulling her close to him. He pulled her into his lap on the floor and let her sob against his chest while he stroked her back. Damn him, how could he have done this to her? He was so angry at himself. He did this to her. He drove her into the arms of another man who had no respect for her. He made her feel like she wasn't worth anything better. He destroyed the love they had shared. He tarnished the time they shared together. How could he make all that up to her?

Josie calmed down. Her tears started to subside. She was starting to breath more normally, until she realized she was sitting in Mike's lap. His arms were wrapped around her and he stroked her back. She was starting to feel completely aroused. She wanted his touch all over her. She moved her head. She lifted it to look into his eyes. She saw the desire there.

He was feeling the same desire. She wanted to act on it, she raised her hand to cup his cheek and turned toward him to kiss his lips. He grabbed her arm to stop her. “Josie, I can’t. If I kiss you again I’m afraid I won’t stop. God, I want to kiss you, but I know you are not ready and I am ready to explode. I promised myself I would keep my distance but I just couldn’t leave you crying on the floor, I had to take you in my arms. But now I need, some distance.”

Josie agreed with Mike. She got off his lap. She moved to the safety of the loveseat. He stayed on the floor waiting until he felt he was back in control of his body. He got off the floor, moved back to the loveseat next to her. She took a drink from her glass, then put it down. “Thank you Michael. I’m sorry.” He shook his head at her, “Josie, I’m sorry. I just can’t help it when I’m near you I want you, I don’t know how to turn it off and honestly, I don't want to. I've thought about you every day. I've never stopped. I am so ready to be with you but I understand you need time to process everything. I am going to try to keep myself under control. You have nothing to apologize for." She looked at him. "I'm physically ready for you Michael, believe that. But emotionally, I need more time." He nodded at her. They sat in silence for a moment. He took another drink. "If you want to start again I would like to hear about your marriage." She nodded and continued.

Josie resumed her story. "After a year of dating we got married at City Hall. Things were fine for a little while. After a few years Jack became very obsessive. He had to know where I was, when I was going to be home. He didn't let me out of his sight for long. As years went on, things got progressively worse. He didn't believe me when I told him where I was.

He was angry with me all the time. He drank but never enough to pass out and stumble about, just enough to get angry. Then he started getting physical." Mike wasn't sure if he was ready to hear her tell this. She looked at him. She saw the anger in his eyes. "I don't have to tell you this Michael. It serves no purpose." Mike shook his head. "No I need to hear it and you need to tell me. We have to talk about it or it will always be between us." Josie nodded in agreement at him. She needed another drink though before she continued. She headed to the kitchen to make another drink. The whole time wondering how to tell him what she went through.

Mike knew Josie was stalling. He got up and followed her to the kitchen. She was standing stirring her drink. She didn't hear him come in behind her. "Josie." She jumped and a small startled yelp came out of her. Mike backed up apologizing for startling her. "I'm sorry Michael. I was lost in thought. I didn't hear you. I'm a little on edge lately. I'm coming back." Mike was totally thrown by her reaction he knew she didn't want to tell him about the beating she endured from Jack.

The truth was Mike didn't want to hear it either but he knew that he had to hear it all. Ted told him most of it but there were things he didn't know. The reports he got were sketchy and didn't have all the details that Josie lived so he knew this was going to be tough for both of them. He sat back down on the loveseat and waited until she was ready.

Josie took a deep breath. She went back into the living room where Mike was waiting. Before she sat down and before she lost her nerve, she started talking. "One day I got home from the diner. I had been working and I was late. He didn't believe I had been working late so he punched me in the face." Her hand went instinctively to her face where he had hit her. "After that I had told him I wanted out. I wasn't going to live that way. He was livid. He raped me. I fought him and I fought him hard, but he just kept punching me. At one point I got away from him and he grabbed me by the back of my head throwing me down. Once I was down he just started kicking me. While I was on the floor he started ripping my clothes off and he had sex with me. I was too bruised and broken to fight. That was when I got pregnant the first time. When I missed my period I wasn't sure what to say to him. So I told him I thought I was pregnant, that I should go to the doctor. He refused, instead he bought me a pregnancy test. It was positive. Things were okay for a week or two. I was starting to look forward to having a baby even if it was his. Then he was enraged one night. He told me I was a whore. He wasn't raising someone else's kid. He told me he'd kill me first." She stopped took a drink and went back to standing across the room. She kept her back to Mike as she continued. "He pushed me down the stairs in our apartment. When I hit the bottom I was dazed but still conscious. He saw me trying to get up so he came down the steps and just kept kicking me in the stomach. Then he lifted me up slapping me across the face. He told me I had better think again before sleeping around."

Mike couldn't listen to this. He stood up and started pacing behind her. "Josie, how did you survive that? What made you stay there and take it?" She shrugged her shoulders. "I didn't have a choice. He was always watching me, waiting for me. I was terrified. I didn't know what to do. People at the diner would ask but I lied to them for fear of what he would do if he knew I told anyone. So people stopped asking and I stopped trying to hide it. Eventually I had a broken arm, fractured foot. I went to the hospital. The nurse there tried to help me but I lied to her because it only made it worse for me. I also went to the hospital for my miscarriage. There wasn't much that could be done. The baby didn't have a chance, not with the beatings I sustained. I don't know if it was the push down the stairs, the kicking or the beating that caused it but I certainly lost the baby. After that I couldn't stand the sight of him. I certainly didn't want him touching me. So the next time he tried to have sex with me I pulled out a kitchen knife. He got it away from me and used it on me. He cut my clothes while holding me by my throat to the kitchen floor. Then once he got my clothes off he held the knife to my throat, when the knife wasn't in my throat his hand was. I preferred the knife there actually because when it wasn't against my throat he used it to put nicks and slices on my body." Josie paused for a moment, she needed to reassure herself that she was still safe. Talking about her ordeal made her relive it. Mike saw her shiver.

Josie continued, "The knife stopped being enough for him so then he used a gun. He would hold the gun to my head and laugh. I used to pray it would just go off, end the misery. He would keep the knife too because once I was tied down he could slice me with the knife then torment me with the gun. He would take the gun down my body and he even took it once and put it inside of me. I was terrified. He saw the fear on my face and he smiled. I tried not to let him see the fear but I was terrified. I never knew what he was going to do next. He had a bag with things he would take out and use on me, it was always a nightmare when he dragged me to the bedroom. I tried so hard to stop him from getting me there but I couldn't stop him." Tears rolled down her cheeks, it nearly destroyed Mike hearing the extent of what she endured and seeing the tears roll down her face.

"I was determined to get away from him, so I tried again to leave." Josie sobbed. "He told me I was a rotten wife and lover. He kept a whore on speed dial because I couldn't satisfy a fly. He opened the door told me to get the fuck out, he even held it open for me. I was out the door, but he was right behind me. He grabbed me to give me a hard shove down the cement steps in front of our apartment. I was bloody all over my face and arms. He came out making a big show of helping me up and back in the house as there were people watching outside. Once we were in the house he took me by the head to the bedroom and tied me fast to the bed. He got the kitchen knife and gun then had sex with me again, the whole time cutting and nicking me with the knife. I begged him to let me go or just pull the trigger. He laughed. He'd told me he'd let me go when he damn well felt like it, but until that time I was his, I belonged to him. He said he would do whatever he pleased because I was his wife and I needed to obey him. Josie's face was blank as Mike watched her. Her eyes held a lost expression, it was tearing him apart inside.

Josie carried on with the story. "I didn't want that life anymore, but I didn't know how to get free. After leaving me tied to the bed for two days with no food, water or bathroom. He untied me, told me to clean myself. I took a shower, when I came out of the shower, he grabbed me throwing me down the stairs. I laid at the bottom in the stairwell naked and shivering partially from the cold, partially from fear. He came down the stairs after me. He told me the next time I tried to leave him he'd put me in the ground." Josie could hear Mike pacing, growling and muttering behind her. She stopped to look at him. His face was red with anger. There was pain in his eyes.

Mike looked at her. "Don't stop Josie. I need to hear this." He was enraged beyond belief. He couldn't believe what she endured, what Jack did to her. He was going to kill him for what he did. Josie faced him. She told him about when she found out she was pregnant again. She tried to hide it from Jack. He had found the pregnancy test. He nearly killed her that time. He beat her and threw her face first against their kitchen island, she caught the island in the stomach. He took the rolling pin and hit her in the stomach. When she punched him in defense he had back handed her and she hit her head on something that sliced her open. She had to go to the hospital for stitches. "I lied to everyone at the hospital because I was terrified." Mike was growling when she told him that. She endured several more beatings and sexual encounters in which he did some things that were unspeakable. She finally miscarried her second child. He didn't take her to the hospital for that one. She just hoped she would have a complication and die. "Josie, how did you survive this? The things he did to you, tying you to the bed, throwing you down stairs, using knives and a gun on you, torturing you during sex? How?"

Josie was watching Mike as he paced her living room like a caged animal. She shrugged. "I thought of you." He stopped to stare at her. "When it got so bad that I thought I couldn't stand anymore, I thought of you. I would go to a place in my head where you were coming to rescue me. I just had to hold on. You were going to save me from it all. When I did that the pain didn't matter so much." He was dumbfounded by her words. She was thinking of him during the worst time in her life, making him her savior. Mike went to her. He put his arms out to her. She went to him willingly and let him hold her while she told him about the last beating and how she got to be free.

Josie and Mike stood holding each other for what seemed like hours. He was mad as hell and he was sorry he didn't save her from that madman. "Josie, I'm so sorry I wasn't there to help you. I would give anything to have spared you all of that. You have to believe me. If I had known, I would have been there." Josie nodded pulling away from him. He instantly missed the contact of her body. "I know. It wasn't your fight. It was mine. It still is. Jack's coming for me. He's called me twice already threatening me. I know it's only a matter of time till he finds me. I will never be rid of him. He's my husband. I will never have the chance to adopt my Rachel as long as he is around. I'll never be free." Michael looked her in the eye. "You will be free. I wasn't able to save you once but that won't happen again. I already sent him a clear message that he was too free you." Her head snapped up. She looked at him. "It was you! Jack told me that someone beat him in prison. He said he was never going to sign divorce papers. Michael, what did you do?"

Mike started pacing again. He told Josie how Ted and Rod told him some of what had happened. He was livid because he had her watched for some time but the men who were watching her were to chicken shit to stand up for her or tell him what was happening. "I made some calls and I arranged for him to have a problem." She looked at him like he was the devil. Mike with a defiant look on his face said,

"What? He deserved it!" She was furious with him, he saw it on her face, and just in case he missed how furious she was her next words summed it up. "Michael Peter Albright! Are you insane? Have you lost your mind? What were you thinking? You tell me you're done with that life and then that easily you slip back into it. Asking for help from your contacts and the people you once knew! They're always going to be there aren't they? You are never going to give that life up are you? Of course you're not. What was I thinking? Damn you!" She was mad as hell at him. How could he do this? That life was supposed to be behind him and now she doubted it ever would be.

"Wait a minute!" Mike shouted. "All I did was make a phone call. I didn't do anything. Besides he had it coming. I already had the riot act from Ted. I promised him I was not going to do anything stupid and I promised I was done with it. I just was so angry and helpless. Josie I didn't know what else to do." Mike went to her and put his hands on her arms. "I promise you I am done with that life. I'm not contacting anyone from my past life, nor do I want to." With that his cell phone rang and he answered it. "What!" The voice on the other end was one of the people he told Josie he would not be in contact with. The person simply said, "He's on his way. Be cautious."

Mike hung up the phone and looked at Josie. She looked at him. "What? Who was it?" Mike told her to sit down. She went to the loveseat and sat down. He came next to her and took her hands. "Ok, you are going to be really mad, but I hope you'll understand. That was a 'former associate'." Josie went to pull away and he held her tight. "Listen to me. Hear me out. He was watching Jack for me. I only did it because I was worried about your safety." Fear flashed in Josie's eyes and Michael wished he could make it go away. "He's coming Josie. Jack's coming. I don't know where he is or how soon, but he is coming our way." Josie went to move away, tears were filling her eyes and Mike just grabbed a hold of her and pulled her to him. She sat there in his arms and he could feel her trembling. It nearly broke his heart.

Josie let Mike pull her against him. He leaned into the corner of the love seat pulling her up against him. Her cheek on his chest, her hand resting on him as well. She felt his heart pounding. She breathed with him, in and out. Jack was coming for her, but in this moment all she cared about was that Mike was holding her. She was never going to be free of Jack. He would always come for her. She needed Mike to be safe. Her fate was already set, but Mike's didn't have to be.

Josie excused herself to go to the bathroom and Mike called Ted. He told Ted what he knew, that he was with Josie now and she knew. When Josie came out of the bathroom she asked Mike if he was hungry. He smiled at her. "Starving, what did you have in mind?" Josie laughed and said, "Michael, I am not dinner." He snapped his fingers and said, "Shucks, rain check?" She laughed. He went to her and gave her a gentle soft kiss. She looked at him afterward. "Food. What would you like?" They discussed different meal options and settled on pizza. They were waiting for the pizza to arrive and when the doorbell rang, Mike went to get it. He opened the door to Rod. He invited Rod in and before he could close the door the pizza delivery was there so Mike waited. Rod headed in to see Josie.

"Hey Josie." She turned surprised to see Rod. She went and hugged him, "What are you doing here?" Rod just looked at her puzzled. "Didn't Ted call you?" Josie shook her head no. "Well he thought maybe I should camp out here for a few nights. We are mapping out a plan to keep you covered at all times. I'm going to start out first. Since Miranda is always on call these days I told Ted I would stay here." Josie was ready to protest when Mike was heading in with the pizza box. "The hell you will. I will stay here with Josie." Josie just stood there looking at the two men. "Look guys. I appreciate all the concern, really I do. But this isn't necessary. Rod, you have a life with Miranda. You don't need to spend nights here with me. You need to be with her. And Michael, there is no way you can stay here. I can't, I mean I wouldn't, or rather, Oh hell, just forget it. It's a bad idea." Mike smiled at her. "I understand Josie, but I'm staying." Josie looked at him. “What about the bar? You have a responsibility to the business and to Max.” Mike looked at her. “Are you kidding me? The hell with the bar and I’m not in love with Max so he can take care of himself.” Rod started laughing and Josie looked at him. “You’re not helping.” Rod stifled his next fit of laughter as he watched the two argue.

Mike took the pizza into the kitchen and left Rod to talk with Josie. “You know Josie, it’s not a bad idea for him to stay here. I understand your concern but I’d feel better knowing someone was with you.” Josie looked toward the kitchen, then back at Rod, “Oh really? Cuz I’d feel better if I was the Lion and not the prey.” Rod started laughing and despite Josie’s being serious, she laughed too. Rod told her he wanted to work with her tomorrow night after work so she should come to the station. They could use the gym there.

He just wanted to review some self-defense techniques with her since she forgot their last appointment. Josie nodded agreement and invited Rod to stay for some pizza. Mike came out of the kitchen with two plates. “I can go get another plate. Really you are welcome to stay.” Rod made his excuses and left them to eat their pizza and debate some more about the sleeping arrangements.

Chapter 18

Mike was not happy. Josie told him it was time for him to go and walked to the door holding it open for him. "Josie, you are not being reasonable. You need me here to take care of you." Josie shook her head. "We've been through this. I will be fine. He is not going to even hit this town for days or maybe weeks. I'm not an injured bird. I'll be fine. You and I both know what will happen if you stay here and honestly, as much as I want that, I'm not there yet. I need to get my life in order and I'm not ready to deal with...." Josie moved her hands in dramatic flair in front of Michael, "all of you." She blushed a little saying that to him and he smiled. He took her in his arms and hugged her. "Ok, you win this round. But there is going to be a time that I'm going to be here to protect you." She looked at him, "Who's going to be protecting me from you?"

He laughed, “I promise you Josie. Nothing before you are ready. I know you are still angry with me and still don’t fully trust me. I can deal with that, for now. I also understand you need some time, after all you’ve physically been through. I need you to know that I would never force you into something if you are not ready. I would never do the things that he did to you, I love you Josie girl. I want to make love to you. I promise I won’t hurt you ever again. I’m not going anywhere this time.” He kissed the top of her head and told her he would be calling her.

Josie closed and locked the door behind Mike. She went to the living room. She sat down to finish her drink. She listened to Mike tonight and he was angry with his mother and himself for a lot of things. He needed to forgive himself. How was he to know the right way or the right path to take to adulthood without a parental figure? He told her while they were eating that his dad left when his mom found out she was pregnant. He never knew his father. "He was a coward. How could he not stand behind your mother? When you love someone that's what you do." Josie looked at him. "Like I would have stood behind you?" Mike looked at her for a moment. "Would you have? Or would you have run off?"

Josie thought about that now and wondered what she really would have done. But to Mike she said, "I guess we'll never know will we?" That was the one thing that haunted her now. She wondered what she would have done back then. Obviously she wasn't as mature as now. Now she was angry as hell at him for what he did, but how could she change it. There was nothing that could be done to change it. Did it change the way she felt about him? That was the main question and the answer to that was no. She still loved him. She still wanted him like crazy but yet she was holding back. Why?

Josie got ready for bed and climbed under the covers thinking about the night she and Mike had talking about everything. He was hesitant about opening up to her. He was a very private person but if he couldn't share things with her then what was the point in having a relationship. She was going to have to talk to him about that. She wanted to be sure before giving her heart away completely that they wanted the same things, that they could talk about anything with each other.

Josie laid in bed thinking until she finally drifted off to sleep. She was deep in sleep. She saw the face she hoped to never see again. It was Jack. He was there in her town, in her apartment and he was coming after her. He had his knife. He was cutting her. He was going to kill her this time. She was fighting him and he was laughing at her. It was like before, she tried to fight and couldn't. She just couldn't defeat him. She tried to run from him and he caught her, pulling her back and throwing her down.

Josie woke up sweating, the blankets in a knot and she could barely breathe. "Damn Jack for ruining my life. I'm not a victim. I won't be a victim. I will defeat him." She sat there on the bed too scared to go back to sleep, so she got up and made some coffee. It was five in the morning and she didn't have to go to work until ten. What was she going to do? She started looking around her kitchen. She had everything she needed, so she started cooking and baking.

Josie made two batches of blueberry muffins and wrapped them to keep them as warm as possible. She brewed up a thermos of coffee and now she was whipping up the filling to her stuffed French toast. She was whisking her eggs, getting her pan all hot and ready for her bread. She was humming to herself. She was in a pretty good mood considering the nightmare that woke her up. She got her French toast cooked and went to get dressed. She would take a shower when she got back. She stacked up all her goodies, got in her car and headed out.

Mike couldn't sleep. He had tossed and turned all night. He gave up the fight at four thirty. He got up. Sitting in the dark apartment, he replayed the conversations of the night before in his head. Josie never gave him a straight answer about whether or not she would have stood by him. He was bothered by that. He was ashamed enough about what he did but her not answering that made him feel even more ashamed. She was a decent, loving person. He didn't want her to feel embarrassed by him or by what he did. He loved her so much it hurt, but if she can't forgive him then he was going to have to let her go again. This time he thought it just might kill him.

Mike was thinking about Josie and decided he needed to work out. He didn't have much to do in jail so he did a lot of working out. He made sure he kept his body in good shape. He thought about Josie and worked out as a way to ward off all his demons. He berated himself every day for the way he left her, for lying to her. He had hurt her. He regretted it and had to live with it every day he was locked in that hell. Mike had always tried to keep in shape, when he and Josie were together they ran a lot and when he wasn't with her he lifted weights at the cabin and kept himself muscular. Now he had a weight bench in his apartment and a treadmill. As far as furniture he had a sofa, chair and TV. His kitchen was in the same room but separated by a little breakfast bar with a few stools. It was nothing fancy, just practical.

Mike started his workout with weights. He was thinking about the things Josie told him about her husband and he was getting angry all over again. The weights felt like they were balloons as the anger coursed through him. How could someone do that to anyone let alone Josie? She didn't deserve all she had been through. He wished he could wipe the slate clean and start all over. Had he been there, had he not done the things he did, she would not have endured all that she did. He would have been with her. They would have had a life together. If only he had not done the things he did. "Damn it Mike! It's over you can't change it." He was angry now and talking to himself. He hopped on the treadmill, started to warm up then hit a stride. He was in a full run in minutes. Sweat was pouring off of him and he pushed himself to his limits. He ran hard and fast. Was he trying to run away from his past or was he trying to run to Josie? Either way he was trying to get somewhere.

Mike's mind was racing as fast as his legs would take him. He was breathing hard. Just when he felt he couldn't take anymore he pushed harder. He thought of all his Josie had endured and he kept running. He wanted to run himself numb. He wanted to run until he stopped blaming himself for all the hell she had been through. He didn't know how long he ran, but he finally slowed his pace to a fast walk, then a slow walk and brought his heart rate back down. He missed the days of running with Josie like they did in the past. They would laugh and sometimes just be quiet while they'd run together. It was a way for them to spend time together away from Escape. He liked to keep her away from there as much as possible. He hoped to be able to run with her again and do many other things as well.

Mike stepped off the treadmill. Then he hit the shower. While he was in the shower he couldn't help but think what was next for him. He thought about looking around for some property to build a home, but he didn't want to do any of that without Josie. However, he didn't want to waste time either. Once she fully opened her heart and arms to him again he was going to have her with him, forever. He wanted her as his wife, his best friend, his everything. His thoughts always went back to her. He wanted her input on decisions, but he also just wanted her by his side. He wanted a life with her. He thought earlier he'd have to give her up if she couldn't forgive him, but now he knew he'd never give her up. He had to prove to her that he wasn't the same man as before. He had to make her see him the way she did in the past and accept who he was now. He would succeed because without her, he was nothing.

Mike was just getting out of the shower, still dripping wet when he heard the knocking on his door. He wrapped the towel around his waist heading for the door. He figured it was Max coming to check in on him. He opened the door to a smiling vision. It was Josie.

"Good morning! Oh my, ummmm, did I oh ah, catch you at a bad time? I well, I can come back when you are not um......" "Naked?" Mike supplied the word to help her. He couldn't help but see she was blushing at the site of his bare body. Josie was completely babbling. Mike reached out to help her with her full hands and turned to take everything in the apartment. He turned back and she was still standing in the doorway. "Josie, it's ok.

You can come in." She stumbled through the door, still not taking her eyes off of him.

Josie was caught so off guard when Mike opened the door wearing only a towel. She couldn't talk or breathe. She definitely couldn't stop staring at him. God, he was gorgeous. She remembered that body and the years have been good to him. Mike had ripples, muscles everywhere he should. He was tan with a broad chest that was so inviting and welcoming. His arms were large and layered with muscles. The towel was just teasing her with hints of what lay beneath it. He was so handsome with the water still running down his chest. She couldn't even formulate a full sentence. She wanted to take the towel and dry off that broad beautiful chest. Damn it if he didn't get her all tangled up in her head. She moved into his apartment. She was trying to look around but she couldn't see anything but him.

Mike knew Josie was uncomfortable, and he couldn't help but enjoy it just a little. "So what's all this Josie? It smells wonderful." His words pulled her out of her trans and she told him. "I couldn't sleep so I baked blueberry muffins. I made some coffee and stuffed French toast. I just have to put it all together and we can have breakfast together." Mike smiled at her. "That is wonderful. I'm starving. Let me get two plates."

Josie watched Mike move around wearing just that towel. She never thought she would wish for anything so hard, but she was wishing for that towel to stop teasing her and just fall. "Don't you want to get dressed?" Mike stopped doing what he was doing and smiled at her. "No, not really. I'm kind of enjoying the way you are looking at me."

Josie was embarrassed then angry. “I’m not, I mean.... Oh the hell with it. Fine you wear your towel and laugh at me all you want. I’m ok with that. I mean you, ummm, well you look. Oh screw it.” She flew to Mike and before he could react she was throwing herself against him. She put her arms up around his neck as she pulled him willingly down into a kiss that seemed to tell the whole story. She was hungry for him. She wanted him against her and she did her best to show him how much she wanted him. Her lips were trying to devour all of him, her tongue reached for his and they danced together, meanwhile her hands were running down his bare back and arms.

Mike was shaking, his body was reacting to Josie, he needed her closer. He picked her up and she responded by wrapping her legs around his waist. He spun her, so her back was against his refrigerator. He pressed himself against her and he reached to touch her. She had completely caught him off guard. He was losing himself in her. He was so hungry for her. He was throbbing and pushing himself against her. He needed her so bad, he didn't know what to do. He finally came to his senses and tore his mouth from hers. "Josie, stop, we can't keep this up, I mean you are killing me. I can't keep kissing you this way. I have to stop. I am going to lose control." She was pulling him to her, "Don't stop, Michael, please don't ever stop!"

There was a desperation in Josie's voice. Mike was not sure what to do about it. He wanted her, but not like this. He needed to stop. He had to find out why she changed her mind from last night to this morning. He didn't want to rush her into his bed, especially if she wasn't going to stay there.

Mike carried Josie to the sofa and he laid her back, gently putting himself over her. "Josie, this is killing me. I would like nothing more than to take you to my bed and make love to you. But not like this. You weren't coming here for this. Besides what changed from last night to this morning? You didn't want me to stay with you last night then you come here this morning and want to be with me? I'm not buying it. What's going on?"

Josie was mad at first but she knew Mike was right. The nightmare she had really set her on edge. She feared Jack finding her and killing her before she could feel the love she had in her heart for Mike. She feared never knowing what love was again before he killed her. Then she saw Mike's naked body and just lost it. She wasn't ready to make love to him. She was hurt and scared about her dream. She just didn't want to feel anymore. She didn't want to miss the opportunity of feeling the way she did with him just one last time. She had no doubt in her mind that Jack was coming to kill her. Josie moved under Mike and she could feel his arousal. He was waiting for her to explain.

Josie looked at him. "Michael, I can't do this with you on top of me only wearing a towel. You have to put some clothes on." Mike smiled at her. "In a minute, first I want to know what's going on in that head of yours. Why did you throw yourself at me?"

Josie's eyes filled with tears that threatened to spill out. She reached up and touched Mike's face with her shaking hand. Softly the words spilled out before she could stop them. "I don't want to die before knowing the touch and feel of your love again. I don't want the last memories of physical contact to be what Jack did to me. I don't even know if I can be intimate with you. God how I want to, but Michael, I'm broken. I don't know if I'll ever be whole again. I don't know if I'll ever be able to make love to you. Not after….." Her words stopped and her eyes dropped away from him.

"Josie, look at me." Mike waited for her to return her eyes to him. He leaned in and kissed her softly. She instantly reacted to him. Her body slowly moved under him and together they deepened the kiss. He moved on top of her pressing himself against her. A soft moan escaped her and her hands moved down his bare back. She was caressing him and kissing him while reaching her body up to him. He softened the kiss and pulled back to look in her eyes.

Mike began, "That was beautiful Josie. Your body responded to me and mine to yours. That is love Josie. That is what we have. Never fear that you can't make love to me. Your body is answering every move mine makes. When you don't get tangled in your head, this will happen. With all you've been through Josie that may take time, and I am going to wait. No pressure, I will wait. I would move heaven and earth to change the past, Josie girl, but I can't. So I will be here guiding you, waiting until you are ready to make love again, but don't worry, you will be able to make love again. Be honest with yourself. You feel it too. You know your body and you are a sensual, loving woman. It will happen." He kissed her one last time and got up off of her.

Josie laid there watching Mike walk away. He was right, her body completely had a mind of its own. She wasn't thinking or stressing out she was just letting the moment happen. She wasn't as broken as she thought. She just needed to leave it all alone. When the time was right she would be with Mike again. She got off the sofa. She tried to clear her head. When Mike returned he looked almost as good as he did in the towel. Josie smiled at him. She moved toward him. Mike opened his arms to her. "Furthermore Josie, nothing is going to happen to you. We have the rest of our lives together so don't even think it isn't going to happen. I will not let Jack hurt you again or take you away from me." He bent his head to kiss her. They found the missing part of themselves in each other's arms.

Josie doesn't know who broke the embrace first but she cleared her throat and looked into Mike's eyes. "I do love you Michael. I never stopped. I can't say for sure what I would have done back when we were younger. I do know that I loved you so much that I believe in my heart that I would have stood by you. Our love was pure and powerful.

I wouldn't have wanted to walk away from you no matter what you did." She turned her back to him and started to get his breakfast ready.

Josie had her back to Mike and all he could do was smile. That was what he needed to know. He needed to know what she thought she would have done back then. He made a terrible mistake not telling her and letting her be there for him. He would never push her away again. He went up behind her and circled his arms around her waist. She spun in his arms and his one hand tangled in her hair. He pulled her to him for a soft and warm kiss. Before he took her lips he said, "Tell me again." Josie smiled at him. "I love you Michael." He took her lips ever so gently and held her to him. His lips moved against hers and she responded to him. "Thank you Josie for my breakfast. I would love to wake up to this, every morning." She was ready to pull away and he pulled her tighter. "I mean it Josie. Whatever it takes, this is what I want. Remember that. You told me you love me, so that makes you mine now."

Josie looked in Mike's eyes. She saw it there, the resolution, the determination and the love that he still held for her. It was all there. He wasn't hiding anything now. His eyes revealed his soul. He was showing her everything inside of him. He released her slowly then went to sit. She turned to him. "I'm sorry Michael for, earlier. I guess when I saw you I just couldn't help it. I had a terrible nightmare and couldn't sleep. You were right. I didn't come here for that. I came here to just see you. I came here because I was scared."

Mike looked at Josie. "What was the nightmare about?" She told him about her nightmare. He was really angry about the fear that Jack put in her. "You know that it was just a dream right? It was not real. I promise you I will not let him hurt you again. Believe me, Josie he is not going to hurt you as long as I can help it."

Josie looked at him, "Mostly Michael, I've been afraid well, afraid that I will never get to feel the way I did all those years ago with you again. Jack is going to find me and he is going to kill me. I'm sure he is. What if he does? What if there is nothing anyone can do to help me and he kills me this time? I'm ok with that except for one thing. I want to feel the way I always did with you, one last time, I want to make love with you and I want to feel your body against mine. I'm so afraid that he will rob me of that chance to just be with you. Hell, I'm afraid he already has robbed me of that. I'm scared sometimes when you look at me like you do and I'm terrified of the physical act of making love to you because of all he did to me. I don't even know if I can make love anymore.

I mean I know what you were saying, my body is responding to you but the actual physical part, clothes off, you seeing my scarred body and having you enter me….." She looked at him, his eyes were filled with tears. "I just don't know if I can have that again."

Mike reached his hand out and placed it over hers, "Josie, I will not let that happen. Jack may have hurt you before, but I will not let him hurt you again. I will not let him rob us of the love we have for each other. I will wait as long as it takes until you feel you are ready to make love. I will be so gentle and patient, I promise you. He will have to go through me to get to you. I will never allow him to steal our time from us." He moved over to her. He was tipping her chin up to look at him. "Josie we will make love again, and believe me I want that, here and now but it's not time. We need to be ready for each other. I am not going to just jump into bed with you out of fear. I will not let Jack continue to control you with fear." He leaned down kissing her lips ever so softly. "I am yours Josie girl. I always have been yours. Jack will not be able to hurt you any longer. When you are ready we will try to make love and if it's not working we'll wait and try again. I will do anything for you Josie. As long as I have you in my life, that's all that matters to me."

Mike stepped back clapped his hands together and smiled at Josie. "Can we eat now?" She laughed and finished dishing out the breakfast. She let her heart slowdown from that last kiss. She was grateful to him for his patience and his control. She was not afraid of him. She knew that he would never hurt her or push her into something she wasn't ready for but she still feared Jack finding her and killing her before she had the chance to make love to her one and only again. She at least was honest with Mike and did not hide her fear.

As they were eating, there was a quick knock on the door. It opened and Max walked in. “Hey Mike are you up? Opps, sorry guys I didn’t know you were here Josie.” Josie stood up. “Come on in and join us. There is plenty of food.” Max looked at Mike and he nodded, so Max continued in to sit down with them. “I would never pass up a meal cooked by you Josie.” She giggled and dished him out a plate of food. The three of them sat there finishing breakfast all the while talking and laughing about the bar. They explained to Josie the silly things that happened during the planning and construction. Josie looked at them. “Who came up with the idea for the tables?” Max said, “That was all Mike. The whole inside was designed by him. The one thing he would not waiver on was those tables. He insisted they be exactly as they are. That was tough and very expensive. This guy is extremely picky." Josie smiled remembering their night in the woods and the conversation they had about making a home from everything around them. Mike talked about a table hand crafted out of the trees from the woods. He really did it. He was talented at designing.

Josie looked at Mike and couldn't resist, "So where did all the inspiration come for the bar. I mean it's really rustic. It's like walking into the woods but without all the bugs, dirt and wild animals." She smiled at him. She thought she had him, she thought she would catch him and embarrass him. However, she had forgotten that nothing really embarrassed him. He spoke his mind. He met her gaze. "The inspiration was you. It was the night I chased you in the woods. If you remember we made love right there behind the Escape club, I stripped you down, laid you on the ground and watched the moonlight dance across your breasts. We laid under the stars. We talked about our place and how we would make it from the things there in the woods. I couldn't stop thinking about that night and the things we did, so that became the motivation behind the bar." Mike just stared at Josie and she was lost back in time to that night again. He saw it in her eyes.

Max, the poor thing, cleared his throat. "You guys know I'm still in the room right?" Mike growled and looked at his friend. "The question is, why are you still in the room?" Max smiled and picked up another muffin, "Because Josie cooked and I'm not done eating yet." He smiled, Josie couldn't help herself. She started laughing. Mike even smiled at his friends' words. Josie thought to herself that the bar was beautiful. Every time she walked in there she felt comfortable and safe. Now that she knew Mike designed it from the memories of their night in the woods she couldn't help but love it even more.

Josie packed her things. "I have to get going guys. I'm going to try and get in a short workout before going to work. I'm going to leave the muffins with you. I'm sure you will have no trouble finishing them off." Mike laughed as Max reached for number three or was it number four? He put the muffin down and went to hug Josie. "Thanks so much for the breakfast, and the beautiful company." He went back to his muffin while Mike walked Josie to her car.

"I really appreciate the breakfast. It was delicious." Mike bent to give Josie a kiss on the cheek. She turned to put her things in the car then turned her attention back to him. "I'm glad you enjoyed it. I love to cook, but it is boring cooking for one." Mike smiled at her and told her, "I'm only a phone call away. I would take any excuse to come see you. If I got fed a home cooked meal in the process it would be a bonus." She swatted his shoulder playfully. He opened the driver's side door for her and before she turned to get in she put her arms around him and hugged him. He wrapped his arms around her and kissed the top of her head. She pulled back. She was going to get in her car but stopped. "Michael, can I kiss you again?" He smiled at her. "Oh hell yeah." He bent in, encircled her waist with his arm while his lips found hers. There they stood completely unaware of anything around them. She climbed in her car and waved as she drove off.

"The little slut. So that's what she's been up to. She's going to pay. I am going to make sure of that. She will pay. She's my wife and she is going to start acting like it soon enough, or I'll kill her. I don't know who she thinks she is acting that way. My wife needs to learn some respect." Jack rubbed his stubbly face and moved into the shadows as Josie's lover closed the door to her car.

Chapter 19

Mike went back up the stairs to his apartment where Max was waiting for him. "Wow! That is some lady. She can cook! I'm ready to swoop in and steal her away from you." Mike laughed at his friend. "Just try, I guarantee it would be the last thing you did." Max laughed at his friend. "So if she was here this morning I'm assuming things went well last night? I mean despite the conversation I just heard, which let me tell you was a little too much for me to handle."

Mike laughed at his friend. He turned serious though and told Max all about the previous evening. He explained the truths they told each other. Mike told Max about the hell that Josie suffered at the hands of her husband. "That son of a bitch!" Max was outraged. "I'll kill him!" Mike said to his friend, "You'll have to stand in line behind me for that." Mike was telling Max about her nightmare, how she came to him this morning. “I’ll tell you Max, it’s hard as hell to turn her away when she is throwing herself at me like that, but it just didn’t feel right. I knew something wasn’t right.”

Max reassured his friend it was the right thing to do. “You know Mike, when Josie is really ready it’s going to be worth the wait. I think you two were definitely made for each other. I mean this place was hot while you too were doing your little whatever it was earlier. I was uncomfortable but yet aroused. Dude, the sparks fly when you two are around each other. It will all work out in due time.” Max laughed. Mike rubbed his face with his hands, “Meanwhile my water bill is going to go sky high from all the cold showers.” Max slapped him on the back, “Preachin’ to the choir my friend.”

Max and Mike sat and talked some more. Mike told Max about Rachel at the orphanage. "She is just the most beautiful child. I can see why Josie loves her so much. I asked Ted if he would speak to the administrator on my behalf. I was wondering since I need all the help I can get, would you be willing to do the same?" Max smiled at his friend. "It would be an honor. You are a good hearted person, you would make an incredible dad. I know you still don't believe this Mike but you made mistakes. You had no one to show you the right path to take. You did what you needed to. You paid your debt and made it possible to close down one large group of dealers. Cut yourself some slack. Besides I don't think the orphanage officials will stop you from adopting that little girl." Mike shook his head. "I can't take that chance not until Josie has all she wants and not until I have her and Rachel in my life." Max shook his head in agreement. They headed to the bar to start going through their inventory and doing orders for the upcoming week.

Josie headed home to get her clothing for work. She changed into her gym clothes. She was only home a few minutes when there was a knock at the door. She went to open it and there was a man standing there with a delivery of flowers. She signed, took the flowers and brought them to her living room. She opened up the cellophane to the most beautiful yellow roses. She opened the card and it read, 'Next we need truth and honesty. This will be the foundation for our future, with all my heart, Michael.' She held the card to her heart and smiled. The man never ceased to amaze her.

Josie called Mike. He answered on the second ring. "Hello." She smiled at the sound of his voice. "Thank you. You are truly sweet."

He said, “I mean every word. No more secrets, no more hiding from each other, the truth and nothing but the truth. I don’t want anything to come between us again.” She smiled. “Thank you Michael. That means the world to me. Do you have time later for dinner?” He chuckled. “Only if you’re cooking.” She agreed that she would cook for him, but it would have to be later in the evening as she had to work till six. Plus, she had plans to meet Rod for some self-defense training. Mike agreed he’d meet her at her house by seven and he would help her put the meal together. Josie loved her job but she found herself in a hurry to get her day over with and the day hadn’t even started yet.

Josie went to the gym. She did some weight training then she thought she’d hit the stair climber before the treadmill. She was working hard on the stair climber when Sarah came in. She waved and headed her direction.

Sarah jumped on the machine next to Josie and the two fell into a rhythm together. Josie was telling Sarah about the flowers she received this morning. She told Sarah about the talk she and Mike had last evening. "Wow, you guys covered a lot of ground last night. That had to be tough on you reliving all you had been through." Sarah responded. Josie shook her head in agreement and told Sarah about her nightmare. "Oh my Josie, you know that no one is going to let him hurt you again. Ted and Rod have been making plans and talking every night for weeks. They've been planning a defense if necessary and besides, you are not the same woman you were before. You've come a long way. You are more fit, you have more muscle tone and you are more prepared for him." Josie nodded in agreement, "But I'm terrified. I am prepared for a lot more physically, but how do I stop the fear?" Sarah looked at her friend and told her, "You are never really over the fear. But use it to your advantage. Don't let it cripple you. Turn the tables and use it against him." Josie was silent for a while. She looked at her friend. "I don't think I can take much more of this torture machine. I think we need to switch to the treadmill." Sarah laughed and agreed.

The girls got into their warm up on the treadmill and were hitting a good stride. Josie was remembering one night when Ted told her to ask Sarah about their love story. She asked Sarah who laughed at first, then got a far-away look about her. She told Josie how the two of them met much like she and Mike. They were young and they met through a group of friends. Only Sarah was there to be sure the idiots she thought were her friends didn't hurt themselves with all the drinking they were doing, and Ted was there undercover.

Josie was so engrossed in Sarah's story, she was losing track of time. Sarah told of her son who had been killed in Afghanistan and how because of all of the lies and secrets Ted never really got to know their son. She told her how they eventually worked through their differences and issues. They were both being stubborn and thick headed, and it took Rod and words from letters they received from their son after his death to finally work through things. "I'm not going to lie to you Josie, it was tough. But what was so tough about it was the fear of giving my heart away again. I didn't know if I could trust him again. I didn't know if I could survive if he walked out on me again."

Josie looked at her friend. "How did you find the courage to give your heart again?" Sarah smiled and told her, "You have to find your own courage there. For me, I always knew Ted was the one for me. I didn't doubt that.

We had been through a lot together, thanks to Rod who gave us a big reality check we were able to get through it. I wish I could give you the answer you're looking for but you have to find that inside yourself. For me, I never stopped loving Ted, so I never really gave my heart away again, it always belonged to him." Josie thanked Sarah for her help then looked at the time. "Oh my God, I'm going to be late for work. I gotta run!" Sarah laughed and yelled goodbye to her friend. She continued her workout and thought about her son. Not a day went by without her remembering his beautiful face and smile. A tear rolled down her cheek and she let it fall. Trent will always be a part of her heart. Josie took a fast shower at the gym. It was a good thing she brought all she needed with her to be ready for work. She ran out of the gym and headed for the office. She was glad she brought her car this morning since it looked like rain, because otherwise she really would have been late. She parked her car at the office and went running in. Miranda was laughing at how frazzled her friend was rushing into the office. Josie apologized all the way to her desk. Miranda was waving it off and told her to relax and get a cup of coffee before settling in for the day. Josie followed Miranda to the staff room and asked her how things were going. Josie gave her the same low down she had just given Sarah.

“Oh yeah, they were like a house on fire. Ted and Sarah wanted to be together but yet Sarah kept pulling away. I liked him instantly. Rod on the other hand, I couldn’t stand the man.” Josie almost choked on her coffee. “What? You and Rod? How could you have not liked him? He’s so sweet and charming.” Miranda snorted. “Oh yeah, sweet and charming. Try cocky, arrogant and annoying as hell. But then throw in those tight jeans, gorgeous body and well you know." Miranda's eyes sparkled and Josie laughed. "Well I guess I'm not alone then with the whole Michael thing." Miranda laughed and told Josie to take her time. She would know when things were right. They headed out of the staff room and got down to the day of work.

Miranda and Josie ran over into their lunch break they were so busy. It seemed that half the town had the flu or some ache or pain that couldn't be simply explained in their minds. Josie was grateful for being busy as she didn't have time to think but she was exhausted from her early morning and lack of sleep. By the time the day was done she didn't have much left in her tank to keep going.

Miranda came out from the back and fell into the chair next to Josie. "Man I am exhausted!" Josie nodded her agreement. "I know, but I have to go meet your man for some self-defense training, then I promised Michael I'd cook him dinner." Miranda smiled at her. "Well I'm glad Rod's going to be with you, because that means I have at least an hour to rest before he comes home. Rod said he wanted a date night or something tonight. He said he has something special planned. I love the man and I love my work, but sometimes it would be nice to crawl under the covers and just cuddle." Miranda looked at Josie who was smiling at her. "Don't even think about telling anyone I just said that, I'll kill you." The two started laughing, then packed up their things to head out. Miranda's pager went off, so she sent Josie on her way. Miranda went back into the office with her change of clothes for the evening with Rod. Then Miranda was forced to go back into her office to answer her page. Good thing she packed a bag. It would save time changing at the office for her evening with Rod.

Chapter 20

Josie showed up at the police station and went looking for Rod. She saw Ted and she told him she was there to work with Rod. Ted told her that Rod was in the gym already. Ted asked Josie how she was holding up and they chatted for a few minutes but then Josie told him she had to get going as she was making dinner for Mike tonight. She still had not a clue what to make him. Ted said goodbye to Josie and she headed off to meet up with Rod.

Josie walked into the gym and Rod was there working out. He didn't hear her come in. He was boxing on the heavy bag and she just watched him. Rod was very good. Josie was surprised at the power he had behind him. Rod was very smooth and he seemed very sure of his every move. "Hi Josie." Rod spoke while he continued his workout. Josie was startled as she didn't realize Rod knew she was there. "I'm sorry. I didn't think you knew I was here." Rod laughed stopping his workout. "There isn't much that escapes me. I may look like I'm not paying attention, but believe me I see more than most people. Hazard of the job, I guess."

Rod got down to business with Josie. They were working on some moves but Rod could tell she was distracted. "Okay, let's take five. What's going on Josie? You seem distracted and that's not good." Josie had told Rod about her nightmare. "I'm scared Rod. I feel better than I have in a long time. I know I'm stronger but I'm really scared. How do I get rid of the fear?" Rod took a drink from his water bottle and took his time answering her. "Josie, it's okay to be scared, but you need to know exactly what you are scared of." Rod paused and let that sink in. "The idea here is to prepare you to defend yourself if necessary. It's also to help you feel more confident which in turn will help you feel less scared if and when you need this training. It's not all about strength, Josie. You could be up against someone twice your size. As long as you have your mind about you and some skills you can beat him."

Josie looked at Rod. "Do you really think so?" Rod nodded. "Let's get back to work. I'm going to show you some moves if someone grabs you from behind. Now relax and remember it's just me. I'm going to grab you around the neck and we'll work through how to handle it. Ok?" Josie nodded in agreement. Rod worked with her until she felt comfortable with the moves he showed her.

Josie grabbed her things to head out. "Thanks a lot Rod. I appreciate all the time you've spent with me. It's been really helpful. I feel better knowing I can protect myself." Rod waved off her thanks, "It's not a problem Josie. I'm glad I can help. Remember you are not in this alone, we are all here for you and we won't let anything happen to you." Josie nodded and thanked him again. Josie hugged Rod and headed to her apartment. On the drive home she thought about what Rod had said, 'you need to know exactly what you are afraid of.' She was fearful of so many things at the moment that she didn't even know where to begin.

Mike was sitting, waiting for Josie on her front stoop. He knew he was early but he wanted to be there when she got home so that she didn't have to go into her apartment alone. Mike knew Josie was scared and he wanted to ease her fear as much as he could. Mike was just sitting there thinking about Josie. This morning he was thinking about her and then she appeared. It was strange how often that happened. Mike was so close to losing his mind this morning when Josie threw herself on him. He wanted to be with her in the worst way but he wanted it to be right, not something that was based on Josie's fear. Mike wanted Josie to come to him out of love. He wanted her to be completely his when he took her to his bed again. Mike remembered the first time Josie told him she was ready. She would have been happy if he'd taken her at that moment. Honestly he wanted that too, but he restrained himself and made it as special as he could. He remembered how she felt under him and how she.... She was here. Mike stood up and waited for Josie to get out of her car.

Josie seemed frazzled. She looked exhausted. "Am I late? Were you waiting long? I'm so sorry, I had a crazy day." Mike laughed as Josie hurried past him to open the door he grabbed her arm to slow her down.

"Josie, honey, please slow down. There is no hurry. Relax and breathe. Mike took her keys from her and opened the door. She went in and Mike followed being sure to lock the door behind him. Josie went to the kitchen. She just stood there for a minute. Then when Mike came in behind her she turned. "I am so tired. I didn't sleep well and it was a crazy busy day. I didn't plan anything for dinner. I feel terrible inviting you here for a home cooked meal when I don't have one for you."

Mikel looked at her and Josie was ready to burst into tears. He went to her and took her in his arms. "Josie, I only came here to be with you tonight. You don't have to cook anything. We can order out or skip dinner and just be with each other. It really doesn't matter to me as long as I'm with you." She leaned into him and she was so relieved that she just melted into his embrace. Mike held her to him and he could feel her relaxing against him.

"I have a deal for you. How bout I whip something up and you go relax?" Josie started laughing, she pulled back to look at Mike. "I don't think so. I like my kitchen. I will make us grilled cheese sandwiches, then we can sit and talk. How does that sound?" He smiled and told Josie that grilled cheese sounded wonderful. She made herself busy making the sandwiches and they talked while she made them.

Mike told her about the day at the bar and that they did an inventory. Things were looking good. "I never imagined that it would be so good. I've hired more staff. We are ordering more as our inventory is going faster than ever. We've had to increase our orders with suppliers and the money is really coming in. We are making a great profit and" He stopped talking and Josie turned to look at him. "What's wrong Michael?" He shook his head, "I'm rambling. I'm sorry. I didn't even ask you about your day." Josie laughed. "You were not rambling. I'm so glad that you are doing so well with the bar. It makes me happy to see you so happy. You are doing well for yourself. You should be proud." Josie walked over to Mike and put her hand on his chest looking up into his eyes, "I'm proud of you Michael." Josie went up on her tiptoes and kissed him softly on his lips.

Mike stood there staring at her. He felt like he just won the lottery. He couldn't ask for better words to come from her lips. He wrapped her in his arms. "Everything I do, I do for you Josie. I want you to be proud of the man I am. I want you to never be ashamed of me." Josie pulled back to look in his eyes. "Michael, I have never been ashamed of you. I know this is going to sound silly to you, but I felt like a queen with you. Whenever we went somewhere I was proud to have you next to me. When I was alone somewhere people would say, hey that's Mike's girl. It stirred something inside me when they said that. I felt important, I felt loved and I felt like I was somebody."

Josie moved back to cooking. She kept her back to Mike when she said, "There was one time I was very upset with you. I understand now that I know the truth but you really had me upset." Mike tried to make light of it. "Was it the night I chased you into the woods and we made love under the stars?" Josie turned and the look on her face stopped him from teasing. "I don't remember, but I do remember the words you spoke to me."

Mike remembered what Josie was talking about. It was a night Mike had an incident with some guys who wanted to buy and he wasn't comfortable, so he was backing out of the deal, it turned ugly. Mike held his own against three guys, but they got some shots in. He had a few cuts and bruises. Josie came to the club right after it all had happened. She was so upset when she saw him. "Oh my God Michael, what happened to you?" Mike was angry about the whole incident and angry that now he had to explain it to her.

Mike looked at Josie now and said, "I'm sorry." Josie turned back to her sandwiches. She said to Mike, "You looked at me and said, 'You know better than to ask me about business, don't do it again.' I will never forget that Michael. I was afraid of you that night, and I had never been afraid of you. I was scared of what had happened to you. I don't ever want to feel that way again." Mike stood there hanging his head. He didn't know how to get Josie to trust him again

Josie put the sandwiches on plates. They went to the living room. Mike placed his on the table and turned to her. “I know I wasn’t always perfect when we were together, but I always loved you, that hasn’t changed Josie, I still love you more than anything. I never wanted anything to happen to you. I never wanted you to find out about what I was doing. I said and did things that I regret now and I promise you I won’t do that again.”

Josie shook her head, “Michael I don’t want promises, I need truth, I need complete honesty, and I need to be able to trust you. I don’t yet. I do love you and the attraction is definitely still there, but how can I just pick up where we left off? I mean you lied to me. I trusted you and you lied. You hid your life from me. You ran out on me without an explanation. You hurt me very badly.” Mike shifted uncomfortably, “I thought we were working through all of this. I thought you understood why I didn't tell you and why I had to leave."

Josie stood up. "I'm sorry Michael. I'm very tired tonight. I don't want to fight." Mike stood and looked at her, "Who's fighting? I thought we were talking this out. If you don't talk to me Josie, I don't know what you are feeling. We had a great night last night a beautiful morning this morning. We've shared a lot but it's going to take time for us to catch up on the last eleven years. We need time to work through all of this. All I'm asking for is the chance to be with you and work through it." Josie just looked at him. Josie walked into the kitchen and put her sandwich on the counter. She came back into the living room. Josie was angry all of a sudden and didn't know why. Was she just locking this all away because she was afraid Michael would disappear again? Or was she really angry with him? Josie looked at him and shook her head. “I wanted to see you tonight, but I’m so tired and well quite honestly I’m angry. I’ve made excuses in my head all these years about why you left me. Most of them are that you left me because I wasn’t good enough or I didn’t do something right.” Mike tried to move to Josie and stop her. “No! Don’t stop me. Just listen.” Mike nodded agreement. “I wanted you to come back so badly. I wanted my life back. I loved you so much and you broke my heart when you didn’t come back. I always wanted the chance to know why you left me like you did. I guess I’m getting that chance now but so much has happened. I’m really angry about the way things ended for us, I’m angry about the choices I’ve made, the path my life took instead of the path it should have taken and part of me is angry with you for that. I’m sorry but I can’t do this tonight. I think you need to go.”

Chapter 21

Mike left Josie's apartment, confused, angry and wondering what happened today to make her so angry. Mike didn't know what to do so he went to see Rod. Mike knew Rod was the last person to see Josie before she got to her apartment, maybe Rod could shed some light on what just happened. Mike pulled up in front of Rod's house and knocked on the door. Miranda answered. "Mike! What are you doing here? I thought you and Josie had plans." Mike grunted. "So did I. Josie asked me to leave." Miranda got very angry, yelled at him and slapped him in the arm, "What did you do to her?" Mike backed up, "Ouch, what the hell? I didn't do anything. We were talking. She told me she was proud of me one minute the next she's telling me I need to leave. Can I come in? I really need to talk to Rod. He was the last one to see her tonight before me. I need to know if she said anything."

Miranda stepped back and allowed Mike in. "Personally if I was her I'd be kicking your ass into next Tuesday." Mike turned to look at her, "Could you not talk to her about me, somehow I don't think your advice would be helpful." Miranda smirked at him, "Maybe she needs to give you a good ass kicking, since you've had your head up there so long." Miranda turned walking away from Mike and yelled for Rod. Mike walked into the living room shaking his head, "What the hell is wrong with all the women today?" Rod came walking in. He was hanging up the phone when he saw Mike. "Hey what's going on?" Mike shook his head, "I was hoping you could tell me. Josie just kicked me out of her apartment. Miranda just gave me an ass chewing. What the hell is going on? You were with Josie tonight. Did something happen? She was fine at first but then she was all I don't know, angry. I couldn't even breathe the right way." Mike looked around the room noticing all he rose petals, and candles. "Awe man Rod, am I interrupting something?"

Rod laughed and moved into the living room he motioned Mike to follow him. "Umm, kind of. But Miranda and I will pick this up later. No worries." Nothing happened when Rod was training Josie, but he did see a lot of anger brewing in her. Josie was trying to tamp it down. Rod didn't want to get into all that with Mike since it was between him and Josie. Rod had formed a bond with Josie. She trusted Rod and he wasn't going to betray that trust. But then again, Rod liked Mike and after the road Rod traveled with Miranda he could sympathize. Men just never seemed to be able to win sometimes.

Mike sat down across the room from Rod and waited. "Mike I can't help you. You need to let Josie work this out. She has a lot to figure out and with the psychotic husband looming in the background she's got a lot on her mind. Just give her time and some space." Mike shook his head. He looked defeated to Rod. "I don't know what to do Rod. I thought we were making headway. I thought Josie was starting to love me again. I was hoping she would trust me to help her deal with the whole Jack thing. I can be very persuasive I can help her remove him from her life."

Rod held up his hands, "Wooh, slow down buddy. This is Josie's problem and she needs to handle it her way. You can't just swoop in and take over. You left her once and she had to fend for herself. She made decisions that she most likely is not happy with herself for and she's angry with you. Can you blame her? You did lie to her, you asked us to lie for you too."

Mike stood up and started pacing as he always did when he felt backed into a corner. "Damn it, I know I lied. Am I going to have to spend the rest of my life making up for that?" Miranda rounded the corner on that last line, "If you're lucky you'll have the rest of your life to make up for it." Mike spun to look at her, "Why do you hate me?" Miranda spun, marched right up to him, "Because you hurt my friend, because she's confused, and angry, because of you. And most of all, listen good because I won't say this again. I like you and I think you are good for her, so get your head out of your ass, and be a man." She smacked him again, she walked over to Rod kissed him then headed upstairs.

Mike stood there and pointed in Miranda's direction, "What the hell dude?"

Rod sat there laughing. “Take it. That is the best compliment you’ll ever get from her. She’s right though. You hurt her. Look I’m not supposed to tell you this. If you tell her, I’ll deny it. Josie asked me to go stay at my cabins for a few days. She needed to clear her head. She also asked Miranda for some time off. She wants to leave now. I’m heading over there to pick her up. I’m going to stay there too so I can watch over her. But I’m going to give her the space she needs to think. Why don’t you give it a few days then come up? We’ll pretend this conversation never happened, you just showed up on a whim.”

Mike was confused, “Josie’s running away from me?” Rod shook his head. “No she’s running to you in a sense. She’s just scared and she’s got a lot in her head to sort out. This isn’t just about you, you know. Josie went through hell, physically and mentally.

You can't forget that Mike." Mike looked at Rod. "I know you are right, but I hate that she has to move away from me to think, it's like she doesn't trust me to understand." Rod shook his head, "Again you don't get it. This is about her and what she needs to work out for herself. It's not about you or trusting you." Mike wasn't sure he understood but, he thanked Rod for the talk as he left.

Mike drove home, he thought about Rod's words 'Josie's running to you. She's just scared. What did that mean? Was she scared of him? What did he do to her? And the part about this had nothing to do with her trusting him, it's about her. What did that mean? He had never meant to hurt her this way. How was he ever to make it up to her? Did he deserve to have the opportunity to make it up to her?

Mike pulled up at the bar and Max was taking the trash out. “Hey man, you’re home early. What’s going on?” Mike looked at him. “I need a drink.” They headed into the bar. Mike sat at the bar while Max fixed him a drink. He spilled the whole story to Max. He listened intently. When Mike was done Max stood up from leaning on the bar shaking his head. “She is one hell of a woman. I think she has been burying her feelings about you leaving for so long that she is just finally letting it all out. Think about all she’s been through Mike. She has scars, emotional and physical. She’s got a lot to deal with and with that crazy man on the loose calling her, how do you think she should be acting? Then add the complication of you, well I agree with Rod. You need to let her figure this out. Give her a few days and go to the cabin like he said.” Mike shook his head. “I’m not going to push her. I’ll give her the time she needs. I’m not going to the cabin after her. I don't want to chase her off." Max shrugged. "Suit yourself." Max walked away to leave Mike to his thoughts.

Josie sat for a few minutes after Michael left. The phone rang and she picked it up. "So you think you can just move on? You little slut! I'm going to teach you and your little lover boy a lesson. You are my wife. You will spread those legs for anyone won't you? Maybe I need to remind you of how to respect your husband, or maybe I just need to get rid of Mr. Loverboy."

Josie was still angry, she yelled at him, "Jack, you go to hell! You can't bully me anymore. I won't let you. Your beef is with me and not Mike so come after me, leave him be. You want me, you want to teach me a lesson, fine come and get me you sick, sadistic son-of-a-bitch. I hate you Jack, do you hear me I hate you! I will never go with you anywhere. You'll have to kill me first!"

Jack was laughing in the phone, "That can be arranged my darling. I'm not going to tolerate this behavior. So you need to work this attitude of yours out and you had better do it fast because I will be coming to take you. Your mine! I always get what is mine. I will kill you if necessary, but you will come with me. I will kill all of them if I have to." Josie gasped, "Oh yeah, I know about all of them. I know where you live and every last one of them. Don't think you can hide. Come with me quietly, no one else will get hurt. Do you hear me?" Josie's tears rolled down her face, then he hung up. Josie called Miranda, asked her for some time off. She needed her head clear. Josie needed to figure out what to do now. Jack knew where she was. He knew about Mike and he knew about her friends. What was she going to do? Not to mention that Josie was feeling so confused and so angry, she just didn't know why exactly.

Miranda could tell something was wrong with Josie. She suggested the cabins to her. She put Rod on the phone with her. But before she did, she said, "Rod will go with you. He needs a break from me anyway." Rod got on the phone. "When are we leaving?" Josie was crying while talking to him. She got so lucky to meet such wonderful people. She couldn't let Jack hurt them. She didn't know what she ever did to deserve them but she would thank God every day for them. Rod told her he would pick her up. She packed a few things including the cards from the flowers that Mike had sent her.

Josie was quiet all the way to the cabin. Rod just let her to her thoughts. Once they were at the cabin he put her in the first cabin on the lot. He was right next door in the second one. Rod gave Josie the tour. Told her he would be right next door if she needed anything. There were drinks in the fridge and snacks in the cabinet. Rod had just stocked things up planning to ask everyone to come up for the weekend, but now that would be put on hold. Right now Josie needed some time to figure out what was in her heart and time to come clean on what was bothering her. Miranda was right, something was going on with her.

Rod went to his cabin to call Miranda. "We're all settled in. I hope you are okay. But you were right, something is going on with Josie. She is very skittish and very withdrawn." Miranda smiled on the other end of the phone, just hearing his voice, but she was worried about her friend. "I survived just fine without you for many years. I think I can survive a few days." Rod laughed a sarcastic little laugh,

"Would it kill you to just once tell me that you miss me and can't live without me?" It was her turn to laugh, "Okay, I love you and I can't live without you. Please come home to me, but first find out what's going on with Josie."

The two started laughing. Rod said, "You know how much I love you don't you?" Miranda smiled. "Yeah I can see how much you love me. It's sitting on my left ring finger." He smiled, "That's right. When are we going to tell everyone else that it's official and I proposed to my beautiful woman." She laughed, "Soon. Right now I want to give Josie a chance to feel whole. I don't want her to feel like we're rubbing her nose in our relationship." Rod shook his head, "You are a wonderful woman Miranda." She laughed, "and you are the perfect man. I don't know any man that would propose then run off on his fiancé at her request to look after another man's woman." Rod thought how much he wished he was home making love to this woman, but he knew there was a lifetime ahead of them for that. She was one special lady, sacrificing her evening for someone else in need. They both said they loved one another then hung up.

Josie laid in bed thinking and crying for the man she loved. Because she knew in her heart she loved Mike with her whole soul, but she cried because she felt so broken that she didn't know how to move forward to love him like she did before. How could she let him touch her and make love to her? After hearing Jack's voice tonight and his threats, the fear of everything Jack did to her, came back full force. How could she have a man touch her that way again? She didn't know if she ever would be able to make love again. Yes, her body was responding to Mike the other day, but how could she let him look at her scarred, broken as she was. Mike deserved better than that. He deserved someone who was whole. She was not whole anymore.

Josie was angry with Mike for leaving her. She was angry with herself for choosing Jack and she was a little angry with Mike because had she known the truth maybe she would have never traveled down the path of Jack. She was also worried about the things Jack said to her. She was putting all of her friends and Mike in danger. Josie, so exhausted she fell asleep crying for the life she didn't know if she would ever have again and for the friends that she had to give up in order to keep safe.

Josie woke up at four am. She couldn't fall back asleep. She put on her workout clothes and headed outside. She needed a run. She went running down the path to the lake.

She ran the length of the lake until she started to feel a little uneasy. It was so quiet and deserted but she felt like she wasn't alone. After that call from Jack she knew she wasn't. Jack knew too much. He was watching her. Josie turned around and headed back to the cabins. Rod was out on the porch when she returned.

"Jesus Josie, you scared the hell out of me. When did you get up and where were you? You shouldn't have been out there alone." She stopped at Rod's porch steps. "I know. I needed a good run but I felt like I wasn't alone. Maybe coming up here wasn't a good idea. I don't know where Jack is and I don't want to put you in any danger." Rod shook it off. "I'm fine but please don't go off by yourself again." Josie nodded in agreement. She went into her cabin to take a shower. After her shower she took some coffee and headed over to sit with Rod on his porch.

Rod was silent for a few minutes then said, “Do you want to talk about it?” Josie sat staring out in front of her. She shook her head, “I don’t know how to fix things.” Rod sat back in his chair and waited. He could tell she was desperate to resolve the issues in her mind, but had no idea how to.

Josie stood up. She leaned against the post on the porch. “I’ve been through hell. I put up with a lot from Jack and my body went through a lot. I don’t know how or if I can separate the real love of Michael from the torture I’ve been through. Then there’s the whole, I’m still married factor that will never get resolved because Jack will not allow me to divorce him.” Josie paused for a few minutes, “and Rachel. I’m so broken could I ever be a good mother to her? And, well this is a biggie.

Jack called me last night. Right before I called Miranda. He's here. He's watching me. He knows about Michael, he knows who all of you are and if I go with him he won't hurt anyone. But if I don't, he'll kill all of you."

"Damn it Josie! Why didn't you tell me?" Rod picked up the phone and called Ted. Rod informed Ted about the phone call and where they were. Rod told Ted to step up security on the bar, Miranda and Sarah. He hung up the phone. "Josie, damn it! I can't protect you if I don't know what is going on." She looked at him, "I can't do this to all of you. Just let Jack take me. You all will be safe. He'll kill me this time and I won't have to suffer like I did before. He told me if I don't "respect him" he'll kill me. Just let him. I want you guys to be safe. I brought the danger here. Just let him have me." Josie started crying.

Rod just listened and was there to just listen. Josie didn't ask for Rod's advice, so he was going to keep it to himself. How could Josie think they would just let her go? Rod, Ted, Sarah, Miranda, Max and Mike would move heaven and earth to make her safe. They all wanted Josie here. She needed to be here with people who cared about her. She was so broken and scared that she felt she didn't deserve all of them. Jack was crazy. He'd give Josie that, but Rod, Ted and Mike would be sure that Jack didn't get her away from them. They would fight with their last breath to protect this woman.

Rod watched Josie, while she talked to him. She faced him but she never once looked at him. She stood there looking at the ground, clutching her coffee mug. Rod noticed how stressed Josie was, her body totally not relaxed, rigid. He did see that around Mike she was relaxed so she wasn't giving herself a break. Most of what was wrong with Josie was that she was scared to trust again. Mostly she was scared to trust herself and her decisions. Rod was deep in thought. He didn't notice Josie looking at him as if she expected something from him.

Rod began speaking. "I don't know what you want me to say Josie. This is your issue. You need to work through it so, work. Talk to me. Tell me what else is going on. What are you thinking? Put the whole Jack thing aside. Let's just deal with you, your feelings, your anger." Josie looked back down at the ground again. "I'm worried about how I will react to Michael physically. I mean, I do love him. I can't deny that. But I don't know if I can have that physical relationship again. I'm scared sometimes even when he moves near me. I don't know what I would do when things turn more, uh you know." Rod was watching her. "No I don't know. Tell me." Josie shot her head up to look at him. Was he teasing her? No by the look on Rod's face he was being serious. "What do you mean? You know what I'm talking about?" "No Josie I don't. Say it." Josie looked back down. Josie couldn't even say it out loud. She moved away from the porch and walked down the steps to her cabin. She turned at the door and looked Rod's direction. She just ignored him and the conversation they were having to practically run through the door of the cabin.

Chapter 22

Rod was concerned he hadn't seen Josie the rest of the day. He was hoping that she was working through her head. He called Ted to check in and found that there was no news on Jack. He was talking to people in town. No one had seen anyone suspicious or lurking about. But Ted and Rod knew Jack was in town. Ted assured Rod that he had things under control. "How is Josie holding up?" Rod shook his head to himself. "Not good Ted. She wants to give in to this lunatic to keep all of us safe. Josie doesn't want him to hurt any of us." Ted was furious, "You told her that we wouldn't let her go didn't you?" Rod told him that he was trying to get to the root of her issues with Mike first as he felt that if she could work past all of that then she would be more confident in herself and feel differently about things with Jack.

Rod hung up with Ted and called Mike. "What's wrong? Is Josie ok?" Rod laughed. "You really need to relax. I just called to let you know she's trying." Mike was quite for a minute, "What do you mean she's trying?" Rod shook his head and spoke into the phone, "Think about it. She's been through a lot Mike. She is afraid. She is trying to get her head around everything, how to feel and how to let go." Rod held back the information of the phone call from Jack for now. Rod felt that Josie needed a chance to work through things. If Mike knew about the phone call he'd be here in a heartbeat. Mike wasn't sure he liked the sound of what Rod was saying but he thanked him for the update. Rod was going to make a sandwich and sit back out on the porch.

Josie stayed in the cabin. She just walked around looking at everything. She was very confused. She knew she didn't need to fear Mike. He would never intentionally hurt her. After all Mike left her to protect her, but it still hurt. Physically it scared Josie how her body reacted to him. It was no different than before but now Josie found herself afraid of the things that were happening inside her. She was afraid at times when he touched her. Josie was afraid she'd never be able to make love to him again. She didn't want to hold him back. He deserved to have better. But yet, she deserved better too. Why should she be alone? If she stayed alone then didn't Jack just win again? But how did she forget all the ugly things that Jack did to her? She couldn't forget the things Jack did to her. She still bore the scars that he gave her. Then there were the threats that Jack made. How could Josie stay and risk something happening to her friends and Mike. She laid down on the bed and covered up. She needed to rest. Her brain was tired.

Josie tossed and turned. She drifted off into a restless sleep. She could feel Jack breathing on her. She heard him laughing at her. He was coming at her. "Did you really think you could escape me? I'm coming to take you home. You belong to me. Don't you ever forget that." Josie tossed and turned. "No I'm not your victim anymore. I'm not going with you. I'll never go with you. Michael, help me." Josie heard Jack laughing again, "He'll never keep you. You are tainted. You are mine. I've taken care of you ever having anyone else. You bear my markings, for everyone to see. They'll see those marks and know that you were touched by someone else, that I had you. You belong to me. You'll never be able to keep a man. You are nothing. You hear me nothing. You're nothing but a little tramp, you liked the things I did to you. No one will want the sick and twisted little whore you are now." Josie sat up screaming, "Noooooooooo!"

Rod heard Josie's screams. He went running. Rod flew through the front door of the cabin. "Josie! Where are you?" Rod scanned the room. He headed toward the bedroom, his gun drawn ready for battle. He went through the door and saw her sitting on the bed crying. She was alone. He stood in the doorway. He didn't know what to do. He waited. Josie was silent but tears were rolling down her face. "Josie, you are safe. It's ok." She looked up at Rod, "Is it ok? I don't know. I'm scared." Rod leaned on the door frame. "Of what? Talk it out. Tell me." Josie stood to look out the window of the cabin. "I'm scared of so many things, but most of all what if I can't love him? What if I can't be with him anymore, I will lose him again. How can he look at me with the scars on my body?" She turned to look at Rod. "I can't survive losing him twice."

Rod waited to see if Josie had more to say. When she didn't say anything more he simply said, "Is that all there is between you, sex? The way I heard it you love Mike, and he definitely is still in love with you. So in my mind there is more to you two than just the physical relationship. If I were you I'd stop worrying about losing him before you even give him the chance to stay. Everything will fall into its place, you just need time. You both need time, together."

Josie listened to Rod. He was right. She was trying to push too much too fast. "I hear what you're saying but how do I stop the feelings that seem to overtake me when I'm with Michael? How do I face him seeing me the way I am now that Jack did the things he did to me? I'm scared. It's so powerful, the love I feel for Michael but yet I get to a certain point then I feel the fear. I feel like I can't breathe. How do

I fix that? How do I risk my heart again, when he knows what Jack did to me? Will he think I didn't fight hard enough? Will he think I wanted those things to happen?"

Rod shook his head, "You can't fix anything and you can't get answers to those questions hiding in the cabin talking to me, running from Mike. You are doing what he did to you, running away. Maybe you should try running to him. Talk to him. He's a stand-up guy. Josie you need to have faith in yourself. You need to dig down, find your confidence. You need to find the strength in you. Don't let Jack make you feel like less of a woman. You are beautiful, strong, and would be the most wonderful mother because you are strong because of the things you've been through. You know that saying 'what doesn't kill you makes you stronger?' Well you lived it. You are stronger than you are giving yourself credit for." Rod turned and walked out of the cabin. She just stood there watching the space where Rod stood. She wasn't sure what to think.

Mike called in his favors with Ted and Max. He missed Josie. He thought since she was away he'd go see Rachel. What better time to have his friends meet with the orphanage? Max rode with him. Ted said he would meet them there. Once they were inside Megan's office Mike was filling out the paperwork. He turned it over to her, "I'm going to see Rachel. I'll leave you two to talk and Ted should be here shortly." Mike went out of the office feeling defeated. He didn't know what would happen next but he needed to see that beautiful little girl, his girl. Mike walked into the play room, well at least that's what he called it. He saw her sitting on the floor alone playing with her dolls.

Rachel looked up and saw Mike. Her smile was so big. She clapped her hands excitedly, “Mike!!!!! We play dolls, come here.” He laughed and headed toward her. Once he was standing next to her she patted the floor. He obliged dropping to the floor with her. He took the doll she handed him, but she crawled into his lap instead of playing. Rachel smiled up into his face, “I missed you! She leaned her head against his chest. He wrapped his arms around her. “I’ve missed you too. I’m here now though. What do you want to do?” Rachel stayed sitting with him for a few minutes. “Would you read to me?” Mike was surprised because usually she just wanted to play dolls. Mike noticed a sadness about her today, and it upset him. He was hoping that soon the sadness could be turned to joy. He hoped more than anything that they would be able to become a family. He helped Rachel up and she went to pick out a book. She came back handing him the book before climbing back into his lap she threw her little arms around his neck and whispered, "I love you. I hope you can be my daddy." Mike sat there and pulled Rachel to him. He didn't want to encourage her but he told her he loved her too, with tears in his eyes. He never saw Ted standing, watching them.

Ted turned headed to the administrative offices. He was ready to fight for this child and these people. They deserved to be a family. Ted wouldn't rest until that happened. He walked into Megan's office and sat down next to Max. He listened to Max and all he had to tell about Mike, the time he served and how it wasn't necessary. Mike shut down a large drug ring and did it without regard to himself. He came forward to shut it down. He served a full sentence for principle. There was no other reason for it. Mike didn't need to serve as long as he did but he wanted no special treatment. Ted waited until Max was done, then he told his story. Ted told her that Mike has a thriving business. He's become an upstanding citizen in this town and the neighboring town, not to mention the money that he donated to the orphanage. He deserved a break, he told Megan, "From what I just saw out there, that little girl deserves a break too. She already loves Josie and Mike. I'll tell you another thing, I won't rest until that little girl comes home to Josie and Mike." Max seconded what Ted was saying. Megan said she would take it all into consideration, but she couldn't make promises. She had to think about the best interest of the child, plus the state had the final say.

Ted and Max left the office. Ted said to Max, "Did you see them together?" Max shook his head no. Ted took him to where he left them. They watched Mike reading to Rachel and couldn't believe the softness that he showed. The joy and delight that Rachel had on her face while Mike read to her. Rachel had her hands on Mike's big arms and her arms moved with him when he turned the pages. When they finished the book Rachel clapped her hands, turned to Mike and put her little hands on his face and squeezed. "Fishy lips!" Mike made fish faces at her and Rachel leaned back laughing and giggling with him. Mike got up off the ground, picked her up and spun her around in a circle, then pulled her close to him and hugged her.

Rachel saw the guys standing watching them and whispered to Mike, "Who are they?" Mike stopped and looked over at his friends. He told Rachel who they were and asked if she wanted to meet them. Rachel shook her head no and clung to his neck. "Rachel, honey it's okay. You don't need to be afraid of them. They won't hurt you. Honest!" Rachel nodded her head but said, “I can meet them later. I don’t want to today.” Mike agreed with her and he took her over to the windows. He told her, “I have to go for now. I will come back soon. It might not be tomorrow but I will be back.” Rachel just held on to him and she patted his shoulder. “I know you will be back. I don’t worry. I just wish I could come home with you and Josie.” She leaned her head on his shoulder. She just held on to him. “Can you bring Josie with you when you come back?” Rachel’s soft voice and her request all but broke his heart. “I will do my very best to do that.” Mike kissed the top of her head as he held on to her. Ted and Max turned to look away as they saw the tears in Mike’s eyes. When they turned they saw Megan watching with tears in hers as well.

Once they were outside, Ted told Mike that Rod called again to check in. He said Josie had a nightmare. She woke up screaming, scared the hell out of him. Josie was fine but she definitely has some serious demons to work through. Mike hung his head and thanked Ted for the update then climbed into his truck with Max. Mike was quiet most of the drive back to the bar. Finally, he said "What should I do Max?" Max looked over at him. "You need to know that. I can't tell you what to do. I can tell you that no matter what she's running from you need to be prepared and understand." Mike shook his head, "I just don't want to be the one hurting her anymore. I've done enough to her." Max shook his head. "You need to go to her and tell her that."

Mike dropped Max at the bar. He decided to head to the cabins. He would talk to Rod and if Josie was willing to give him a few minutes then he would take it. If not, he would just wait until she was ready. On the way to the cabins Mike thought about all the times they spent together. He could remember her smile. She smiled all the time back then. She deserved so much more than he gave to her. He was selfish. He should have gotten out of that life sooner. He had to find a way to make it up to her. There had to be some way to make this up to her. He loved her and he never stopped but that's not enough. Mike had to prove to her he was worth it. Mike would spend the rest of his life trying to prove it to Josie.

Chapter 23

Rod heard the truck coming. He heard the squeak from the shocks, he heard the motor. Mike's truck wasn't exactly quiet. He really needed to get a better vehicle to drive, but he liked that truck. Rod stood up on the porch and watched as Mike pulled up. Rod looked at the other cabin but saw no movement. Not since Josie's nightmare and the talk they had. Rod waved as Mike pulled up to park. He walked off the steps to meet him. Mike didn't waste time. "How is she?" Rod shrugged his shoulders and just let it at that. "I heard you were at the orphanage again? How'd that go?" Mike took his hand through his hair and shook his head. "It was hard. Every time I go in there and see that little girl I fall more in love with her. I just hope they can find a way to let us have her. Ted and Max stood up for me today. They didn't really say how it went but I'm going to try and stay positive." Rod shook his head in agreement. "I just wish I knew what to do for Josie. I hate that she is hurting. I wish I could make her see how much I love her. I just need a chance." Rod shrugged, "You need to ask her. Look I'll clue you in a little. Remember the hell she went through from that husband of hers. It's going to be a tough road. It won't be easy. It's going to take patience."

Mike looked at him, "Josie's afraid of me?" Rod shook his head, "No. She's afraid of how she reacts to you. Then the fear comes from what she's been through, what her body has been through and what she looks like now compared to before. She fears what your reactions to her will be knowing what has been done to her. You need to get her to talk to you." Mike turned and looked toward the lake. "I know but how?" Rod shrugged, "She's right over there." Rod pointed in the direction of the cabin Josie was in. "I don't know if she'll talk to me." Rod shook his head, "You won't know unless you try." Mike shook his head moving toward the cabin.

Josie was sitting on the bed, thinking about Mike, wondering if things would ever be simple again. She longed to sit holding him and just being with him but how? She didn't think she was ready for more. Being with him confused her. Being without him made her sad. She just didn't know what to think. She heard a vehicle coming but she didn't feel like seeing anyone so she just stayed in the bedroom. Mike was always on her mind now. He was all she could think about. She was just worried about how to go forward with their relationship. She was scared of how her body reacted to him, and she was scared of getting more physical with him, then not being able to follow through. She was scared of him seeing her body, all the ugly marks and scars. What if after Mike saw the marks and scars he ran away from her. She would lose him again. Mike deserved better than her, he deserved a whole woman. She just didn't feel whole anymore. But, she thought to herself, if I'm thinking he deserved better than me, then I guess I'm doing to him, what he did to me. He placed me on a pedestal, there was nowhere for me to go but down. Was she doing that to him now? She was making decisions about his life, without consulting him. Just like Mike did to her.

There was also the whole Jack thing. Josie worried that Jack would hurt Mike, or kill him. She felt like she'd never be free of Jack. This meant she'd never be free to be completely with Mike, not the way she wanted to. Josie dreamed about getting married to him. She would wear a white dress, hold beautiful flowers in her hand. She would walk toward Mike and see nothing but her future in front of her. She would smile at Mike as he watched her come down the aisle not being able to take his eyes off of her. They would have a minister perform the ceremony then Mike would whisk her away for a honeymoon. There was no need to go anywhere fancy because they would never leave their room. Josie had no reservations in her dream. Why couldn't her dream just be real? She heard a knock at the door, and went to answer it.

Mike hesitated in front of the door. He knocked twice and waited. He looked over toward where Rod had been and he was gone, looked like he was on his own. Mike stood waiting and he heard her turning the knob to the cabin door. His breath caught and his heart pounded.

Josie opened the door, she whispered, "Michael." He looked at her face and it was the most beautiful thing he'd ever seen. "What are you doing here?" Mike looked at her and smiled, "Would you believe just passing by?" Mike smiled at her and Josie couldn't help but to laugh. "Josie, all kidding aside. I need to know what's going on. I want to help and I can't help if I don't know what to do." Josie nodded her head and stepped back to let him in. They went over to the sofa in the cabin and sat down. They were both silent until Mike spoke. "Why are you running away from me Josie?"

Josie hung her head down and simply said, "I'm scared." Mike moved closer to her and took her hands in his. "Why? I would never hurt you. You have to believe me." Josie looked up at him with tears falling down her cheeks. "I know you wouldn't hurt me. But I'm afraid I would hurt you." Mike just stared at her. He didn't understand. He waited for her to continue. "I'm married. I will never be free to be with you as I want to." Mike stared at her. "Josie I promise if it's the last thing I do, I will make sure you get a divorce from that maniac. He doesn't deserve you. You don't have to worry about that. You've always belonged to me, no matter what you always will." Josie pulled her hands away and she was crying harder. She got up moving toward the fireplace in the cabin.

Mike stayed where he was. It took everything he had inside him to stay put. He wanted to go, wrap his arms around Josie and hold her until the crying stopped. She started talking quietly. "Michael, you don't understand." Josie tried to compose herself. She had to tell him. "I'm not whole anymore. I feel like I'm not good enough, like I can never fully be with you." He sat there trying to understand what she was saying. He didn't understand so he waited for more from her. Josie wrapped her arms around herself and continued. "When you touch me, I feel like I'm seventeen again. All I can think about is more. I want more of you. Then I move in to kiss you. You hold me so tight and touch me, then the fear comes back. My mind goes back to Jack, all he's done to me and I panic. I start to feel terrified. My body responds to all you do to me, but my mind starts racing, fear rises up inside of me."

Mike sat there. He didn't know what to do. Josie turned to look at him and she saw the love in his eyes and the pain. He blamed himself for all she'd been through. "Michael," He stood up and moved toward her. "I want to be with you. I want my dreams to come true but I can't offer you all of me because I'm already married. I'm terrified to even try to make love to you and I don't think I'll ever be able to have children. I'm not whole. I'm broken, I'm scarred I don't know how to be whole again." Josie reached out her hand and ran it down his face, "You deserve better."

Mike stood there. Was Josie serious? He reached up and took her hand from his face and kissed the palm. Mike took a deep breath. "Josie, I deserve all you are willing and able to give me. You and you alone is all I've ever wanted. All I've ever needed. I don't care if we can never marry, but I promise you we will. I know we will make love Josie, but on your terms. I will wait forever if need be, but I will never force anything that you are not prepared for. I promise you that. I never want you to fear me."

Mike moved and took Josie's other hand in his. "As far as having children, I'll adopt all the kids in that orphanage if it will make you happy, starting with Rachel. Every child there who needs a home will be ours. I will raise them with you and that is all the family I need. I would love to see you carry our child, but that is not something that will make or break us. We've been through hell Josie. You more so than me, so stop torturing yourself further. Everything will come in due time. I don't expect you to fall into my bed tonight, but I do expect that one day you will trust me enough to make love to me again. The scars scare me but only because they are the pain you had to bear, not because they make you any less beautiful in my eyes. That my love is the truth, simply and honestly, the truth. I love you all of you, now and forever."

Josie stood and listened to his words. Tears were completely blurring her vision. "It's not fair Michael. It just isn't fair. You deserve so much more. You deserve a woman who can show you her love and affection, not me who gets so far and leads you on to snap the door closed right when things are getting heated." Mike pulled her to him. She struggled at first to move away. He held her tight and said, "Josie please, I love you so much. I will take whatever it is you have to give me. I can wait. I will wait. I will never push you further than you are ready for. Please give me the chance to prove it to you." Mike pulled back to look into her eyes, "Please."

Mike and Josie stood there staring into one another's eyes for what seemed like an eternity. Josie was the first to turn away. Mike held his breath. She moved to clear her head. She was so confused. She turned and walked away from him. He stood there and waited. She was playing back what Mike had said. Did he really mean it? Could she take the chance again? Mike broke her heart once, would he get tired of her and walk away again? No Mike loved her, and all this nonsense was just her insecurity. It was her fear. Josie was tired of living in fear. Jack wasn't going to win, not this time.

Josie turned back to Mike. Her lip was quivering and all she could do was hold her hands out to him and whisper his name, "Michael," He moved quickly to her. He bent his head and kissed her gently. When he pulled back Josie finished her words to him, "I love you. I never stopped." Mike took Josie's head in his hands and she could see the tears in his eyes. He kissed her again.

In the cabin next door, Rod came back out to the front porch. He sat and waited. He didn't see Michael come back out and he heard no yelling. He picked up his phone, "I'll be home tonight beautiful. Warm up those lips."

He hung up the phone and smiled to himself. Rod knew that all Michael and Josie needed was time. They needed to ease into this relationship and they needed to just take their time. They belonged together, they always had. Otherwise they wouldn't have found each other again.

Mike pulled Josie back to the sofa to sit down. He pulled Josie to his side and held her. "Josie you scared me. I didn't understand what had happened. I'm so sorry. I didn't even consider all you had been through. I promise you nothing before you are ready." Josie moved as close as she could to him. Her head was resting in the crook of his neck. Josie felt safe, protected and loved. Mike was gently running his hand up and down her arm.

Josie felt like everything was right. She placed her hand on Mike's chest, gently and slowly moving it back and forth. She could feel her heart pounding in her chest, she was determined to not be afraid. “I’ve always loved you Michael.” She moved her head to look at him, “Always!” Mike kissed her again, and again. He needed to hold her closer. He pulled her onto his lap and she curled into his arms. Mike kissed her neck and he nibbled on her earlobe. She giggled and pulled away. She looked at him, she saw the desire there and it made her heart thump harder. She went to move away. He held her steady. “It’s ok Josie. We are just making out like we did when we were kids. No worries. I held back when we were younger, I can do that now, never before you are ready. I promise.” Josie saw the promise in his eyes. He held her and they kissed until they both felt like they were going to explode. She was kissing his neck and moved up to kiss his lips, “Michael,” “Hmm,” Josie moved her lips across his cheek and she mumbled, “I think I need to go for a run. I uh, think we both do." Josie kissed him once more then pulled back to look at him. Mike blinked a few times and shook his head clear. "Ok, but not here. Let's head back to town." Josie nodded and went to pack her things. Mike headed out to find Rod.

Mike walked over to him and climbed the steps to the porch. Rod was smiling at him. "So it went well I take it?" Mike laughed and nodded. "Thanks for all your help Rod. You're a good friend." Rod stood up and shook the hand that Mike had stretched out to him. "Anytime." Mike explained that he and Josie have a long road to climb but they are going to do it together and from the beginning. Mike told Rod that they wanted to head back to town. They were going to go for a run together. Rod went and gathered his things while Mike went to help Josie. Rod met them at the front of the cabins. He locked up his cabin first then went over to their cabin and locked it as well. Josie hugged Rod. “Thank you for your patience and your help.” Rod hugged her back and said, “No problem. Just remember, he’s a stand-up guy. No worries. But you have to tell him about the phone call. He doesn’t know.” Josie pulled back and looked at him as she climbed into Mike’s truck. Rod reached out a hand to Mike, “One step at a time. Everything will fall into place.” Mike shook his hand, “Thanks.” Mike climbed into his truck and away they went.

Chapter 24

After stopping at Mike's apartment for him to change they headed to Josie's so that she could put her things away and change as well. They stepped out onto the sidewalk. Josie said, "Are you ready?" Mike nodded at her. He fell into step behind her. The town was quiet so they were able to move off the sidewalk and run side by side in the street. They were running and Mike was impressed at how well he was able to keep pace with her, so far at least.

Josie was running at a mild pace. She wasn't sure how much Mike had been running so she didn't want to push too hard. He was right with her though so she thought she'd see what he had in his tank. Josie sped up a bit and Mike stayed right with her. She started running harder and he was still with her. They were matching pace for pace. She was breathing heavier and she heard Mike breathing more labored as well. She kept pushing and they were running at full pace.

Mike hung back a little and slowed his pace to follow Josie. He wanted to watch her move. He watched her stride. He watched her muscles with each movement she made, and yes he was watching her ass. Mike was so busy watching Josie he lost track of how far they were running. He moved back beside her, "We're almost at the bar." Josie looked at him and winked, "I'll race you." She took off and Mike had no problem bringing up the rear.

Josie stopped at the back door to the bar and waited for Mike. He was only a few paces behind her. "You did that on purpose didn't you?" He came up beside her, "Somehow that run didn't do anything to cool me off." He moved in and gave Josie a quick breathless kiss and swat on the behind. They laughed as he opened the side door to the bar. Mike took Josie in to get some water. Once inside Josie was looking around. “Water first then I’ll give you the tour.” She came up beside Mike and took his hand. Mike took her into the bar area and Max turned toward them. “What the hell? What were you guys doing?” Josie laughed. “Running.” Max waved at them, “What for? All that sweating, heavy breathing. I could find better things to sweat and breathe heavy for.” Max laughed. Josie and Mike looked at each other and Max couldn’t help but do a silent fist pump to the heavens. Max saw the sparks and knew they were getting there.

Mike walked Josie around the whole bar, pointing out all the little details that he put into it. He ended taking her into the back showing her the storeroom and then his office. Once Mike took her into his office he closed the door and pulled her back up against the door. He bent to kiss her and quickly their kiss became a little heated. He stopped and rested his head against hers, gasping for air. “I could die with that kiss. You make me crazy Josie. I love you so much.”

Josie just enjoyed the feelings running inside of her. She couldn’t believe that she was able to be here with him and not feel guilty about not going any further than she was comfortable. She did feel bad, because she knew he wanted more, but she knew he wasn’t mad about stopping.

Mike saw the look coming over Josie and he tilted her head to look at him. “No pressure Josie, just expressing what I feel. Don’t pull away now.” She looked at him and smiled. “I’m not going anywhere. I promise Michael.” He pulled her to him, they kissed again, gently at first but he deepened it. He felt Josie’s tongue touch his, they tangoed inside their mouths and she was reaching for him.

Josie was pulling Mike to her tighter and rubbing her hands down his back and around his ass. She was pulling him so close he was afraid his arousal would scare her off. He kept his hands on either side of her for fear of scaring her. He let her use her hands to explore. She was pulling her hands up his sides and reaching to touch his arms. The knock on the door had her shrieking and pushing him away from the door. Mike grabbed ahold of her and steadied her. Once Josie was steady he went and all but pulled the door off the hinges.

The young bartender was standing there unaware of what he had interrupted. He stepped back at the gruff, "What?" Came out of Mike's mouth. The young man came to say that he would be in this weekend. The other job he was working didn't need him. "I know you had asked me, with the band coming this weekend I knew it meant a lot to you to have extra hands on deck, so I checked they said they were covered, so I'm available all night." Mike thanked him and told him to go get ready for his shift. He scampered away as Josie dissolved into fits of giggles as she sunk down into his chair. Mike stalked over to her. "Just what is so funny?"

Josie was so busy laughing that when Mike picked her up out of his chair it caught her totally by surprise. He lifted her and turned to sit in his chair, then pulled her onto his lap. She was straddling him and was unsure what to do. "Relax Josie. It's all good." He pulled Josie to meet his lips and he picked up kissing her where they had left off. He however, this time took advantage of their position and was running his hands over her body. Slowly, up and down her back, as she pressed deeper to him and tentatively rubbed herself against him he became a little greedy with his hands. Mike ran them down her sides then rounded her ass, as he grabbed both cheeks he pulled her against him and he heard the moan roaring out of her throat.

Mike was losing himself in Josie and he was so afraid to scare her off but he had to try. Mike brought his hands around to her stomach and moved slowly up to her breasts. He felt her lean into his hands at first, then he felt her stiffen. Mike stopped instantly and pulled his lips from hers. "Ok, girl. Relax. It's all good."

Josie was breathing so heavy. She had a look mixed with desire and fear. "I'm sorry." She breathed out, "I'm sorry." Mike held his fingers to her lips, "Shhhh, Josie. Nothing to be sorry for. We are fine. Relax." Josie relaxed back against him for a moment. "My body is ready for you Michael. I just wish my head would catch up." Mike chuckled and held her to him. "All in due time Josie girl, all in due time."

Mike and Josie ran back to her apartment. He came in for some water and they kissed a little more. Then Mike told her he needed a shower. So he kissed her one last time. He told her he would see her in two days. Mike wanted her to come to see the band this weekend. She promised she'd be there. After Mike left, Josie took a shower and thought long and hard about him. She thought about how her body reacted to him. It's so natural and it feels so right. Why couldn't she just get her head to turn off and cooperate? He's been so good about this and she could feel how hard (literally) it was for him to be so close without going any further. She didn't want him to stop but yet she felt her heart race and fear creeped in. Josie just needed to find a way to let go of the fear and to tell Mike about the phone call from Jack.

Josie called Miranda after her shower. Josie said she could come to work in the morning, but Miranda told her to take the day off since she would be at the hospital and only had a few office patients. It was nothing she couldn't handle. So Josie thought if Rod wasn't too busy maybe he could set aside an hour to work on her self-defense moves again. Miranda told her to make it 2:00pm. Josie hung up with her then thought about what she would do with her day. She thought maybe she would treat herself to a nice dress to wear to the bar Saturday night. Then she could warm up with a workout at the gym and meet up with Rod. Josie was excited for tomorrow to come. She would find the perfect dress for Saturday night. She wanted to knock Mike right out of his socks.

Chapter 25

Josie went to the same shop where she bought the black dress. They had nice things for reasonable prices. Josie tried a few dresses on and she found one she really liked. It was plain. It was a shirt dress, burgundy in color, had a simple gold chain belt around the waist with buttons all the way down the front and Josie loved it. She saw some shoes with high heels, she thought for Michael she'd give them a try. Josie put the shoes on with the dress. She looked in the mirror and with the heels, it really made her legs stand out. The dress only came to mid-thigh so it was a little short for her liking but she really liked the way it looked on her. She only hoped that Mike would like it too. She took it home and checked out her jewelry. She found some simple gold earrings and a gold heart necklace. She was all set.

Josie was going to take a run but figured she would run to the gym do a work out, then see how she felt. If she still needed a run she would do so after the gym, but she was hoping to go to see Rachel. She missed her and wanted to hold her in her arms. Rachel was such a sweet little girl. She hoped that someday she'd find her forever home. Josie thought choosing Mike would most likely hurt her chances of adopting but since she couldn't get a divorce, Jack would be the reason that she wouldn't get Rachel. If only she and Mike would have been able to stay together. Jack wouldn't be an issue. No sense going down that road as it's the past now. Josie changed into gym clothes and headed for a workout. Thinking about Jack made her second guess even going to the orphanage. As she was going to the gym it struck her, Mike mentioned Rachel at the cabin. How did he know about her? It didn't dawn on her until now, but he definitely mentioned adopting all the kids at the orphanage and Rachel. She needed to talk to him, she needed to find out how he knew. She still needed to tell Michael about the Jack phone call too.

Josie was doing her weight training and working the circuit when she heard two women talking. "I'm telling you that guy is hot. His arms are so muscular. His body is just on fire." The other woman said, "Oh yeah, the way he pours drinks and smiles at you, well it just melts my heart." Josie wasn't sure who they were talking about but she tried to listen in. "I heard that he owns the Heartbreak. That's an even bigger ace in the hole." The other woman chimed in, "You never see him with a woman either. He's gotta be single! I'll bet he's dynamite in the sack." Josie could hardly contain her laughter. Josie just kept going about her business. The women continued their talk about the "guy at the Heartbreak."

The first woman continued, "He has such gorgeous blonde hair. Oh how I'd like to run my fingers through it." The second woman chimed in, "Yeah, I'll bet it's silky soft. Oh what dreamy blue eyes he has too. I could sit at the bar all night and watch him."

Josie almost fell off her weight bench. She'd had enough. She walked over toward the women. "Excuse me, are you guys talking about Michael from the Heartbreak Bar?" They both looked at her and nodded. "Do you know him?" Josie nodded, "Yes I know him, and he has a really jealous girlfriend, so I'd be careful." They both looked at each other, "Hey thanks for the tip." She smiled sweetly, "Anytime." She turned leaving the gym, she knew now she was taking that run. She was going to run to the Heartbreak and make sure her Michael was aware of all the lust he was stirring up around town.

Josie was running a good pace. She liked to start out slow easing into hitting it hard about halfway. She had her headset on so she was totally in her head with her run. She didn't let her mind wander she just concentrated on the run. For once she was feeling at peace. Josie felt like her life was coming together, even though she was afraid of the intimacy with Michael she felt safe with him. So for once she wasn't second guessing herself. Her only worry now was Jack. She was breathing harder really pushing herself. She was over halfway to the bar.

Josie was starting to get an uneasy feeling. She felt like someone was watching her. Like she was being followed. She turned her head slightly to look over her left shoulder. She didn't see anything unusual. So she kept going. It was the middle of the day. Jack wouldn't dare try anything in broad daylight. Besides she didn't know if it was him or not.

She thought she would challenge herself, try to get out of her head, she pushed even harder, she hit a pace that was a little uncomfortable for her, she dug deep. She kept the pace going until she could see the parking lot of the bar. Only then did she slow slightly then finally hit an easy jog the rest of the way.

Josie walked in the main door to the bar. She saw Max but not Mike. “Hey Max, where’s the big guy?” Max looked up at her, immediately pouring her some water. “He’s upstairs.” She took the water thanking him. She was going to go out the main door when he stopped her. “Head up the back.” She cut through the bar, out the side door and up the steps to his apartment. She knocked waiting. He came to the door all sweaty. “Josie. I was just thinking about you.” She looked at him smiling. “Nightmare?” Mike smiled. “No I was running on the treadmill.”

Mike bent to give her a kiss stealing her water as he did. He guzzled it down. “Hey! Max gave that to me.” He looked at her, his eyes dancing, “Well, run down and get us some more.” Josie slapped his chest and moved inside his apartment. Mike went over to the refrigerator, grabbed two bottles of water. “So what brings you out here to see me? Couldn’t stand to be away from me? Needed to see this sexy thing?” Mike moved toward Josie teasing her.

Josie took the water bottle from Mike thinking two can play this game. “Actually I was making sure you weren’t throwing me to the curb. I mean with the hot body you have, the beautifully soft and silky hair you have plus those gorgeous blue eyes, the women of this town are ready to beat your door down.” Mike looking puzzled, quirking an eyebrow at her. “I don’t understand.” Josie started laughing. She told him the story, by the end he was laughing with her. Mike reached out and pulled Josie to him. "So how jealous is this girlfriend of mine?" He leaned in kissing her. Josie wrapped her arms around him. "Very." She went for another kiss and intensified it. She wanted Mike to know how much she loved him. He pulled back from her kiss. "Josie, no worries. You are the only woman I have eyes for. I only want you." Josie looked at him. "Good, because you are the only man for me." She pulled Mike in again. They were kissing and touching each other like their lives depended on it.

Josie pushed herself to Mike and couldn't get close enough. Mike had his arms around her, he couldn't get enough. He hoisted her up, she wrapped her legs around him. She was holding him so tight he could hardly breathe. Mike moved across the room with her and laid down on the sofa with her. Once they were stretched out on the sofa together. He said to her, “Josie, I don’t know how much of this I can take. I’m trying but we need to slow down.” She looked at him and nodded. “I’m sorry, you just, I mean I can’t, I don’t know why I can’t ever speak when you are this close to me. It’s like I lose my brain and just turn into putty.”

Mike laughed he brushed a hair off Josie’s cheek. “I love you Michael. I hope you know that. It’s not that I don’t want to make love to you. I’m just scared.” Mike looked into her eyes, “Josie I would wait forever for you. I just need more of you. Every day I just want more. I understand, I will wait as long as it takes for you to feel safe. I love you Josie girl. I never stopped.” He bent and kissed her gently on her lips. “Oh Michael. What did I do to deserve you?” She pulled him to her they were kissing again. She was pushing herself against him and she was wanting more of him, but yet she wasn't sure she could follow through. She reached down between them. She wanted to touch him.

"Josie! Please don't!" She looked at him. "Let me help you. I want to touch you. I need to touch you." Mike nodded. She reached inside his shorts. She felt him all warm, hard, thick. She heard him moan as she wrapped her hand around him. She was so turned on with him in her hands. She was not sure how or what to do for him but she felt okay with him. Mike wasn't forcing anymore on her. He was giving her the freedom to move, to touch. He bent to kiss her. Her hand was instinctively moving. Mike was moving with her until he was starting to lose control. "Josie we have to stop! I'm not going to be able to hold back."

Josie kept stroking him. "It's okay Michael. I want you to feel relief, I want to help you. If I can't completely make love to you yet, I want to at least do this. Let it go." Mike leaned in to kiss her again. His elbows braced on either side of her, he moved with her. He was moving faster and Josie kept stroking him. He tore his lips from hers, "God in heaven. I love you Josie." He erupted in her hands and she continued to stroke him gently till the end. He laid on her panting. "God Josie, what you do to me. I'm sorry, I couldn't stop."

Josie held onto Mike and started to cry. Tears were just spilling over her cheeks. "Shit!" Mike swore and went to move off of her. She grabbed him and held him to her. "Michael, I have to tell you something." He wiped at the tears on her face. "Please don't cry Josie. Please! Anything, you can tell me anything."

Josie took a deep breath, she pushed him to sit up. He moved and sat next to her and waited.

Josie started, "The day I went to the cabin, before I planned to go there I got another phone call from Jack." Mike stood up. "Why didn't you tell me? What did he say?" Josie looked down at her hands in front of her. I didn't want you to know. I didn't want anyone to know." He waited for her to explain more. She looked up at him. "He's watching me. He evidently saw us together, he threatened you and all my friends. If I go with him no one will get hurt." Mike was furious. "You're kidding right? Josie please don't listen to Jack. He's not going to get to you or anyone else." Mike sat back down next to her. He saw the fear in her eyes.

"Josie, I promise you, Jack's not going to hurt you and he's not going to hurt any of us." She smiled a weak smile at him and nodded her head. “I hear what you are saying but I can’t help but worry. I don’t want anything to happen to my friends or you. I wouldn’t be able to live with myself.” He took her head in his hands. “Nothing is going to happen to any of us. Please don’t worry Josie.” She nodded at him, “I need to get going. You have to get to the bar and I’m going to train with Rod.” He stood and walked with her to the door. He bent down and kissed her, she smiled at him. “I’ll call you later Josie.” She said, “I’ll be waiting by the phone.”

Josie headed home. She ran home and was on cloud nine after her time with Mike. She was feeling more and more comfortable with him. Maybe they could try soon. She really wanted to be with him but just didn’t want to start the ball rolling, then pull away. She was almost home, she heard a car behind her. She turned in time to see it headed right for her. She ran off into the grass, stumbled and fell. Her heart was racing and the car just sped away. Jack. She knew it was him. He's trying to rattle her. She got up, brushed herself off and finished her run. She'd be damned if she'd let him stop her. She headed right to the police station to meet with Rod.

Chapter 26

Rod looked at Josie as she walked in, he was concerned. She was disheveled and had dirt on her clothes. “Josie, what happened to you?” She stopped in front of him and looked mad as hell. “Someone tried to run me over.” Rod was shocked, “What? Where?” She told him and he was outraged. “Calm down Rod. It’s ok. I’m fine. But now I know he’s here and watching for sure. I need to be prepared.” Rod looked at her, “and so do we.”

Rod was going over moves again as if someone had Josie from behind. She worked hard with him and listened to all his advice. Josie was grateful for the time he gave her. She wanted to be sure she paid attention to everything. When they were done, they sat down and drank some water. “Do you feel comfortable Josie? If not, we can do it again.” She shook her head. “I got it Rod. I just thank you for all you're doing for me." Rod waved that off. "It's important to me that you can defend yourself. I watched Sarah once when she was being held at gunpoint. Scary shit. But she handled herself well and the rest is history." Josie was shocked. She knew nothing about this. Rod told her the story about how Sarah became a hostage. Ted watched helplessly. Rod got himself close and when the gun was fired at Ted, he jumped in front of the gun and took the bullet in his shoulder. "The doctors told me I wouldn't be able to fire a gun again. I go to the gun range every day. I'm getting more accurate every day. I am a cop. I need to be able to fire my weapon when it counts." Josie was glad that Rod was sharing with her. "I trust you Rod. I know when it matters you'll be able to be accurate." He patted her leg, "Thanks Josie."

Josie and Rod sat a little while longer and talked. "I told Michael about the phone call from Jack, before I left for the cabin. He was angry, but he didn't say much. I told him how Jack threatened him, my friends. I also told him that Jack said if I go with him no one will get hurt." Rod shook his head, "What did Mike say to that?" Josie didn't answer at first, but a tear slid down her cheek. "I will never forgive myself if something happens to any of you." Rod put his arm around her, "Let me worry about that. You just think about making this place, this town your home." Josie leaned in and kissed Rod's cheek. "I don't know what I did to deserve you, this town and Michael, but I sure am grateful. Rod smiled at her, "We truly are the lucky ones Josie."

Josie needed to take a shower. She needed to get home. Then she was going to just stay in. She didn't want to risk Jack being around and following her to the orphanage. With that thought she looked at Rod. “How did Michael find out about Rachel?” Rod looked at her a moment but didn’t say anything. “When Michael came to the cabin to talk to me, he mentioned about adopting all the kids at the orphanage and Rachel by name.” Rod chuckled, “I don’t think Mike could handle all those kids.” Josie smiled and laughed at the thought of Mike with children. Rod grew serious for a moment. “I told Mike about Rachel. The night Mike revealed himself to you, I went to the bar to tell Mike about the phone call you got from Jack. I also told him what an incredible woman you were, how you met Rachel at the hospital and fell in love with her. I told Mike about you wanting to adopt Rachel but were scared because of Jack. Mike automatically said, he would be no good for you too. I told Mike that I wasn’t putting that thought out there to give any second guesses to the relationship. I just wanted Mike to be prepared for fatherhood, since you two belonged together."

Josie couldn't breathe for a moment. "Oh my God, so Michael knew about Rachel before he approached me. He knew that I wanted a family?" Rod nodded. He was unsure if it was fear in her voice or hope. "Josie, Mike loves you. He would move heaven and earth for you. He would do anything to get you Rachel, even if that meant walking away." Josie let the tears fall down her face. "I can't let him go Rod. As much as I love Rachel, I can't lose him again." Rod nodded. "So don't give up. Fight for them both." Josie stood up, Rod beside her. He pulled her into his arms and hugged her. "Don't ever give up on your dreams Josie."

Josie got home and before she could get in the shower there was a knock at the door.

She went to the door, checking before opening it. She saw the young boy again with flowers. She took the flowers from him and headed to the living room. She unwrapped them. This time she had a dozen red roses. The card simply read 'I love you more than words can say. Always yours, Michael.' She smiled and held her breath. Her life was finally coming together. Rod was right, she needed to fight for love, fight for her dreams. With her Michael by her side, there was no way her dreams, their dreams couldn't come true.

Josie smiled on her way off to the shower. She was in the shower, thinking about her time with Mike today. She really wanted to hold him close to her. She didn't want to be fearful of what was coming next. She wanted to be whole for him. She wanted to be able to show him how much she loved him. She stepped out of the shower. She was getting dressed when her phone rang. She ran to the phone, thinking it was Mike. "You little whore. Who do you think you are? You are married to me, what were you doing with that other guy? I warned you, I'll show him who you belong to. You are mine and always will be. I'm coming for you Josie. Just you wait. I'm coming, and if anyone gets in my way I will kill them, including your lover boy." Jack hung up and left her trembling.

Josie hung up the phone. She called Rod immediately. Rod told Josie to stay calm he would be right over. Rod hung up the phone. As he was walking out the door he called Mike. "Jack called her again and tried to run her over today." That was all he got out and Mike said, "I'm on my way." Rod got to Josie's apartment first. He knocked on the door and waited. "Josie it's me, Rod. It's ok. Let me in." She unlocked the door and threw herself at him. "He's going to kill me. I know he is. He will kill Michael too. I have to protect him. I can't let him get hurt." Rod held on to her, moved inside the apartment and closed the door behind him. Rod helped her into the living room holding on to her while she cried on the sofa.

"How can Jack affect me like this. I'm prepared to stand up to him but yet he scares the hell out of me. I turn into a crying crazy mess." Rod just patted her shoulder. "It's ok Josie, it's natural to be afraid. He's hurt you and you are scared of him. We will get him. He won't hurt you again." Josie needed a drink to calm her, she went to the kitchen to get something and she heard Mike.

Rod didn't lock the door because he knew Mike was coming. He came barreling through the door yelling for her. "Josie, where are you? Are you okay?" She came out of the kitchen, “Michael,” she threw herself in his arms. He was angry, “Why didn’t you call me? You should have called me.” Josie cried, “I don’t want Jack to hurt you. He saw us together. He knows about you and he said he would kill anyone that got in his way. I can’t let him hurt you. You have to leave. Please Michael.” Mike held her while she cried and she was barely standing. He scooped her up and carried her into the bedroom. He laid her on the bed. “Josie, relax honey. It’s okay. Jack’s not going to get me or you. Relax honey. I’m not going anywhere, I love you. I will never leave you again.” Josie cried harder. “Please Michael, don’t let him hurt you. I can’t live with myself if he hurts you.” She was sobbing and a complete wreck. Mike held her for a few minutes, then as she calmed some he moved. “I need to go talk to Rod. I’ll be right back sweetheart.”

Mike went out to Rod. "What the hell happened? She is a mess. She keeps telling me to leave." Rod told Mike what Josie said. Rod told Mike that he called Miranda. He thought Josie should have a mild sedative to relax her and help her get some sleep. He heard the reaction to the nightmare she had at the cabin and he envisioned she would not be sleeping well tonight. "Good idea. I will stay here with her tonight. I don't want her to be alone." Rod nodded. "You go sit with her, I'll wait for Miranda." Mike turned to go back to the bedroom. Rod stopped him, "Mike," He turned to look at him. "She told me at the cabins that she wanted me to just let Jack take her. She wanted to protect us. She wanted to protect you. She, God help us, she wants to go off with that madman, to save all of us." Mike's face hardened, "The hell she will." He turned and went back to the bedroom to hold her.

Josie laid crying quietly on the bed. Mike sat down next to her and brushed the hair out of her face. He rubbed her back and just spoke softly to her. “Josie, it’s okay. Jack’s not going to hurt you. I promise you he won’t. I won’t let him.” She sat up. “No Michael. You have to go. It’s not safe for you to be with me. He will kill you. I don’t want him to hurt you. You have to go. Please, I can’t stand the thought of something happening to you. Michael, please you need to go!” Mike wrapped his arms around her. “I’m not going anywhere Josie. I’m not leaving you, and you are not leaving me.” She cried in his arms. She only ever loved this man. All she wanted was to protect him. “He’s crazy Michael. He is crazy. I don’t want him to get near us. I don’t want him here. Why does he have to be here?” Mike sat with her and just held her while he rubbed her back.

Miranda came into the room and Mike handed Josie off to her. He left the room to allow Miranda to talk to her and soothe her. He heard Miranda explain she was going to give her a mild sedative to help her get some sleep. Josie was protesting but Miranda was handling it. Mike went back out to the living room and saw Rod hanging up the phone. "What's next?" Rod held his hands up. "Relax Mike. We will watch her. We can't do anything until Jack makes a move. So far he's been careful and only making moves on her when no one can see him. He calls her on the phone when no one is here. We can't do much yet." Mike was enraged. "What do you mean yet? Does he have to kill her before something is done? This is insane. He can't get near her! He can't!" Mike was running his hand through his hair and pacing the floor. "She's all I ever wanted and needed. I can't let anything happen to her." Rod spoke, "We won't let anything happen to her. You need to trust me." Mike nodded and headed into the kitchen to make himself a drink.

Miranda came out of the bedroom and moved over to Rod. Rod kissed her and hugged her then they turned to look at Mike. Mike noticed something was different with them. "What's up with you two? You seem so, I don't know happy." Miranda laughed, "Is there a law against being happy big guy?" He held up his hands, "No, back off I don't want any trouble." Rod laughed. "I'm dying to tell someone. Miranda spun around, "Rod, no!" He ignored her protests and told Mike that he proposed and she accepted. Mike grinned grabbing Rod's hand then hugged him. "Congratulations man!" He moved to Miranda, "Hey, don't touch me!" He hugged her anyway and she smiled. "You can't say anything. I haven't even told my best friend." Mike crossed his heart with his finger, “My lips are sealed.” He looked at Rod. “Are you sure about this? She’s a firecracker.” Miranda smacked him, “Hey I’m standing right here in the room you know.” Mike rubbed his chest where she hit him, “Ouch, see what I mean?” The three of them started laughing.

Mike walked the two out to their cars and thanked them both. Miranda told him if Josie needed anything to call. Mike promised he would. “One thing Mike. That girl in there would sell her soul for you. She told me she would go with that crazy bastard just to protect you and us. She’s not worried about herself. She’s worried about something happening to you and all of us.” Mike looked at her and said, “What is she thinking? Without her I have no life. Why is she so hell bent on going with him, to protect me? I don’t deserve her.” Miranda patted his shoulder. “The two of you deserve a life together. Don't you forget that." She moved to her car door and got in.

Mike went back into the apartment, he locked the door. He called Max filled him in on what was going on. He promised he would be back to the bar the next day to get ready for the band set up. Mike walked back to the bedroom and watched from the doorway as Josie slept. He went to sit on the bed next to her and she stirred slightly. He took his boots off, loosened his jeans, then climbed into the bed with her. He pulled her against him and held her while she slept.

Chapter 27

Josie dreamed of Mike. He was so loving and caring. He touched her and her body immediately reacted. He could stir things inside of her that she never felt before. She longed to be held by him, to have him buried inside of her. She dreamed of the days when they would run off to make love in the cabin, or the times that they couldn't wait to get to the cabin and ended up in his car or even in the woods. One time all those years ago they didn't even make it into the car. They were teasing one another while they were at the club. Josie wore a dress which she rarely wore so he was surprised. They were kissing in the club and Mike was getting aroused. She looked at him and said, "Let's get out of here."

Mike nodded taking Josie's hand to pull her out of the club. Once outside he said to her, "You are killing me in that dress. I'm dying to take it off of you." She moved in closer to him and whispered, "I'm naked under this dress." His eyes grew wide and he picked up his pace. They got to the car and instead of opening the door for her he pressed her back against the door. He touched her nipples and they pushed against the fabric. He growled deep from within, he pulled her leg up around his hip. He slid his hand over her thigh and slipped up to her bare ass. He tore his mouth from hers and swore, "Jesus, Josie." Mike looked around and the club was quiet, no one in the parking lot. He hiked her other leg up to his waist and he placed his hands on her bare ass and carried her to the hood of the car. Once there he placed her bottom on the hood and quickly undid his pants.

Josie protested slightly, "Michael, this is insane. What if someone pulls in or comes out of the club." He groaned and pulled her to him,

"Then they are going to get an eye full. Damn what you do to me Josie. I can't wait, I have to have you now." He pulled her in and within seconds he was inside of her. Josie lifted her hips, wrapping her legs around him. He was devouring her mouth and he had placed his hands under her to lift her to him. Josie was dissolving in his arms. She needed more. She arched her back and he helped her lay back on the hood of the car. She had placed her feet on the front bumper and was pressing up to him. Higher and higher, he drove her and deeper and deeper he went.

Mike took his hands down her breasts. They peaked under the light weight fabric of her dress. He was so turned on he couldn't hold back. "God I love your body and how it responds to me. I feel you wrapped around me, squeezing as I slam into you. I can't get enough. I just need more. He took his hands and grabbed her hips pulling her hard into him. Josie's back arched up off the car and she exploded around him. She tightened around him and he came hard inside of her. She was still so hot and turned on. She wanted to do it again.

"Michael, I never want this to end. Please take me to the cabin, I want to feel all of this again, now." Her words were instant arousal for him. He was starting to get hard again. She felt him. Josie sat up. She grabbed his hips and pulled him to her, "Or we can just go again, right here." She pulled his head down to her and playfully bit his lip.

Mike pulled out of her, he didn't even bother zipping his pants, he helped her off the car and in the passenger seat. He slid behind the wheel of the car and drove like lightening to the cabin. On the way there, Josie moved close to him and reached down to touch him. He groaned and hit the gas pedal harder. She was enjoying the feel of him in her hands. She could tell she was driving him crazy. “Damn it Josie. You need to stop that.” She grinned at him and said, “Why?” “You damn well know why. You are killing me. We aren’t going to make it to the cabin if you keep that up.” She smiled and said, “Exactly what I’m trying to do, keep it up that is.” With that he pulled up at the cabin, slammed the car into park and turned off the car. He grabbed the back of her head and mashed his lips to hers, plunging his tongue deep within her mouth. She climbed onto his lap. He was moving them out of the car.

Josie’s back hit the door to the cabin as Mike fumbled for the door knob. Once it was open he entered the cabin and headed straight for his room. He opened the door kicking it shut behind him. He lowered her feet to the floor as he pulled the dress up over her head. Sure enough she was completely naked standing in front of him. “Oh my God Josie!” He turned to lock the door. On his way back to her his clothes were hitting the floor. He picked her up and laid her on the bed. He was stroking her nipples with the back of his hand, driving her wild inside.

Josie was tired of waiting. She moved up and over Mike. “Tell me you love me Michael.” He brushed the hair off the side of her face and said, “I love you Josie.” She moved and centered herself to take him. Josie was teasing him now. She took a little of him inside her. When Mike moved to deepen it she pulled up. He was left staring at her puzzled. “No rushing this. I want to make love to you. My way.” He groaned and grabbed her ass in his hands trying to get her back where he wanted her. She shook her head, "My way tonight. Please Michael, give me this."

Mike nodded, "I can't deny you anything Josie girl, you know that. Your way." Josie took just the tip of him back inside her. She was only allowing him a small sample of her sweetness. Mike was trying so hard not to move. She saw the concentration on his face. She rubbed his chest and brought her hand down to where their bodies were joined. His eyes followed her hand as she slid him a little more inside of her. She reached between her legs and felt him there. She felt where their bodies met and joined. "Oh God Josie, what are you doing to me?" He was quickly losing control. "I'm feeling you. I'm touching us, I want to feel you go inside of me. It feels so good when you are there. I want more."

Josie slid down a little more. She was now touching more of herself than Mike. She saw his eyes flare, she took his hand with hers, "Feel it Michael, feel us together. He moved his hand against her and he slipped a finger inside of her. She arched her hips and he felt her take more of him, he was tired of waiting for her. He moved his hands around her hips and pulled her down as he pushed up with his hips. "Feel this Josie. Feel me." She rocked her hips against him and kept rocking until she was ready to burst, then she stopped and pulled him out of her.

Mike looked at Josie. There was fire in his eyes. "What the hell?" When he looked her in the eyes she drove him all the way back inside of her and he filled her completely. She rocked again and she couldn't hold back any longer. Her back arched and the colors of the rainbow exploded in front of her. Her body was tingling all over and she yelled his name, "Michael," He drove his hips up and up and up. He too had reached his end. She felt him explode inside of her and she collapsed on his chest.

Mike felt Josie stirring beside him. She must have been dreaming. He pulled her tighter to him. He was aroused lying there holding her but he would deal with it later. She just needed to be protected. His Josie. He would not let anyone hurt her again. She had to believe that. If it was the last thing he did, he'd be sure that Jack paid for what he did to her.

Josie was still dreaming. They laid in bed holding each other and whispering words of love. The door flew open and Jack came in pointing a gun at Mike. "I told you I would kill him. You are mine, you whore." Josie was grabbing at Mike. "No Jack, no. Leave him alone. Please, just take me I'll go, just don't hurt my Michael."

Mike knew as soon as Josie started thrashing about something was wrong. She started yelling, “No Jack,” then she was yelling his name, “Michael.” He shook her to wake her. “Josie, wake up. I’m here, wake up.” She opened her eyes and looked at him. “Michael!” She threw her arms around him. She was crying, “He has a gun, don’t let him hurt you. You gotta get out of here.” She was trying to get out of the bed. He held her down. “Josie, it’s okay. No one is here, there is no gun. We’re both fine. Look at me!” He pulled her back to look at him. “Breathe, honey. Just breathe.” He was holding her face between his hands and she was starting to wake up more coming out of the dream she was in.

“Oh my God Michael! Jack can’t hurt you.” Her hands were grabbing at the front of his shirt. “He just can’t. I can’t lose you again.” She buried her face in his chest and he rubbed her back. “Please Josie, don’t worry. He’s not going to hurt me or you. I promise you. I love you so much, I will never let him hurt you again.”

Mike held Josie until she calmed down. He laid her back on the pillows and took his place beside her again. She was facing him. She reached out and touched his face. “I was dreaming about the night we made love on the hood of your car. The night you drove like a maniac to the cabin to do it again.” She was smiling at him. “Hey wait a minute, if I remember correctly someone wasn’t leaving me alone while I was driving. It’s a wonder I made it to the cabin. I was ready to pull the car over and make love on the side of the road.” She laughed. “It was always special for us wasn’t it Michael? Every minute we shared always meant something didn’t it?”

Mike still saw the hurt in Josie's eyes. "Yes Josie girl. Every second I spent with you was embedded on my heart. I kept those memories, that's what pulled me through. I told Max that you were the one thing that could make jail seem like home. Every time I thought about you, I wasn't in that cell. I was like this holding you. I couldn't think of anything else while I was away from you." Josie looked at him and saw the honesty there. "But then why Michael? Why didn't you come back for me?"

Mike shook his head. "I did Josie, you were gone. I came to check up on you to see that you were happy, then I was coming here. When I got to where you lived you were gone. The house was empty and the neighbor told me you packed up and left. I figured once I got settled at the bar, I would find you again." Josie looked down away from him. "You mean it? You were going to find me?" Mike reached down and tilted her chin up. “Look at me Josie.” When Josie looked into his eyes Mike saw the tears there. “I mean it. But you found me first. I’m going to make it forever. Remember that.” Mike leaned in and kissed her lips softly. “Now lay back down here and get some sleep.” Josie shook her head no. “I’ll be right here Josie. I’m not going anywhere.” “Promise?” He smiled at her and said, “I promise you forever.” She laid back and closed her eyes, “I love you Michael, forever.” He smiled and pulled her up against him again.

Chapter 28

Mike woke up and Josie was gone. He panicked and jumped out of the bed, yelling her name, "Josie, where are you?" He didn't know where she was. He went to the bathroom but the door was open. Then he heard it. She was singing. He walked toward the sound. He found her in the kitchen. He stood in the doorway watching her move about and listening to her sing. She never sang for him like this before. She really had talent. He cleared his throat, she spun around and looked at him.

Josie was out of bed but left Mike sleeping. She didn't want to wake him. She went to the kitchen and was going to make something for breakfast. She looked at the calendar hanging on the refrigerator and said, "Oh my God. It's today." She ran to the phone and called the flower shop. She had an important delivery of flowers that had to arrive today. After she ordered the flowers she sat there thinking about Michael. He stayed with her all night and held her in his arms even though he wanted more. He really did love her. He was nothing like Jack. Mike was warm, caring, affectionate and full of love. Jack was full of hate and evil.

Josie was thinking about the dream she had last night. She was not brave enough to go naked under her dress but she was going to go shopping this morning to get some beautiful new underwear and a matching bra. Tonight was the night. She believed Mike and she trusted him with her life. She loved him and tonight would be special. She was going to make love to him again. She smiled to herself and started making her Mike a breakfast fit for a king.

“Michael, you’re up.” Josie looked at him and her eyes went to the opened pants. Wow what he did to her. Mike didn’t miss the shift in her eyes as he walked to her. He took her in his arms and kissed her. “Don’t you ever do that to me again. You scared the life out of me when I woke up and you weren’t in bed.” Mike was holding her. He was so close and so damn sexy. It took all Josie had in her to not move in on him now. Josie stretched up to kiss him again then she patted his ass. “I have a breakfast to cook. I wanted you to have a big wonderful breakfast because you have a big day ahead of you.” Josie smiled at him then turned to move back to her cooking.

Yes, Mike did have a big day ahead of him. He had to get the bar set for the band. He had to make sure everything was in order and working properly for the band. The lights, the acoustics and the electric. This was the first band he was bringing to the bar. He was hoping this was the start of many more to come.

Josie brought Mike out of his thoughts. “Grab a cup of coffee and go sit on the love seat. I’ll bring breakfast.” She smiled at him. He went over and kissed her on the cheek then down her neck as he slipped his arms around her waist. He just held her while she worked on the eggs and pancakes she had going in two separate pans. “You are going to spoil me Josie. I’ll want this, every morning.” Josie leaned back against him and sighed, “I’ll give you whatever you want as long as I can have every morning like this with you.” Mike turned her around to look at him. “That is a deal lady. I can make good on that. Take my words to the bank. I’ll be here every night into every morning as long as you’ll have me.”

Josie reached her arms up around Mike’s neck. She pulled him down to kiss his lips and she went for the demanding full force, I want you and I need you kiss. She parted his lips with her tongue. She demanded control of their kiss. Mike pulled her up against him, his hands squeezing her ass, grinding her against him. Within seconds he lifted her and she had her legs around his waist. Mike was pressed against her and he was losing control. He turned putting her ass on the kitchen table and was ready to start tearing into her clothes. That was when reason jumped into his head. Mike tore his mouth from hers and swore, "Damn it Josie! You are killing me. I can't do this right now. I, oh God, I need a cold shower. You drive me wild in seconds."

Josie smiled up at Mike. "I'm sorry, but I'm really not. Now get out of my kitchen because you are making it way too hot in here." Mike moved back and grinned at her, "You are going to be the death of me woman." Josie laughed over her shoulder at him and went back to her breakfast before it all burned. Mike took a coffee cup and went into the living room. Once there his cell phone rang. It was Max. Everything was okay at the bar but he wanted to confirm the set up time for the band and wanted to go over a few other issues. Mike told him to hang tight, he was going to have some breakfast then he'd be back to the bar. "No, I'm not bringing you a doggie bag Max." Just then Josie came through the door and said, "Yes you are." Josie laughed and Mike growled into the phone a goodbye since Max heard her response.

Josie sat down next to Mike and they ate their breakfast in the living room. Since being in the kitchen turned a little too heated she figured the living room would be a little safer. "I don't want to keep you here Mike. I know you have a lot to do today. I have a little shopping to do anyway." Mike looked at her, "Josie, promise me you don't go anywhere without someone with you." She looked at him, "I'm okay Michael. I don't need a babysitter. I'm going to go to the gym and then shopping. After that I'm coming home to get ready for tonight. I'm not going to fall apart again. I'm done letting Jack rattle me." Mike shook his head, "No! You need to promise me you are not going anywhere without someone with you. Promise me Josie or I'm not leaving."

Mike was angry and Josie was not sure how to respond. "Okay Michael. I'll call Miranda and ask her to go with me." He nodded, "Thank you. Call her now before I go." Josie got up and called Miranda, who said she was going to come over anyway. She added that she'd be happy to hit the gym then shopping with Josie. Josie relayed Miranda's acceptance of the shopping trip.

Mike helped Josie clean up and she, true to her word fixed a plate up for Max. He was getting ready to leave her when he took her in his arms. "Josie, I'm sorry. I just don't want you to be alone right now. I know Jack is out there. I don't want him to hurt you. You need to be more careful right now." She nodded, "I understand, but it's like I'm becoming his prisoner again." Mike looked at her and nodded that he understood. She was right. This wasn't going to be a solution. Jack was going to find time to do whatever he was going to do. They just had to be prepared. Mike left her with strict orders to not open the door for anyone but Miranda. Josie laughed at him and ushered him out the door.

Josie changed her clothes, put on her workout gear and waited for Miranda. Once she arrived she was full of questions. "So Mike spent the night? Well are you going to spill the beans? What happened and don't leave anything out!" Josie laughed at her. "Come on, let's go to the gym." Miranda followed her out the door, "Seriously, you are not going to tell me anything?" They walked to the gym and Josie was laughing at her friend. "Nothing happened. Honest. He was a perfect gentleman. He just held me while I slept. I had a nightmare, he woke me up and sat with me until I fell back to sleep."

Miranda looked at her, "For real? I don't believe you." Josie laughed at her, "If you want details you'll have to wait until tomorrow morning. Don't you breathe a word to anyone, but I have special plans for tonight." Miranda was all but skipping to the gym now. "I knew it wouldn't take long. You and he were made for each other. I'm so excited. Okay so my turn. I told Sarah last night." She reached out her left hand and showed Josie her ring. She gasped,

"Holy crap! Miranda that is incredible. I want details now, when? How?" Miranda was gushing, and she rarely gushed. But she told Josie all the details, including how the night Rod proposed she sent him off to take care of her. "Miranda! Why didn't you guys tell me what was going on? I feel terrible." Miranda smiled. "Don't, it was so much more incredible when he came home." They laughed and talked more as they entered the gym.

Josie and Miranda did their workouts and while on the treadmill Josie told Miranda her plan. She told of the plain burgundy dress and how it buttons almost like a shirt and that it has a gold belt that drapes around the waist. She told Miranda what she wanted was a lacey burgundy bra and maybe a thong. She hated them and didn't wear them but she thought it would be the perfect thing for under that dress. Miranda was laughing. "He is not going to know what hit him." Miranda paused and smiled, "Why tonight? What made your mind up?" Josie smiled, "That's a secret."

The girls finished their workout, heading to the store. Josie found exactly what she was looking for. They walked back to her apartment. Miranda left. Josie took a shower, and carefully laid out her outfit for tonight. She headed to the kitchen where she made something special just for her Mike for tonight.

Josie was going to go to great lengths to get ready tonight. Her make-up and her hair had to be just perfect. Josie picked up the phone and made a phone call to Max. She was going to need a little help to make this happen tonight.

Mike was barreling through everything that needed to be done. He wanted this to be perfect tonight. He was such a perfectionist when it came to the bar. He stood back and looked around the place. The band had just arrived and started setting up. Mike was watching them when he heard the front door open. Mike turned and saw the young boy coming with flowers. Mike went over to him. “Michael Albright?” Mike nodded. The boy handed the flowers over to him. Mike walked to the bar and unwrapped the flowers. There were a dozen yellow and red tipped roses. They were the fire and ice roses. He opened the card. ‘I haven’t forgotten what today is. I promise you the fire will be reignited tonight. All my love, Josie.’

Mike stood there for a minute. What was Josie talking about? What was today? Mike went to the calendar and looked at the date. He smiled and just then Max came around the corner. “Flowers? For me? Awe Mike you shouldn’t have.” He laughed and Mike laughed. “You ass, they’re from Josie.”

Max smiled, "What a girl! I told you if you didn't make her yours I'd steal her away." Mike glared at his friend. "Not on your life."

Josie was singing and putting on her make-up. She had it almost perfect. Then she started on her hair. She curled her hair, piece by piece with the curling iron. Once each strand was curled she pulled part of it up with a clip. She was almost ready. She sprayed a little perfume behind her ears, between her breasts and at her navel. She stood up and took off her robe. She dressed in her new undergarments, she slid the dress over her head, put on her jewelry and belt. She looked at herself in the mirror and said, "Get ready Michael. I'm running back to you. I hope you are ready. I hope I am too." Josie put a little lipstick on, slid on her high heels, grabbed her bag, purse and the box sitting on the kitchen counter just as her doorbell rang.

"Holy smokin' hottie!" Rod was standing at Josie's front door to escort her to the car. Ted was whistling from the driver's seat and Miranda and Sarah were smiling from ear to ear. Josie blushed at all the fuss the boys were making as she climbed into the car. "What's the special occasion Josie?" Ted asked. Miranda spoke for her, "Evidently it's a secret. She wouldn't even tell me. What's in the box?" Josie just smiled, "I told you it's a secret. Oh by the way guys, I don't think I'll need a ride home tonight." The girls oohed and aahhed and the guys just grinned. "I'll be sure the paramedics are close by the bar tonight and I'll notify the fire department so they don't run out when they see the smoke coming from the bar." Rod laughed as he said the words. Josie smiled, she couldn't wait for tonight.

Once the group arrived at the bar, Josie told them she was meeting Max at the side door. So they headed in before Josie. Max was there waiting for her and hurried her up to Mike's apartment. He told her to just turn the lock when she was done and slip in the side door. He would leave it propped open. She shook her head, "No Max, I'm going to go in the front door. It's okay. I'll be fine." She put the box on the counter and took her bag to his bedroom. She set up the candles exactly where she wanted them and had the lighter ready to go for when they came back upstairs tonight. She looked around and said, "Perfect." She left the apartment and locked the door as Max told her, then headed to the front door.

Chapter 29

Mike was behind the bar. He saw his friends come in but no Josie. He was concerned, but everyone waved and just headed for their table. He was getting their drinks together. He was taking them over to the table. "Hey guys. Where is ....." The words trailed off as the front door opened and Josie walked in. Every eye in the bar was on her. Mike almost dropped the drink he was placing in front of Miranda. "Whoa there, big fella." She took the drink. He didn't even acknowledge her. Mike left the tray and all at their table to head straight for Josie.

"Josie, oh my God you look gorgeous." She smiled at Mike and put her arms around his neck. "Nothing but the best for you Michael." She moved to kiss him and her friends were applauding. She laughed as she pulled away. Mike stood there unable to move.

“Josie, how in the hell am I going to be able to work tonight with you looking like that.” She pulled away from him and shrugged her shoulders and smiled. Mike went to the bar and looked at Max. Max shook his head, “I keep telling you, I’m ready to swoop in. She is looking killer in that dress.” Mike shook his head at his friend, “That dress sure the hell shouldn’t be legal.” Max looked at Mike, “Buddy, those legs, them eyes and that body shouldn’t be legal.” Mike scowled at his friend. “That’s my woman you are ogling.” Max laughed and slapped his friend on the shoulder, “Face it man, every guy in this bar is eyeing that beauty up. But she only has eyes for you. Damn shame, ugly mug like you getting the beauty.” Max walked away shaking his head. Mike just stood there staring right at Josie.

Josie sat there with her friends and they were discussing Miranda and Rod’s wedding.

Evidently they had waited long enough and they were going to get married at Rod's cabins, right by the lake. Miranda was telling them that she wanted Sarah and her to stand up for her as bridesmaids and that Ted was going to the best man. The girls were so involved in the planning that they were not paying any attention to the activity brewing around them. Ted and Rod were watching and all the single guys in that room were watching every move Josie made. One brave soul came toward the table and Mike saw him coming. He headed straight for the table and cut the guy off. The poor boy didn't stand a chance. He said excuse me to Mike and tried to move around him. Mike blocked him. "I don't think so. Go sit down, and tell all your friends, that is my woman. No one goes near her. Got it?" The kid shrunk away and was back with his friends all of whom were looking at Mike as if he was the devil. Mike grabbed the tray he had forgotten earlier and looked down at Josie and her legs she had crossed. He growled and walked away. All the girls laughed.

The band was incredible. The bar was packed and despite the distraction of Josie, Mike was having an awesome night. The money was flowing and the band was on fire. He hoped they would come back again. They were exceptional. They took a break halfway through the night. He saw the singer go over to his friends table. He shook hands with Ted and Rod. Then the guys introduced him to the women. He chatted with Josie for a few minutes. Then he headed to the bar for a drink. Mike nodded to him and handed him the soda. “This is a great crowd Mike. I’m glad we were able to come in here. I hope we can do this again.” Mike agreed and told him they’d have to talk later about setting up another date. As the guy was walking away he stopped, “You are one lucky guy. That lady of yours is incredible." Mike's eyes shot over to Josie and he grinned, "Yeah she is one hell of a woman."

The band was wrapping things up and the singer was thanking everyone for a special night. Mike went into the back to start getting ready for closing procedures. The he heard the singer say, "We have a special request tonight and I'd like you all to welcome Miss Josie Morris to the stage to help us with our final number." Josie was at the side of the stage with her heart in her throat. She took the stage and went to the center of it. She took the microphone and said, "Thank you. This song is a special surprise for my boyfriend on his special night. Happy Birthday Michael." He came out from the back room to see his Josie standing in front of everyone ready to sing.

The band started playing, Adele's, Lay Me Down and Josie was looking right toward

Mike. He was moving from behind the bar and out into the tables. He was so focused on Josie and her words. What was she saying? The song went on and he kept drifting closer and closer to the stage. He was standing in front of her as she continued the song.

Josie looked down at Mike as he now stood right in front of her. She locked eyes with him as she sang out the last chorus of the song. The fire was burning her up inside and the fire was burning in his eyes as well. Her voice strong, solid and silky as she finished singing to him.

The bar erupted into whistles and applause, the lead singer took the microphone from Josie and Mike climbed up on the stage and took her face in his hands, kissing her in front of everyone there. He leaned down to her and said in her ear, "Josie?" She said, "I'm all yours Michael, tonight if you'll have me. I want to be in your bed and wake up in your arms." Michael pulled back and looked into her eyes. "Oh hell yeah...are you sure?" He bent and kissed her again. Josie smiling, nodded her head yes and he took her hand, then led her off the stage.

The singer stopped them, "Anytime you want to sing with us Josie, you got it. That was smokin'." Mike turned and grinned but kept moving with his woman. They stopped at the table with their friends and they hugged Josie and told her that was awesome. The guys were looking at Mike like he was a lucky devil. Miranda said the words everyone else was thinking, "Damn, I need to get my man home. That was hot." They all laughed and said goodbye.

Mike was pulling Josie so fast through the bar Max was having trouble stopping him. "Mike stop, wait!" Mike turned around and looked like he wanted to murder his friend. "What?" Max took a step back. "Look I know you're in a hurry and all but you gotta pay the band." Mike stopped and looked at Max then looked at Josie then back to Max again, "Fuck!" Josie couldn't help but laugh behind him. "It's okay Michael. I'm not going anywhere. Why don't you give me your key and I'll head up to your apartment? I need to freshen up anyway." Mike turned to her, he took her in his arms. "I swear I will be two minutes and don't touch anything on yourself, you are already hotter than I can probably handle." He bent, kissed her and handed her the keys. She winked at Max and held up her hand and mouthed the words, five minutes. Max nodded and Josie disappeared.

Josie headed up the steps to the apartment and unlocked the door. She dropped her purse on the chair, headed into the bedroom. She lit all the candles she brought with her and folded the blankets of the bed down. She then went back into the kitchen area and opened the box. She took out a round layered birthday cake she had made for Mike. It was her homemade chocolate cake with buttercream icing. She put one candle on the top, when she heard him barreling up the steps she lit the candle and stood waiting for him holding a can of whip cream.

Mike thanked the band and apologized for running off but he had other things to attend to, and they all smiled and laughed. Mike didn't even care to stick around and comment. On his way through the bar Max said, "Don't do anything I wouldn't do." Mike stopped and said, "Oh believe me I plan on doing that and more." He turned and headed out the side door and up his steps to the apartment. Once inside there were no lights on but a glow came from the bedroom and Josie was standing next to a cake with a candle. "Happy Birthday Michael." He smiled. "I can't believe you remembered." Josie smiled. "I never forgot. Come over here and make a wish. Blow out your candle." He went to her and kissed her. "I already got my wish." He kissed her again and then turned to blow out the candle.

Josie was trying to slow her heart beat down. She felt like her heart was going to pound out of her chest. Mike turned back to her after blowing out the candle and he was kissing her neck and up to her lips. He was ready to devour her there. She felt his need. She was trying to slow him down. "Don't you want some cake and whip cream Michael?" He stopped to look at her like she was nuts. "As delicious as that cake probably is, I want what you have more. Maybe we can take the whip cream along?" He looked at Josie as if she were his prey. She pulled out of his grasp and said, "You need to slow down Michael. You're going to strip a gear." She put the whip cream on the counter and started backing away from him.

Mike laughed and followed her as Josie was backing out of the room, headed toward the bedroom. He followed her every movement. "Baby, I've been waiting for this moment for so long I only have one gear and that gear is vavoooooommmmm."

Josie laughed and started unbuttoning her dress. Top button first and slowly stepping back toward the bedroom. She got halfway down the dress and Mike was ready to pounce. She stopped him with her words. "Don't you think you better go lock the door?" He stopped, "Shit!" He turned and headed to the door to lock it. Josie finished unbuttoning her dress and stood with it hanging open. When he appeared in the doorway she slid the dress off her shoulders and let if fall down around her feet. She was still wearing the high heels.

Mike stood there staring at his Josie. That dress was incredible on her but the view he had now was glorious. The delicate undergarments, the candles twinkling over her body. Her body was incredible. Her breasts were just barely covered by her bra. The material was completely see through so he saw her nipples pressing against the fabric and the underwear she wore left very little to the imagination. The triangle of material that covered her was see through as well and the strings that went over her hips he knew came together in the back to slide down the crack of that gorgeous ass.

Josie was standing there letting Mike drink her all in. "God you are beautiful Josie, and you are all mine." He headed toward her and he could see the flicker in her eyes, it was desire mixed with a little fear. Mike knew she'd need him to slow it down but he didn't know how slow he could go. He had his hands on her in seconds. He took them down her sides and her hips and then around to her bare bottom. He kneaded her ass with his hands and pulled her against him. "Can you feel that Josie? Do you feel what you do to me?" She nodded her head and he took her lips. Softly at first and then he delved into that warm moist heat to meet her tongue with his.

Josie took her hands down Mike's stomach to his waist. He could feel her body trembling. He pulled back. "Don't be afraid Josie." She responded by unbuttoning his jeans and releasing the zipper. Mike put his hand up to her face and kissed her lips gently. "If you need to stop Josie, please stop me now. I don't think I can turn back if I go much further." Josie shook her head. "I'm not afraid of you, Michael. There is no turning back. We are just moving forward. There have been too many wasted years without you. I want you, I need you and I love you." She was pushing his pants down over his hips and he was impatient to get out of his clothes.

Mike let go of Josie to pull off his boots and pants almost falling over in the process. He pulled his shirt over his head and had her hoisted up with her legs around his waist. She reached up pulled the clip out of her hair. He heard her throw it across the room but couldn't take his eyes off of her. Her hair was falling around her face. While he held her she reached around unclasping her bra as she set her breasts free. She threw the bra across the room as well.

Mike went to the wall by the bed first. He pressed Josie's back up against it and kissed between her breasts first. Josie arched her back and pressed her breasts out to him and he answered. He had one of her nipples in his mouth instantly. He was running his tongue over and over it then he moved to the other breast to do the same. Josie was arching her back off the wall toward him pressing herself out to him and pulling the back of his head tighter to her. Josie was losing her mind. She wanted more. Mike grabbed ahold of her as he spun her to the bed. He laid her down, slowly sliding over her, covering her body with his.

"Josie, I've dreamed of this night for so long. I don't know how much control I'm going to be able to have, but I am going to try my best. I want this to be so good for you." Mike pulled himself up and grabbed her panties. He slid them over her hips and down her legs. When he got to her feet he saw that the heels were still in place. "These shoes, God how they made your legs look walking across the floor. I hate to take them off, but I want you completely naked. He slipped the shoes off and they hit the floor with a thump. He stood taking off his underwear, then was back down between her thighs. He reached with his hand first. He rubbed her and caused shock waves through her body. He slipped his finger inside her. She tensed up.

"Easy Josie girl. It's just you and me. I'm trying to love you. Don't worry, I'm not going to hurt you. Nice and easy sweet girl." Josie's heart was in her throat. God she wanted him, but him being down there touching her was bringing back horrible memories. No, she wasn't going to do this. This was her Michael. He loved her and wants to touch her, she's safe in his arms. Josie reached down and touched his hand, his finger still inside of her but not moving.

"Yes Michael. Touch me, feel me, make love to me. I'm ready, I'm ok." Josie pulled his hand and moved his finger inside her further. She was ready for him. He locked eyes with her and he whispered her name. She slowly lowered herself back down to the bed and let him explore. Mike wanted to feel more of her, but first he needed just a taste. He moved in and suckled her, then pulled her legs over his shoulders and grabbed her bottom to pull her to him. He stuck his tongue inside of her and he saw her raise off the bed. He kept moving his tongue and plunging as deep as he could. She was so soft, so warm and so sweet. She was his now, all his. He had to have her.

Mike rose up and came over top of her. "Oh God Michael. I had forgotten what this was supposed to be like. I'm ready, take me, now. I need you." Josie was ready to burst she was in agony waiting for him. He was ready too. He looked at her lying there. He couldn't believe she was real. He took his hand and brushed over her one last time then he moved his hips in and plunged into her. She cried out his name. Her legs wrapped around him and he was rocking deep inside of her. There was nothing slow about their love making. It was hard. It was desperate. It was needy. Josie whimpered, "Michael, yes....I need more." Mike was answering, he pushed deep inside of her growling at how she felt wrapped around him. "Jesus Josie, you're so tight around me. God I can't hold back much longer. It feels so good." She was raising her hips to meet his every thrust when she couldn't hold back any longer, she was chanting "Yes, Michael, yes." He pressed hard into her, he felt her tightening, and squeezing him as she all but screamed his name and it was all he needed, as one they climaxed together exploding. He felt her pulsing around him as he moved slower, trying to extend her orgasm. He watched her face as she fell back down to earth. He felt his release down to his soul, pulsing into her. She felt like she was flying and he felt like he was finally home.

Chapter 30

Josie and Mike were wrapped up in each other lying in the bed together. Neither one spoke, neither one moved other than to gently stroke one another's arm or back. The movement was more of a reality check to be sure they weren't dreaming. Josie was the first to stir she came up on her elbow and looked at him. "Do you want some of your birthday cake?" Mike laughed at her. "Sure, but only if you serve it as you are." She looked at him and scowled. "Is that a challenge?" He reached up and kissed her lips, "Oh hell yeah." She got up, headed to the kitchen, got him some cake and brought the whip cream can back to the bedroom. He smiled at her, "Do I get a drink too?" Josie rolled her eyes at him heading back to the kitchen and grabbed two bottles of water. She stood beside the bed holding the two bottles of water. "Is there anything else you want?" Mike reached out grabbed her arm and pulled her to the bed, then reached for the whip cream can, "Oh hell yeah."

Mike was kissing her as soon as she hit the bed. Josie laughed. "I thought you wanted some cake." He smiled, shook up the whip cream can to spray onto her nipples. He started licking and then suckling first off of one nipple then the other. "I can have my cake later. I'm sure it's delicious Josie girl, but I love what I have right here. Josie smiled, "Whatever you like my sweet Michael."

Mike and Josie were both unable to get enough of each other. It seemed that as soon as they cooled off they were back at it again. Mike drove her to heights she'd never known. He was stroking her body with his hands, raising her desire. He sucked on her nipples causing them to erect peaks, then he would tug gently biting the nipples. She moaned his name, holding his head to her. His hand rolled down over her abdomen, reaching between her thighs. He stroked her wet folds, slipping easily inside of her. He used his thumb to press on her clit as he pressed as deep as he could inside her. He looked up at her face as she gasped, God, it was the sexiest sound he'd ever heard. Her hips were lifting and rocking against his hand and she was getting close to an orgasm. He could see it on her face. He could feel the urgency in her motion. "Cum for me Josie, let me make you feel good. Let it go." He lifted his fingers up against the wall deep inside hitting her at just the right angle. Her hips bucked. She moaned, his name flowing over her lips. "Oh God Michael, yes, God, don't stop!" Mike smiled at her words, never would he stop, nothing will ever stop him from touching her again. She was his.

Josie's hips slowed, Mike's strokes slowed and he slipped from inside of her. He kissed her neck, nibbling his way up the side of her neck, to nibble gently on her ear. He whispered in her ear, "I'll never have enough of you Josie." He slid over top of her and gently eased inside of her. Her hands came down his back, stroking gently sliding to touch him. She looked into his eyes smiling at him. "I never want you to stop making love to me Michael, never." She took her hand down his face like she had done the first night he came back to her and so many nights in the past. Assuring herself that he was real, letting her fingers touch his face, love pouring into her soul. Their lovemaking was a slow steady meeting of body and soul. Mike pushed deep inside her and held himself there. Josie rocked her hips feeling him deep within her. Her neck arched and he took advantage of her exposed neck, sucking, licking and nipping her skin.

Josie couldn't stand it, she wanted more. She pushed against his chest and Mike mistaking it for panic, pulled back and away from her. "Josie," That was all she needed, she pushed him back against the bed and straddled his hips. She took him in her hands and stroked him slowly before sliding him back inside her where she wanted him. Mike groaned at the feel of her hands on him, then let a tense curse slide out as she slid him back inside of her.

Josie sat over him, rubbing her hands over his chest as she slowly rocked her hips sliding him in and out of her. Josie played with his nipples on his chest and then bent to kiss and lick them. "Jesus Josie, what you do to me." His hands were tangled in her hair and he was pulling her to his mouth. She raised her hips to slide slowly back down against him. She did this several times, as Mike kissed her lips, thrusting his tongue against hers, moaning inside her mouth. Josie pulled away from him and sat back up to stare down at him. “This is how it should be forever, Michael. I want this forever.” Mike reached to where their bodies were joined and rubbed her clit as she moved over him. “Yes, baby. I’m going to give you forever. I promise you that.” She rocked her hips harder, faster to match the building desire within her. Mike raised his hips to hers pressing harder, deeper within her. “Damn baby, I’m so close I can’t hold back much longer.” He didn’t have to with his words Josie’s body shuddered and her head fell back and she was moaning as she rocked herself through her orgasm once again. Mike deep inside her felt himself slip and before he could think, spilled himself deep within the only woman he’d ever loved.

Josie was glad that she was with Mike again. She never wanted to be without him. She laid in his arms so she could hear his steady breathing. He was falling asleep. "Happy birthday, Michael. I love you." He pulled her closer and kissed the top of her head, "Thank you Josie. I will never forget this birthday. This is the year I got all I've ever wanted. I love you too." He pulled her in and tucked her against him. "Go to sleep Josie." She laid there her backside up against him and his arms wrapped around her waist. She was where she belonged. She was loved and finally with the love of her life. Everything was perfect.

Jack stood out in the shadows looking up at the apartment. "I'll wait. Our time will come. You won't get rid of me that easily you whore. Your man will see his end too. I promise you that. Enjoy now because soon there will be hell to pay for your actions Josie." He was not a patient man but he would wait for now. He wasn't going to be told what to do and he certainly wasn't leaving this town without his cheating wife.

Josie was dreaming again. She was seeing Mike's face and he was saying something to her. "What Michael? I don't understand what you are saying?" She looked at him and he was yelling, "Run Josie!" It was too late Jack had his hands on her and he was pulling her to the bed and quickly tying her hands and lying on top of her. She was thrashing about kicking, crying and screaming, "Michael help me! Michael! Where are you? Help me! Don't let Jack take me again, don't let him!" He was laughing and saying, "Michael can't help you anymore, you belong to me. Forever Josie and don't you forget it." Josie broke free and was running from him.

"Josie! Breathe! Josie, it's me Michael! Wake up!" She felt someone shaking her and she was on the verge of panic. Her eyes flew open and her hands were flailing. She finally was coming awake, focusing gradually and it was Mike that she was fighting. "Michael?" She turned her head looking around the room as best she could since Mike had her pinned down. "He's here!" Mike let go of her arms and smoothed her hair out of her face. "Shhhh.... Josie. It's okay. He's not here. It's just us. You are safe."

Josie laid there silently. She knew Jack was here in town. She could feel the evil. She could feel the chills running through her. She shivered. Mike pulled the blankets over them pulling her closer. "Come here Josie girl. I got you." She laid there in his arms and enjoyed it while she could. She knew that it wouldn't last. Jack was coming for her and she wasn't sure if she would survive this round with him. But one thing was certain, she would go with him if it meant her Michael was safe.

Josie got out of bed heading to the kitchen. She looked in the refrigerator and there was no food there. She found the coffee and made some. After her nightmare she couldn't fall back to sleep. She just laid there with Mike holding her and listened to him breathe. She was not sure what she would do without him, but she knew she couldn't let Jack hurt him. She never wanted him to hurt Mike. That would kill her. She sat there stirring her coffee never hearing Mike get out of bed.

Mike wrapped his arms around Josie and she nearly took his head off. "Jesus Josie! It's me!" She spun around and looked at him. "I'm so sorry Michael. I didn't hear you get out of bed." He was bare chested and had his jeans over his hips without being zipped, nothing else on underneath. He was a vision to her. Josie was wearing her dress with none of the buttons fastened, and nothing underneath. She wrapped her arms around Mike's waist. "I'm sorry!" He stroked her back. "It's okay sweetie, but you are fine. I promise you." Mike pulled her back to look at him. She smiled up at him. "I know. I'm okay, you just startled me that's all."

Mike walked over to the counter to get some coffee. He turned his back to Josie. "Oh my God Michael! Did I do that to your back?" He had scratches all down his back. He turned to her grinning. "Oh yeah baby! It was all you!" He walked back over to her and put his coffee back on the counter, he took her in his arms, "and I'd take more of them as long as I can have all of you again." She smiled up at him. "I don't know how you do it to me but I can't control myself with you." He shook his head. “Don’t even try, just do whatever you want. I can take it baby.” He bent to kiss her he pushed her dress off of her and he carried her back to the bedroom again.

Mike was suckling on her neck and Josie yelled. “Hey don’t you mark me up! I gotta go to work you know.” He kept suckling then said, “I don’t care! Anyone that sees it will know you are my girl.” She laughed and let it go. “I think everyone at the bar last night knows I’m your girl. You scared the life out of that poor young man that was trying to approach me.” He looked at her, “Serves him right.” She swatted him. “Michael, he was harmless.” Mike responded, “And he’s going to stay harmless. You looked so amazing last night Josie. I can’t even tell you what it did to me to see you walk in that bar. Your body is incredible. You are so sexy and every inch of you turns me on.” He was looking at her and she was feeling uncomfortable. She tried to pull away or pull the covers up and he stopped her. “Why are you hiding?” She was pulling away from him completely, he didn’t like it. “Josie! What is going on? Why are you pulling away from me now?”

Josie sat up trying to pull the blankets over her. “You don’t understand. Stop looking at me!” He was getting angry. “Why? What don’t you want me to see?” She was crying and she was so tired from not sleeping. She stood up dropping the blankets. She turned toward him and pointed. “This is what I’m hiding! Look at me! I have scars and marks all over me. I don’t want you to see them. I hate to see them. It’s a constant reminder that Jack touched me, that he’s still out there and I’m still his wife. It’s a reminder of all the hell I endured at his hands and it’s ugly. I’m ugly when I’m not covered up. In the candle light it's fine, but in the daylight, well it's not as forgiving."

Mike was out of the bed like lightening striking. He hit is knees in front of Josie. "Damn it Josie! If I could change it, I would, but I can't. I know Jack hurt you and those scars you bear I have to live with the rest of my life because it is my fault they happened. Mine! You did nothing wrong to deserve this." He ran his hands over the scars and he looked up at her with tears in his eyes. When he spoke again, his voice was rough with emotion and cracking. He didn't hide it. "I was a coward! I never told you the truth. I never trusted that you would love me no matter what. I didn't want you to see me behind bars and I didn't want you to feel obligated to wait for me. I thought I was doing what was best for you. I fucked up! I did this to you and yet, you came to my bed. You opened your heart and your body to me. Don't close me out now. Don't run away from me. Not now! Not when we are so close to having what I wouldn't allow us to have so many years ago." A tear rolled down his cheek and Josie reached down to wipe it away. "Come back to bed with me Josie. Let me see you. All of you! Let me kiss the bad memories away." He stood up and she moved with him back to the bed. He laid beside her where he took his hand down her body and stopped at each mark on her. He touched each one with his hand, then traced each with his finger, then took his lips pressing a kiss against each one.

Josie was trembling as Mike touched her. The scars were hard to bear. She hated seeing them. Most of them came from Jack cutting her, but some came from the beatings. He would hit her with things or throw glasses at her until they broke. Then he'd throw her down on the broken glass until she was cut and bleeding. The memories of each of those scars was more painful now seeing Mike look at them. “I can’t bear to have you look at them. I hate that I was so weak, that he was able to do this to me.” Mike looked at her, “Josie, you weren’t weak. You are the strongest woman I know. To survive all of this took strength and courage.” He continued looking at her and he was raging inside with anger. Someday he would find Jack and God help him when he did.

Mike worked his way down Josie’s torso touching each scar and then kissing it. Once he got to her navel he licked it. He went down between her legs. He was kissing her and licking her. She had forgotten all the reasons why she had been upset. He was devouring her and she was arching her hips to him. He was making her head spin and she reached down to pull him closer to her. He took her legs pulling them up over his shoulders and he lifted her beautiful, toned ass squeezing it as he raised her up to get a different angle. His tongue was stroking her and making her crazy. He moaned against her, whispering against her, "So good, baby, you taste so good." She felt the tidal wave that was ready to crash over her. "Oh Michael! I can't breathe, oh God!" He just kept stroking her while she whimpered, begged, then half screamed half moaned her release. He licked her till he felt her come down, but didn't give her long to recover as he came up and over her. He needed her now. He drove into her. She was instantly ready for him. He was pumping in and out of her and she was rising up on the wave again.

"Michael, oh my God. It's happening again." He chuckled, "Yes Josie girl. I'll always take care of you. As many times as I can." She had never experienced any of these feelings, well not for a very long time at least and certainly not since she had been with Mike years before.

Mike was fierce now, he was growling in his throat and he was trying to erase the memories of what Jack did to Josie. He was trying to leave her with only the thoughts of him inside of her and the memory of him kissing each one of those scars. So she would see that they didn't matter, she didn't need to hide them from him. "Cum with me Josie, oh God! Just cum with me!" He was ready but he held back. He saw her rising to him and he heard it, the strangled cry in her throat and he buried himself inside of her. They came apart in that bed together. Josie had tears rolling down her face. Happy tears, tears of completeness. They were tears of extreme bliss and exhaustion, and tears knowing that she wouldn't have this forever.

Mike laid his head on Josie's chest and slowed his breathing. "God Josie! I can't get enough of you." She was slowly catching her breathe. "You are going to have to get your fill soon or I'm not going to be able to walk." He pulled her close and nuzzled her neck. "Okay, hint taken. I'll run you a warm bath and I will leave you alone. How about I run and get us some breakfast to go with that cake I have out there?" Josie laughed and agreed. Mike ran Josie a warm bath. He got dressed then he came to her to tell her the bath was ready. He couldn't resist. He scooped her up into his arms. "Michael! What are you doing?" He grinned and carried her into the bathroom. "I'm taking you to your bath." He took her and gently eased her into the water. He kissed her lips and told her he would be back soon. She laid back in his tub just letting the warm water run over her. If only this could last forever! Damn Jack!

Chapter 31

Josie finished her bath. She got dressed with the clothes she brought in her bag. She was packing up her things to go back to her apartment. She wasn't sure what was going to happen next. She didn't really think that out. She had wanted to just stay right where she was but she liked living in town. She was close to work, her friends and shopping. She also liked being out here and the quiet. It was a short drive to the mountains, which made it all the more appealing. She was pretty much torn. She knew she wanted to be with Mike, but did it really matter where they were? He needed to be close to the bar. She could drive to work and town. If he wanted her to she would move with him. She didn't mind giving up her apartment and location. She just wanted to be with him.

Mike came back to the apartment and when he walked in he saw her bag sitting on the sofa. “Where are you going?” Josie looked at him. “I suppose I’m going to go home after breakfast. I don’t know, why?” Mike put the bag with breakfast down and he turned away from her. “I guess I thought, well I don’t know what I thought.” Josie busied herself taking the food out of the bag and putting a slice of cake down for both of them. Mike came over to the counter and stood there waiting for her to stop. Josie kept moving, trying to find something to keep her busy. She didn’t know where this conversation was going. She couldn’t find anything else to occupy her so she sat down at the counter and waited.

Mike was thinking about what next. He couldn’t ask Josie to give up her apartment. But would she want him there? He didn’t like living above the bar. He would give that up in a heartbeat. Her apartment was small so he could keep unnecessary items here and take just the essentials with him. He looked at her now as she settled and stopped avoiding him. "Josie, I want us to be together." She looked at him and nodded. "I would like that too."

Mike looked at her, "What if I moved in with you? I know your place is small but I wouldn't need all my stuff, just the essentials. I was thinking about buying some land. I didn't yet because I was hoping that we would make that decision together. We could decide where to live. I would have a house built for us." Josie was looking at him like he was crazy or so he thought. "Josie? What are you thinking?"

Josie looked down for a brief moment then looked at Mike. "I think that it sounds like everything I've ever wanted. I just can't believe that all this is real. Michael, I've waited a long time to be with you. I've wanted to live with you for so long. I wanted to marry you, have a home and children." She paused and he reached for her hands. "I want all that too. I will wait if you're not ready, but I thought after last night we were ready to move forward." Mike got down on his knees in front of her. "I want to marry you Josie. Will you marry me?" Josie looked at him like he was crazy again. She started to cry. "I'm already married." She covered her face and cried.

Mike stayed on the floor knelt before Josie. He forgot about Jack. Damn him! He got up and went to the bedroom. He found what he was looking for in seconds. Of course he did because he only looked at it every day. He went back to her. He knelt back down in front of her. "Josie please look at me." When Josie finally looked down at him he started to speak.

"I know you are still married. That won't be forever. I will make sure of that. You will be free of him one day and when that day comes," Mike reached in his pocket and pulled out the ring box he'd had since he knew her all those years ago. It was stored in a safety deposit box until he was released from jail. He opened the box and looked at her. "I want you to be my wife Josie. I've always wanted that. I've had this ring since before I went to jail. I wanted to give it to you so many times, but I just didn't feel like I had the right back then. I wasn't the man you deserved. I realize now I was all kinds of wrong and I want to start now, never taking another minute for granted. Please Josie, tell me you'll marry me."

Josie was crying again and was torn from looking at the ring and him. She was so surprised. Mike really had loved her all those years ago. He was asking her for promises that she didn't know if she could keep. "Michael,

I've always wanted to marry you. Nothing would make me happier, but..." Mike stood up, "No buts! That was a yes to me." He slipped the ring on her finger and he kissed her. "I don't need any buts Josie. I know that this is the way things belong. You wear my ring. This is my promise to you. It will happen." She nodded and she hoped in her heart he was right. "Yes Michael, I've always wanted to marry you but I hope you know I have no guarantees. I don't know if I'll ever be free to marry you and I'm not sure I can have children which I know you want. As far as where to live, that is easy, I want to live wherever you are. That is home for me." He smiled at her last words.

The two sat and ate breakfast, Josie couldn't stop looking at her hand. She smiled at Mike. Even if it was never to happen at least she knew her Michael wanted to commit to her.

He loved her and wanted to be her husband. They decided for now they were going to stay at Josie's until they figured out everything else. He told her it was because he wanted her to be close to work and her friends. Truthfully, Mike wanted her close to Ted and Rod for protection.

Josie and Mike left after he packed up some of his clothes. He would come back later to get some more things. Right now he wanted to go wherever Josie was. He drove Josie in his truck to her apartment in town. Josie and Mike were putting his things away and she was smiling the whole time. She had almost forgotten about Jack.

After putting Mike's things away, Josie told him they needed to go to the grocery store. He told her okay, but he wanted to make one stop first. She couldn't imagine where he wanted to go. So she went willingly with him and when he pulled up in front of the orphanage. She looked at him in surprise. "Michael! What are we doing here?" He looked at her. "I have been coming here to see Rachel. I know how important she is to you and I needed to see her, to meet her. I needed to see who she was and what we thought about each other. So I've been coming as often as I can. I met with Megan Tate. I filled out a request for adoption and I had Ted and Max come see Megan on my behalf. I told you Josie, I want you to be happy. I want you to have everything you want. I have been working on this because I didn't know what would happen. I mean would they approve me or would I be what stands in your way of getting her?"

Josie shook her head. "I've missed Rachel. I have been distancing myself from her because I knew I needed you in my life and with Jack not letting me out of my marriage I knew that I would never adopt her with the threat of him. Plus, I wasn't sure if you would be a factor if I finally was free of Jack. I didn't want to not be with you. I made the decision to try and move forward, to let Rachel maybe be adopted by people who would love her like I did." Mike sat there and watched Josie. "I want you to go in and see her with me. I think somehow, some way we will find a way to have our family, and Josie, Rachel is a part of that family. I love her so much. I can't even think about giving her up." Josie had tears in her eyes and she nodded. "I would love to see her with you. I imagined you two together, now I get to see it for real. I can't believe you did all this for me. I must be the luckiest girl in the world." He took her hand and kissed it. "I'm the luckiest man alive and once I have you as my wife and Rachel as my daughter, there isn't anything more I could ever ask for."

Josie and Mike walked into the orphanage hand in hand. They stopped at the administration office, checked with Megan to be sure they could see Rachel. But Megan had asked for a moment of Josie's time. She told Mike to go ahead. Once they were alone Megan told Josie what Mike had just told her. He filed an application and Ted and Max came in to speak on his behalf. She looked at Josie and said, "Honestly I didn't think there was a chance for his application to be approved. Especially since you two aren't married. Then I saw them together and well, I put in a good word for him as well. Josie, I can honestly say that Rachel has never responded to anyone the way she responds to you and she is extremely cautious with men, but she just adores Mike. From what I saw the feeling is mutual. I am going to do all I can." Josie thanked her and headed off to see Rachel.

Josie stood in the doorway and watched Mike with Rachel. They were sitting and chatting. Rachel was sitting in his lap and she was squeezing his face. She was intently talking to him and his full attention belonged to that little girl. She was talking away and Mike was smiling at her. Then he was tickling Rachel and she dissolved into explosive giggles. Mike looked up and saw Josie watching them. He stopped tickling Rachel, bent down and whispered to her.

Rachel looked up, saw Josie and lit up. She was on her feet and running. Josie reached down and scooped Rachel up into her arms. "Mama Josie! I was worried about you. I missed you. Have you been very busy? Daddy Michael said you've been real busy working hard. He also said you've been singing. Sing fireflies!"

Josie laughed trying to keep up. She told Rachel that she had gone away for a few days to some cabins. She was delighted and clapping her hands "I want to go to cabins too. When can we go?" Josie looked at her then at Mike. He shrugged at her. Josie walked over and sat down next to where Mike was. "Rachel. I can't just take you to the cabins. I would get into a lot of trouble. I love that you love Mike and me so much that you call us Mama and Daddy, but we can't be getting ahead of things here. I don't want you to get your hopes up sweetie." Rachel looked at Michael then at Josie. "I know where I'm going to live. It's okay, you may need more time than me to adjust, but I know I am going to be with you and Daddy Michael."

Josie looked at Mike for help and he had tears in his eyes. She knew he would be no help. "Sing fireflies!" Josie obliged and

Michael and Rachel were swaying in front of her. She couldn't help but smile. They said goodbye to her, were leaving the orphanage, headed to the grocery store.

Mike knew Josie had been extra quiet. Going through the store she was very distracted but he didn't want to get into things in public. He would wait until they were back home. Josie picked up a few things at the store and was trying to formulate what she needed but she just couldn't focus. She kept thinking of that little girl. The way she looked at Mike and her. How could she ever break Rachel's heart? There was no way she would get custody. That lady told her they needed to be married and with Jack still in the picture there was no way for them to be married and together as a family.

Mike and Josie got home, quietly putting away the groceries. Josie was reaching to put something away when he came and took it out of her hands. He pulled her to look at him. “What is going on Josie? You’ve barely said two words since we left the orphanage. Talk to me.” Josie looked at Mike and told him about the conversation with Megan. Mike’s reaction to this was elation and Josie just thought that he was missing the big piece to this problem. It had nothing to do with him. It was her problem. She was going to be the reason that they couldn’t have Rachel. The mistake she made by marrying Jack. That was going to continue to haunt her.

Mike drove Josie to the gym because she said she needed to work out. He told her he’d be back in an hour and to stay with people. She nodded and he went to do a few errands. He was true to his word and was back in an hour. He watched her on the treadmill. She was determined, self-assured and a million miles away as she ran on that machine. He just wished she would see that now that they had each other nothing was going to stand in their way. He would just have to make her believe.

Josie finished her workout. When she stepped off the treadmill she saw Mike. She wondered how long he'd been there. She felt a little better after her workout but she still was feeling a little confused and hopeless. They got into Mike's truck and drove to the apartment. When Josie opened the door she gasped.

Josie looked around the room and all she saw everywhere were the fire and ice roses like she had sent to Mike. There were dozens of them everywhere. "Michael!" He came up behind her and wrapped his arms around her waist. "Welcome home baby." She turned in his arms and kissed him. He lowered her to the floor and there in the middle of their living room they made love, surrounded by the beautiful aroma of those roses. They took their time, there was no hurry with their lovemaking. He took great pleasure and pride in touching every inch of her body, and she was getting acquainted with him and the sensuality she had lost after being with Jack. Josie moaned as Mikel touched her. She loved the feel of his hands on her body. She loved the feel of him inside of her. Once they had stripped off their clothes Josie felt a little uncomfortable. She was trying to feel sexy, she was trying to feel like the seductress that Mike deserved. She was just feeling a bit inadequate. Mike could feel the shift in her. He could see the look on her face. She was trying to feel beautiful even though she didn't think she was anymore. She kept trying to hide her body against his and he wasn't having it.

Mike pulled her over on top of him, "Make love to me Josie. I want you to set yourself free." She was trying to move away from him. "No, damn it Josie girl. You are in there somewhere. Come back to me." He took her head in his hands and he kissed her. "It's just you and me, no one watching and nothing is right or wrong. You do what feels good to you. Just like early this morning. Except the sun is streaming in the window, and yes I am going to look at your body, I'm going to see you, all of you, but you are going to take charge. I'm just along for the ride." He slid his hands down her sides and he laid them on the floor. "I'm yours, what do you want with me?" She had tears in her eyes. He had given her so much and he had done so much for her, she had to do this. She needed to do this. But what if.....No she was not going down that road. Live like there was no tomorrow. That was what she needed to do.

Josie straddled Mike's waist and she slowly raised herself up to look in his eyes. She reached her hands out to touch him. She started with his face. She ran her fingers through his hair and then down his face. She rubbed her hands over his shoulders and down his arms. She touched his chest. She ran her hands down his chest to where she sat astride him. This was her moment with him. This was what she had dreamed of for so many years. She was going to not regret this moment. She wasn't going to waste it. Josie was finding herself again. She rubbed herself against him and felt his immediate reaction. She wanted to feel him. She sat back to explore him. She touched him at first like she wasn't sure then she took a hold of him feeling him in her hands. She felt how solid he was. He was ready for her and she wanted him too, but she waited a few minutes just trying to get more courage.

Josie moved back over Mike, she guided him inside of her. She was just sinking into him and he waited for her. He didn't move he let her take the lead. He wanted her to do whatever she needed to do in order to feel whole again and to feel how beautiful, she was to him. She was starting to move her hips and she was rocking on him. She was letting herself get lost in the feel of him.

Josie took her hands to her body and was running her hands down her body. She was touching herself her breasts, reaching down her abdomen. She was letting herself go and Mike couldn't take anymore. He reached out to take her breasts in his hands. He rubbed her and peaked her nipples. Her head went back as she rocked her hips harder on him. He was ready to lose it. He wanted to move with her but he didn't dare. She sank down and tried to get more of him. She was surprised when there was more. She shifted sinking down farther. She was rocking a little more steadily and he lifted to meet her. He made her eyes flare. He saw her in there. His Josie girl. She wasn't hiding anymore and she was coming to life on top of him. He needed her to stay with him. He held her hips and pulled her to him as he thrust up into her. She was ready to explode. "Michael, you make me feel more than I ever thought I could. I love you!" With that she exploded around him and he thrust up into her and met her explosion.

Josie laid on top of Mike, curled up on his chest. She didn't want to move him out of her, she didn't want to break the contact. Mike was gently brushing his hand over her shoulder and back. He didn't know how he could have been without her for so long. His whole life was finally just starting to come together. Now all he needed was to make her his wife and have Rachel embedded in their family. Then all would be right and worth the sacrifices he'd made. They laid there until finally Mike shifted her, when she met his eyes, he said, "Let's go to bed baby. I just want to hold you in my arms."

Chapter 32

The alarm rang. Josie shut it off and looked next to her. Mike laid their sleeping stirring only slightly when the alarm went off. She got up, took her shower and got dressed for work. She was in the kitchen cooking breakfast when he came in. He was moving for the coffee when he dipped his head to give her a kiss, then mumbled a good morning. She giggled and kept scrambling the eggs.

"How come you are so beautiful and chipper in the morning?" Mike said to Josie. She laughed at him then answered, "Because I had a wonderful night. For the first time in a long time, I didn't have a nightmare wake me from sleep. I have a beautiful day ahead of me. I slept in the arms of the man I love. I pretty much have what I've always wanted, why wouldn't I be chipper?" He smiled at her and took a sip of his coffee. She had a point.

Maybe he'd finally become a morning person. Oh hell no he thought to himself. "Okay you win. You can be chipper but I'll be chipper after two more of these." He raised his mug at her and she laughed. "Get dressed. Breakfast will be ready in a flash. I gotta get going so I'm not late for work."

Mike went to get dressed then came back to the kitchen to eat. The two of them sat and talked over their breakfast about the plans for later. She was going to meet him at the bar tonight and stay at his place so that he could be at work and she would be close by him. He didn't want to leave her alone.

She kissed him goodbye heading back to the kitchen to clean up the dishes. She heard the knock on the door. Honestly he would forget his head if it wasn't attached. She gave him the key. He must have forgotten it. She raced to the door, flew it open expecting to find

Mike only Jack was standing in front of her. She quickly recovered trying to slam the door but he was in the doorway and kicking it closed while grabbing her by the throat. “Is that anyway to greet your husband? What have you been up to you little tramp? I saw him leaving so I know you are alone. He was here all night. I guess he likes having leftovers.” He laughed at his own joke and was pushing her up against the entryway wall. She was in a panic. First trying to move his hand so she could breathe and second because she didn’t know what hell he would bring this time.

“Jack!” Josie gasped. “Let me go! I can’t breathe!” She gasped and all he did was squeeze harder laughing. He let his grip loosen as he pushed her up the steps into the living room. He looked around while he still had a grip on her. “Well what do we have here? Flowers? Awe how sweet!” He pushed her down roughly to the ground. She banged her head on the table and tried to get up. He put his foot on her saying in the voice she hated. "Stay down! When I want you to get up I'll tell you."

She was not going to be Jack's victim. She yelled at him, "This is my home and you are not welcome here." She pushed his foot off of her starting to get up. He grabbed her by the arm pulling her the rest of the way up, then punched her in the face. "Who do you think you are talking to? You will respect me. I am your husband you little cunt!" He Josie was enraged. slapped her this time across the face. She felt her lip split and the blood start to trickle down her chin.

Josie wasn't going down without a fight she surprised Jack by swinging and punching him. He stumbled back for a second she thought Josie wasn't going down, she would get away. She headed for the front door and he caught her by the back of her head slamming her into the front door face first. She heard the click of the knife Josie and she shuddered. He pulled her away from the door back to where they had been. He had her with his arm around her throat, keeping the knife within eye sight. “You want to play. Let’s play.”

Jack took the knife and cut Josie’s arm. The blood was warm running off of her. “How many more slices would you like? I can keep going.” She wasn’t going to go down without a fight. She stomped on his foot then kicked his shin. He still held onto her but he was mad now. He flung her and she wiped out the table with some of the roses. She felt the pain of the shattered vases on her side and back. She tried to get up and he kicked her. She flew onto her back. He now stood on her throat with his foot. “You think you can fight me? You are sadly mistaken. I thought you had learned your lesson before. I guess you think you are something now. Strutting around town with that guy. I'm sure you can't stop thinking about me when you are with him."

Josie huffed out a laugh as best she could. "More like you never enter my mind. Michael touches me in ways you never could or will." Jack bent down ripping her shirt off of her, he then moved pulling her to her feet. He pushed her against the wall and the glass on the picture she had hanging there broke from the contact of her head hitting it. He had her seeing stars after that blow to the head. But it was worth it she thought. After slamming her into the wall he dropped her and she crashed down on the floor again. Josie felt the glass under her. She had some pain in her back so she was sure there was glass there as well. Jack stood over her and she could hear him seething. He was really mad. She didn't look up at him she just sat there trying to get her bearings back. God please help me she thought!

Mike was so happy driving back to the bar. He couldn't wait for tonight. He was going to clean up the apartment today to make room for her to hang some clothes and store her things. He wanted to get some groceries and to tidy up so she didn't feel like she had to clean.

Miranda was at the office early. She wanted to get her things in order for office hours and had a consult to go over with one of the other doctors who was working this morning. She needed some files and couldn't remember where Josie put them. She called Josie's house but there was no answer. She didn't leave a message as she figured Josie would be there in a few minutes. Her house was only two minutes from the office. Miranda went to get some coffee and was thinking about her afternoon rounds at the hospital. She figured she would go to her office for a few minutes and look again on her desk for that file.

Josie heard the phone ring. Or was that her ears ringing. No, it was the phone because it stopped. “My friends will come for me Jack. They aren’t afraid of you.” He laughed. “They should be. Don’t you worry about them. If they come, I’ll be ready for them. Either way I’m not leaving here without you. So you better figure on coming peacefully with me.” It was her turn to laugh. “Peacefully? Like hell! You’ll have to kill me and drag my dead body with you because that is the only way I’m going with you. I hate you! You are a miserable son of a bitch and the sorriest excuse for a human being I’ve ever met!” In seconds she was down on the ground. He slapped her first, then knocked her on her back straddling her. He pulled at her breasts and she was swinging her hands at him. He took the knife to her throat. "Don't make me do it Josie!" He cut her neck ever so slightly and she froze.

Jack held Josie down by her throat and took the knife to her abdomen. He enjoyed marking her. He made several cuts before he looked at her. "Remember me? I'm your husband. You had better start remembering how to speak to me and how to act with me. He bent down to kiss her mouth and she bit him. He reared back and punched her. He got up moving to the front door. He had a bag there that she didn't see when he first pushed her inside. He took rope out and she got up trying to run from him. He caught her and dragged her to the kitchen to tie her to a chair. He tied her mid-section and arms down and she was kicking him every chance she got. He tied her legs to the chair then untied her mid-section. He decided to just tie her hands to the chair. He took the knife and cut the top of her pants and then ripped them the rest of the way off of her.

Jack was circling Josie and watching her. She'd changed. Something was different about her. He sat astride her lap. "What is different about you Josie? Something has changed. It really is turning me on. I think I need to get our love nest prepared." He pulled her head to the side, kissed and then bit her neck. Josie tried to move but couldn't. "I'll tell you what changed. Michael changed me. He treated me with love. He touched me lovingly and he made love to me. He is the man you will never be." He grabbed her throat angry now. "How dare you? You are a little lying whore. He will never be the man I am. I kept you in line. I made sure you understood I was the boss. He has let you walk all over him. No respect. Don't worry though. I'll get you fearing and respecting again."

Jack leaned down and grabbed the speculum out of his bag. Josie's eyes widened. "Ahh, I see you remember this. I will have to use this first and flush you out. Lord only knows what kind of trash that piece of shit left behind. I don't want any of his junk on me." Jack leaned down picking up the knife again. "Maybe I'll have to cut some of you to remove all the shit you've got in there now. He probably isn't the only one that you've had visiting you, just the only one I've seen. Although I have seen the way you look at that cop. He's always hanging around too. Maybe you like having two at once." He bent down and took out something like a dildo. He raised it up to her, "Maybe we need to try this. I'll have you my way and we can jam this up your ass. Looks like you have some new interests. I'm a fair man, I'll give you what you want."

Josie reared back and spat in Jack's face. "You are nothing to me. You can do all you want to me Jack, but I'm telling you now, you mean nothing to me. Everywhere you touch me just remember Michael was there first and he was there last." She saw the anger across his face and she kept going. "He's ten thousand times more of a man than you'll ever be. I will remember his touch until the last ounce of torture you give me. Until you kill me, Michael will be all I think about. Don't ever doubt that Jack. You are a mistake, a huge giant asshole of a mistake I made. I wish I'd never met you."

Jack stood over Josie and grabbed her throat. "You piece of shit! You are nothing but an ungrateful little whore. I am going to teach you a lesson you'll never forget." He went to work hitting her. He slapped her first in her face. She turned and looked him straight in the face, defiance clear on her face. He slapped her again and she turned her head back to look him in the eye again. "Go ahead Jack, keep going. I can take whatever you got. I've known the love of another man, you mean nothing.

Jack got off Josie's lap and moved behind her. He pulled her by her hair and almost snapped her neck off her shoulders. "You shut your hole Josie or I'll shut it permanently." He pushed her head back up roughly. He moved back in front of her and punched her in the face. He turned like he was going to leave the room surprising her when he turned back around. He brought his leg up to her chest and kicked her as hard as he could. Josie felt the air go out of her and her chair flew backwards.

Josie must have blacked out. She came to and Jack was not there. She thought maybe he'd left she tried to move. Her arms were pinned underneath her. She hit her head on the kitchen floor when he kicked her chest. She couldn't move. Her head was pounding and she couldn't feel her hands or arms. She lifted her head slightly and saw him coming from the direction of the bedroom. She closed her eyes and cursed. "What the hell did I do to deserve this? Please God help me!"

Jack sneered, "You can plead all you want but no one is going to help you now. You belong to me Josie. Start to comprehend that." She was tired of his abuse, "Like hell I will. I will get away from you. I will never be with you again. You, sick bastard! I hate you! Do you hear me, I hate you!" He stood over her and he kicked her, she took the kick to her side and one to her shoulder. She cried out in pain. He pulled her chair back up punching her again in the face.

Jack looked at Josie sitting in the chair with just her bra and underwear on. He reached his hand under the cup of her bra roughly fondling her breast. “Oh yeah, I’ve missed these.” Josie couldn’t help herself, “Why did your cell mate bubba not have big enough one’s for you?” He pulled his hand out of her bra and backhanded her across the face. He walked away from her and Josie breathed a sigh of relief for a moment.

Jack walked back to the bedroom grabbing his gun and knife. “I can’t believe the way she is talking to me. She is a piece of shit. I’m going to show her who’s boss. I’m going to have her begging me for more. I’m going to kill the stupid cunt after I have my way with her and hear her beg me to spare her miserable life. I don’t need this whore. I’ll find me a real woman. One who knows how to respect her man." He turned and went back to the kitchen.

"No Josie's not with me. I thought she was on her way to work." Mike was in his apartment and cleaning up. When his phone rang he thought it was Josie. When he picked up it was Miranda. Miranda was asking him if Josie was with him? The last time she was late for work it was because of him.

Mike cursed, "Damn it, Jack's got Josie." He hit the steps of his apartment and all but jumped to the bottom. He never even stopped to shut the door. He jumped in his truck, jammed it into gear and floored it toward Josie. Miranda was trying to calm herself and him, "I'm sure she just got side tracked. I'm sure she'll walk in any minute." She could hear the revving engine and the squealing of tires. "Yeah, I hope, but just in case, call Rod. Tell him to get Ted and meet me there. I'll be there in minutes." He threw the phone down and continued driving like his life, no her life depended on it.

Jack moved back into the kitchen he took the knife and laid it on the table. He showed Josie the gun. He took it and held it to her head then drug it down her body to her abdomen. Josie couldn't help but shudder from the cold steel of it. "I knew this would make you change your tune." Josie shook her head and laughed. "No Jack, I'm just hoping it goes off." He took it and pushed it against her underwear. "Maybe we need to get those chains out and play. I'll get you all revved up with this inside of you. I have some new toys I bought just for this occasion. Trust me, you are going to love it."

Josie heard the truck quietly she said, "Michael!" "You think he can save you? Guess again, I'll kill him. He has no business touching my wife. He will pay." He moved out of the room and she didn't know where he went. Several things happened all at the same time. Josie heard the door crash and the sirens screaming, then she heard Michael shouting her name.

The door crashed as Mike didn't stop to use a key, "Josie! Josie! Damn it where are you?" She screamed from the kitchen, "Michael!" He headed toward her and he stopped in the doorway. "Michael, he's......Noooooooooooo!" Mike crumbled to the floor. Jack was standing behind him with the gun. He struck Mike with it twice over the head. Josie was crying and screaming for Mike. "It's time we leave here and finish our business without interruptions. You have plenty of time to make up for." He stepped over Mike then turned back and kicked him in the mid-section. Jack pulled Josie's precious

Mike's limp body up and punched him in the face. "That's for touching my wife."

Jack went to Josie untied her and she scrambled off the chair toward Mike. She was trying to touch him and Jack was already at her pulling her up. He was dragging her to the living room with his precious bag in his hand. "So much for your hero." Josie heard more cars outside. Jack did too. "God damn it!" He pulled her up in front of him. He tucked the gun in his backside and pulled the knife back out of the sheath on his hip. He held the knife to her throat. "Be a good girl Josie, and no one gets hurt. You tell them you're leaving with me." Rod and Ted entered her apartment. Both had their guns drawn.

Jack was laughing. "Now we have a party!" Rod looked at Josie and spoke, "Josie, are you okay?" She was crying, all she said was, "Michael." Rod's eyes never left hers.

"Look at me Josie! Look at me!" She focused on Rod. Ted was talking to Jack. "You are never getting out of here with her. Hand her over to us." Jack laughed. "No I don't think you understand. She's mine and she is leaving with me. Aren't you Josie? Tell them. Get out of my way, or I will kill all of you." Ted shook his head. "That's not happening, Jack. So let's settle this. Let her go." Jack took the knife against her throat and cut. "No you don't understand. I will kill her." Rod shuddered. He felt so damn helpless. "Josie," he said through gritted teeth. She did not stop looking at him. A calm came over her seeing Rod. "I'm okay Rod." Jack looked over his shoulder and saw movement from lover boy. He pulled Josie so that his back was not to Mike. He had all three of the men where he could see them now.

When Jack moved, Josie's eyes moved to Mike. He was moving and trying to get up.

"Michael!" She yelled. He was on his hands and knees shaking his head. He got up and was headed toward Josie. "Mike, no!" Ted hollered. Jack kept the knife to Josie's throat and reached behind him to pull out the gun. He aimed it at Mike. Josie yelled, "Michael! No! Stop!" He stopped and looked at her. She said, "I'm okay, but I won't be if you come charging over here."

Jack sneered. "Move it over with them lover boy!" Mike started moving toward Rod and Ted. Josie watched in agony as the gun was still trained on Mike. She didn't dare move or make Jack angry now. "Your lover boy takes commands better than you do. Does he think you have a golden pussy, or is he just a pussy himself?"

Mike turned. "Who's holding the fucking gun? Who beats on women? Put it down and we'll see who the pussy is Jack. I guarantee you it's not going to be me." Josie looked at Mike then at Rod. Ted was trying to get Mike out of the line of fire. Josie looked at Mike, she tried to hold it back but a tear slid down her cheek as she said, "Let them go Jack. I'll go with you, just let them go!" Mike's eyes flared. "The hell you will! You are not going with him." He lunged like he was going to go for Jack. Ted grabbed Mike and held on to him. "Mike, stop! Relax! Let us do our job. Stop!" Mike stopped fighting with him. "Okay! Okay! Let me go!"

Josie turned her stare back to Rod. He never left her. He was focused on her. He watched the moves of Jack and he was concerned. The man was not at all rational. He looked back at Josie. "You got this Josie. Just stay with me." She looked at Mike and he was angry and also looking helpless.

Josie knew she needed to get out of this and back to Mike. She knew if she made Jack mad he'd lose control. Hopefully it would be enough to pull off a miracle. "Jack you are not getting out of here. Just let me go." Jack pulled the knife tighter on her throat leaning his head to her ear, "No Josie, you belong to me and you are coming with me."

Josie looked at Mike, as he said, "She belongs to me. She never belonged to you. You don't deserve her." Jack was tightening his grip on her. The knife was pulled tight to her throat. His other hand with the gun was around her waist and pointed in the guy's direction. Jack was distracted with Mike and Josie turned her attention back to Rod. He looked at her and mouthed, training, think! She was watching his eyes and she knew what he was saying. He trained her on what to do when someone had her from behind. But the knife made it harder. She shifted slightly and Jack switched his arms. He pulled down the hand with the knife and was using it to cut her abdomen right in front of the men now. The arm with the gun now held her at the throat.

Josie didn't even flinch as Jack cut her this time. Her concentration was on Rod. She heard Mike moving trying to break free of Ted's grasp. She heard Jack laughing, "Do you like that lover boy? How bout some more? Josie likes it when I cut her. How do you like looking at all of her marks? I did that, I've touched her." He laughed more and Mike cursed at him, "You are one sick son of a bitch. I'll kill you once I get my hands on you. Let her go, let's go a few rounds."

Jack laughed at Mike. "Ahh…. How tempting, but do you see this body? This is what I kept thinking about in jail. I'm finally going to have it again. Maybe you want to watch?" Josie heard Mike and he was ready to lose control. She turned briefly in his direction. "Michael! Stop! He's baiting you. You're better than that." She looked Mike in the eye and he settled. She had steel in those eyes. His Josie girl was strong. He needed to be strong for her. He needed to not lose control right now.

Josie turned her eyes back to Rod. She started baiting Jack. "Where are you going to take me? We don't have a home any longer." Jack pulled his arm tighter across her throat, "Whose fault was that you whore?" He cut her abdomen again, "You should have still been there waiting for me to come home." Josie laughed. "Why? I never loved you Jack. I hated you. I only had love for one man in my heart."

Jack pulled Josie's head back with the force he squeezed on her neck. "I found your 'trinket box' you thought you were hiding. I knew all your stories of your precious Michael. God, I had to endure them for the whole first year we were dating. He's nothing Josie. I don't know why you carried such a torch for him." Jack snickered and looked in Mike's direction. Josie didn't miss a beat. "He was more of a man than you are. He never had to beat me to get hard. He never had any trouble giving me what I needed to be satisfied. He never once had to use vibrators and tools to get himself or me off. I've had multiple orgasms in one night, I screamed his name, begged him for more while he fucked me harder than your pencil dick ever could. Tell me again Jack, who's the real man?" Josie watched Rod. He felt the anger brewing in Jack. If they were going to do this, it had to be soon or she was done for.

Rod looked at Josie. "Do you trust me?" Jack turned his attention back to the man speaking now. Mike was looking between Josie and Rod. He didn't like what was going on. Jack evidently didn't like it either. Josie stone faced, "Always," was her only response. Jack moved and pulled the gun to Josie's head. The other arm now pulled snug around her waist, the knife pointing out to the side.

"Don't get any ideas there, don't try to be a hero. I'll kill her!" Jack said with authority in his voice. Josie knew this was it, she spoke, "If you were going to kill me you would have done it years ago. You don't have the balls. I know first-hand what you're so not packing. Go ahead Jack, do it! I'm dead if I go with you so just pull the fucking trigger!" She never looked away from Rod as she screamed at Jack.

Rod nodded ever so slightly at Josie. Jack was getting angry with the situation and her mouth. Who did she think she was talking to? He leaned into her ear and said, “I told you that you had better find some respect.” She said with a calm voice, “I told you, you will have to kill me to take me with you.” Jack was really mad now. She was disrespecting him in front of others. He would make a mistake soon.

Jack pulled Josie tighter to him. “That can be arranged!” Mike was flinching and Ted was holding him back. Rod was keeping steady and she saw him shift his stance and his arms slightly. Rod nodded his head to his left and she was ready.

Jack was ranting at Josie but she wasn’t listening. She watched Rod. He was focused and his focus was now on Jack. Josie was ready. “I may have been your victim once. But that ends here.” She elbowed him as hard as she could. He loosened his grip enough for her to shift to her right and then a gun went off. All

Josie heard was Mike screaming her name. She hit the ground and Mike was on top of her. He was pulling her up into his arms. She saw blood on her left shoulder. She didn't feel any pain. She looked and saw Jack lying on the floor. She knew. Rod shot him. Mike was pulling her up trying to move her out of the room. "Is he dead?" Rod was standing over Jack with the gun still pointed at him. Mike looked over at Rod and he nodded. He pulled Josie over toward the kitchen with her back to the men. "It's over Josie. He's dead." She fell into Mike's arms and started crying. She was sliding to the floor and he went with her.

"You came back for me. You saved me from being taken by him." Mike held Josie and whispered, "You saved yourself Josie girl. You saved yourself." She sat in his arms and she heard more sirens. Rod came over to them. Josie started to get up. Mike helped her. He took his shirt off and put it on Josie. Once his shirt was in place she reached out to Rod. He took her in his arms and hugged her. "Thank you for trusting me." Josie laughed a little laugh, "Thank you for practicing and for being my friend, my guardian angel. How can I ever repay you?" He squeezed her in his arms one last time and stepped back to go tend to business. He paused only a moment, "Stay in town, make this your home."

Mike stood there watching the exchange but didn't ask any questions. He took Josie back in his arms. "Let's get out of here." He ushered her past the body of her husband and went outside. There were more police outside and one of the other officers gave her a blanket which Mike wrapped around her. Josie had to wait until everyone was done with questioning. When the coroner came and took out the body he stopped and asked her, "Is there anyone I should contact?" She shook her head. The man continued on his way and climbed in the van. All she could think was good riddance.

Chapter 33

Rod and Ted took Josie and Mike to get checked out at the office in town and wanted them to go to the hospital. Josie insisted she wanted Miranda and only her. Miranda and one of the other doctors were waiting. She had rooms ready for both Mike and Josie and was pacing the office floor waiting for them to arrive. Once they hit the door, she looked at Josie and said, "Holy shit! What the hell?" Josie waved her off. "I'm okay. It looks worse than it is." Miranda helped her into the treatment room and took Mike's shirt off of her. Once she pulled the shirt off of Josie she saw the cuts to the abdomen. "Jesus Josie!" She took Miranda's hands. "I'm okay. It's fine. I may have some glass in my back though."

Miranda looked at Josie's back and her eyes filled with tears. She needed to pull herself together and told Josie she'd be right back. She left the room and met Rod in the hallway. She fell into his arms. “How could someone do this to her?” Rod hugged her. “It’s okay Doc. He’s not going to do it again. I took care of it.” She looked at his face and he had a stony look about him. “Thank God you are all alright. What happened? Where is Jack?” Rod looked at her. “I shot him. He’s dead. Is Josie okay? I didn’t take him down fast enough. I didn’t get there soon enough to keep him from hurting her.” Miranda kissed him nodded her head, “She’s going to be fine. She’s bruised, battered. She’ll be sore, but she’s alive because you got there. You did your job baby, to serve and protect. Don’t doubt that.” This was the first time Rod shot someone, that she knew. Hell, this was the first time he fired his weapon other than training and practice since he was shot. She was going to have to deal with one patient at a time. Miranda moved away from Rod. “Don’t go anywhere. We’ll talk after my patients are taken care of." He nodded to her and she moved off toward the other room. Miranda could hear Mike yelling at her partner. She moved off in that direction.

"Mike! Enough!" She barked at him and he stopped fighting with the doctor. "I just want to be with her." Miranda nodded her head. "I understand, but first let him finish with you. I am still working on Josie. She wouldn't want you to see her like this so give me a chance to fix her up a little. Okay?" He nodded agreement and mumbled, "I'm sorry." She looked at her partner and said, "He'll stop being a pain in the ass now." He smiled at her as she left the room, to go back to Josie.

Josie was sitting waiting for Miranda. It was finally over. Jack was dead. She was free. She should feel something, but all she felt was relief. Was she a bad person? How could she not feel something? He was her husband?

Miranda came in and saw the look on her face. "Okay Josie, talk. I want you to tell me what you are thinking. No filter. Just let it out. I'm going to clean these cuts and bandage you up." Josie was sitting there and nodding to Miranda. She didn't flinch while Miranda worked on her.

Miranda couldn't believe the strength of this woman. "Miranda, I'm a horrible person. I feel nothing but relief that he's dead. Is that terrible? I mean it's a human life and he was my husband. How can I not feel something? I am so happy he is gone. I'm finally feel," Josie paused and said, "free."

Miranda paused from her work. "Josie, you are allowed to feel relief that he is gone. Look at what he has put you through. Your body, your mind and your soul are scarred by him. You are one tough lady. You can rise above this and you do not need to feel guilty.

You did nothing to deserve this. He was the sick one. You have every right to be happy. I believe you're in a bit of shock right now too, so give yourself a break." Josie looked at her friend. "You are right and I know it in my head, but I feel so confused. What do I do now? Jack needs to be buried or something." Miranda patted her leg. "One miracle at a time sweetie. Let's get you patched up and give your mind time to settle." Josie told Miranda what had happened. Miranda was concerned for Rod and she started asking questions about Rod's demeanor. Miranda knew she was going to have to deal with him next.

Josie told Miranda without Rod and all the training he gave to her, she may not be sitting there. Josie told Miranda how Rod kept her calm, focused on him and she took her cues from him. "Miranda, he is special. Your Rod, he will always be a dear friend to me. He took a lot of time to train me and he talked to me. He even came with me the night he should have been with you. The night he proposed." Miranda looked at Josie. "He is definitely a keeper. I'm glad he was able to give you the support you needed. Just keep him in your mind now. I have a feeling he is going to need some support. It's been a long time, if ever that he used deadly force." Josie nodded and told her friend, "I will be there for him. I owe him and he is the greatest friend I'll ever have. He gave me my life back." Miranda patched Josie up and told her she didn't appear to have any broken bones. The x-rays were negative for fractures. Miranda wanted her to be careful for the next few days. She most likely had a concussion. She should really take it easy. Miranda assured Josie that she would be fine at the office without her. Miranda headed out in the hallway to talk with Mike.

Chapter 34

Rod had been waiting to talk to Josie alone. He used the opportunity to slip into the room while Miranda talked to Mike. Josie was lying back on the table and had her eyes closed. She opened them when she heard the door. "Rod! I'm so glad it's you." He came up beside her. "Are you okay Josie? I'm so sorry it took so long to get Jack. I just didn't want to chance missing. I needed to get his rhythm, I had to be sure. I didn't want to hurt you."

Josie nodded at Rod. "I understand completely. You don't need to worry. I thank you for freeing me, for keeping me grounded. I don't think I would have been able to stay so calm without you. I will always be grateful to you." She reached out and took his hand in hers. "That makes two of us." Mike was standing in the doorway. Rod looked at him and looked back at Josie. "I will let you two alone." Josie didn't let go of his hand. "You talk to me Rod if you need to. I don't want you to suffer with this. I think Jack caused enough suffering. We are all free of him now. So thank you." She pulled him toward her and hugged him. Quietly she said to him, "You are my best friend. You truly understand me. Thank you." She kissed his cheek and with that Rod pulled away to look at her. "Same here Josie. You say I kept you calm and grounded, well that was you. You were very brave. You had a confidence about you. It was good to see. So happy you are okay."

Rod turned to leave the room and Mike stopped him. "I owe you everything Rod." Rod turned looking at Josie, then back at Mike. "No, you just need to take care of Josie now. She's one tough lady and very dear to my heart." Mike smiled at him, "You bet I'll take care of her. She is very special. I'll never let her go again." Rod opened the door to leave and Max was pushing his way in. "What the hell happened? Josie! What? Are you okay?" He ran up next to her and was wanting to touch her but didn't quite know where." She smiled at him. "I'm okay Max. We are all okay. I just have some cuts, a possible concussion, I'll be bruised, swollen and sore, but I will be just fine." He continued talking to her and asking what happened. She told him the story while Mike and Rod continued their conversation.

"Rod, I owe you big man. Josie means the world to me. I could have lost her today. If you need anything, you call me and I'll be there. From here on out, you owe me nothing at the bar. I can never repay you for all you've done for me." Rod looked at Mike, "I didn't do anything you wouldn't have done for me. We are friends. We both care about that lady over there. She's a special woman." Mike looked at her and said, “She sure is.” Mike turned his attention back on Rod, “Do I need to worry about the bond you and Josie have?” Rod grinned at Mike. He shook his head no, then thought for a second. “Actually you do. Fair warning Mike. She’s like a sister to me. I’ve grown very fond of her. As much as I like you my friend, if you ever hurt her again, I will hurt you.” Mike held his hands up in surrender.

Mike said, “Never again will I do anything that hurts her. Thank you for being honest with me. Sorry I had to ask.” Rod nodded, “My heart belongs to Miranda. I sold my soul to that woman a long time ago. Josie, well she’s just, well, there are no words, she is just Josie.” Mike nodded, there were no other words that needed to be spoken.

Max and Mike helped Josie to the truck. Max said he’d meet them back at the bar. Mike didn’t want her going back to her apartment.

He would go there later and get their things. Right now he needed to settle her in at his apartment. He scooped Josie up in his arms and climbed the stairs with her. He walked through the opened door and took her right to the bedroom to lie down.

Mike laid down next to her and he breathed for the first time in hours. “Damn Josie, I thought I was going to lose you. I was so scared. I am so sorry.” She looked at him concerned. “For what?” He looked at her and he had tears in his eyes, “For lying to you, for subjecting you to Jack and for not being able to save you from him.” She reached her hand out and touched his face “Michael, please don’t do this to yourself. I am okay, Jack is dead and it is the past. We are free. Unless of course you’ve changed you mind about marrying me?” Mike grinned at her, “Not on your life baby.” He leaned in gently to press his lips to hers.

Mike laid there holding Josie while she was resting. He told her about some land he found and he wanted to start building on it right away. He didn't want to wait any longer to be with her and to start their life together. She agreed. "Start building. It sounds perfect Michael, just like you." He was hoping she would say that. He had a meeting scheduled with a builder tomorrow. Now he just needed her to heal. The land was on the side of town where the bar was. It was out of Wellsprings and in Kellersville. It was tucked back, mountain views and privacy for them to do whatever they pleased, wherever.

Mike didn't want to leave Josie alone but he needed to go get some of her clothes from the apartment. Max knocked on the door holding food, asking how she was doing. Mike said she was resting. He needed to run some errands but didn't want to leave her alone.

Max willingly went to sit with her. Mike left heading to her apartment first. He called Ted asking if he could go and get some of Josie's things. Ted said he would meet him there. When Mike pulled up Ted was waiting for him. "How is she?" Mike told him she's doing good. She was just sore, her face was bruising and starting to swell. She had a really bad headache. All in all, she was one tough cookie.

Max knocked on the bedroom door and peeked in. Josie was propped up on some pillows just looking at the TV. It was turned off and she was just staring at the black screen. "Josie, it's Max. Are you ok?" She turned to look at him. She smiled but the smile didn't quite reach her eyes like it usually did. Her face was bruised and swollen, but she patted the bed. "I'm fine come sit with me."

Max walked toward Josie and sat on the bed next to her. Max was never short on words but today, he didn't quite know what to say. "Do you want to talk about it Josie?" She looked at him and touched his hand. "There isn't a whole lot to say. I've been running from him for a while now and scared to death about the day he found me. That all ended today. I'm free for the first time in years." Max couldn't help but think she sounded depressed about being free. "Josie, what's really going on? What are you not telling any of us?" A tear slid down Josie's cheek and she looked at Max. "Where is Michael?"

Ted and Mike walked into the apartment. Ted pulled all the officers out so Mike could get some personal items for Josie. The men didn't mind the break as Taryn from Soups and Such had shown up with sandwiches, hot soup, and drinks for the men in uniform working to keep the town safe. Mike looked around at all the broken glass, the blood and the roses all over the floor. Ted saw his expression. “Mike I have to warn you, before you go to get her things. Jack had started setting up the bedroom for her. It’s pretty, well unreal.” Mike looked at him. “What do you mean?”

Ted went on to explain to Mike that the officers found chains, more knives and gags. “Son of a bitch!” Mike was wanting to kill him again. “That sick bastard! Thank God Miranda called me. What if she hadn’t? What if he’d gotten her away from us?” Ted shook his head, “We could stand here and what if all day. The fact is that he didn’t get away with it. He was stopped. Josie suffered some but at least it’s over now.” Mike agreed. “I think she suffered more than we all know. She amazed me today. I always knew Josie was strong but what I saw of her today, well she was really something.

Ted looked at Mike. "These women of ours truly are the strong ones."

Mike turned to go get Josie's things. "Try not to move too much around in there. We need to do some more documentation and then all that stuff will be collected and put into evidence. We should be done by tomorrow so if you want to come back then for more you can. We'll actually probably be done here tonight." Mike nodded and headed into the bedroom to get a few of her things for the next few days. Even though he knew what he would find, it still didn't prepare him for what he saw. He looked around. He was angry and completely terrified.

Max took out his cell phone. "I can call him if you want Josie." She shook her head. "No, Max. I'm fine. I just, well I didn't want him to hear me." Max shifted on the bed feeling a little uneasy about what Josie wanted to share. He waited for her to be ready to say whatever she needed. "I waited so long to have Michael back in my life. I dreamed about it, I fantasied about it." She paused and Max nodded for her to continue. "The past few days have been more than I ever dreamed about. Michael is my everything. But I realized today that I always dreamed of him coming in and rescuing me, like a fairytale." She looked at Max. "But today I saw the woman in me that didn't need rescuing. I saw the woman who was ready for whatever came her way." Max looked at her slightly confused.

Josie wasn't making sense to Max. What was she saying? He waited for her to finish, thinking maybe she had more than a concussion. Josie smiled at him, "I know you think I'm crazy. Maybe I am but Max for the first time in a long time I was taking care of myself and protecting Michael. For many years

I blamed him for my life, for the pain and for the lack of love in my life. Today I realized that Michael wasn't to blame I was." Max was going to speak up and decided to wait for her to finish. Josie smiled at him. "Today I realized that I am in control of my life. Not Jack and not Michael. I am strong now, I am not the same woman who cowered to Jack for all those years. I'm finally finding myself and making my life all I've ever wanted."

Max still wasn't sure he understood, "I'm just so glad you are okay Josie. I don't understand what you are saying because to me you've always been strong. When Mike told me all the hell you've been through I couldn't believe you survived it. I knew then just how strong you were." Josie shook her head, "No it's more than just surviving it Max. It's that I've finally taken responsibility for my choices. I've finally stopped blaming Michael for leaving me and I feel like I can finally have my dreams. I stopped having a pity party for myself. I stood up to Jack. I didn't just let him do the things he did to me. I fought him and I stood up for myself. Today, I was important, I was beautiful and I was worth something. No matter what he said to me or did to me he couldn't break me. I was free." Max finally got it.

Mike saw the chains and he could not imagine his Josie chained up in them. He saw the tools laid out. There were knives and all kinds of other objects including some in which he knew were why she had been so timid in bed at first. He had an assortment of torture equipment and Mike was glad he never got the chance to use them. He grabbed the clothes and headed out of there before he completely lost it.

Mike was on his way back to the bar when he got a phone call from the contractor. He was clearing the land and wanted to see the plans. Mike had them in the truck so he headed over there. Mike went over everything with him in detail and said, "I want it done in three months, four at the maximum. I need to get Josie settled and fast. I don't care how many men you have to put on the job, just get it done. I can help during the day but right now I can't tell you when. I need to be with her for a little while." The contractor nodded, he said he would do his best. Mike wanted to move forward with their lives. The past was over and done except for one small detail.

Mike went to the morgue before heading back to the apartment. He wanted Jack out of this town and back where he belonged. When he got there he was surprised to find that they were already shipping Jack back for burial. "I don't understand. Who?" The man looked at Mike and said, "Rod from the police department and Miranda. They told me they wanted him out of here immediately. We will send the autopsy report to his, um, Mrs. Morris." Mike growled at the man. He headed to Miranda and Rod's. He couldn't believe they took care of everything. He had to go see them. Mike called Max first and he said that Josie was doing well. They had been talking and he should go do whatever was necessary.

Max hung up the phone and looked at Josie. "I understand Josie. I can't imagine the pain you felt when Mike left you all those years ago. I know how hard it is when someone you love betrays you, lies to you and isn't who you thought they were. You feel like you don't matter. You feel like you are worth nothing and it doesn't matter what happens to you." Josie looked at Max. "It sounds like you've had experience in love." Max shook his head not wanting to talk about his troubles. "You are an incredible woman. Mike is the luckiest man alive." Josie smiled at him, "Thank you Max, but I think we are both pretty lucky." Max looked at Josie. "There is just one thing I don't understand." Josie looked at him with a serious look. Max turned and grinned at her, "What do you see in that ugly mug?" They both laughed and Max knew she was going to be alright.

Josie looked at Max, "So are you going to tell me about her?" Max grinned and said, "Who?" Josie looked at Max, "Really? You think I haven't seen the looks, the flirting, the smile she brings out in you?" Max grinned, "Taryn." Josie smiled, "Yes, I knew it. So spill. I deserve something good to delve my mind into." Max grinned and started telling Josie about the woman who was capturing his thoughts. “Do you know Josie that she set up sandwiches, soups and drinks for the officers at your apartment. She wanted to help but didn’t know what to do, so she loaded up the stuff from her families’ restaurant and went to feed the men working to process everything.” When he paused, Josie knew he was regretting bringing it up. She wanted to lighten the mood. “It looks like I’m going to need to talk more to this woman and get to know her better. But did you say she brought food?” Max smiled, “Yes there is a bag on the counter in the kitchen. I guess Mike was too busy worrying to be sure you ate.”

Max was hoping that Josie would want to be friends with Taryn. He thought Josie was just what Taryn needed right now to help her sort her mind out. Little did he know that Josie and Taryn already were becoming friends, talking and sharing secrets with each other.

She already knew before pumping Max for information that Taryn was quite taken with Max, and vice a versa.

Chapter 35

Rod answered the door. He saw Mike standing there. “Is Josie okay? What’s wrong?” Mike shook his head, “Nothing is wrong. In fact, everything is going to be great. I can’t believe you guys. You and Miranda are the greatest friends in the world. I was just at the morgue.” Rod shook his head. “That piece of shit needs to get out of this town and fast. He doesn’t belong here with our good people.” Mike shook his head in agreement. Mike told Rod that Jack was being sent out today. Rod invited Mike in. “How are you feeling?” Rod shrugged, “I’m okay. I just wish I could have stopped Jack sooner. The hell that Josie went through again.” Mike shook his head, “Yes I know, I feel the same way but it is a lot better than it could have been.” He told Rod what he had seen in the bedroom and Rod stood up pacing. “I know I was at the apartment and had to help collect the evidence. It really made me crazy. I can't believe she endured so much. How did she survive it?"

Mike told Rod that one time Josie told him that she thought of him to get through those times. "But I don't know how that could have helped. She's stronger than she gives herself credit. I failed her in so many ways, but I'm not going to fail her again. I proposed to her. I am going to have the quickest wedding ever. I am not wasting time. I've started construction on a house for us and all I need now is to bring Rachel home."

Miranda came in and heard the information Mike was sharing with Rod. "You can't have a quick wedding. She had that once. She deserves her dream wedding. Let Sarah and me help with the planning. I promise it will be fast but she deserves so much more. Where and when?" Mike shook his head,

"Miranda you've already done so much. I can't ask you to do that." "Damn right you can't ask because I'm telling you that's how it's going to be. I have to get to the hospital but give him the details. The wedding is on." She went and kissed Rod. She stopped in front of Mike. He stood up and looked at her. She was a tough bird but he was starting to see a softer side of her. He waited and instead of the usual smack he got from her she hugged him. "Don't get used to this." She pulled back and smacked his arm anyway. Out the door she went. Rod watched and was grinning at the interaction.

Mike sat back down and laughed. "I guess we are surrounded by strong women." Rod nodded. "Can I ask you Rod, what happened between you and Josie in that apartment? She was focused on you and you asked her if she trusted you? I don't understand." Rod sat back and told Mike that they had several talks while he was giving her private self-defense lessons. “There is something about Josie that I can just relate to. I feel almost like she’s my little sister. Somehow since I first met her I’ve felt connected to her. I can’t explain it other than we just connect.”

Mike looked at him. “I’m glad you say you think of her like a sister, because I can see a connection with you guys and it worried me. Even though we had that talk at Miranda’s office I still thought I had some competition.” Rod laughed. “Josie is a beautiful woman, but my heart belongs to Miranda. You are safe, but I do love your Josie. She’s going to always be a part of me and my life. I told her a lot of things about me some Miranda knows and some she doesn’t. But trust me she’s like a sister to me.” Mike looked at Rod. “Why did you ask if she trusted you? It sounds like you guys do trust each other already."

Rod told Mike about being shot, being told he'd never fire a weapon again. He told him about his practicing, he told him that Josie knew all that while he stood there holding the gun on Jack. "I was holding back. I was afraid to pull the trigger. I didn't want to hurt Josie, but I couldn't let Jack hurt her anymore. I knew she was there and I wanted her to use her training to give me a little breathing room. I signaled her what to do and she focused on me. She was ready. She is one smart, brave lady."

Mike couldn't believe what he had just heard. She was willing to risk her life to be free. She just wanted the hell she lived over with. Mike's phone rang. While he answered it Rod went and got some drinks. Mike hung up. "That was the orphanage. Rachel is wanting to see Josie. They can't seem to calm her down. I have to go over there." Rod looked at him, "Can I tag along?" Mike nodded and they headed over there. Once they arrived Megan took them to Rachel.

Rachel looked up and saw Mike, "Daddy." She ran to him and he scooped her up in his arms and held her. "What's wrong sweetheart?" Rod watched the interaction from the door with Megan. Mike went and sat down holding her. She was crying. She had her little arms wrapped around Mike. "I missed you and mommy. I wanted you to come here and they told me you couldn't. They said that you aren't my mommy and daddy, that I have to stop calling you that. I told them that you are my mommy and daddy, that you will come for me. I love you, Daddy. When can I come home."

Mike thought his heart was going to break. He just watched his Josie suffer at the hands of a madman, now this. The tears were in his eyes and he pulled Rachel tight to him. "I do love you Rachel, but I can't bring you home. Not unless they give me permission. There is nothing that Josie and I want more than to bring you home."

Rod looked at Megan and said, "How can you deny that they belong together. They are a family already, they love each other. That man would do anything for that little girl. Why?" Megan looked at him and said, "I'm trying. It's the best I can do." Rod shook his head, "It's not good enough. Mike and Josie are getting married. Her estranged husband was just killed so that marriage is over. It allows them to finally move forward. He is having a home built for them and that home includes Rachel. I want that little girl at their wedding. I want her there as their daughter. You need to make it happen. If you can't you call me, and I will. That little girl has suffered enough and so have Mike and Josie. They deserve to be a family." Megan nodded and walked away.

Rod walked over to Mike and Rachel, "I would like to know if I could meet the beautiful princess Rachel. I've heard so much about her that I just have to know who she is." He sat down next to them and Rachel peeked over at him but clung tighter to Mike. He was rubbing her back and said, "It's okay Rachel. This guy is going to be a very big part of your life when you come home with us. This is Uncle Rod. He is a really good guy. I promise you, he would never hurt you." She peeked at him again and loosened her grip on Mike. "Does Mommy know him too?" Mike shook his head. "Josie and Uncle Rod are very good friends. He protects Josie and has done a lot of nice things for her. He is also going to marry Dr. Porter.

You remember her from when you met Josie at the hospital."

Rachel's eyes lit up. "I liked her. She was super nice. She's funny and she has lollipops in her pocket. You are going to marry her?" Rod nodded. "So you looooovvvve her?" Rod nodded laughing at how the little girl drug out the word love. Rachel was quite a character, Rod absolutely loved her already. "Are you going to come here and get some kids too?" Rod looked at her and said, "I don't know. But if we do I know someone who can help us pick out some really nice kids." Rachel smiled and reached out her hand to him. Rod took it gently so as to not scare her away. "I will make sure you get the best kids here. We will all be able to play together and my mommy can sing to your kids too. We can have tea parties and play dolls. We'll have so much fun." Rod and Mike were laughing.

Rachel looked at them as if they were crazy. “Why do you laugh at me? I am serious, I am so good at playing dolls, and I know all the kids here. I will tell you who to stay away from, like Bobby. He’s mean. He isn’t a nice kid to have cuz he takes my dolls and says he’s going to not give them back. Then, well I don’t want to talk about the other kids, I want to know where Mommy is and when I can see her?”

Mike hugged Rachel to him and told her that Josie was not feeling well so she probably wouldn’t be over to see her for a little while but he promised to be back to see her. He made her promise to be a good girl and to not give them a hard time there. He also told her, “I love you Rachel. Remember I want only what is best for you. If they tell me that I am the best thing for you I will be here in a heartbeat. But if not then you will have to do as they say. Sometimes things don’t work out like we think they should, but it's only because what we want isn't always what is right."

Rachel looked at Mike. "I know but I also know that you are supposed to be my daddy. I love you." She hugged him and kissed his cheek. She went to Rod and gave him a big hug. "Nice to meet you Uncle Rod. I can't wait to see you again. Maybe you and Dr. Porter can come visit me. I like Dr. Porter." Rod laughed. "I know she has lollipops in her pockets. I'm going to have to search her later because she never gives me any." Rachel giggled. "You only get them when she stops to visit you in the hospital, silly. She always comes visit us sick kids and give us lollipops before she goes back to work, making the grown-ups better." Rod smiled and bit back a laugh as Rachel rolled her eyes at him as if she couldn't believe he didn't already know what she was talking about. "You are going to be seeing us soon

Rachel. You certainly mean a lot to Josie and Mike. They will do all they can to bring you home. But I'm sure I can talk Dr. Porter into coming over to visit. Maybe you can introduce us to some of your friends." Rachel smiled at him touching his face. "Do you know how to make fishy lips too?" Rod made a silly face at her and she dissolved into giggles. She looked at Mike, "I like Uncle Rod, he's silly." She walked away leaving both men sitting there staring after her. Mike looked at Rod, "Now do you see why we love her so much?" He shook his head, "You got it tough dude. Two head strong women in your life. You are in for a rocky road." Mike smiled and said, "I can't wait for that ride."

Chapter 36

Josie recovered from her bruises and cuts. She was fixing up Mike's apartment, making it her home. She was ready to start getting back to work now that she wasn't as bruised and battered. She had started running a little but hadn't been outside running yet. She was using Mike's treadmill. She would sit watching him running while she recovered. She really missed it. She was ready to head out and go for a good run. It was a beautiful day. She was getting cabin fever. She put on her running clothes and headed out. Mike had been spending his days at their home they were building. He had taken her to see it when it was just framed. It didn't look like much then but it was going to be theirs. She thought she would run to the house and check it out. It wasn't far from the bar, but the opposite direction of the town of Wellsprings. It was still close enough to run from there to Wellsprings. Mike wanted to keep us close to town but give us the privacy we loved.

The weather was perfect and Josie was hitting a slow run. She wasn't in a hurry. All Josie wanted was the exercise and fresh air. The past month had been hard trying to put the demons to rest from Jack's attack. So was going back in her apartment to pack her things up. She knew she'd never be able to live there again. She was trying to get used to being with Mike full time. He was definitely a handful but she loved having him with her every day. He was treating her like a china doll that might break. Josie was getting tired of that.

All in all, Josie thought she was doing okay. She had some nightmares which Miranda said were normal considering what she had been through. Miranda was concerned about the lightheadedness also the tiredness she was feeling but Josie said it was just adjusting to a different way of things. She didn't seem overly concerned so Miranda let it go. All and all her life was getting back too normal. She hadn't been to see Rachel. Josie didn't want her to see the bruises. She was planning on going to see Rachel soon though. Before she knew it she was standing in front of her soon to be home.

Mike saw her approach and he went over to her. He leaned down to kiss her. "What do you think?" She couldn't believe how much work they got done in the last month. The walls were up the siding was going on and the roof was done. "Oh my God! It looks like a real house. This is ours?" Mike stood proud next to her and shook his head. "Come on I'll show you inside." He took her hand and she went with him. He was walking her around showing her all the rooms. The rooms had walls up but no finished touches yet. He walked her into the kitchen. It was huge. “Oh Michael. This is beautiful. It’s so big in here.” He smiled, “I wanted plenty of room for you to cook. I know how you like to cook and I wanted room to entertain our friends and space for our family.”

Josie was looking around a little overwhelmed. “I don’t know why we need all this room Michael. It’s just you and me.” He shook his head. “I’m not giving up Josie. I will not give up on having Rachel and more kids.” She shook her head. “Josie, don’t give up on me. I want us to have the life we deserve. We have all the love in the world to share. There isn’t anyone out there who deserves a good life more than you. I will find a way to get you all you want and deserve.” She smiled up at him and moved to him. “I have you Michael, I don’t need anything more.” He saw the sadness in her eyes. He knew she was just telling him what she thought he needed to hear.

Mike finished the tour showing her the upstairs with a master bedroom and three more bedrooms. The layout was perfect. The space was more than she could have ever dreamed. It was perfect. She wanted to get out of his way so she headed back to the apartment. She took a shower and then there was a knock at the door. She opened it to find Sarah. Josie welcomed her in and hugged her friend. "I wanted to come and take you shopping." Josie looked at her surprised. "What are we shopping for?" Sarah smiled at her, "Wedding dresses."

Josie looked at Sarah like she was crazy. "What?" She was smiling from ear to ear. "Okay, here's the deal. Mike told Rod he proposed, Miranda overheard so we are on bridal mission. Miranda and I want you to have the wedding you and Mike deserve. We are helping him put it together. I want you to have the perfect day and part of that is the dress." Josie sank down into the sofa. She couldn't believe her ears. Mike was building their home and planning their wedding. She was sitting around doing nothing. Sarah walked over to Josie and was concerned. "Josie, you do want to marry Mike don't you? I mean this is what you want, right?"

Josie was silent and Sarah didn't know what to think. She waited and no answers were coming. She was starting to feel a little uncomfortable. She watched Josie. She could see a thousand different emotions running over her face. She just sat and waited. Josie looked at her friend finally speaking. "I don't know what to say. Everything is just so overwhelming. I mean finding Michael again. Then he proposes to me and I'm still married.

My crazy husband shows up and gets killed. Michael buys land and starts building a house for us and now a wedding. It's all happening so fast. I feel like I'm steamrolling through my life these past few months."

Sarah sat waiting, she could tell there was more coming from her. "It sounds like I'm complaining. I'm not. I'm extremely happy, I just feel like Michael is doing everything for me and I haven't been doing anything." Josie sighed, "I mean, when is this wedding? Where is it? I don't know anything." Sarah laughed. "There really isn't a set date as of yet, if you want we can help you with all the details. This is your wedding Josie, we just wanted to help. We didn't want to leave things up to him. You need to have the wedding you always dreamed of. Mike just wants to get married and keep moving forward, which is fine but for how long you two have waited to be together we felt you deserved a dream wedding."

Josie shook her head. "I don't even know what that is. I just always wanted to be with Michael. That's all that mattered to me. The how and the planning didn't seem to matter. Now that I know it's happening, it seems so surreal. I don't want anything fancy because that's not us, but I do agree with Michael. I don't want to wait. I'm ready for my life with him to be real and I'm more than ready to be Mrs. Michael Albright."

Sarah sat for a moment, she took her friends hands in hers. "You know Josie, every moment counts. Losing my son. Trent taught me that. I don't regret a moment of the life I had with him. I regret the time that Ted lost getting to know his son, but you can't live life on regrets. You need to move past that. You need to just grab hold of what you have and make every moment matter. Trent lived a short life, but he lived it doing what he wanted. He taught me how to live."

Josie listened to her friend talk about her son and how brave she was. How could she have handled losing her son? What did Josie have to complain about? Losing a son, that was worse than anything she ever endured. She squeezed her friend's hands. "Let's go get a wedding dress and plan a beautiful wedding, but quick." Sarah smiled and hugged her friend. They headed out to start their shopping. Sarah filled Josie in on what she knew so far about the wedding which wasn't much. "All I know is he's going to have it at the bar. It's going to be small with just immediate friends and he was going to just have a very small reception at the bar with some music and food." Josie smiled and said, "It sounds perfect. I don't need fancy, but I would like something more than just a justice of the peace.

I think that you guys and Max of course should be there and the people from the office. The people from the diner I worked with and the employees at the bar should be there too. What do you think?" Sarah said, "It sounds perfect."

At the shops in town the girls found some beautiful dresses. Sarah thought Josie would want a more traditional wedding dress but Josie wasn't having it. She wanted a simple dress that was elegant and beautiful but not formal. They weren't formal kind of people. She just wanted something that would make Mike remember how she looked for the rest of their lives. She wanted him to forget all the horrible things that Jack did to her. She wanted him to see her, his wife as a beautiful woman giving herself to him. That's what she was looking for. She put on the last dress she had picked out and looked in the mirror. She walked out of the dressing room and Sarah's eyes filled with tears. “It’s perfect.” Josie nodded and the two of them started crying.

From the dress shop Josie wanted to go to the florist and the bakery. She picked out the flowers. They were going to be the fire and ice roses with some other flowers for accent. She also was getting some flowers for the tables that matched in the colors of her bouquet. Josie and Sarah went to the bakery. They picked out a tiered cake with simple decorations of flowers on it. Josie didn’t fuss much, she liked things simple. Josie and Sarah talked as they stopped for something to eat in town. Josie was starving and needed to eat as she just wasn’t feeling well.

Miranda came in and saw Josie and Sarah sitting in the diner. “Hey guys. How was shopping?” She came and sat down. They ate lunch together catching up. Sarah and Josie told Miranda about the dress, flowers and cake.

She was impressed. "Wow sounds like you two got a lot accomplished. Some of us had to work." They all laughed. Josie told her she was looking forward to getting back to work. Miranda couldn't wait either. It was tough without her at the office, but she needed time to heal, emotionally as well as physically.

Josie looked at Sarah and Miranda. "You guys have been friends a long time. But from what I've heard there was a third in your group. What happened?" Miranda looked at Josie with sadness in her eyes. "It's been a long time. The story is not ours to tell. That has to come from the source. But can I just say that it's not the way Sarah or I want it. We love and miss our friend. Taryn was so full of life, so much fun and she pulled away from us. The rest you will have to ask her." Sarah looked at Josie and said, "We heard that you've been talking to her. Has she said anything to you?"

Josie shook her head, “No. I’ve been waiting for her to open up to me. I don’t want to push her. I’ve only talked to her briefly here and there, but I do believe, I’m going to stop in and see her about the food for the wedding. What do you guys think?” The two women smiled and nodded their agreement. Josie grinned, “Also if I’m not mistaken, I believe our Max is smitten with her.” Miranda’s jaw dropped and Sarah gasped covering her mouth in surprise. Miranda recovered and said, “No shit!” The three laughed and Josie spilled what she had observed.

Josie knew a lot more than she let on. Taryn had told her what tore her from her friends. She also told Josie how she missed them as well. Josie wasn’t one to tell anyone someone else’s story. She knew when the time was right Taryn would tell them how long she and Josie had been talking and if she didn’t that was fine too. Josie also only told the girls the things she observed with Max and Taryn, not what Max had revealed. The ball was in Taryn's court. Josie was very fond of her though. Josie hoped that she would open up soon about her life. They were talking about going for a run sometime. Josie would love having a female to run with, instead of bugging Mike all the time. Plus, he had enough to do. Josie needed her own friends and life too.

The women talked through their lunch and the conversation came to rest on Miranda and Rod's wedding. "So when is the big day for you guys?" Sarah asked her friend. Miranda shrugged and said, "I don't know. Right now I have a lot on my plate. The hospital is wanting me to take a full time position. I already turned them down once, but I'm so unsure. They obviously want me or they would have given up and moved on. Taking the position though would mean giving up my part in the practice. I'm not sure how I feel about that. I mean it's an awesome opportunity for me but it's going to be more time being away from Rod."

Josie looked at Miranda. "What does Rod think?" Miranda said, "That's the hard part. He tells me it's my decision. How can it be my decision when it will affect both of us?" Sarah smiled and said, "He wants you to have what you want. He doesn't want you to hold back. That's a smart man." Miranda looked at her, "But we're in this together or so I thought, so how do I make the decision alone?" Josie shook her head, "You're not making the decision alone. He is telling you he supports you no matter which way you go. He is a good man. He will always stand behind you, not in front of you blocking the way." Miranda was silent. The three of them sat quietly for a little, each thinking how lucky they were to have the men in their lives.

Miranda had to head back to work and Sarah needed to get back to Ted as he was watching Bella. She dropped Josie off back at the bar. Josie went into the bar to see Max. She went in the side door and Max was out stocking the bar. "Hey Josie." He stopped moving to kiss her cheek. Josie had been getting better at the personal contact. She still flinched a little but it was obvious she was trying not to pull away. "Did you finally give up on Mike and come running to me?" She laughed, "Awe Max, you know I'd leave him in a heartbeat if I thought he could handle being without me." They both laughed. She went to sit at the bar and watched him work. "So what's on that pretty little mind of yours?"

Josie sat there for a minute. "I feel like Michael has been doing so much for me and I haven't done anything for him. He's building this house for us. He's planning our wedding. Is there anything he hasn't done for me?" Max shook his head, "You are thinking about it all wrong Josie. He's trying to right the wrong from so long ago. He wants the life you guys should have had so many years ago. He's trying to make sure he doesn't waste another minute. He's not doing anything more for you than what he feels you deserve. He wants you to be happy and he wants your life together to start now."

Josie smiled at Max. "You are all he talked about Josie. You were what got him through. He hated being away from you but he told me he didn't have the right to be with you until he served his time. He felt like after he served his time he could start fresh, like he would finally deserve you. Everything he ever did, he did to change his life for you. You've been the only thing that mattered to him since the day he met you. He would walk through fire for you."

Josie smiled at Max and thought she'd press ahead. "So how are things going for you Max? Have you talked with Taryn?" Max looked at her, "Yes. I have been seeing her quite a bit lately, which I think you already know." Josie smiled. "So are you going to tell me about her and you?" Max grinned, "I'm sure you know Josie. That woman is amazing. She's been through a lot, but I've been taking things slow." Josie looked to Max. "I know more than I tell anyone, but I will tell you that Taryn has confided in me. Don't tell her I've told you. I didn't even tell the girls at lunch, I played dumb, but I know her story. You are a smart man, taking things slow. Don't give up on her Max. I like her, you are exactly what she needs."

Max looked at Josie smiling. “Taryn is amazing, beautiful, somewhat naïve but in a perfect way. She makes my heart beat so hard against my chest. She makes me laugh harder than I have in a very long time. She makes me believe in trust and love again.” Josie smiled at Max, “This makes me so happy. I’ll be cheering for you both.” Josie thanked Max for the talk. Max smiled, “Same here.” Josie headed upstairs to think more about what she could do for Mike. There had to be something she could do for him.

Chapter 37

Mike was done working at the house. He had to get back to the apartment and shower so he could get to the bar and work. He was exhausted from the last month of working at the house then the bar. He hadn't spent much time with Josie as there just wasn't enough time. She had been fixing up the apartment and making it home for now. She really had come a long way since, well since Jack. Mike hated thinking about it. He was grateful that the bruises were starting to heal and so was Josie's mental status. He walked in the house and he could smell her lasagna baking. She must have been busy today.

Josie was in the bedroom straightening up when Mike came in. She went and kissed him. He was all sweaty and dirty but she didn't mind. "Hi sweetie. What have you been doing besides making lasagna?" She smiled.

"Planning our wedding. I got a dress and flowers and a cake. Sarah told me you've been working on the wedding." He smiled at her. "I was trying to take care of it so as to not stress you out. I just can't wait to make you my wife Josie. I hope you're not mad." She smiled and said, "At first I was, but now I understand. I can't wait to be your wife Michael." He leaned down and kissed her again. He mumbled something about having to get to work and went off to get in the shower. She took the lasagna out of the oven and covered it with foil to keep it warm. She called Max and said that Mike might be a little late for work tonight. He laughed and said no problem.

Josie headed to the bedroom taking her clothes off as she went. She heard the water running and she quietly entered the bathroom and climbed into the shower behind her Mike. She reached out and touched his back.

Mike was letting the water run over his achy body and he was thinking about how he couldn't wait until the house was done so he had more time to be with Josie. They hadn't made love since before the attack. He didn't want to push her. He knew she had been through a lot and he wanted her to heal. He turned to let the water run over his neck and head. When he felt something on his back. He spun around and saw Josie standing in his shower naked. "Josie!" "Were you expecting someone else?" He smiled, "There could never be anyone else." She came up close to him. "I think you need to get cleaned up." She took the soap in her hands and lathered up, then started to wash him with her hands. She started at his neck and shoulders running her hands over him leaving a soapy lather behind as well as a tingling and burning everywhere her hands touched him.

Josie was so aroused. She was running her hands all over Mike's body. She had forgotten how solid he was. Every inch of him was so muscular and from being outside working on their home. He was bronzed from the sun. His body was so beautiful to her and she was enjoying this time of getting to know him again. She had him turn and she ran her hands over his back. She could feel his muscles flinching under her touch. He was getting aroused as well. She continued washing him and took her hands down the back of his legs, reaching around to wash the front of his legs as well. She stood back up and had him turn around again. Once he turned she knew he was aroused. There was no denying it. She took her hands over him and washed him gently.

Mike's hands were shaking as they came up to touch Josie's face. "Josie, you are killing me." She shook her head and said, "No

Michael, I am loving you." He bent down and kissed her forehead and moved down to take her lips. He was losing himself in that kiss and her hands rubbing him. He didn't know how much more he could take. She reached around him and told him it was time to rinse. She took her hands over him again to help free him of the soap she had just put on his body. She took her time and was not in a hurry at all with him. Once she felt all the soap was removed she turned off the shower and opened the curtain to get his towel.

Mike couldn't take it. He was going to explode if he didn't have Josie. He reached for her and she slipped away from him. She grinned at him, "You are all wet Michael. I need to dry you." She was killing him. She took the towel over his body and patted him dry all the way down to his feet. He took the towel from her and started drying her. Once they were both dry she moved over to him and reached her arms up and over his shoulders, she stood on tiptoe to move toward his lips. "Now that you are all clean, it's time for bed Michael."

Mike crushed Josie's mouth to his and he grabbed her beautiful ass in his hands. He was trying to guide her out of the bathroom and ended up pushing her against the sink instead. He lifted her up onto the sink as he moved closer to her. He was kissing her neck and down her chest. He started licking and suckling her nipples as she pulled his head tight to her. He reached down between her legs which parted easily for him and he felt her. She was wet and ready for him. She wanted him and the warm silkiness of her was more then he could stand. He pulled her off the sink and onto him. He held her to him while he went quickly to the bed. He came down on top of her on the bed and instantly she was moving under him. They were both on fire. They had missed this connection. They had missed the feel of each other.

Josie was pulling Mike closer to her. Her fingers were digging and scratching his back. His mouth was over hers and taking each stroke of her tongue with his. She tore her mouth from his and looked in his eyes, “I love you Michael. I’m so in love with you. Oh God! I can’t hold back.” She gasped and he pushed harder into her as she exploded. He was right there with her. He rolled to the side pulling her with him as he didn’t want to move from within her yet, but he didn’t want to crush her under him. “God Josie, I missed that. I didn’t want to push you until you were ready. I’m sorry it went so fast.” Josie smiled at him, “Michael, we need to make more time for this. That was incredible.”

Josie and Mike laid in the bed and she heard his stomach rumble. "You didn't eat lunch again did you?" He smiled at her. "I was too busy. I want our house to be done. I want our life to begin." She was rubbing his chest. "Michael, our life already began. It started that first night you came up to me in the bar. We were always meant to be together. So now we are." He knew she was right but he wanted more. "I want us to be married. I want us to have that house and family. I want it all for us Josie." She reached her hand to his face. "Sometimes you want too much Michael. I'm a simple girl. All I need in this life is you." She moved to kiss him and he stopped her. "I don't deserve you Josie. You know that?" She shook her head at him. "You deserve so much more Michael." Before he could protest she kissed him. She got up, dressed and told him she needed to get his dinner ready.

Mike laid in the bed for a few minutes and played over what Josie said, 'You deserve so much more Michael.' What did that mean? He couldn't even imagine that she wouldn't be enough for him. She was all he wanted and all he needed in this world. He got dressed to find her and ask her what she meant. He found her cutting into the lasagna and she was dishing it out. It looked so good. He couldn't wait to eat it but first he needed an answer. He turned her to look at him. "What did you mean by that Josie? You are all I need in this life. I can't imagine anything else I would want." She looked at him and said, "Children Michael. I can't give you children. You deserve a family and you're building that big house for what? You want children. I can't give them to you. I had two pregnancies that both ended in miscarriages but after those miscarriages I never got pregnant again. I can't get pregnant anymore. Which means I can never fully give you all the things you want and deserve."

Mike shook his head at Josie. "Josie, all that doesn't mean anything to me, not if I don't have you. I take you how you are and if we can't have our own children then there is Rachel who I would want whether we could have children or not. Also I want a son. We can adopt. I would love any children as long as I have you by my side to raise them."

Josie had tears in her eyes. This man in front of her was her destiny. She belonged with Mike, forever. She smiled at him. "I can't wait to be your wife Michael." He kissed her and they sat down to eat. She was laughing at how he devoured her lasagna. He was rushing around the apartment while she cleaned up dinner and she fixed a plate to take down to Max later.

Mike headed down to get to work and Josie worked around the kitchen. After cleaning up the kitchen she headed into the bathroom to clean up after their lovemaking. She fixed the bed and she thought about the man that filled her thoughts every minute of every day. She finished cleaning up and grabbed the plate of food for Max then headed down the stairs to the side door of the bar. She went in and found Max. She handed him the plate and he grabbed her and kissed her cheek.

Mike came up behind Mike. "Let go of my woman!" He let go of Josie and turned to Mike. "If you don't marry her soon, I am going to steal her away." Mike growled, "I'd like to see you try." Max went off to eat his dinner laughing at his friend and Mike walked Josie to a seat at the bar. "Do you want a drink Josie girl?" She shook her head. "Just a diet cola." He looked at her surprised but got her the diet coke she asked for. “You okay?” She smiled and said she was fine, but she thought she may need to have Miranda run some more tests. Her head and stomach just weren’t right. She knew the concussion could cause her headaches but she wasn’t really suffering from headaches just lightheadedness and nausea. There must be some ill effects from the concussion.

Chapter 38

It was time for Josie to head back to work. She was up early and ready to go. She couldn't wait. She missed the office and having something to do. She loved working but she was going to miss going for her runs in the morning and seeing Mike. The house was almost done. She was so excited. They had started ordering furniture and getting things to decorate. It was so exciting. Mike couldn't believe how excited she was about decorating the house and getting the furniture. He told her they had to be careful of cost for right now, but they could order some of the things she wanted. He insisted on ordering furniture for Rachel's room. He had a bed with a canopy on order. He was making it a real princess room for her.

Josie couldn't help but get involved in it and have fun with getting the decorations for

Rachel's room. It was so hard to not think about adopting her but Josie was afraid of getting hurt by being turned down. All the furnishings for Rachel's room were there and Mike ordered light pink paint for the walls. Once it was finished being painted Rachel's room would be the first to be finished. He really did love that little girl.

Josie walked into the office and to her desk. "What a mess!" Miranda came around the corner and smiled. "Still wanna be my friend?" Josie laughed and started sorting through the mess that Miranda created. She had charts everywhere and notes galore. It was going to take her days to sift through this. Josie just started plunging into the mess. She made piles. There were charts that just needed to be filed, charts with orders on them that needed to be processed and then there were the notes that she needed to get through to find out what exactly was needed.

By lunch time Josie was halfway through the disaster. She was still working when Miranda came in and said, “How bout some lunch?” Josie stopped and looked up at Miranda. She stood up and the room shifted slightly and Josie sank back into her chair. “Josie, are you okay?” She shook her head and said, “I think I’m just hungry. I haven’t stopped all morning.” Miranda looked around and was thoroughly impressed by her progress. They headed to the lunch room.

Miranda looked at Josie. “I finally decided on a date for the wedding.” Josie smiled so big and clapped her hands. “Hooray! When?” She said I want to have it in July. I want to do it 4th of July weekend. I figured with all the fireworks Rod sets off in me, it’s appropriate. We are going to have the wedding at the cabins. We both just love it there, and it's just going to be close friends, so basically just you guys. We'll spend the weekend at the cabin and just enjoy being with our friends."

Josie was surprised. "No big reception?" Miranda shook her head. "Rod doesn't have family any longer and I don't have family who matter. I haven't spoken to my sister or my mom and dad in years. I don't plan on starting now. That book has been closed and shipped. I'll invite my brother. He's living in Kellersville, not far from you guys. We've just started talking more. Our family life wasn't the greatest, but he and I were close once. I'm hoping to be that way again. I've missed him." Josie didn't understand why Miranda wouldn't want to try and see all of her family but it wasn't Josie's business and Miranda was the type of person who told you only what she wanted to reveal. She kept most of her life very private. “Well then we had better get planning. You only have a few months to pull this together.” Miranda shrugged her shoulders and said, “Not much to plan. It’s going to be very simple. Just like us.”

Josie headed back to work. She had pretty much put her desk back in order by the end of the day. She was cleaning up and getting ready to head out of the office for the day and not a moment too soon. She was exhausted. She couldn’t wait to go home and take a nap. Mike would be working so she could rest for a little while. He wouldn’t miss her. He could grab something to eat from somewhere or there were leftovers in the fridge. She needed to rest up because the wedding was coming fast. She only had a few more weeks left before she and Mike finally became husband and wife. She had everything all lined up and the planning was mostly done.

This is all except the decorating which they would do that morning. She was ready and so was Mike. She was done. She hit the lights off and locked up the door. Finally, time to head home.

Max was getting the bar ready and he had filled the ice bin behind the bar when Mike came in. "What else do you need?" Max shook his head, "I think we are good. All ready." Mike was surprised how under control things had been. He had a good staff. Everyone really stepped up for him since everything happened with Josie and while he had been spending so much time trying to get their house built.

"Max," Mike stopped working and looked at his friend. "I can't tell you how glad I am to have you working with me. You have been taking control and handling all that's been thrown your way. I can't tell you how much I appreciate it. I know I haven't been here a lot and I am sorry. I am planning on making myself more available. The house is almost done and the wedding is coming up soon. It's all going to finally be complete." Max laughed and shook his head. "Mike, you have a staff and me for a reason. We need to keep this place running. We all have a job to do. You are the boss, now that this place is off the ground, you don't have to be here twenty-four- seven. I'm here to pick up for you and besides when we really need you, you're here. During the week we are slow so it's no big deal."

Mike looked around the bar. Everyone was setting up different areas of the bar. Max was right, he had a staff who he paid to take care of things. They all were doing the jobs they needed to. Max was right. The weekdays were slower, however business was increasing. He had been running the numbers and there was definitely an increase. He was really happy with how things had been turning out with the bar. He couldn't complain. "Well still Max, I owe you. You've been good to me all these years, and you've been there for me with Josie. I don't think I'll ever be able to repay you." Max smiled at his friend. "No repayment necessary, just treat her right." Mike nodded. "I intend to. So, well I guess what I'm trying to say is, will you be my best man at the wedding?" Max grinned. "Hell yeah!" The two shook hands and then hugged. They had been through a lot together and even though Max knew Mike while he was in jail, he never thought ill of Mike. He knew Mike was a good person, just mixed up and trying to find his way.

Mike hung at the bar for a few hours and around nine business seemed to slow down. Max was talking and smiling with Taryn. She seemed to be coming around a lot. Josie was talking with her at the gym and Max seemed completely into Taryn. Mike went to Max telling him he was going to head upstairs to check on Josie. Mike went up and all was dark and quiet. He walked to the kitchen and thought it was odd. There were no dishes. She hadn't eaten dinner. He went into the bedroom and there she was. She was sound asleep on the bed still in her scrubs. The poor thing was exhausted. He let her sleep and he headed back to the living room to watch some T.V.

Josie woke up still in her scrubs from work. She heard the T.V. in the living room. She looked at the clock it was nine-thirty. Josie was surprised that Mike was home, but she was going to make the most of it. She stripped out of her scrubs and walked naked to the living room. She leaned in the doorway of the bedroom looking toward him on the sofa. She moved until she was standing in front of the T.V.

Mike never heard her but he damn sure saw her naked standing in front of the glow of the T.V. “Holy shit Josie! What are you doing?” She moved toward him and climbed on his lap straddling him. “What does it look like I’m doing?” Josie pulled at his shirt pulling it off of him. Mike raised his arms and leaned forward for her to easily remove the garment. She reached for his pants and she unbuttoned his jeans and pushed the zipper down. “Does this make it clearer, Michael?” She reached into his pants and grabbed ahold of him and he was ready to lose it. “Oh yeah, it makes it crystal clear.” Mike moved quickly flipping her onto her back on the sofa. He stood dropping his pants to the floor and kicking them aside.

Josie watched Mike drop his pants to the floor, then he moved quickly over her. When his body covered hers she looked into his eyes before she pulled him to her lips where she gently kissed and nibbled his. She took her tongue tracing his lips before she pressed inside of them. Once she was in his mouth she tangled her tongue with his. She felt his hips moving over her. She reached down between them and stroked him gently. Mike tore his lips off of hers, "Jesus Josie, you can't do that. I won't last." She grinned back at him, she pulled her legs up and threw one over the back of the sofa. She gently placed his tip against her and rubbed it back and forth.

Josie held Mike in her hands and she was driving him wild. She was rubbing him against her. She was hot, wet and Mike didn't know how much more he could take. She moved her leg over the back of the sofa to allow him more access to her and he was ready to press deep inside of her. Mike sat up pulling slightly away from her. He reached behind him grabbing the two throw pillows Josie had placed on the sofa for "decorations". He lifted her ass up and stuck the pillows underneath her. He moved back over her. "Sorry Josie, I have to feel you. If I wait much longer it's going to be too fast and I need to savor this." Mike pressed his tip against her and slowly started to slide into her.

Josie was trying to take more of Mike, she wanted him deep inside of her, but Mike wasn't having it. "No Josie! I want you to feel me, I want you to feel me fill you. Slowly, I am going to ease inside of you until I fill you, until I hit that spot deep within you that makes you explode and moan when I rock against you." Josie was moaning already turned on by his words. Mike reached between her legs as he was slowly entering her. "I want to rub you here," Josie moaned, "Ahhhhh yes Josie girl, I want to rub and circle you until you are jerking underneath me from the spasms that are waiting to erupt inside of you. Feel me, do you feel me?" Josie gasped. "Michael, I can't breathe."

Mike moved his hand from between them, he bent his head down to kiss her. It was an urgent meshing of tongues, Josie was pulling his neck tight, he felt his resolve slipping, he tore his lips from hers and moved to her nipple. He sucked it into his mouth, circling the nipple with his tongue and then moving his tongue back and forth over the stiff hard peak. Finally, he nibbled the nipple and she gasped underneath him. He slid himself a little deeper inside of her. He was almost at the end of her control, but he was also almost deep within her. He had one more nipple to suckle and bite then he would be buried deep within her.

Josie felt the sparks flying as Mike first suckled her one breast and nibbled the nipple, now he was doing the same to the other. As he nibbled the second nipple she felt him slide deep inside of her. She felt him hit her deep within and her hips rocked, rubbing his tip deep against her and she started quaking. Her body was shivering. "Oh my God, Michael!" He moved back to hover over her lips. "Shhhh, Josie, I got you. Let it happen. I want you to lose control, I want you to explode so hard, I want you to squeeze me tight when you cum and I want to be the one that makes you scream from pure pleasure." Josie's hips were rocking and she felt him deep within her. He owned her soul. Josie was shuddering underneath him.

"More Michael, more……" Mike heard her. He pulled back from inside her then pressed deep in again. Josie's hips rose to him as he hit her deep again, she said, "Oh God yes, again." Mike not disappointing her he did it again and again. Josie was shuddering as Mike kept pumping into her. "Michael, oh my God, Michaaaaaeeeeelllllllll!" She was losing the battle, she was pulsing and Mike felt her tighten around him. Her hips raised to him and her whole body shook with her release.

"Yes, Josie, let it go." Mike pumped in and out of her intensifying her release and bringing his on. As he felt the last of his restraint slipping, he heard her. "Oh my God Michael, I'm going to do it again, ohhhhh God I feel it." Mike tried to hold himself back from his release to let her cum again, but he was losing the battle as she rocked her hips and pulsed around him. She was squeezing him with every pump he made. “Oh God Josie, I’m trying to hold back but I can’t much longer. I need to feel you squeezing every ounce of me into you.....God Josie, I love you so much.”

Mike’s last ounce of control left him and he exploded inside of Josie. He pressed himself deep inside her and left her squeeze around him, her hips rocking beneath him and he felt her trembling under him. “Michael, oh Michael it’s happening again.” Josie’s hips were rocking faster and he held himself as deep as he could inside her until her moan tore through her lips and her hips finally came to rest on the pillows he placed under her. Mike bent and gently kissed her lips.

“Damn Josie, that was beautiful.” Josie looked up at him. “Michael, oh Michael.” Tears were flowing out of her eyes and he thought he hurt her. He went to move only she held him tight. “No, don’t move. I’m okay. It’s just that I haven't felt that in a long time. You've made me feel things I didn't think I ever would again. Michael, I love you so much. I don't know how I survived without you for so long." He looked in her eyes, "You will never spend another minute having to be away from me. I will never leave you again. Never, Josie. I want to lose myself in you as often as you'll allow me, I want to bring this kind of pleasure to you always and forever. This is how it is supposed to be, this is how it will be forever. My Josie girl, I promise, forever."

The next few weeks passed like a blur. Mike was busy getting the house ready. Josie was working and sleeping a lot. He was concerned but he knew there was a lot of stress for her so he let it go. She was working some days with him at the house trying to get things set to move in so he understood why she was so tired. They were so close to finally having it all.

He kept pushing on. They had fallen into bed most nights completely exhausted. He would still pull her naked against him and some nights he would feel her respond. On other nights he knew they were both beyond exhausted, then he would hold her tight to him and just sleep. Josie was at work the Wednesday before the wedding. One minute she was fine and the next she was on the ground. She didn't know what happened. She woke up in an examination room and Miranda standing over her with a puzzled look on her face. "Josie, you are back. You scared the life out of me." She just looked at her, "I don't know what happened. I was fine then I got dizzy and then I don't know what happened." Miranda said, "Okay Josie, but I think I need to take some blood work and check you out." Josie agreed. "One thing. You cannot tell Michael." Miranda looked at her and shook her head.

Chapter 39

Mike's cell phone rang and he picked it up. He was standing in the finished house. He was looking at Rachel's room. "Are you kidding me?" The voice on the other end of the phone just gave him the best news of his life. He called Max immediately. Megan Tate of the orphanage had just called and told him that there was paperwork that needed to be completed but he and Josie were going to be approved to adopt Rachel. He was so excited he forgot to ask when they could do the paperwork and if Rachel could come to the wedding. He couldn't contain himself. He called Rod to tell him as well. Rod was ecstatic. He was telling Rod that he wanted to surprise Josie but he forgot to get all the information from Megan. Rod told Mike not to worry. He would work it out and he'd be sure Rachel was at the wedding.

Mike only had to keep it a secret for a few more days. The wedding was coming fast and he now had everything he needed. Josie made it clear to him that the night before the wedding he was staying at the apartment and she was going to stay at Miranda's. She didn't want to stay at the new house for the first time without him. She didn't want him at the house either. The first night they would spend at their home would be their wedding night. Mike promised her and he was making sure everything was ready for them there. He was going to have flowers, champagne and candlelight. They hadn't made love for a few weeks now as they've been so busy and Josie had been so tired. Mike knew this was going to make their wedding night even more special. He wanted their first night as husband and wife to be perfect. Now knowing that Rachel was theirs was going to make it even more special.

Rod called the orphanage. The staff told him that he could come and get Rachel for the day of the wedding then bring her back afterward. Once Josie and Mike were married, they could come and sign all the papers then take Rachel home. Rod called Sarah he told her to find a flower girl dress but keep her lips sealed. He was going to need her help to pull this off. Since Miranda would be busy with Josie he could slip out, get Rachel and take her to Sarah's house to get ready. Sarah was squealing with delight and promised her secrecy. She would find the perfect dress.

Josie was still so tired but she was getting excited about the wedding. She wanted everything to be perfect. The bar staff was incredible. They volunteered to come in Sunday morning to decorate. Josie had dropped off all the decorations and explained how everything should be placed. They were happy to take care of things. Josie made sure to go around thanking each one of the staff personally for all their hard work at the bar, and also for their wedding. The staff all adored Josie and since she and Mike had been together, they liked him a lot more. She and Mike both would see the decorated bar for the first time as they were getting married. Neither one of them would be doing the set up and Max promised to not let Mike into the bar until it was time to have the ceremony. Josie was happy. She couldn't wait to spend their first night in their new home. Finally, Josie had everything she wanted, if only she knew what was wrong with her. She had a feeling that something was definitely wrong though. She would wait for Miranda's tests before letting panic set in.

Mike paced the apartment. Finally, the day he'd waited for was here. He was going to marry Josie today. It came quickly but yet seemed like it took a lifetime to get here. It was a beautiful day and soon he would have his wife by his side. He couldn't wait. Sarah and Ted were going to bring Rachel to the apartment to see him before the ceremony. He couldn't wait to see his soon to be daughter. The day was going to be perfect.

Miranda got up early and made breakfast for Rod and Josie. Okay Miranda didn't cook. She took frozen waffles out of the freezer and placed them in the toaster. It was the thought that counted. Rod was heading out early to do some errands but promised he'd be back to change and pick them up. He was being secretive but Miranda let him because he never kept anything important from her. Sometimes the little surprises were the best so she would let him go for now. Rod ate and was out the door before Josie got out of bed. Once

Josie was up Miranda heated up the breakfast (aka frozen waffles) she had made earlier, they sat down to talk. Miranda had Josie's file in front of her.

Josie looked at her friend. "Are you kidding me?" Miranda shook her head. "No, I wouldn't kid about this." Josie had her answer about why she had been so tired. She was totally in denial and didn't let it sink in. She got up from the table and told Miranda, "Not a word, okay? I don't want Michael to know about this. Not yet." Miranda shook her head and Josie headed upstairs to take a shower and start getting ready. This was her wedding day. She wasn't going to think about it until after she and Mike were married. She would wait and she would tell Mike afterward. No sense in ruining the planning of the wedding by rushing over there now. She knew what Mike's reaction would be and there would be enough emotions with the wedding today. Besides she needed to check the autopsy report she had been given months ago to see what secrets that held.

Miranda got ready for the wedding then went to help Josie. She was just finishing up with Josie when Rod returned. Rod was in the bedroom changing she heard him cursing while he thumped around the room. Miranda heard him go down the steps to the living room. He was quick. Miranda told Josie she looked beautiful and she would see her downstairs when she was ready. Miranda went downstairs and whistled when she saw her soon to be husband. "You look awfully handsome." Miranda went to him and kissed him. Rod smiled at her. "You look spectacular, but it's really not fair to the bride to look as good as you do." She grinned at him, "Flattery will get you everywhere. So later, I'll let you see what I have on under this dress." Rod grinned at her.

"I'll be counting the minutes and copping a feel." They were kissing when Josie came down the stairs.

"I'm ready." Rod and Miranda both turned their attention to Josie and smiled. Rod told her how beautiful she looked and Miranda said, "Let's get you married to the man of your dreams. You've both waited long enough for this day." Josie smiled. She stopped before heading out and asked Rod for a moment. Rod stopped and Miranda headed out to the car. "I know it's late notice but I've been thinking. Rod you mean so much to me. You are like family to me. I never had anyone in my life other than Michael that believed in me, encouraged me and made me feel important." Rod shifted and said, "I understand. Josie you are like a sister to me. I love you very much. You and I have quite a bond and I'll always be here for you." Josie shook her head. "I love you too, as a brother." She smiled at him and continued. "I don't want to walk into that bar by myself today. I was hoping that, well I was hoping that you would represent me and give my hand in marriage to Michael. It sounds old fashioned but, that's me."

Rod looked at Josie and she never saw him cry but a tear rolled down his cheek. "Josie, this is truly an honor and I would be happy to do that. It means a lot to me that you asked me to do this. Wow!" Josie went to hug him and Miranda came back in the house. "Are we doing this today or not?" Josie laughed while hugging Rod and then the two separated and Miranda saw the emotion in her fiancé wondering what was going on. Josie turned to her friend, "I hope you don't mind but I'm going to borrow your man today." She looked at Josie and said, "You're not planning on running away with him are you?" They all laughed and Josie told her friend about Rod's role in the ceremony.

Josie was starting to get very nervous. She had waited a long time for this day. She just needed to calm down. On the way to the Heartbreak Bar, Josie was thinking about Mike and the road they had traveled to get here. It wasn't an easy one, but it had been worth every bump and bruise. She had great friends now and family with these people here and she couldn't be happier. After the wedding she had some things to tell Mike but she was sure that things would be okay.

The three pulled up at the bar and Sarah was waiting for her. Ted had already moved inside with Rachel. Everything was set. Max popped his head out the door to see if they were all ready. Miranda was Josie's maid of honor. Max and Miranda were walking in together. Max looked at Josie. "Are you sure you want to do this? We could still run away together." Josie laughed, "I've waited my whole life for this moment so I'm sorry but I'm going to have to turn you down." Max smiled and kissed her cheek. "He's a lucky guy. Mike has a wedding gift for you though before you go in. He opened the door and out came Rachel. She was all dressed up and her hair was beautifully put up with flowers in it. She grinned at Josie. "Mommy, I'm going to be the flower girl at your wedding to Daddy. Daddy said that after the wedding I have to go back to the orphanage but then tomorrow you have to sign something, then I get to come home to see my room that you fixed up for me. Daddy says it's all official and we are a family for real. Can you believe it? I told you I was going to have you as my Mommy. I knew it!"

Josie was looking at Rachel like she was kidding. She looked at Max. He nodded his head. “It will be official after you both get married and go to sign the papers.” She started to cry and she reached down to hug her daughter. Rachel smiled at her mother. “Is it time to marry Daddy now?” They all laughed and Josie wiped the tears from her eyes and said, “You bet it is.”

Mike stood at the front of the bar. He waited to see his Josie. He couldn’t wait. He was shifting back and forth. He could barely stand still. Ted looked over at him and said, “Dude, knock it off. She’s coming. Relax.” Mike looked at him. “I’m trying. I just need to see her.” With that the doors opened and Max and Miranda came in. Next the door opened and there was his daughter. He smiled with pride watching her come toward him. Finally, his heart was in his throat. The door opened and there was Josie. She was holding onto Rod’s arm and she was looking straight at

Mike. He would never forget a second of this moment. Her dress was long and silky. It shined as she stood there looking at him. It was simple but absolutely beautiful. It clung to every curve of her body. It hugged her in all the right places. It had thin straps that came over her shoulders and it dipped low at her chest with little waves in the silky material at her chest. God how he wanted to touch her. Her hair was up and had such beautiful curls that fell over each other. She had on her butterfly necklace. He had never seen anything more beautiful than Josie.

Josie's heart was pounding in her chest. She was concentrating on moving. She came through the door and paused. She looked at Rod then looked for Mike. When she saw him she held his eyes and was ready to walk toward her future. Rod squeezed her arm and steadied her, "Ok Josie, this is it. Are you ready for your dreams to finally come true?" Josie turned to him for a brief moment and smiled, "You bet I am. Let's go big brother, give me away to the man of my dreams." Rod patted her arm and with that they were off. Within seconds she was by Mike's side, but it felt like a lifetime till she got there. There were tears in his eyes. He couldn't stop looking at her. The minister asked "Who gives this woman to be wed to this man?" Rod stood with pride next to her and said, "I do." He leaned down and kissed her cheek, then handing her off to Mike he said, "She is yours now, take care of her." Rod backed away. Mike turned to look at his soon to be wife. She had tears in her eyes watching him.

Mike took Josie's hands and said, "You are the most beautiful woman in the world." The minister cleared his throat and started the ceremony. Josie just looked at his face. This was going to be the face she looked at for the rest of her life. She was ready. She wanted this man in her life forever. He had tears in his eyes and he was squeezing her hand so tight. The minister was talking but all she could do was look at her Michael. She didn't hear a word the minister was saying. Her heart was pounding so hard and she couldn't focus on anything but her Michael.

Mike stood there holding her hand. He couldn't believe that this day was here. He was ready to sweep her off her feet and run out of there with her. He just wanted to be with her. She was so beautiful. She smiled at him as she held his eyes. He was truly the luckiest man alive. The minister was talking and he was having a hard time focusing on anything but Josie. The minister finally was at the vows and Mike was ready.

"I understand that Josie and Mike have prepared their own vows to one another. Mike couldn't wait, he was ready to pledge his heart to her. "Josie, from the first moment I met you so many years ago I knew you were the only woman for me. I have waited a lifetime for this moment and I want you to know that no matter what life throws our way, I am yours. I stand here before you today to promise you all the things in life that you have always wanted and dreamed of. I will move heaven and earth for you. I will not rest until your life is as full as you've made mine. You have given yourself to me, twice heart and soul. You have introduced me to our daughter. Today I am a completed man after I officially say I do. My heart belongs to you both. I promise you I will be here for you from now until my last breath. Josie Ann Williams-Morris, you are the air that I breathe and the love in my heart, I thank you for loving me and becoming my wife today."

Josie was crying. She was listening to her Mike profess his love and it was the most beautiful thing she had ever heard. She reached her hand out to touch his cheek, then as she always did she slid her hand down his face. He smiled at her, now it was her turn. "Michael Peter Albright, today is a day I have always dreamed of. It's a day I never thought would happen. I waited a lifetime for you and now I get to spend the rest of that lifetime with you. I have loved you since the first moment I met you and I never stopped loving you. You are in my heart, you are my soul and you are my world. I stand here before you today as a woman completely in love with you. I would give you my last breath and I promise you I will love you until that last breath. You are my strength, my rock and the father for my daughter. We are the luckiest women in the world to have you in our lives. I promise you this life we will live will be filled with surprises, unpredictability, joy and everything you will ever need to complete you as you complete me. I love you so much. I am proud to stand before these people and declare you my one, my only, my everything until my last breath."

There was not a dry eye in the room. These people witnessed the complete and total commitment of two people so in love that they felt it in their hearts as well. The couple standing before them had only stared at one another the whole time as if no one else was in the room. They completed each other and that was obvious. Rachel couldn't contain herself any longer. "Daddy! Kiss Mommy, she loves you!" Everyone laughed.

Mike leaned over and winked at his daughter then said to Josie, "Our daughter wants us to kiss." Josie smiled at him. Mike continued "I'm not going to disappoint her." Josie's Michael grabbed her and dipped her in his arms. He kissed her to the sound of thunderous applause. The minister didn't even get the words out and he was kissing her. He pulled her upright and she swayed a little. He held on to her until she was steady. Mike could feel her back, so he knew her dress had no back to it. He couldn't wait to get a look at it. Josie and Mike turned to their friends and the minister said, "I want to introduce you to Mr. and Mrs. Michael Albright." They all cheered and clapped and then Rachel was in front of them. Mike hoisted her up in his arms and she hugged both of them. Josie looked to Miranda, who came over and said, "Let's go get a drink and sit down." Josie went with her to get a drink of water. Mike followed with Rachel.

The happy couple sat down and let everyone come to them. Josie was holding Rachel and they were talking about her room and how they couldn't wait to have her there.

Rachel was understanding and was fine with not going to the new house that night but Josie promised her first thing in the morning they would be at the orphanage to sign the papers and bring her home. She was curled up in Josie's arms.

Mike got up and circled the room. He was talking with Max and some of the other staff members. Max said, "Aren't you going to dance with your new wife?" Mike looked over at Josie while she was holding their daughter. "You bet I am. I just hate to disturb her while Rachel is sitting with her. Max said, "We can take care of that. I understand she adores her Uncle Rod. So he can dance with her while I dance with Miranda. It will be a group dance." Mike nodded and headed to the DJ and asked him to play their song.

Josie heard the song come on. She looked up. Mike was there. Rod took Rachel while Mike le Josie to the dance floor and into his arms. He pulled her close. She tucked her head into his chest while they swayed to the music. "Are you happy Josie girl?" She looked up at him, "Completely." He leaned down and kissed her lips. She continued to look into his eyes as their song ended. The music had stopped but he still held her. "You really do look beautiful Josie. That dress is perfect." She smiled as she knew he would like it. It was a silky spaghetti strapped white dress. It dipped low exposing most of her back and rippled in waves at the chest. It was a full length dress more traditional wedding dress. Josie wasn't sure about how it clung to her body, but she knew Mike would like it. Josie had to admit her curves had started to look good even to her lately.

"The dress is perfect, and it is going to be even more perfect once I can get it off of you and my hands on you." Josie smiled at Mike. "Come here." He leaned down and she whispered in his ear, "I'm naked under this dress. Watch as I walk away, no panty lines." He didn't let her go. "Josie, you had better be joking." She shook her head no. Mike groaned. Josie laughed and he muttered, "You are killing me." She pulled away. She felt his eyes on her trying to take the dress off of her as she walked away.

The wedding went on with dancing and music. Josie and Mike cut the cake and Rachel was getting sleepy. Miranda and Rod offered to take Rachel back to the orphanage for them and Josie and Mike said good-night to their little girl. She didn't cry when she left them because she knew she'd be seeing them tomorrow morning. She hugged them both, told them she loved them then went off holding Uncle Rod's hand smiling up at him. Miranda was holding the other hand but Rachel just adored and loved Rod.

The last guest left and Josie was cleaning up while the staff protested. They wanted her to sit down and relax not clean up. Mike saw her cleaning up. He went to Max who was with Taryn wrapping up the food. Mike told Max he was going to take Josie home. Mike wanted the staff who stayed and cleaned up to be given a bonus and Max said he would take care of it. He then went over and took his wife in his arms. "Mrs. Albright, I want to take you home." She smiled and nodded her head.

Chapter 40

Josie and Mike got into the truck and she moved over close to him. She had her hand in his lap and she was kissing his neck. They made it to the house in record time. He came to help her out of the truck and once she was standing in front of him he kissed her. "I've waited a lifetime for this Josie. But now I finally have something to offer you. We have the bar and our home. Tomorrow we will have our daughter. I finally have a purpose in this life and I have you by my side. Welcome home my beautiful wife." He scooped her up and carried her into their home. He didn't stop for her to look around he figured there would be time later for that. He carried her straight to their bedroom.

Mike put Josie down inside the door to their room. "Are you really naked under that dress?" She smiled at him as she pulled the dress up and over her head. She was standing there naked. She slipped her feet out of her shoes then walked right up to her husband. "I told you. Have I ever lied to you?" She reached up and slid the jacket off her husband's shoulders then she unbuttoned his shirt. She slid that off his arms as she walked around behind him. She was touching his back as she leaned in leaving a trail of kisses across it as well. She came back in front of him, unbuckled his pants and left them hit the floor. He stood frozen just watching her. She stopped in front of him. She took a few slow steps backward toward their bed. "Make love to me my husband. I want you to make love to me as your wife. I've waited so long for this. Come to me."

Josie was almost to the bed when Mike came up in front of her and took her face between his hands. "You are so beautiful Josie.

I can't believe that you are my wife, finally." He kissed her then laid her on the bed. He took his time touching, his hands didn't stop. They were caressing her breasts and his mouth took them one at a time suckling, licking them until he had her wriggling beneath him. His fingers moved down between her legs. She was so soft there and she was pressing against his hand. He didn't disappoint her. He slipped a finger inside of her moist wet heat. She was pushing against him and they started their familiar rhythm. He wanted to taste her. His wife, she was his, he needed to taste her.

Mike moved down between Josie's legs. She moved her legs to accommodate him. "Oh Josie. I will die making love to you." With that he moved in and started licking, suckling and making her wild beneath him. He peeked his tongue inside of her. The heat of if drove Josie wild. Her climax was building and he knew it was coming. He reached under her, squeezed her beautiful ass lifting her to him. He was stroking her with his tongue and she was pushing herself to him. He felt her and heard her. She was his. She was shaking rocking into him. She was ready to give all of her to him and as he delved deeper into her he felt her release spill around him.

This was Mike and Josie's night. Now they could have it all. Mike moved up and over her. He wanted her to cum with him. He wanted her to tighten around him in climax he wanted to bring her that joy and feeling over and over again. He moved in and kissed her neck. He trailed kisses across her chest. He raised up to look in her eyes. He slowly entered her. "I'm yours Josie, take me. Take all of me forever." As he slid into her he felt like he was home. Together they made the most of their new bed and they made love as husband and wife in their new home.

The morning came Josie and Mike woke up in each other's arms and smiled. Not only were they husband and wife but today they would get their daughter. But before that happened Mike wanted to make love to his wife again. But Josie had other plans. Mike moved toward her and was ready to start touching her. She reached out and grabbed his hand. "You had your moment Michael. This morning is mine." She smiled at him and rolled to mount him. She straddled his body and leaned into kiss him. "This morning I am going to make love to my husband." She pulled herself up and looked into his eyes. She ran her hands over his body, down his arms, she rubbed her hands up his chest and then she reached down and took him in her hands. He was rock hard. He was excited and ready for her. She was ready for him too.

Josie moved up to take Mike and let her body slide over him like a glove. She loved the feel of him entering her. She wanted to feel it again. She pulled herself off of him, looking him in the eyes as she slowly slid down him again. God how he made her feel. She felt beautiful when she was with him. There was no shame any longer with her scars. She was free with him. She reached up and touched her breasts. "Touch me Michael. I want you to touch me." His hands replaced hers and she moved her hands to where they were joined. She pushed her hands against his skin between them and felt the heat. Their bodies came together where her hands were. It completely turned her on thinking about how they were joined. She raised up again and pulled him out of her.

"Josie, please don't stop." She leaned down to kiss his lips. "I wouldn't dream of stopping Michael." She sat back up and raised above him again. One last time she needed to slide him into her. She slowly took him. Inch by inch and as she did so she took his hands in hers and covered her breasts with them. He was rubbing her nipples into taut little peaks and her hands held on to his while he did. She sank down and took more of him rocking her hips back and forth. She could feel her climax mounting. She wasn't ready for it. But she couldn't wait to feel him explode inside of her. She rocked harder and sank down further to take more of him grinding her hips into him.

"Jesus Josie." Mike was dying beneath her. He was so close to spilling everything inside loved the feel of her in his mouth. She rocked faster against him and he knew she was unraveling too. His hands were on her back. He slid them down to her beautiful bottom. He squeezed her in his hands and pulled her to him as he raised his hips to her. Her head fell back and a strangled cry of ecstasy came from her lips. That was all it took. He was spilling into her as she squeezed every last ounce out of him. They both fell to the bed panting and satisfied. It had been almost five months since they made love the first time and every time they made love it was always different.

"Oh my God Michael! I want to do that again, but I can't breathe." He laughed and pulled her in kissing her forehead. "Ah, my Josie girl. We have forever to continue doing that." She snuggled up against him. "Good. I love to touch you and I love your hands being on me. I can't wait to see what we do next." Mike chuckled. "Neither can I my beautiful wife. Neither can I."

Mike and Josie both got up and dressed. They were so excited to get their daughter that they decided to wait and get Rachel then they could go for breakfast together as a family. They went downstairs and Josie went to the kitchen to make some coffee. Mike went to the living room and waited for her. She met him there and they walked around their new home. It was beautiful. She had decorated it so perfectly for them. He made her a coffee table like the ones from the bar from a tree trunk. She decorated the rest of their home around that. It was like bringing the woods inside. It was perfect for them.

Josie went back to the kitchen and was fixing them more coffee, when Mike came in behind her. He reached up and cupped her breasts from behind. Instantly they were pressing against the fabric to peek under his direction. She leaned her head back and rested it against his shoulder. She pressed herself back toward him and then reached her arms behind her to pull him tighter to her. His hands slid inside her jeans and were playing a familiar song with her as he leaned down to kiss her neck.

Mike unbuttoned her pants running his hands over Josie's soft, sweet ass. He was kneading it in his hands and he said, "I love to look at your ass Josie. It's as perfect as you are." He went down on his knees behind her and kissed it, gently nibbling on it. While he did that he reached between her legs and started to play with her again. Josie couldn't believe the way he made her feel. She was so turned on by everything he did to her. She was so aroused that she didn't think she could take much more.

"Michael," Josie's breathing was erratic and she was trying to move with him. He released her and stood up behind her. She heard the zipper to his pants go. She felt him enter her. He was pulling her to him as he pumped into her from behind. He took his hand and was letting his fingers play over her soft sweet center. “Josie, God you are perfect. I can’t get enough.” His actions were faster now and he was pushing her further and further. Driving deeper inside of her as she pressed harder back to him, bending herself so she was pressing herself up for him to take. It was a more brutal coupling than they’ve had, but Josie was so turned on there was no fear. She rode his movement, grinding back into him. She was ready to ride over the edge with him when he stopped. He pulled out of her and before she could react he spun her taking her mouth and driving back inside of her. She pushed her arms against the counter and pulled her legs around him with her ass resting on the counter.

Mike needed her. He wanted more. He lifted Josie's behind off the counter and across the room. He pressed her back against the wall. Josie arched her back pressing further into him. He was driving her higher and she was ready to crash around him. He was driving faster and harder into her and she answered every drive. "Michael," she yelled out, "don't stop! God don't stop!" She was exploding around him again. He kept driving into her, he was afraid he was hurting her but he couldn't stop. He felt her release and he pushed harder until he was growling. He took her mouth and kissed her roughly until his release was done.

Mike leaned his head against Josie's. He still held her against the wall. He lowered her legs and together they moved to the floor of their kitchen. Both completely spent holding each other. The floor was cold but they were both so hot they didn't mind. Mike was the first to break the silence. “I’m sorry Josie if I hurt you. I couldn’t stop.” Josie smiled at him. “You didn’t hurt me Michael, you made me feel things I’ve never felt before. I completely lose control around you.” Mike laughed, “I think I’m the one who loses control. I guess we are going to have to be careful now with our daughter joining us.” Josie smiled at the reminder that they soon would be parents. She laughed. “I guess we are going to have to tone it down a little.” Mike smiled at her and wondered how he was going to keep his hands off. Mike laughed, “Or plan a lot of sleepovers with Uncle Rod and Aunt Miranda.” The two laughed at the thought.

Still in the kitchen, Josie climbed on top of Mike. She looked down at her husband and said, “I want to make love again. I want to feel you deep inside of me right here, right now.” Mike smiled at her and said, “I need a minute....but God I want that too." Josie leaned down and kissed him. She pressed her tongue inside his mouth, she teased his tongue and danced around it. She pulled back and looked in his eyes. "Let me help you get there." Josie sat up still straddling him. She reached her hands to her breasts. She rubbed her hands over her breasts, rubbing her nipples into peaks. Mike was growling. He reached his hands up and she swatted at them. "Watch me Michael. Watch me and follow my hands." She slid her hands down her stomach to where she rested on him. Josie took her fingers over herself. "I'm wet Michael. I'm ready for you. See how I slide over myself. See how swollen I am from our love making. Watch as I rub myself." Josie was rubbing herself and he could see her rising to a climax. Mike felt himself rising too.

"Josie you are killing me! I need to touch you." Josie smiled at Mike and pressed her finger inside herself. "You want to do this?" Mike cursed, "Jesus Josie! I need to touch you." He moved his fingers to her center and pressed inside of her as she moved her hand out of his way. Mike was pressing inside of her with his fingers and she was rocking back and forth on him. Her head fell back and she was gasping. "Yes Michael, yes….I'm ready." Mike pressed deep inside of her and he felt her tighten around his finger. "God, I love you Michael." He felt her shuddering around him and he pulled his fingers out of her to stroke her clit making her gasp.

Josie felt Mike remove his fingers though her body was still quaking from her orgasm. She rose up as he stroked her making her body want more. She slid over his now hard erection. She held herself back as she wanted to drive him deep inside of her, but she went as slowly as she could. Mike's hips were trying to rush her and she rose up away from him. "Damn it Josie!" She looked him in the eye. Mike stared deep within her eyes. "I need you Josie, please." Josie smiled at him. "You have me Michael. Just take me, slowly, gently, feel all of me...."

Josie slowly started to ease over Mike. "Feel me stretch for you. Feel me slide around you. Feel me throbbing. Feel me fill myself with you. Do you feel it? Do you Michael?" Mike was in sweet ecstasy. "Oh God yeah! I feel you, I need to move Josie. I need to slam inside of you, I need to press deeper." Josie pressed herself down around him, "Like this?" Josie could feel him completely fill her. He was pressed deep inside of her. She gently rocked him against her as he continued to stroke her. She was gasping with each rocking of her hips and each stroke of his fingers. He was pressed so deep inside her. He was touching deep within her. "God Michael, do you feel that?"

Mike felt it deep within his soul. "Yes Josie, I feel it." He pressed up to her and she moaned. Mike slowly moved his hips to accentuate the pleasure for her. She looked in his eyes and he saw the desire there, the pleasure and he wanted her release. He was still stroking her between their bodies when he found the spot that made her soar. He started circling it slowly with his finger. "Yes, Michael." His name caught in her throat. He knew he was driving her higher. He kept stroking her slowly. "Michael, faster, harder." Mike slowly kept stroking her, "No Josie, I want to savor this." Josie's moan tore at him. Her head fell back and her hips rocked wildly. Mike felt himself rising and didn't know how much more he could take. “You drive me crazy Josie. I want you to cum around me. Cum for me Josie.” Mike increased the pressure on her and he lifted his hips to her slowly. She gasped, “Michael, yes, yes……Miiiiiiccchhhaaaeeeeel!” His name was a scream off her lips as he felt her squeezing him. He felt her throbbing around him and her breathing was erratic.

Josie was spinning after the mind blowing orgasm Mike just gave her and she heard him curse, “Holy shit!” Next thing she knew she was on her back on the kitchen floor and Mikel was over her and pressing deep within her. She pulled her legs up and Mike hooked one of her legs with his hand and he was driving in and out of her. Josie felt herself building again. The excitement, the pressure, him filling her. It all drove her wild. She raised her hips to meet his thrusts. “Christ Josie! I can’t stop, damn you drive me wild.”

Josie was just as wild as he was. "Harder Michael, harder, I'm ready again."

Mike's growl tore out of his throat. He drove harder and deeper inside of her. "God Josie, I don't want to hurt you, but you drive me wild. Cum with me again baby......ummm, yes Josie, I'm ready, I'm going to lose myself in you." With that he pressed deep and hard inside of her. He exploded inside of her. She felt his release and it triggered hers. "Ahhhhhhh Michael.....God yeah......" She pushed her hips to him fast and hard as her release came with his. Mike felt her throbbing, squeezing him, and he fell spent against her. "Jesus Josie. You are going to kill me." Josie chuckled underneath him and said, "I know, I feel the same."

The two laid there catching their breath. They started to get cold on the floor. Mike stood and helped Josie up off the floor. "You know Josie, I will never be able to step into this kitchen without remembering this." Josie smiled. "Yes, I know." Mike smiled at her, he took her lips with his. He swatted her naked ass, "Let's get dressed and get our daughter." Josie smiled at him, "Definitely."

Mike and Josie were at the door to the orphanage before they were opened, even after their delay in the kitchen. When the staff opened the door they went right to Megan's office and she smiled. "I knew you would be here first thing but since it is technically your honeymoon I didn't expect you this soon." They all laughed, Josie blushed and Mike was aroused seeing her blush remembering their love making this morning. Megan nodded and started to get all the papers in order. When the last one was signed they stood up, Mike reached out his hand to the woman then turned to his wife and said, "Let's go get our daughter." Josie smiled and took his hand to get Rachel.

The three of them walked out of the orphanage and headed to the diner for breakfast. Rachel talked the whole time, Josie and Mike laughed at the exuberance she showed when telling them all her stories. When breakfast was done they paid the bill, headed back to the truck and home. Josie couldn't wait for Rachel to see her room. Mike carried her up to her room and made her close her eyes before he would open the door. Once inside her room he told her to open them. She squirmed and squealed. He put her down, she ran around the room touching everything. "Is this really where I get to sleep? I mean, all by myself and everything? These are my toys?" Mike and Josie stood in the doorway with their arms around each other smiling, nodding yes to all her questions. She threw herself on her bed. “Mommy and Daddy I’m so happy to be home.” Josie had tears in her eyes and she smiled up at Mike who had matching tears in his.

Josie told Mike that she had some tests done by Miranda because she wasn’t feeling well. So they needed to meet Miranda at the office this afternoon for some more. He was concerned but Josie was fine other than a little tired lately. He couldn’t imagine that anything was seriously wrong. He couldn’t let himself believe it. Josie told Mike that Rod would meet them there to take care of Rachel while she had the test.

Josie and Mike went to the office and into the treatment room. Once Miranda was in the room Mike looked at her a little fear in his eyes. “What’s going on with Josie? I mean she’s okay right?” Miranda nodded. “Yep she’s better than okay.” Mike looked at Miranda then Josie. Josie looked at him. "Michael, I don't know how it happened but I'm pregnant." He sat there and stared at her. "You mean, but I don't understand? How did, no I know how but, I'm confused?" Josie smiled at him. "I didn't understand either. I found the autopsy report and in the report the coroner indicated surgeries. Jack had a vasectomy. He didn't want me to get pregnant again evidently. I never knew." Mike sat there for a few moments looking in disbelief. He looked at Miranda again, "Are you sure?" She sneered at him, "Well of course I'm sure, but hang in there big guy because you are going to get to take a look."

Josie sat on the table. She laid back and Miranda started the ultrasound. "By the calculations from Josie I believe that she is around four and a half months. We should be able to tell the sex of the baby at this point. So let's take a look." First Miranda did Josie's measurements and they listened to the baby's heartbeat. Mike was off the chair and by Josie's side. He put his arm around her neck and shoulders and held her hand with his free hand. "What's that? Is that the heartbeat?" Miranda told him yes. She was moving the machine on Josie's belly and Mike was glued to the little monitor. "Here is the head, and everything looks like it is coming along fine. But this here is what Mike will be most interested in." Miranda paused, Mike squinted and looked at the screen. He looked at Josie. "What is it?" Josie laughed. Miranda smiled too. Josie looked into his eyes as she said, "It is your son."

Mike watched Josie getting dressed. He was sitting in the chair not moving or saying a word. She moved over to him. "Michael? Are you okay? I mean you haven't said a word."

He pulled her into him and kissed her stomach. He pulled her onto his lap. "Oh my God Josie! I'm over the moon. We are going to have a baby." Josie had started crying. "Yes Michael, I finally found something I could give you. We have each other, our daughter and now I'm giving you what you've always wanted. A son." He kissed her and held her to him. Mike shook his head, tears in his eyes. "Oh Josie to think of all the hell you suffered and that you were pregnant with our child when Jack had you in his grasp. It scares me to think I could have lost you both."

Josie pressed her lips against Mike's forehead. "It's over Michael. We both survived and are fine. You heard Miranda. We're fine. Jack is gone. We are husband and wife. We are truly starting our family, with Rachel and now our son." She took her hand to his face and drug her fingers down from his forehead to his chin. She stopped at his chin and pulled his face to look at her. "I love you Michael." She bent to kiss his lips gently but Mike was so consumed with emotion he grabbed her hair pulling her head back. "Oh my God Josie, I love you. You are my world." He crushed his mouth to her and the door flew open.

Rachel came running through the door. She stopped and looked at her parents disappointed. Josie and Mike pulled themselves apart to look at her. "What's the matter Rachel?" She moved closer to them and said, "Aunt Miranda said that I'm going to have a baby brother. I thought he was in here. Where did he go?" Mike and Josie started laughing. They opened their arms to pull Rachel close. It was going to be a long four and a half months answering her questions. But Mike couldn't wait for each glorious day. He was excited to watch Josie grow with his child inside of her and he couldn't wait to hold him. Mike was waiting for Josie and Rachel to say good bye to Miranda and Rod. He was deep in his thoughts.

Mike started his life without much of anything. He made mistakes. He paid for them but finally he had the things in life he always dreamed he would have. He had Josie, his daughter and soon he would have a son. He didn't know why he was so lucky but he would spend the rest of his life thanking the good Lord for what he had. He would never regret anything in his life because it all brought him to this moment and in this moment life couldn't be more perfect. That is except one thing. Now he knew that Josie can get pregnant, Mike wished he'd made the house bigger. He wanted to fill it up with their babies. Josie walked toward Mike and smiled at him. She was happier than she had ever been. She was so glad that their life had turned out this way. She was so in love with him and all the things that held her back were no longer an issue.

They had their beautiful daughter. The daughter she thought she would never have. Josie brought her hand to her stomach, which had started to expand into a tiny baby bump but she never gave a baby a thought. It was Mike's baby that grew inside of her. Her life didn't turn out how she planned. It was better than she had ever dreamed it would be. The family climbed into the truck. Josie looked at Mike and he reached over to touch her belly. She put her hand over his and Rachel was chattering away. This moment was perfect. Mike smiled at her and said, "It's time to take my family home." Josie nodded with tears in her eyes. A lifetime they waited and now they had everything.

Epilogue

Mike had been working at the bar less and less. With his family at home he didn't want to miss a minute. He would work until seven, then he would go home to help get Rachel ready for bed. When he would walk through the door, she screamed, "Daddy!" His heart melted every time. Josie joked that she had him wrapped around her finger. He hated to admit it, but Josie was right. There wasn't a damn thing Mike wouldn't do for his daughter. Tonight was no different. Mike walked in the door and Rachel ran to him yelling "Daddy!" He scooped her up into his arms nuzzling her neck as she tried to squeeze the life out of him. Mike laughed against her neck and she giggled. "Daddy! Mommy said, this weekend I get to have a sleep over at Aunt Miranda and Uncle Rod's. She said that you two are having a date night, whatever that means." Mike looked over at his wife who was cradling their son in her arms. He was latched onto Josie's breast and Mike could hardly contain his look of envy.

Mike's eyes hit hers, "Is that right? So what are we going to do on this date night?" Josie smiled at him. "I have a nice dinner planned with an even better desert menu." Mike looked at her with desire raging in his eyes. He cleared his throat as he told Rachel to go up to start her bath. Rachel bounded away happily singing to herself. Mike moved toward his wife and son. He bent to kiss his son's forehead then lifted his gaze to his wife.

Josie smiled at him, "Trevor will have to stay home with us, but Dr. Mattson gave the green light. I've missed you and I don't want to wait another minute to have you." Mike growled at her taking her lips with his. When he pulled away he said, "Are you sure it's okay?" Josie laughed, "Do not question the doctor!" He looked down at his son, "Sorry Trev, Daddy is going to be sharing that gorgeous nipple this weekend." Trevor moved in her arms, protesting Mike's words. Josie smiled down at their son, "I don't think he likes the idea." Just then Rachel yelled, "Daddy, let's go, my bath is getting cold." She smiled at him, "Your princess awaits." Mike took her lips one last time before turning toward the stairs toward their daughter. "You've been saved for now baby. But this weekend you are mine." Josie smiled at him saying, "I'm counting the seconds." Mike growled a curse under his breath stomping up the stairs.

The night Trevor was born was much like every other day of their lives. Crazy! Mike was at the bar working. Josie was at home when her water broke. She called Rod and Miranda. They came to the house to get Rachel, then Josie called Mike. Max put him on the phone. "Yeah baby. You okay?" Josie smiled, "Not exactly. It's time Michael." He was dumbfounded as Trevor wasn't due for another two weeks. "Time for what Josie girl?" Max heard his response and said excitedly, "It's time! Mike, you dumb ass! The baby." Josie laughed through the phone. "Shit! Josie, is it? Shit! Max...." Max was yelling go! Josie was laughing as it sounded like a comedy act gone wrong.

Mike got to the house and took Josie to the hospital where Dr. Mattson met them. Miranda turned her over to him after doing the ultrasound for them. Dr. Mattson was the OBGYN in the practice, so she needed to get used to him. Josie did fairly well with him. It was hard at first but she learned to relax with him as she got to know him. Miranda was always there for her and helped her through her appointments with him. But after a while

Josie didn't need to lean on Miranda for support. With every day that passed with Mike Josie found herself getting stronger and stronger. She was almost back to the Josie she was back when she and Mike first met.

Mike got Josie to the hospital before he had a complete meltdown. Josie laughed at him the whole time. He was terrified. He was scrambling all over the place. He was completely out of sorts. Josie had never seen him that way. She took his hand in hers, "Breathe Michael. Babies are born every day. This is going to be fine." He looked at Josie, she saw the fear in his eyes. "Michael, everything will be fine. Just relax." Mike nodded at her, but she knew until the baby came out, he heard the cry and they were both okay, Mike wouldn't take a deep breath.

Josie heard Rachel and Mike upstairs playing in the tub. Mike was singing along with

Rachel and both were completely off key. She smiled down at Trevor. “Your sister and father cannot sing to save their lives. I sure hope you get your Mamma’s voice.” She drifted back to her memories. When Trevor was placed on her chest, Josie cried from pure happiness. She never thought she’d experience holding her child right after birth. Mike who she had seen cry on only a few occasions, was reduced to racking sobs. Josie was happier in that moment than she ever thought she could have been.

When all was said and done and Mike held their son for the first time. He was tucked into the bed next to Josie. She passed Trevor to Mike and he was terrified. “Josie, I don’t think I should be holding him. What if I don’t do it right? I don’t want to hurt him.” “Shhhhh, Michael. I am not going to be the only one holding this baby.” She placed Trevor in his father's arms and held her breath. Mike looked at his son in complete awe. She would never forget that look on his face. Until her last breath she would always remember that look of completeness. Josie never thought this would happen for them, but now that it had, she couldn't wait to have another child. She smiled at her husband and son, "Michael, I think we are going to need to add on to the house. I want more babies." Mike looked at her and grinned. "Oh hell yeah baby, I'll give you a dozen." He moved to kiss her lips gently then turned his attention back to his son.

Trevor whimpered in Josie's arms. He was done nursing. He was ready for bed. She got him ready to put him down laying him in the bassinette in the living room while she moved about picking up a few toys and things. Mike came down the stairs and wrapped his arms around Josie. She rubbed against him causing him to moan. "Did Rachel go to bed?" Mike was kissing her neck and murmuring, "Ummm hummmm." Josie reached her hands around to pull him against her. "Oh, Michael....I can't wait for this weekend." He turned her in his arms pulling her tight to him. "Neither can I baby. I can't wait to touch every inch of you, to sink deep inside of you again."

Josie groaned. "Michael, condoms." He grinned, "Absolutely, I'm already prepared. I told you I can't wait, I've been planning. I think I have about four boxes." Josie laughed at her husband, "I love you." Mike smiled at her, "I love you too baby." Just then Trevor made his presence known and Mike groaned. "Son we are going to have to talk about this." Josie laughed as Mike went to pick up his son. Seeing him hold their son brought tears to her eyes, it made her heart beat faster. It also stirred something deep within her.

Finally, life had given Josie all she needed to be happy for the rest of her life. Sure she wanted more children now that she knew she could have them, but that could wait. Right now her heart was full with her daughter, her son and the man who gave it all to her. Life couldn't get any better than this moment right here. Josie finally found herself in this town, with these people, with this man and her children. Today and everyday moving forward she moved closer and closer to the woman she buried deep down long ago. She was shedding the woman who was hurt, battered and abused.

The love of this man has made Josie feel safe, loved and desired. The power of his love pulled her back to the strong woman she always was before. She would never forget where her scars came from, but she would never again be afraid of her husband's touch. Her daughter would grow up protected, loved, cherished and her son would learn from Mike how to respect a woman, the right way, to cherish her and to protect her. There was no doubt in Josie's mind that her children will always be loved, wanted and Rachel would never think that she was not part of them. Josie and Mike may not have created her physically, but she helped make them complete. There was no doubt in Josie and Mike's mind that without Rachel, their lives would not be complete. Josie couldn't help but think it's funny how things work out. I guess somehow love always finds its way.

PREVIEW TO
LOVE IS ALWAYS ENOUGH
Chapter 1

Max Bennet was leaving the house he had resided in for almost 20 years, shutting the door to a house, not a home. It never was a home to him. Honestly, as the door closed he felt happier than ever. He took his suitcase, got in his truck and hauled ass to his new beginning in North Carolina, leaving Mellbourne Maine and the bad taste it left in his mouth. At least he'd be closer to home, where his family lived. He left to find himself so many years ago. He hadn't been home since. Well he hadn't been home since he made so many mistakes in his life that he felt like he still didn't know who he was. Ironically that was why he left Pleasantville, South Carolina and his parents' farm at eighteen. He didn't want to admit his failures.

Max had been a prison guard for the last, God too long. It was all but 20 years ago when the warden came into a steakhouse Max was working in. Max had pulled into Mellbourne full of ideas, hopes and dreams of an eighteen-year-old. He was waiting tables and earning his keep, living in a shitty little efficiency apartment, but what did he care. He didn't need much, just a bed, kitchen and bathroom. It wasn't like he knew anyone there and he didn't need a fancy, expensive place to lay his head. When he wasn't working he would go out to the bars in town to see what Mellbourne had to offer. The job opportunity the warden laid out sounded promising. Good money, and let's face it Max was built like a brick shit house, he could handle himself. He also was quite good with a gun. The family used to shoot back home all the time, beer cans, soda cans, occasionally fruit. He and his brother loved hunting and shooting. It was time they spent together doing something other than farming.

Max wasn't a playboy. He wasn't looking to bang a girl and walk away. That wasn't his style. He was raised to respect women and he held them in high regard. He dated back home growing up. He wasn't an angel. He had sex with women, but it was consensual and it was only with the woman he was dating at the time. Ok, so he dated a lot. Women liked him. He liked them, but he wasn't the flirt. He was the one who normally ended up being the clueless bastard when they moved on. He started dating his first girlfriend at age fifteen. Yes, he was young to date, but he had looks that drew women to him. His black hair, blue eyes and the body of a man who worked hard and worked out harder were the things that pulled the women in. Max's serious nature was what usually pushed them away.

Max's last girlfriend before he left home told him one night, "You know Max, you need to lighten up. If you would just let yourself have a little fun instead of trying to plan the rest of your life maybe relationships would stick." Max was dumbfounded, "I thought women wanted to get married and have kids. I'm not a player Regina. That's just not who I am. So basically what you're telling me is if I would whore myself out, play the field and just fuck 'em and leave 'em, I'd have all I need?" Regina looked at him, "I didn't say that, but shit Max, you are freaking hot as hell, you rock what you got below the belt but you're too serious too fast. We've been dating, what two weeks?" Max looked at her, "Seriously, we've been together a month Regina." She chuckled, "Yeah, whatever. See what I mean? You know it's been a month but to me it's only been weeks. But that's not really the point."

Max was getting pissed, "So what is the point Regina?" "Reggie, and stop with the Regina bullshit. I've told you before, I hate that name. The point is Max, you're ready to go buy an engagement ring and lock my ass down. I'm not there. I'm nowhere near there. Neither are half or ninety percent of the women you've dated in town. We're eighteen for fucks sake. I have a hell of a lot more, well fucking to tend to before I settle down and start pumping out kids." Max couldn't help himself. He snorted derisively at what she just said and she rolled her eyes. "Regina, come on. If I rock what I have below the belt, why don't you want to keep dating? Do I not satisfy what you need?" "Yes Max, sex isn't the issue. You are too serious, I want to have fun, live a little. I'm not made to be a farmer's wife. Maybe you need to get out of this town, give yourself a chance to see what's out there. Then come home to the farm and maybe settle down. Live a little, party, have dirty hot sex Max. You don't need to lock a girl down right away." Max just stared at her. She put her hand on his arm and pulled him to her. She kissed him gently on the lips. "I'm sorry to walk away Max. I will miss our chemistry, but I need more. Come back in a few years, we'll see where we are." Max just shook his head at her. "Have nice life Max. Good luck finding what you're looking for." Max just watched her go, just like all the women before her. Well good for him, at least he knew it wasn't about the sex, but bad news, how do you change the fact that all your life all you've wanted was to find the one?

So the one thing Max gained from his past 20 years of prison guard work was he met one of the inmates there who was a decent guy. They became friends over the years. Yeah, go ahead laugh. The guy made mistakes. He paid dearly for them. In fact, he paid a higher price than anyone really knew. Mike Albright, was a prisoner at the correctional institution. His time was finally coming up and he wanted a fresh start. Max put some feelers out with a guy he knew back home who was into real estate. He found an interesting prospect. There was a bar in Kellersville, North Carolina that a man was selling. He only wanted it sold to someone willing to fix it up and keep it as a bar. Mike had a good business sense, and he knew what he wanted to do with the space. Max wasn't a book man, or figures, he was a worker. Let him get his hands dirty and he was happy.

Max drove thinking about the past, the old girlfriends, the house and town he left behind, the job he left. Was he going to miss it? Hell no! Although he still hadn't learned to loosen up. Max knew Mike's back story, but Max never told him his. That shit just wasn't worth the time. Someday Max would find what he wanted in life, and fuck Regina. Yes, that's right Regina not Reggie. Fuck the past he just walked out on too. Some woman would love having the old-fashioned, one-woman man, uptight Max. But wait, was he really uptight just because he wasn't a flirt, and wanted a life with someone, not just a roll in the hay so to speak? No, he was a fun guy. He wasn't all business, was he? "Oh hell, fucking Regina! That was over 20 years ago, just let it go Max." He chuckled to himself when he realized he was talking out loud.

Once Max arrived in Kellersville, he went right to the bar, to settle up some questions about lay out and repairs. The owner was letting him start working on it before the papers were signed. Mike unfortunately had another few weeks until he was released and could get out there. He paid the owner extra to let us start the work. The papers were all drawn up, all they needed was the final settlement and signing of the paperwork. The owner gave Max the keys and told him to take care of the place. He'd be coming back in a few weeks to meet with the lawyers and Mike.

Mike and Max had discussed their plan at length. Max had all of Mike's plans, so he was ready to start digging in, tearing stuff up and making the new life he needed, for both of them. Max worked hard on the bar. He had specific instructions from Mike on what he wanted. Max was working hard to have things lined up for when Mike arrived. Mike was due to be there within a week or two. Mike said he had one stop to make before heading to the bar once he was a free man. Max didn't question him, nor was he going to. He already knew it had to do with his girl he left behind when his world crumbled. Max sure hoped that Mike would have better luck in the love department than he did. The last few months Max didn't even try anymore. There was no sex, in his relationship. There was no trust, no love, hell there was just nothing. He got himself tested for everything under the sun. He wasn't taking chances with how promiscuous the woman he'd been with was. If he found someone, he wanted to not take chances with her, she didn't deserve to get anything from him. He had the papers to prove he was clean and now he was well on his way to building something new. It wasn't just a house and town he was running away from. It was lies too.

There was an apartment above the bar which was roomier than Max's old apartment, but he left that for Mike. Max rented an apartment in the town next to Kellersville which was Wellsprings. It was a small apartment but for just him it worked. It was basically just like what he'd started out in back in Maine. Once Max got settled he called the lawyer back in Maine who was handling finalizing a few things and gave him the address. He wanted that part of his life over. As far as he was concerned it was over, the paperwork was just a formality. The day he closed the door on that house, it was over for him. Hell, the day he found out about the cheating it should have been over, but he was a fool, he stuck it out. Afraid of failure, he didn't want to fail. He left home to find himself, so far all he did was find a lie. There had to be something better out there.

Max really liked the town of Wellsprings. It was kind of an old town, the brick roads, the circle with a fountain in the middle of town. A park that had a bike trail and jogging trail. There were plenty of restaurants, which was good because Max didn't cook. There was also a gym. Max had a gym at his old house, so he definitely wanted to get the membership at the gym so he could keep working out. He loved the physical labor with farming back home. He loved working with his hands building and fixing things. He also loved hitting the gym hard, to keep pushing his limits. He had plenty of time to workout back in Maine, in fact he had also done a lot of boxing. Working in the prison system it helped him react quicker and it was also a hell of a work out.

Max put money into the bar and he and Mike were partners. He left the decisions to Mike. He was just a silent partner. He really didn't want claim on anything. All he needed was enough to keep him going. Max wasn't a fancy man, and didn't like all the expensive things. He was happy with his jeans, t-shirts and boots. There was only one thing Max wanted and he was going for that today. He was ready for his Harley. He had wanted one for a long time. He had the money, so what the hell. The bike didn't really fit in with his life back in Maine, but then again neither did his pick-up or him. Now it was time. Well beyond time if you'd asked Max, for him to have the things he wanted. He worked hard, he saved money, he also sent money home to his folks. He had a nice nest egg even after shelling out cash for the bar. He wasn't a millionaire or anything but he was comfortable.

Max took a time out between deliveries to the bar and headed to the Harley dealer to look around. He may not know what he wanted in life but he knew what he liked and wanted in a bike. He walked around the showroom. He sat on a few bikes until a salesman approached him. Max wasn't one to be bothered. He liked to look around by himself if he needed help he'd let you know. The guy walked off said he'd be around if Max had any questions. He had been there about an hour looking around. He took his time looking over each bike and its features. Max found one that he liked. It wasn't fancy but it was what he liked. Max flagged the guy down to make his purchase. He had to go back the next day for them to detail it and shine it before pick up. Max would have to have one of the guys in town drop him off to pick it up. He couldn't wait to ride his new bike.

Max went back to the bar and started digging in. The floors were a mess. They needed to be ripped out and replaced. Max wanted to wait for Mike for that decision, but the floors were a total loss and needed to go. He was surprised no one had been seriously hurt on them. There were chunks missing out of them and rotted out spots. Max didn't want to waste time. The bar needed to get fixed so they could get it up and running. He thought a light wood would look great in the bar, especially with all the other natural wood accents that Mike had planned. The two weeks passed by quickly and Mike arrived on scene. After Mike's arrival it is was sun up and sun down work at the bar. It didn't take long for Max to realize he'd made the right choice working with Mike. He was detailed, professional and together they made a great team. The bar came together and within a month they were having the grand opening.

Max enjoyed working. He liked to keep his hands busy. He didn't want time to think. When Max wasn't working at the bar he would go to the gym in Wellsprings and work out. He enjoyed keeping in shape, lifting weights and taking in the sights. It was a small town, with very few single young people running around.

Max had met a few people here and there at the bar, some nosey sorts but some real decent folks. Max had made friends with the chief of police in town and one of his deputies. They came out to the bar with their ladies to see the progress being made. They were nice people and he enjoyed talking with them. The ladies, he would run into at the gym now and again. Miranda Porter was one of the local doctors who dated Rod Marks the deputy in town and her friend was the chief Ted Blake's wife, Sarah.

Miranda was a real ball buster. She liked to harass Max. The ladies were at the gym one day while he was there and she came over to see how things were going. "So Max, how's the bar?" Max shrugged, "Still going." Miranda laughed at his response as Max was a man of few words. "Jesus Max, what the hell do you feed those things? Your arms are huge.

Seriously dude, what the hell?" Max shook his head and laughed. Sarah stood next to Miranda smiling at the exchange. Max curled his arm and smirked at Miranda, "Well normally I give them whatever they want, usually a tasty steak or occasionally a bossy, smart mouthed woman." They all laughed and the exchange was over. Max however noticed a woman across the room watching them. He wondered what her story was? Then he thought, screw that, he didn't need another entanglement, although she was quite intriguing, she had something that drew Max's attention.

Max noticed that Miranda and Sarah were at the treadmills talking to the woman. He figured at some point he would meet her and see if there was something about her, or was Max just lonely? He kept lifting his weights, doing the workout program he designed for himself. There was no way he was going out of his way for another woman again. There was no reason for him to get involved with anyone. He had no desire at this point for the complication. Whatever her name was, could remain a mystery.

Chapter 2

Rod came out to the bar one night on his own. Max strolled up to the bar with a draft for him. “Hey, flying solo tonight?” Rod grinned, “Shhhh.....I wasn’t here.” Max laughed. “Needed a break did you?” Rod laughed and the guys bantered back and forth for a while. Max got him another draft and the detective in Rod came out. “So where are you from?” Max told him then told him he was a corrections officer at the prison Mike had been at. “Interesting. So is that how you met Mike?” Max being defensive, “Yeah, and he’s a hell of a guy. Never had any trouble with him and he never should have served the time he did. You’re not here to hassle him are you?” Rod held his hands up, “Dude, relax. I’m curious is all. Miranda says you’re at the gym all the time. She was curious about you asking me all kinds of questions. I don’t know the woman is crazy sometimes. I love her to pieces but, damn women gotta know everything." Max laughed. "At least she cares, and pays attention." Rod's eyebrow shot up. "Elaborate." Max shook his head. "Nope, not going there. So are there any facilities near Wellsprings that offer boxing?" Rod sat up, "You box?" Max grinned, "I used to back in Maine. Loved it, found it as a good release. Kept me in shape." Rod grinned. "Ok, if you promise not to crush me, we can box at the gym at the police station. There is nowhere in town. I have a bag and stuff in the police gym. I love going at it but can't find a sparring partner. Last one I had I kind of, well let's just say, they didn't move fast enough." Max chuckled. "You're on my man. Name when and I'll find the time."

Max took his empty beer and with a wave Rod was off to head home to his woman. They were an odd couple, but you could tell very much in love. Miranda was flirty, and opinionated, shall we say. Rod was more on the quiet side. He worked undercover years back but now just worked on the force after they busted open a drug ring and cleared out the department of dirty cops. He had been shot from what the rumor mill stated around town, and he was placed on desk work until recently. Word around town was he had a temper but it very rarely reared its head. However, there were a few incidents on which no one had elaborated in his presence. Max was glad for the chance to start sparring again. Rod told him he could come before his self-defense training class tomorrow. Things were still slow at the bar, so Max knew Mike would be good with it.

Max got up the next morning and went to the gym to warm up for meeting Rod later that day. He was at the gym by 5am. You would think a guy who worked in a bar could sleep beyond 5am. Nope, not him. He was up and ready to go. He rarely missed a workout. He walked into the gym and damn near couldn't move. She was there again. She was stretching on the mats just in front of where he normally did his workouts. She was a vision to behold. She had beautiful blonde hair that kind of went every which way. Her eyes were blue like the ocean, so clear it was like they opened her soul. She hid pain in those eyes. She seemed guarded, shy. Her body was curvy, but in all the right places. Ok, well yes she had a little more than curves but damn. She was not his type at all but yet here he stood, not being able to put one foot in front of the other and his heart was beating out of his chest like he'd just finished his workout instead of just coming in the door. What was it about her? This was insane. Max shook it off and headed back to the mats. As he was going to pass her she moved and bumped into him. She nearly fell at the impact from them hitting. He reached out and grabbed her arm. She pulled back so quickly that she nearly fell again. Max moved to steady her but she gained her balance and righted herself, "I'm good, thank you. Sorry about that." She moved so fast away from him without making eye contact that he wasn't able to reply.

Damn crazy women. The girl acted like Max was going to molest her, as if. He proceeded to start his work out and tried not to look her way, however his eyes seemed to have a mind of their own and he watched her as she moved on the treadmill. He watched her as she seemed to lose herself in her headphones and whatever music was playing in her ears. He wanted to know what that music was. Max shook it off again and got back to his work out. The woman needed to stay a mystery, he wasn't interested.

Max went down the street to the diner and grabbed some coffee, a bagel with cream cheese, scrambled eggs and a side of sausage after his workout. He needed some fuel for his sparring with Rod. He needed it after trying to forget the woman from the gym. After eating Max knew he'd be early meeting with Rod but he didn't have anything else to do so he headed to the police station. When he got there, he was told Rod was already in the gym. The officer showed him the way and when he walked in Rod was sitting like he was meditating. As if he knew Max was there he took a breath in and then let it out as he got up to slowly move toward him. "How's it going Max?" Max just stared at him, "Does that shit help?" Rod grinned at him, "Meditation?" Max nodded. "It helps me find my center, helps keep me grounded. I enjoy it." Max grinned, "Maybe you need to teach me about that." Rod laughed, "Come on, let's warm up."

Rod and Max started punching on the big bag to warm up. Then moved to the mats to start sparring. Max was impressed. Rod wasn't a little guy, but smaller than Max was, and he was good. Better than the guys in Maine. "Damn, you are good at this." Rod grinned, "When you're a cop every edge helps. Plus, like you I find this helpful." Max held his glove up in signal to stop. "What do you mean?" Rod shrugged, "Seemed to me like you had some issues you were trying to work through." Max shook his head, "What are you a mind reader?" Rod shook his head, "No. I just pay attention. Seems like you have a host of anger locked up. Wanna talk about it or spar?" No hesitation Max moved back into stance, "Spar." They went at it for a while. Max wasn't sure what time it was, but he and Rod were both sweating and Max could feel his muscles screaming.

The young lady walked into the gym and heard the hitting and grunts. She was quiet so as not to disturb them and she tried to blend quietly into the room. No one else had arrived yet for the class. She'd been coming to classes for years. She hadn't missed one yet. She needed these self-defense classes as much as she needed the air in her lungs. When she moved into the gym at the police station, she watched the two men taking swipes at one another, grunting, both men sweating. She'd heard the noise of them hitting each other and was frozen. Their bodies were both a marvel to look at but the force of what they were doing and the size of them made the fear rise in her. The man from the gym, she recognized. He looked angry. Rod had been instructing the self-defense classes as long as she'd been coming. He never seemed to want to look her in the eye anymore. Then again, she never wanted to look herself in the eye anymore either.

The quiet woman stood frozen in her spot watching Max and Rod, hit, move, hit move, grunt. They went on like that for a bit. She heard noise coming from the hallway and more women filtered in from the police station for their class. The men continued. It was as if they had no idea anyone was in the room. Miranda, and Sarah came through the door and in typical Miranda fashion she let out a whistle of complete appreciation and all the women laughed. That's what it took for the men to break concentration. When the man from the gym stopped, his eyes landed on her. Her heart speed up, just like earlier in the gym and she automatically assumed it was the fear coming, only this felt different somehow.

Rod grinned at the woman letting go with the wolf whistle. "Babe, really?" Miranda laughed, "Come on, ladies really they are hot aren't they?" The women all started laughing and agreeing. Miranda moved to the men, squeezed one of the python arms on Max then moved to Rod and ran her hands over his sweaty bare chest. She leaned in, "This one is taken." She kissed him in front of the women when all the laughs and whistles started again. She pulled back, "This one ladies, is fair game. Aren't ya Max, baby?" Max held up his hands, as the women in the room started applauding and whistling. Max moved his eyes to the silent woman in the room and grinned at her.

Max finally was able to make his way through the women after thanking Rod and Miranda for outing him to the women of Wellsprings and beyond. From the doorway before he left he looked toward the woman trying to hide herself in the throng of women and he stopped. "Ladies, don't forget if you haven't already, stop out at the Heartbreak Bar. Bring the husbands, boyfriends or whatever out for some drinks, music and fun. It's totally redone inside and no more riff raff in the bar. Mike has done an amazing job turning it around." With that he broke his gaze from the woman and scanned the room with his eyes before turning and heading out.

About The Author:

Ivy Blacke is from Pennsylvania and always enjoyed reading, writing and using her imagination. She dreamed of publishing a book one day and decided to take a chance and started writing and hasn't stopped.

She enjoys sharing her stories with friends and family who have encouraged her to share with everyone because they laugh, they cry and they love the creativity of her writing.

She is married to a man who supports her in her love of writing and she loves that he tries to understand her creative side and encourages her to write what's in her heart.

Made in the USA
Middletown, DE
24 December 2019

81897104R20459